DARK ROAD HOME

D0957207

Books by Elizabeth Ludwig

From Bethany House Publishers

___

EDGE OF FREEDOM

No Safe Harbor
Dark Road Home

ALSO BY ELIZABETH LUDWIG

Love Finds You in Calico, California
*Died in the Wool**
*Inn Plain Sight**
*Where the Truth Lies**

*with Janelle Mowery

EDGE OF FREEDOM, BOOK TWO

DARK ROAD HOME

A NOVEL

ELIZABETH LUDWIG

BETHANYHOUSE

a division of Baker Publishing Group
Minneapolis, Minnesota

© 2013 by Elizabeth Ludwig

Published by Bethany House Publishers
11400 Hampshire Avenue South
Bloomington, Minnesota 55438
www.bethanyhouse.com

Bethany House Publishers is a division of
Baker Publishing Group, Grand Rapids, Michigan

Printed in the United States of America

Library of Congress Cataloging-in-Publication Data
Ludwig, Elizabeth.
    Dark road home / Elizabeth Ludwig.
      pages cm. — (Edge of freedom ; Book Two)
    Summary: "Hunted by dangerous enemies and betrayed by those they loved, can Ana and Eoghan, 19th century Irish immigrants in New York, forgive the wounds of the past and learn to trust again?"—Provided by publisher.
    ISBN 978-0-7642-1040-2 (pbk.)
    1. Young women—Fiction. 2. Irish Americans—Fiction. 3. New York (N.Y.)—History—19th century—Fiction. I. Title.
PS3612.U33D37 2013
813'.6—dc23   2013010858

Scripture quotations are from the King James Version of the Bible.

Cover design by Koechel Peterson & Associates, Inc., Minneapolis, Minnesota

Author is represented by MacGregor Literary, Inc.

13 14 15 16 17 18 19   7 6 5 4 3 2 1

*To Dylan . . . and all those like him
searching for a way home.*

PROLOGUE

The Celt's long strides sliced through the mist rising from the moor. Like waves the damp fog swirled and rolled from his legs. Overhead, gray clouds squeezed out one fat, icy raindrop that missed the brim of his brown derby and landed with a splat on the end of his nose. He slashed it away with the back of his hand.

A fitting morning to match his foul mood.

But beyond the next bend lay his destination—a modest manor, elegant but not sprawling, nestled on a choice piece of farmland. His feet devoured the remaining distance, carrying him to a wide staircase with stone steps and a curving banister.

His grip on a pearl-handled walking cane tightened as he lifted it to strike a matching set of oak doors. At the second knock, the doors parted and a pert housekeeper draped in black from head to foot poked her head out.

"Can I help you, sir?"

"The master of this house, is he in?"

Her eyebrow lifted. "Aye, sir, but Mr. McCleod does not take visitors at this hour—"

He cut the words from her mouth with a sharp glare. Voice

low, he lifted the cane and touched the handle to his forehead. "Tell him The Celt has come with business to discuss."

Her firm chin dropped a finger's span. She lowered her voice and spoke his name cautiously. "The Celt?"

Ah, good. An appropriate amount of fear. He nodded. "That's what I said. Now, you will fetch him for me, aye? Dinna tarry. You understand my meaning?"

Eyes wide, she nodded, ruffling the edge of her cap. "Aye, sir."

"Good." He lowered the cane to thump against the floor, then motioned past her to a room that opened off the hall. "Is that the parlor?"

Again she nodded.

"I'll wait there. Go on with you now."

In answer she whirled and sped up the stairs. He followed suit, the tails of his overcoat flapping, and swept through the hall into the parlor. The woman was sufficiently cowed. She would not keep him waiting long.

Indeed, the hands of the mantel clock had only crept forward a few paces before the door behind him opened with a whoosh. Biting back a smile, The Celt turned from the cheery fire.

He and Brion McCleod had never met, but The Celt made it his business to know about men of power—their strengths and weaknesses. McCleod was impatient, brutish and loud, with a quick temper and perpetual scowl. He loomed in the entrance, his untucked shirt drooping sloppily over his trousers.

"Who are you, and what do you mean frightening my staff half to death?"

Arrogant fool. His identity was a well-guarded secret. Were he to answer McCleod, the man would be dead before nightfall.

The Celt savored the name on his tongue, anticipated how

the speaking of it would rip the self-assurance from the lout's bullish shoulders. "Lucy McCleod . . . your niece . . . is alive."

He could almost see the name rolling through the man's brain, feel the flush that crept over his cheeks as it was processed. Finally, McCleod's mouth opened and he gaped like a bass on a hook. "W-what did you say?"

Ah, disbelief mingled with dread. "Lucy McCleod," he repeated. "Daughter of Shamus and Adele McCleod. Sister named Brigid. Names sound familiar?"

"Of course they do. He was my brother—his wife and children, my family."

"Then you will be relieved to know that one of your family, the eldest child, is alive and well."

"You have proof of this?"

McCleod spoke slowly, formed each word carefully. The man would be an easy mark in a game of poker. "Would I have come if I didn't?"

To his credit, McCleod collected himself quickly. He strode to the door, closed it tight, and then turned on his heel and returned to the fireplace. His blue eyes, so pale as to almost appear gray, narrowed, and he drew himself up through his barrel chest until he stood nearly as tall as The Celt. "Forgive me. Your claim has set me back, for certain. If indeed the news be true, I would be most pleased. But due to the nature of the revelation, I must insist you tell me how you know of it and what proof you have that she is who you claim."

"Pleased?" The Celt scratched his chin. "Not the sentiment I expected you'd feel when you learned of Lucy's existence, what with the stakes as they are."

Aye, that was subtle enough. McCleod was measuring him, struggling to gauge what he knew, and how he knew it. As if to confirm this, McCleod leaned forward, a large vein protruding on his neck.

"Who are you?"

He shrugged and unwound a long woolen scarf from around his neck. "Some questions are better left unanswered, aye? Sufficient for you to know that I am someone with a very long, very deep grasp of history."

The Adam's apple in McCleod's neck bobbed, and his eyes, still gauging, swept The Celt from head to toe. "And what has that to do with me? What ill wind has brought you to my doorstep?"

Leaving the fire, The Celt circled a padded camelback settee, his cane dragging the floor with his left foot, thumping with his right. "I have a proposition for you, Brion McCleod, one that could prove mutually profitable, I think, considering the year which it be."

McCleod dragged his fingers through his hair, looking suitably distraught, just as The Celt had hoped. Perhaps the old priest had been right all those years ago. He smothered a confident spark. Pride always preceded a fall. He'd learned that well enough.

McCleod's hand cut through the air. "I dinna ken your meaning. Speak clear, man. What is it you want from me?"

The Celt lowered himself to the settee and folded both hands atop his cane. "Your question is ill-spoken. Better first to ask what I can do for you."

McCleod's brows formed peaks across his wrinkled forehead. "Aye? And what is that, pray?"

He took his time answering, relishing the look of dread that kindled in McCleod's face as he listened. "Nine years ago, a *bairn* came into my care. A bonnie enough lass, though frightened and scarred. A fire, I think it was, that claimed her mother and sister but spared her. Her father, of course, died years earlier in some sort of farming accident. Aye . . . that's it. If my figures are correct"—he tilted his chin and pretended to count—"that would make her not quite nineteen. Am I right?"

McCleod swallowed, then opened his mouth to take a breath. "You are mistaken. Whoever this lass is, she is not Lucy McCleod. My niece is dead."

The Celt pinned McCleod with an unblinking stare. "Is she now? And would you be willing to stake your name, your land"—he thumped the floor with his cane—"this house on that certainty?"

McCleod eased toward a writing desk next to the window. No doubt he had a weapon of some sort hidden in its drawers.

The Celt sighed and stood. "Killing me does you no good. Your niece will still be alive and of proper age to claim her inheritance, assuming she doesn't ruin your reputation first— a very troubling concept with someone of your political aspirations, no?" He let the words sink in before lowering his voice to just above a whisper. "Only I can tell you where she is and how to find her before that happens."

He quirked an eyebrow, measuring the desperate gleam in McCleod's eyes with the distance of his twitching fingers to the desk drawer. He brought the cane up, running his palm over its smooth length until it settled on a notch just below the handle.

"Well? Do you care to hear my proposition or shall I be on my way?"

For a sliver of a second he thought he'd guessed wrong, that McCleod would reach for the drawer and his scheme would be foiled by an unpredictable Irishman. But then McCleod's shoulders slumped. His hand fell to his side. He returned to the fireplace and sank onto a chair opposite the settee.

"Where is she?" he rasped through tight lips. "Where is Lucy McCleod?"

The Celt smiled. The lass's name was no longer McCleod,

or Lucy for that matter, but that information would come later. For now, one bite of the pie at a time. "America. Your niece is alive and well and living in America."

A scowl took shape on McCleod's face. "America is a broad place. I assume it be the narrowing of it which will cost me."

Finally the real purpose behind his visit. Laying aside his coat and cane, The Celt returned to his place on the settee. He and Brion McCleod had much to discuss.

Much to discuss, indeed.

1

Sometimes, in the unguarded moments just before she woke, Ana imagined she could once again feel the flames searing her flesh.

She dispelled the fiery images in two rapid blinks, but the bitter scent of smoke coiling through her singed hair made her heart race. She lifted her hand, holding her breath until her fingers closed around strong, healthy curls. Sagging into her pillow with relief, she drew clean smoke-free air into her lungs.

No pain. No blinding, scorching heat that baked her insides with each burning breath—just sweet fresh air.

The blankets fluttered from her shoulders as she sat up in the bed to devour with her eyes the pale papered walls dotted with small perfect rosebuds. Crisp cottage furniture, not darkened by soot or sullied by ash, glowed in the moonlight streaming from the floor-to-ceiling windows.

A choked laugh bubbled from her throat, oddly haunting in the quiet room. Reaching down, she clasped the coverlet and drew it to her chin. She wasn't in a burning cottage. She was in Amelia Matheson's boardinghouse on Ashberry Street in New York, far from the village in Ireland where she grew up. And the keening wail that sent shudders coursing down her back was the wind outside her window, not a child's voice pleading for help that she was powerless to give.

Her fingers shook as she withdrew a match from the tin atop her dresser to light the oil lamp next to her bed. The match sputtered and then sparked to life, even that feeble flame creating uncomfortable heat against the red, puckered skin on Ana's hands. She lit the lamp quickly and waved the match out.

A pocket watch lay next to a book of poems on her bedside table. Ana flipped open its lid, directing her eyes away from the tiny portrait cradled opposite the watch face.

Four fifteen.

Dawn was still hours away, but she'd get no more sleep this night. Sighing heavily, she cast the covers aside and reached for the floor with her toes.

"Ah!"

Shivering, she drew them back, wrapped the blanket around herself, then lifted the lamp from the table and scooted from the bed. Out the door, past Cara's room—

Meg's room, she corrected silently. Cara and Rourke no longer lived at the boardinghouse. They owned a beautiful home across town close to Rourke's office. Breda, too, was gone, moved in with a family in need of a housekeeper and cook.

She crept past Meg's room before descending the stairs and winding down the hall to the library. The door opened with just a touch, and a candle flickered from the table nearest the window. Ana lingered on the threshold, her fingers curled about the edges of her makeshift robe.

Clearing her throat, she peeked inside. "Anyone in here?"

Tillie's head appeared around a tall wing chair, her unbound dark hair tumbling across her arm. "Ana? What are you doing awake and about at this hour?"

14

Ana pressed farther into the room, leaving the lamp on a desk near the door. "I could ask the same of you."

Tillie shrugged and disappeared behind the chair. Mindful of the fire burning brightly in the fireplace, Ana skirted the hearth and dropped into another chair a satisfactory distance from the blaze.

Small, petite Tillie looked even more waiflike with her legs drawn up beneath her nightdress and her long tresses splayed about her shoulders. Ana held up a corner of her blanket. "Cold?"

Tillie accepted the offer with a grateful nod. With just a small bit of wrangling they managed to spread the blanket over them both, a dip in the middle where it spanned the two chairs.

Once the room returned to stillness, Ana turned her attention to the crackling fire. Not liking how it whispered, she shivered and looked at Tillie. "How long have you been awake?"

"An hour. Maybe two."

"Bad dreams?"

Tillie nodded.

Ana shrank into her chair. "Me too."

The fire popped, spitting a burst of sparks up the chimney. Tillie slipped from her seat, grabbed a poker and prodded the logs into a pile, then adjusted the screen to keep stray ashes from escaping.

Ana released the tension from her shoulders and smiled through the gloom at her friend. "Thank you."

Rubbing her hands over her arms, Tillie nodded and scrambled back to her seat. "Have you plans for this Saturday?"

Ana shrugged. Saturdays were idle, so apart from her list of household chores, she had no plans.

Tillie hugged her blanket-draped knees, her teeth working

her bottom lip and her brow drawn in a frown. "Meg has me thinking," she said at last.

"About?"

"The shelter at Our Lady of Deliverance. Father Ed runs it."

"I know the place," Ana said, prodding her with a nod.

"Meg says there are over forty women living there, some of them sick, or running from abuse and in desperate need of a place to hide." Her eyes gleamed as she twisted a lock of her hair round and round on her finger. "A lot of them are simply alone in the world and looking to start a new life."

Ana smiled indulgently. "That be a weighty topic for this hour of the morning, don't you think? Wouldn't that be something better discussed when we're both more alert?"

Tillie's gaze, so direct as to be piercing, fastened onto Ana. She felt a twinge inside her chest—similar to the uncomfortable pricking of conscience she used to feel as a lass after she'd spent time in the confessional. "Sorry. Go on."

"I'm thinking I'd like to help, maybe volunteer an hour or so after I leave the milliner and on the weekends."

"Doing what?" Ana's heart raced faster with each word Tillie uttered.

She lifted her hand in a wave. "Dishes, laundry, cooking . . . whatever they need." Reaching across the span between their two chairs, she grasped Ana's fingers tightly. "I'd like you to come with me. Will you?"

There it was—the question she'd been dreading. Ana pulled her hand free and jerked up from her chair. The blanket rippled to the floor, but neither she nor Tillie bothered picking it up. Ana skirted the heap and flitted to the window.

"Why is it my help you ask for, Tillie? Why not Amelia, or Meg? You know I . . . I do not attend church."

"I'll not be asking you to." Her lips bunched in a pout as she uncrossed her legs and joined Ana at the window. "These

16

women need our help. So what if the shelter be housed in a church? It's a building, Ana. Nothing more. Surely you wouldn't mind helping now and again."

Tillie didn't . . . couldn't . . . understand. And why would she? It wasn't as though Ana had ever bothered to explain her reluctance about attending Sunday services. She rested her hand against the frosted windowpane, letting the cool glass soothe her scarred flesh, and closed her eyes. A moment later, Tillie's warm fingers squeezed her shoulder.

"Ana, the reason you refuse to attend mass with us, why you won't set foot inside a church . . ."

She hesitated and Ana shivered.

Her voice lowered to a whisper. "Is it because of the nightmares?"

Searing, screaming flames. Her mother's pale face. Droned prayers falling from the lips of a faceless priest—

Ana jerked her eyes open and wrenched from Tillie's grasp. "I-It's complicated, Tillie." With each step across the library floor she avoided the flapping terror that closed her throat, but it wasn't far enough. Never far enough to take her beyond its clawed reach.

Tillie snagged her arm, forcing Ana to meet her gaze. "Complicated or no, have you never wondered why, after all these years, they still haunt you? Maybe if you talked to Father Ed—"

Anger straightened her spine, sped her breathing. "I know why they still haunt me, Tillie. Because what happened to my family was horrible—something no child should ever have to live through. And afterward I was alone! No priest, no . . . *God* to hear or answer my prayers. Just a stranger the priest paid to put me on a ship and escort me to an orphanage a thousand miles from home. Have you any idea what it feels like to be that alone?"

Pain shimmered in the tears falling from her friend's eyes, cutting the wretched words from Ana's tongue. At her midsection, Tillie's hands wrung the wide, wasted folds of her nightdress.

Ana took one step toward her and stopped, horrified by her arrogance and self-pity. "I'm so sorry, Tillie. I didna mean—"

Tillie gave a low sigh and let her hands slide to her sides. "We both have things we need to let go of, Ana. Maybe finding time to help another—maybe it'll help us move on. My Braedon . . . he would not have wanted me to spend my life pining for him and our child. Neither would your mother or sister want you looking back and missing them."

But she had moved on . . . hadn't she? An entire ocean, in fact. Ana swallowed the lump in her throat and pulled her hands close to her body, hiding the scars beneath her crossed arms. "Maybe you're right. I'll . . . think on it."

"Promise?"

Though her insides trembled and her knees felt weak, Ana smiled. "Aye."

Tillie's hand, so small compared to Ana's, moved in a pat. "I'll stop by there tomorrow—" she glanced out the window, where the sky had just begun to glow a light pink—"today actually, after I leave the milliner shop, and see what work they have to be done."

"Tillie," Ana warned, grabbing her wrist before she could dash out of reach, "I said I'd think on it."

Thankfully her eyes were brimming not with tears but with merriment. "I know you did, dearie."

"I may decide that volunteering at the shelter is not for me."

"Of course."

Ana frowned, the sleeves of her nightdress billowing over her arms as she propped her fists on her hips. "And you wilna be disappointed if I decide not to go?"

Tillie leaned forward and pressed a kiss to Ana's cheek. "Good night, dearie. I'll see you in the morning."

Ana gestured out the window toward the lightening sky. "It's morning already."

"Aye, but if we're going to work extra hours at the shelter, we'd best try to wrangle a few more winks before breakfast."

"Tillie—" Ana protested, too late.

She whirled, her nightdress swirling about her heels as she darted from the library. In seconds, her tapping footsteps faded to silence on the stairs.

Moving to the window, Ana freed the sigh trapped in her lungs, her breath forming a crystal cloud on the glass.

Tillie was right about letting go, but some things were dug in too deep, and entering a church . . . she hadn't done that since she was a young lass. True, Tillie carried a grievous burden of her own, and Ana had no desire to see her friend pained further. But why should it matter if she exposed her wounds to a priest or if she chose to bear her anguish in silence?

Both fists curled, she banged the library window so hard the glass rattled. She wouldn't do it. No matter what Tillie said or how she pleaded, Ana would never again set foot inside a church.

Ever.

— ❊ ❊ ❊ —

The sun peeking over the rooftops of Canal Street pried at Eoghan's eyelids, dragging him from his liquor-induced slumber on tearing, tenacious fingers. Groaning, he rolled from his stomach onto his back, gradually becoming aware of the cold, hard steps where he'd lain awkwardly through the night.

Blinking, he peered up, up, up . . . past ivy-covered walls to a gleaming silver steeple that pierced the sky like a sword.

A church?

A derisive snort blasted from his cracked lips. This had to be Kilarny's doing, with his twisted sense of humor.

He rocked to a sitting position, taking a moment to brace his throbbing head between his palms. Normally he avoided the taverns, avoided the danger of dulled senses, but last night . . .

Last night he'd hoped tipping back a few mugs would soften the Fenians' resolve against him, maybe even convince Kilarny to remember Ireland and better times—when all that mattered to either of them was helping the Fenians achieve Irish independence from England. . . .

And when he wasn't viewed as a traitor.

His hand slid to cover his aching jaw. At least they hadn't killed him. That was something.

Behind him, the door creaked open, followed by a decidedly feminine gasp. "Wha—? Father Ed, come quick!"

The woman's strident voice hit him broadside. Eoghan screwed his eyes shut and clutched his head against a wave of renewed pounding.

"Father Ed!"

Twisting, Eoghan lifted a pleading hand toward the dour-faced woman. "Madam, please."

Her eyes narrowed as she stared at him. She blew out a "humph" and folded her ample forearms over her black-clad bosom. "My name is Sister Mary, lad, not madam."

"Sister Mary, then," Eoghan said, stifling another snort as he went back to cradling his head.

"Are you drunk?"

"What?"

Her booted feet pounded the steps as she circled to stand in front of him. Leaning down, she braced her hands against her hips and looked him square in the eyes. "I said—" she paused, punctuating her next words with an ever sharper glare—"have . . . you . . . been . . . drinking!"

"Aye!" Eoghan exclaimed, hoping the admission might somehow convince her to stop talking, then grimaced. Shouting was definitely a bad idea.

She straightened, disapproval etched in the creases ringing her stern lips. "Humph. Better the son of a gambler than a drinker, me ma always said."

"And neither one very fitting for a child of God," a deeper voice added firmly.

The hostility melted from Sister Mary's shoulders faster than butter on a hot biscuit. "Father Ed . . . of course . . . it's just . . ."

She pointed at Eoghan, her finger traveling with her gaze over the stains on his shirt. "Well, see for yourself."

A lighter step scraped the stairs behind Eoghan, and then a kind-faced man with red hair ruffled by the wind squatted in front of him, his hand extended. "Hello, lad. Welcome to Our Lady of Deliverance. My name is Edward Murphy—Father Ed to my parishioners."

"Oh . . . en Hamilton," Eoghan said, changing the oath he'd been about to mutter into a strangled pronunciation of his name when he saw the priest's eyebrows lift. He took Father Ed's hand and gave it a reluctant shake, wincing as the movement sent fresh pain charging through his temples.

"Looks like you've had quite a night." He pointed at Eoghan's jaw, which by the feel of it bore a rather ugly bruise.

"To put it mildly."

"And you slept out here, on the church steps?"

Eoghan nodded, not that he could remember.

"Lucky you didn't freeze to death," Sister Mary chimed, her frown returning. "It's cold for October."

"Come now, Sister. A kind word never broke anyone's

mouth." Father Ed rose to his feet and offered his hand to help Eoghan. "Besides, weren't you about to head for the market?"

The ill-tempered nun gave a grunt that jiggled the rolls on her hips. "Aye, that I was."

"I doubt Sister Agnes will be pleased if she's forced to wait on the potatoes for her stew."

Whoever Sister Agnes was, the mere mention of her name was enough to drive the frown from Sister Mary's lips. Swaying in his shoes, Eoghan bit back a groan. Another nun worse than this one?

Sister Mary's head bobbed once, twice, and then she barreled down the steps. "I'll be back in an hour," she called over her shoulder, moments before she disappeared around the wrought-iron fence surrounding the church. Bolted to the hinges was a wooden sign that bore the name *Our Lady of Deliverance* in faded yellow letters.

Squinting to make out the smaller words scrolled beneath the name, Eoghan leaned forward and nearly toppled down the steps.

Father Ed caught him by the elbow. "Easy there, lad." He tapped his fiery red head and grinned. "No sense adding to the bruises on your nugget, or another tear to your coat."

Eoghan tugged on the tattered hem of his tweed jacket, shame heating his cheeks. "No, I guess not." He cleared his throat. "Well, it was nice to meet you and . . . her." He motioned in the direction Sister Mary had taken.

Father Ed smiled kindly.

"I guess I should be going now." He turned to move down the steps.

Father Ed stretched his hand toward the church door. "Are you hungry?"

"What?"

"I dinna suppose you've had a chance to break the fast?"

Eoghan's stomach rumbled in response. In fact, he'd missed far more than just breakfast. He didn't know what kind of cook Sister Agnes might be, but the thought of a hearty meat-and-potato stew was enough to make his mouth water. He shoved his hands into his pockets, reminded by the lint that clung to his fingernails of his plight.

He lowered his gaze, surprising himself with his honesty. "I do not have any money."

Or clothes, or a place to stay.

Father Ed clapped Eoghan on the shoulder. "Ach, then 'tis lucky for you that I have plenty of work needing to be done around the church. You're a godsend, for sure and for certain."

"I'm anything but a godsend, Father." Again, Eoghan was startled by his own honesty. What was it about this priest that lured the truth from him before he could even think?

Father Ed shrugged and climbed the steps to push open the door. "I suppose that remains to be seen, eh, lad? In the meantime, what say you come inside? We'll work out the details of your employment after we've put some meat in your belly."

Eoghan licked his lips, tempted almost beyond reason by the offer to staunch the quivering in his limbs brought on by hunger.

"Well?" Father Ed tipped his head toward the entrance. "You coming?"

Throwing his head back, Eoghan narrowed his eyes and stared at the steeple piercing the sky. So, it was a church. What did it matter if it meant earning enough sustenance to carry him through another day?

"Aye, I'm coming." Feet dragging, he followed Father Ed to the door. A moment later, he did the one thing he swore he'd never do again.

He set foot inside a church.

2

Ana clung to the wrought-iron bars of the fence surrounding Our Lady of Deliverance. The smell of new paint taunted her nose, and fresh oil glistened from the hooks pinning the church sign to the fence, so it no longer squawked when prodded by a brisk wind, like today. Below the name of the church had been painted FATHER EDWARD MURPHY in crisp, straight letters.

"*. . . have you never wondered why, after all these years, they still haunt you? Maybe if you talked to Father Ed . . .*"

Ana clutched the bars tighter, the name rolling on her tongue. Tillie thought Father Ed could help. But to get to him, one had to pass through a pair of forbidding oak doors.

"You all right, Ana?" Meg's face, plain though it was, shone with kindness as she peered around the bars at Ana. "You look like you swallowed a moldy biscuit."

Ana grimaced and uncurled her fingers from the fence, one by one. Indeed, her breakfast did sit like a stone in her stomach. "I don't feel well is all. Maybe we should come back another time."

"And leave Tillie to work in there all alone?" Meg caught Ana by the hand and tugged her around the fence to the steps. "We couldn't. Not after everything she's done for us so's we could spend the day at the shelter." She gave a toss of her head that set her jaunty curls to bouncing. "Besides, 'tis only one Saturday we agreed to, not a month of them."

"Aye, and I still do not ken how she managed to wrangle that much," Ana grumbled, her toes curling inside her boots as she climbed the first step and stopped. Overhead, the steeple jabbed the sky like an accusing finger, pointing to the One she had rejected.

Who rejected me, she reminded herself angrily, giving vent to her surging emotions with a stomp of her foot.

Hitching her skirt, Ana churned up the remaining steps. "Come on then, let's get this over and done."

She didn't wait for Meg, but gave the door a hearty beating with her fist. Her bravado fled when the door opened a crack and a pair of beady eyes looked her over from head to toe.

"No need to pound. The doors are not locked." The crack widened, filled almost full by a starched black habit. It rustled crisply as the nun wearing it jerked her thumb over her shoulder. "If you're in need of a place to stay, the shelter is around back."

Heat flamed in Ana's cheeks. "A place to—? No, ma'am. I mean, Sister . . . ma'am. I . . . that is, we . . ." She staggered to a halt and gestured weakly at Meg.

The nun's eyes grew narrower with each flustered word. Scowling, she folded her arms and tapped her booted foot. "Well?"

To Ana's relief, Meg stepped around her and stretched out her hand. "It's me, Sister Mary. Megan Riley." With her free hand she patted Ana's arm. "And this is my friend, Ana Kavanagh. We're here to volunteer in the shelter."

The woman's face transformed from dour to delighted in an instant. Her voluminous sleeves billowed as she flung her arms around Meg in an enthusiastic hug. "Megan Riley? It is you! Why in heaven's name didn't you say so? Come in, come in." She pushed the door open and swept to one side, jabbering and clucking. "What a delight to see you again, lass. Did Father Ed know you were comin'?"

Meg shook her head and linked her arm with the nun's as they walked down the wide center aisle between pews, chatting like old friends.

Ana followed more slowly, avoiding looking at the statues of the saints that adorned one wall and the Virgin Mary the other. Overhead, the vaulted ceiling snagged the sound of her footsteps and hurled them back down on her head, making them sound unnaturally heavy and loud. She swallowed hard and kept moving. Though the polished pews she passed invited her touch, she kept her fingers tucked tightly into the folds of her skirt.

Finally she reached the front of the church, and there hanging above the altar was a gleaming gold crucifix.

Ana froze, pinned to the floor before her Judge. Of their own accord, her eyes drifted upward, from the pierced feet to the intricately carved beard and beyond, to the outstretched hands.

She sucked in a quivering breath, bracing for the condemnation that was sure to flow her way.

Instead she felt only sorrow as she gazed at the Man's carved face, at the beads of blood and sweat that poured from the twisted crown on His brow—

"Ana?"

She jerked her head toward the sound of Meg's voice.

"You coming?"

Both she and Sister Mary eyed her intently, Meg with a quizzical bent to her smile, the nun with a wider, more knowing grin.

Ana rubbed her sweat-soaked palms down her skirt. "Aye, I'm coming." Resisting the urge to shepherd one last glance at the crucifix, she scurried to the door where Meg and the sister waited. "Sorry."

The nun gave a surprisingly gentle pat to Ana's shoulder. "No need to apologize, lass. God's house is just the place for those in search of something. Maybe later you can come back into the sanctuary by yourself. Sit awhile and pray, if you like."

"No," she said, quickly enough and with enough vehemence to invite a surprised glance. Though her mouth was dry, she swallowed and forced a smile. "We came to work. 'Tis about time we got started, isn't that right, Meg?"

Indeed, she had deeper reasons than mollifying Tillie for coming, but since no one had asked, she saw no reason to say more. Squaring her shoulders, Ana stepped through the door into a wide hall framed on both sides with paintings of various sizes. Rather than take in the figures depicted in them, she kept her focus on the large room that opened off the end. Cheery voices drew her, and by the time she crossed the threshold, some of her discomfort had disappeared, though the priest, she noticed, was nowhere to be seen.

"Ana, there you are!" Tillie rushed around a table laden with savory smelling breakfast food and grasped both of Ana's hands firmly. "Thank you for coming."

"Thank Meg." Ana tipped her head at the woman emerging from the hall on Sister Mary's arm. "If it weren't for her, I might not have made it past the gate."

Tillie laughed, the merry sound drowned amongst the chatter of the shelter residents. The clamor grew as a few of the women recognized Meg and moved to surround her with glad welcomes.

Tillie tilted her head to whisper in Ana's ear, "You're here. That's all that matters."

Grabbing Ana's hand, she spun and led the way back to the serving line. The women working there parted to make room, and within moments Ana had a spoon in her hand and was busily dishing out hearty helpings of bread and fried potatoes. After breakfast, she and Meg lugged buckets of water for the dishes while Tillie maneuvered a broom around the large kitchen. Ana met Sister Agnes during the cleanup, who though less talkative than Sister Mary, seemed likable enough.

"Here," Sister Agnes said, jamming a plate piled high with leftovers under Ana's nose. "Take that to the hired man round back." She jabbed her thumb toward an exit near the rear of the church kitchen. "You'll find him in the stable tending to a few chores while Father Ed is gone."

Her wits cut from under her, Ana stared at the plate clutched in her fingers. "Father Ed is . . . gone?"

"Went out to the island—Ellis, that is. He does that from time to time, usually once or twice a week to check on refugees for the shelter."

"Refugees?"

One eye closed in a wink. "That's what Father Ed calls 'em."

Ana's heart sank. So much for speaking with the priest. The day was for naught. "I see."

"Go on," Sister Agnes urged with a wave of her apron. "The food's cold enough as it is—no sense dallying about while it sprouts icicles. He's a good-looking lad, tall and lanky. Goes by Derry. If you don't spot him straightaway, call out for him, right?" She patted Ana's cheek before grabbing her by the shoulders and spinning her toward the door. "There's a good lass. And I hope you don't mind waiting for Derry to empty the plate before you come back inside. Otherwise he'll leave it, and one of them wooden-headed cows will likely smash it to bits."

Wait. Cows. Bits.

The orders rattled like pebbles inside Ana's head. Though she had no idea where she was going or for whom she was searching, her heels scraped across the kitchen, out the door, and down the steps toward the stable.

Across a broad courtyard, one half of two livery doors gaped, spilling the scent of animals and fresh hay into the air. Ana sniffed gingerly, then poked her head inside and took a look around. It was warmer inside the livery, but not unpleasantly so. On a cold winter day, she imagined it could be quite pleasant surrounded by cows and hay, and soft, fuzzy lambs.

She eased deeper into the livery's dim recesses. In the stall closest to the door, a cow lowed a greeting, and farther away, a shovel scraped the wooden floor. "D-Derry?"

Her voice caused a stir amongst the hens, pecking corn from the hay strewn haphazardly around the entrance. Clawed feet scrambling over worn wooden boards accompanied the flapping of wings for a moment before returning the stable to relative quiet. Ana shifted the plate to one hand and shoved the door wide to let in more light.

Drawing a breath, she managed a shaky "Hello?"

"Down here."

Midway down the row of stalls, a pile of hay erupted into a dusty cloud above the stall wall. Ana eyed her burden critically and then did her best to shield the food from what dirt and chaff she could manage with one hand. "Are you Derry?"

"Aye, that's me. Leastwise, that's what the sisters call me. Who's asking?"

At the gruff voice, a knot of nervousness formed in Ana's belly. She swallowed and tried to sound cheery, though her feet remained rooted like saplings to the spot near the door. "I brought your breakfast."

"Breakfast? I didn't ask for any breakfast."

29

A head popped up over the stall wall. Even from this distance, Ana felt herself snared by the glittering hazel gaze shooting out from beneath a ragged tweed cap. The man's face was pleasant enough, but gaunt, the cheekbones too defined, as if he'd only just recovered from a lengthy illness. She lowered her eyes and nodded. "Sister Agnes sent it."

Instead of leaving the stall, the man merely leaned a shoulder against the wall. "There's a bench near the door there. Leave it. I'll eat when I finish mucking."

Ana glanced at the rickety bench. Like the rest of the place, it was covered in dust and bits of hay. She shook her head and held up the plate. "I brought no napkin to cover the food. It's likely to get a most unsavory sprinkling of dirt if you don't eat it now."

The stubborn man only grunted and proceeded to cross his arms. "Let me guess . . . Sister Agnes told you to wait on it so you could return the plate."

Ana simply shrugged and held the plate higher. Though it had been years since she'd been to church, she still wasn't keen on the idea of lying while inside one—or near one, as was the case.

A chuckle drifted from the man's throat and rumbled her insides. He straightened and then sauntered—for there was no other way to describe his gait—out of the stall to the entrance where Ana waited.

"I'll take that."

At the brush of his fingers, Ana instantly averted her gaze and moved back a step. Maybe he'd hurry. Maybe he was a fast eater and she could finish this unpleasant task and return to the kitchen—

"Um . . ."

She could lift her eyes no further than the cleft on his chin. "Aye?"

He hesitated and shuffled from foot to foot. When next he spoke, his tone had softened to something less than that belonging to a bear. "I . . . uh . . . don't suppose . . ."

"Is something wrong?"

He cleared his throat. "Have you by chance got a fork hidden in your sleeve?"

"A fork?" Ana scanned the plate of cooling potatoes and eggs, and the hearty crust of bread. No fork. Had she thought to bring nothing besides the food?

"Unless you mean for me to eat with my hands."

"I'm sorry, I . . ."

"Never mind."

The man curled long tapered fingers around a slice of potato and brought it to his mouth. Transfixed, Ana's gaze followed.

"There you are." His hazel eyes twinkling, he shrugged and offered a lopsided grin. "Sorry about my temper just then. Mucking stalls tends to put one in a foul mood."

Heat fanned from Ana's cheeks, down her neck, to her toes. There was something startlingly familiar about the man's smile, but rather than try to place it, she clasped her hands behind her back and turned to go.

"Wait. I did not mean to embarrass you."

At the touch he placed on her arm, Ana immediately stiffened. "I'm not embarrassed," she snapped, directing a pointed glare at her elbow. When he released his hold, she resumed. "I simply have other chores to be tending."

"I see," he said, drawing out the words in a saucy manner she found disrespectful. Adding further injury, he garnished the insult with a smirk.

Ana drew a deep breath and fought a swell of anger. "I'm not so old as Father Ed's cow, but neither am I a schoolgirl to be so easily embarrassed."

"Of course you're not." He quirked an eyebrow and brought another sliver of potato to his lips. "Old, I mean," he added before popping the food into his mouth.

"Or embarrassed," Ana insisted, crossing her arms.

He chewed thoughtfully, then frowned. "Not so certain on that point."

"Excuse me?"

"One would think you'd be inclined to stay if you were truly as hardened as all that."

Ana gritted her teeth, realizing as she did that truthfully the man—Derry—she corrected mentally, had done nothing to inspire such wrath. Helpless to tamp it, she plopped onto the bench, dust and all. "Fine then, I'll wait. Suits me better to sit out here anyway."

She cast a scorching glance out the barn door toward the steeple. This was all *His* fault—His way of punishing her for breaking her vow and setting foot inside the church.

With new direction for her anger, Ana ignored Derry as he claimed the dusty spot next to her on the bench and proceeded to wolf his breakfast.

"I don beleef I caw ur nem."

"Was that English or something else?" Ana asked.

Derry grinned wickedly, swiped his sleeve across his mouth, and swallowed. "Sorry about that—forgot me manners. I said I don't believe I caught your name."

"Kavanagh."

"Kavanagh?" His brow lifted, as did his voice.

"Miss." Ana jutted her chin away from his wheedling gaze. She'd seen his kind before—devilish rakes with little or no regard for a lady, though she had to admit to a certain amount of surprise at seeing him employed in a house of worship.

"Well, Miss Kavanagh, it's a pleasure to make your acquaintance." He set aside his plate, rubbed his palms on his trouser legs, and offered his hand.

Ana hesitated. He had not yet seen her scars—at least, she didn't think so, but if she accepted his handshake . . .

Burying her fingers in the folds of her skirt, she dipped her head. "A pleasure."

"Ach . . . me manners again. I'm afraid it's been too long since I've enjoyed feminine company." He rose and swept the cap from his head. "Name's—"

"Derry. I know," Ana interrupted.

He wagged his finger. "That's *Mr.* Derry."

Ana glanced up at him, a warm blush heating her cheeks at the amusement in his hazel eyes. He was mocking her!

She jumped to her feet. Plate or no, she refused to remain in his presence a second longer. "Well, Mr. Derry, it has been—" the lie died on her lips—"interesting," she improvised. "However, I believe I'm needed inside. Please see that you don't forget to return the plate to Sister Agnes."

She started to motion, caught herself, and clasped both hands at her midriff. "Good day."

"But—"

Thankfully, Ana did not trip as she scurried out of the stable, across the yard, and back to the church.

"Wait," the voice behind her called. "It was a jest only. I'm not really called Derry. My name is—"

Ana slammed the door, cutting off the rest of the man's speech. What made him think she cared what his name was? He was the hired man, and she'd offered him food.

That was all.

Because Sister Agnes had asked her to.

And yet . . .

The quivery, breathless feeling in her chest lingered long after she, Tillie, and Meg gathered their things and left the church. Like a living thing, it dogged her steps out the door, down the sidewalk, all the way to the boardinghouse. Even there, she found herself hard-pressed to shake the memory of that haunting hazel gaze.

Enough of that, Ana admonished as she hung her cloak on a row of hooks inside the boardinghouse door. It made no difference to her who the man was, or why his presence had shaken her so. She squared her shoulders and marched down the hall, past the parlor, and toward the kitchen to help with dinner. After all, she had no intention of ever laying eyes on him again, because doing so would mean returning to the church. And that was something she refused to endure again.

Ever.

— ✸ ✸ ✸ —

The Celt watched from his carriage window as three young women scurried up the steps to Amelia Matheson's boardinghouse. They were all attractive in their way, but the tallest one, the one with riotous curls spilling down her back . . . she had caught his eye. At the top step she stuck out one hand and opened the door with an awkward twist—unusual when compared to her otherwise graceful movements.

He settled back against the velvet seat and rapped his cane on the roof of the carriage, sending it into jolting motion. Aye, that was the lass. She'd grown into quite a beauty. It was unfortunate that he'd have to use her, considering all she'd been through.

He flicked a piece of ash from his sleeve, annoyed that here in New York, as in Dublin, there was no escaping the dirt and soot of the city.

Innocent as the girl was, however, there really was no other solution. He needed Brion McCleod. Lucky for him, McCleod needed Ana Kavanagh.

He stared out the window, admiring the turning foliage on a row of giant oaks as a new thought struck him. In essence, that meant they both needed Ana.

They just needed her dead.

3

Eoghan muttered to himself as he speared a pitchfork of fresh hay and lobbed it into the stall he'd spent the previous hour mucking. Wasn't like him to make a proper heel of himself on such short acquaintance. Then again, he hadn't *asked* Sister Agnes to send a girl to deliver his breakfast, especially not a slip of a girl with enormous brown eyes that rounded like a wounded puppy's when he snapped at her. And her hands . . .

He jabbed the pitchfork into another mound of hay and flipped it into the stall. He hadn't wanted breakfast at all. What he'd wanted was to be allowed to work off the food he'd consumed the day before and then be on his way. If it weren't for the wages Father Ed had promised, enough to sustain him long enough to come up with a new plan for ingratiating himself with the Fenians, he'd have been gone with the sunrise.

Satisfied with the depth of hay on the stall floor, Eoghan leaned the pitchfork against the wall, then rested his back next to it. The job, normally an easy one, had taken him most of the day, but that was due in part to the condition of the barn.

On top of the general labor to clean it, he'd repaired and filled the feed bins, restocked the loft with hay, and mended not one or two, but three stall doors.

For sure and for certain, Father Ed had not exaggerated when he'd told Eoghan the church was in need of a handyman. But now that he'd finished in the barn, had he worked himself out of food and lodging?

He grimaced as he latched the door and swung for the church steps. Aye, and had it not been but yesterday that he'd been reluctant to accept the job in the first place?

That was before he sampled Sister Agnes's cooking. He sighed with pleasure as the warm, yeasty fragrance of baking bread greeted him when he entered the kitchen. Ach, but the scent brought back memories of his childhood—before he'd been tainted by betrayal and blood.

He took a deep breath, his mouth watering at the thought of dinner, but before he could take one step toward the dining room, Sister Mary appeared and shoved a broom into his hands.

Her brow lowered in a glower. "Is that chaff I see clinging to them boots?"

Eoghan backed out the door onto the steps. "Chaff? No. Just a wee bit of dust is all." He moved the broom lazily over the tops of his boots. "I had no intention of sullying your floor. I fully intended to clean up before I went looking for you."

She narrowed her eyes. "For me?"

"Aye, to tell you what a bonnie smile you have, and what an angel you are for always sneaking me one of Sister Agnes's rolls when she's not looking."

Growling, Sister Mary jerked the broom from Eoghan's hands and replaced it in a narrow closet before stomping to a tray of cooling bread. She plucked one from the center and dropped it into his eager palm. "There, and get on with you now, before Sister Agnes catches me feeding you like some stray pup."

Eoghan stifled a laugh with a bite from the warm, fluffy roll. Pure delight melted over his tongue, almost as pleasurable as the verbal sparring he'd enjoyed earlier with Miss Kavanagh. Perhaps Sister Mary could tell him who she was. Instead of leaving, Eoghan settled onto a high stool.

"I finished with the repairs to the barn."

"Good. Father Ed will be glad to hear it." She grabbed a pail and miniature flat-head shovel, then went to squat before the stove. Reaching in, she scraped the ashes into the pail. "It's been in need of repair for a long time. Father Ed is a dear, but he's hopeless with a hammer."

"Lucky for him, there isn't much call for one in the pulpit."

"Depends on who you ask," Sister Mary said, her mouth curving in a pert grin.

Eoghan answered with his own grin. He liked this sassy old nun, who often spoke her mind yet consistently found ways to temper her words with humor. Plus she was absent of the guile that plagued most women. There was an innocence about her, a sincerity of heart which no doubt explained the habit—few though there were who could wear it.

"Me da would argue a hammer upside my head might have done me a bit of good," he said ruefully. He stuffed another bite of bread into his mouth and chewed thoughtfully.

Sister Mary shrugged. Finished scraping out the ashes, she jammed the spade into the pail and rose. Hopping off his stool, Eoghan took the pail from her and carried it outside to pour on the compost pile. Mixed with manure and straw, it would make good fertilizer and keep the church's fall crops from freezing. When he returned, Sister Mary had replenished the wood in the stove and was fanning a small fire to life. Satisfied the blaze had taken hold, she shut the door and then dusted her hands on her apron.

She tipped her head toward the uneaten half of his roll. "Finish that and then come join me in the sanctuary. I've got some work in there I need you to see to."

The sanctuary? He'd already spent a day and a half avoiding the place. He jammed the rest of the roll into his mouth and followed Sister Mary out of the kitchen. At least he hadn't worked himself out of a job.

She pointed to a short flight of steps that wound along one wall and finished at the pulpit. "Them stairs creak so loud on Sunday morning, they're enough to wake the parishioners. Think you can do anything to fix them?"

Eoghan laughed and hooked his thumbs in his pockets. "Aye, I reckon I can."

"And the windows." She pointed upward at several leaded glass panes. "A couple of them have cracked, and more threaten to break if we don't do something about the leaks in those seals." She shivered and ran her plump fingers down her arms. "The way the wind whistles through here in winter, one would think we were holding services in an icebox. 'Tis a miracle no one has froze to death."

Judging by the bits of mortar collecting on the sills, she was likely right. Eoghan brushed the pieces to the floor and nodded. "Might take me a couple of days, but I can patch them up for you."

Sister Mary's rosy cheeks lifted in a smile before she turned to amble back toward the kitchen. "Don't you fret about how long it takes to finish. You just see to it that this room stays nice and toasty come the first snowfall. I'll take care of the rest."

The priest's threadbare garments and worn shoes flashed through Eoghan's brain as he trailed her to the door. "By 'the rest,' I take it you mean Father Ed?"

She snorted. "The man worries too much. Never have seen God fail to provide a nickel when we need it. He sent you, didn't He? And just when we thought the place would fall down round our ears." Pausing with one hand on the knob, her stern tone dissolved into a chuckle. "To think I almost tossed ya back into the street. 'Twould have been like the blind man turning up his nose at Jesus."

The words pricked his spirit. He wasn't accustomed to being thought of as a godsend, and this made twice in almost as many days. He caught her sleeve before she could disappear into the hall. "Sister Mary, do you have a moment?"

She eyed him curiously. "Aye, lad. What's on your mind?"

"Why me? Why not one of the men of the church? Surely God could have sent one of them, or Father Ed could have asked for their help."

Her brown eyes, which at first he'd thought looked beady, softened with compassion. "Who can claim to know the mind of God, lad? Not I. I only know that He sent you here for a purpose, and glad I am He done it."

"And the women—the ones who come to volunteer—does He send them, too?"

The fabric of her habit rustled softly as she rested her back against the door. Framed by the cowl, her face looked kind, even angelic. "I suppose so. Why do you ask?"

Unsure how to answer, he shrugged. She motioned toward a pew, then sat down and slid over to make room. Hesitantly, Eoghan claimed the spot next to her. It had been years since a warm wooden pew had welcomed his backside. Even so, the feeling was oddly peaceful, the place surrounding him, inviting.

"I met a girl today," he began. "She's young. Pretty. But her hands are scarred."

The puzzlement cleared from Sister Mary's brow. "Ah, that one. Aye, I met her, too."

"Has she been here before?"

"Not that I can remember. Meg brought her, I think."

"Meg?"

"Megan Riley. She stayed with us when she first came to America."

"And the other? With the . . ." He wiggled his fingers. "What's her name?"

Sister Mary paused, and her lips parted in a knowing grin. "She did not tell ya?"

No, and he'd spent the better part of the afternoon trying to guess. Heat crept over his neck to his ears. "I'm afraid I may have left her with a poor first impression of myself."

"Not you." Her cheeks quivered with mirth as she leaned over to bump his shoulder. "Think how you and I first met."

He rolled his eyes. "I'd rather not. The bruises are still fresh."

"Lucky for you, Father Ed appeared before I could add to them."

He rubbed his knuckles over his scalp, thinking of the time or two when he'd witnessed Sister Mary wielding a heavy wooden spoon. "Lucky indeed."

Warmth radiated from her touch as she reached to pat his shoulder. "What did you do?"

"To make her angry?"

She nodded.

Eoghan scratched his temple. "I'm not sure, exactly."

His befuddlement unleashed her laughter. The cheerful

sound echoed from the rafters, then reached down and tickled his own sense of humor.

"Well now, and ain't that the way of it?" she said between gasps. "Women all tangled up in their emotions and men chasing after them trying to figure them all out." She laughed some more and then finally managed to run her fingers under her eyes to stem a flood of merry tears. "Ach, wait until I tell Father Ed."

"I'd rather you didn't," Eoghan said, sobering. "I've embarrassed myself enough where he is concerned." He lifted the collar of his borrowed shirt and grimaced. His own shirt had been too bloodied and torn to save.

"Ah, lad. You don't need to be embarrassed with Father Ed. Despite his faults, I've never met a kinder, more understanding man."

"Still, I'd rather not have to explain how a shy lass whom I've met only once managed to capture my fancy," Eoghan said with a snort.

"And is that what she's done?"

Her eyes fairly twinkled as he looked at her. He'd say no, but why then had a bonnie lass with a bashful smile, who hid her hands in the folds of her skirt when she thought he wasn't looking, consumed his thoughts?

The teasing melted from Sister Mary's face. "Her name is Ana Kavanagh."

Ana. He repeated the name silently to himself.

"She seems like a sweet lass. Lives in a boardinghouse on Ashberry Street with Meg and another of our volunteers, Tillie McGrath."

Eoghan froze. "Wait . . . Did you say Ashberry Street?"

She nodded. "Amelia Matheson owns it. She's one of our parishioners and another kind soul. I met her when . . ."

Sister Mary continued on, but he'd stopped listening.

Bracing both hands on the back of the pew, he pulled to his feet and crossed to the window, his boots thudding on the hardwood floor. A boardinghouse. Ashberry Street. It couldn't be the same place and yet . . . it had to be. The owner?

He whirled, cutting off Sister Mary mid-sentence. "Who did you say runs the place?"

She blinked. "You mean Amelia?"

He gave an impatient nod. "Her. What's her last name again?"

"It's Matheson." Sister Mary's brows lowered as she pushed from the pew and stood. "What's wrong, lad? What have I said?"

"Nothing. You've said nothing."

Fists balled, Eoghan clenched his jaw. It wasn't Sister Mary's fault, after all. She couldn't know the days and weeks he'd spent waiting, hoping—following a trail that had led him to Amelia Matheson's door, behind which he'd thought to obtain peace at last and found instead . . .

Bitterness washed over his tongue. He hadn't found peace. No happiness or reconciliation. Ashberry Street offered one thing and one thing only.

Betrayal.

— ❊ ❊ ❊ —

Groaning like a woman in labor, the deck of the *Etruria* pitched forward and back, then heaved from side to side. Knuckles white, Brion closed his eyes and grasped the edge of his bunk.

Blast this infernal boat! Two weeks and he'd nary left his bed for seasickness. Hadn't the steward promised they'd be making landfall soon? He'd already missed the appointed meeting with The Celt when he arrived in New York. Yet here he lay, his insides as roiled and tossed as the sea outside his porthole.

Clutching the edges of his shirt together tightly, he swung his feet to the deck and rose on shaking legs. The wall tilted to meet him. He leaned against it gratefully and inched toward the door, ignoring his cabin mate—a rail-thin bug of a man whom The Celt insisted accompany him—who huddled under his blankets as sick as Brion was. At least the moans had ceased sometime during the night. That was something.

"Steward!" Brion threw the door open with a crash. "Where are you?"

"Have . . . we landed?" The low rasp drifted from across the cabin. A weak rattling cough followed, the sound of which scraped at Brion's raw nerves.

"Steward!" he bellowed again, closing his ears to the young man's pathetic whimpering. If it hadn't been for the fact that his presence added some pleasant amenities to the trip, Brion might have pitched him overboard days ago.

A white-coated steward wove down the passageway, legs apart to keep from being bounced from wall to wall. Watching him made Brion's stomach roll.

"You called for me, sir?"

Swallowing against the burning at the back of his throat, Brion nodded. "How long before we reach land?"

"Should be any day now." The steward placed his hand on Brion's shoulder and squeezed as though to urge him back to his bunk. "Mind if I help you, sir?"

Brion growled and shrugged from his grasp. "You said 'twould be 'any day now' yesterday."

"That is true, sir, but this storm has slowed our passage."

As if to prove his point, the ship swelled beneath Brion's

feet and just as quickly dropped away, leaving him weak-kneed and nauseous.

"There now," the steward urged, "you see? It can't be helped. Best to wait out the remainder of this voyage in your bunk like your mate, over yonder there." He gestured to the lad's still form. "I'll check on you both before dinner, right?"

What could he say? Brion staggered across the cabin and flopped onto the plank that substituted for a bed before the next wave hit. Moving as though to tuck him under the sheets, the steward grabbed the blankets and reached for Brion's feet. Brion motioned him away with a snarl and a glare that sliced through his snide English demeanor. "See that you inform me the moment we're in sight of land."

The smug smile faded. "Will do."

"And take that mess." Brion pointed to a tray of food that his cabin mate had left untouched. "It's beginning to stink."

"Of course, sir," the steward said, bending to retrieve the tray and then pausing at the young man's bedside before he carried it from the room. "What about you, sir? Is there anything I can get for you?"

The whelp said nothing. Brion snorted. Now he slept, after keeping him awake half the night with his incessant moaning. He tossed onto his side and yanked the cover over his head.

"Mr. Whitham, sir? Can I get you a glass of water, perhaps a crust of bread to help settle your stomach?"

"Heaven's sake, man! Leave him be. He's resting is all," Brion shouted from his side of the cabin.

His curiosity piqued by the silence that followed, Brion poked out from under the covers. Still balancing the tray in one hand, the steward clutched a corner of Whitham's sheet with the other, his eyes round and his mouth agape.

Brion dragged himself up to sit. "What is it? Surely you've seen a man sleep before. Why are you standing there gaping like some infernal fish?"

"Sir . . . young Whitham . . . Mr. Whitham is . . ."

Brion dropped his gaze to the young man's pale face, his wide, glassy eyes, and the cracked lips where bits of foam had begun to collect. He lifted one corner of his mouth in disgust. "What's wrong with him? Is he dead?"

Dropping the tray, the steward backed from the cabin, his eyes flitting from Whitham to Brion as if they somehow shared the same plight. "Sir, I must ask that ya not leave this cabin, leastwise until I can fetch the ship's doctor and . . . and have 'im take a look at ya."

Funny how the bloke's proper English accent broke down when he was nervous, or frightened. Brion scowled. "Why? What business have I with him? I'm motion sick is all, unaccustomed to riding the sea."

"No, sir. It isn't seasickness." Grasping the knob, the steward gave a yank and then stumbled into the passageway.

"If not seasickness, then what?" Brion growled, beginning to feel uneasy over the steward's hasty departure. He threw aside the covers and leaned over the side of the bed. "Steward, get back here and tell me what is going on. And what about Whitham? You can't leave him here!"

Retrieving a key from his pocket, the steward fitted it to the lock in the cabin door, then braced himself. "Please, sir. Wait here. I'll be back shortly."

Brion eyed the key clutched in the steward's hand. "You're locking me in? Why? For what purpose?"

"I won't be gone long, I swear. Just going to fetch the doctor, and maybe the captain."

"Why?"

"Because . . . I'm afraid . . ."

"Aye?"

The door slammed shut, and the key scraped in the lock. A moment later, the steward's muffled voice drifted through the cracks. "I'm sorry, sir, but your cabin mate, Mr. Whitham . . . I'm afraid he's died of cholera."

4

Ana scraped the last bit of orange flesh from a pumpkin and then set the empty rind aside to be cut into a bowl for baking. Pumpkin custard. Her mouth watered at the thought of the sweet, spicy scent that would soon fill the kitchen. The seeds, too, were delicious when roasted and lightly salted. She couldn't wait to show Cara, who'd promised to stop by for a visit later, after she and Rourke had tended to a few tasks at the office where he worked.

Laverne, the boardinghouse cook and housekeeper, shuffled into the kitchen bearing a tray with the remnants of Amelia's afternoon tea. "How ya coming with that custard?"

"Just fine," Ana said, lifting the bowl to display her prize.

Laverne's head bobbed with pleasure. "That'll make a nice dessert, sure enough. Need me to fetch you some eggs?"

Thanks to the lamps Giles had rigged in the barn, and the warmer than normal temperatures, the hens were still laying. Ana nodded and pointed to the counter. "I've a couple there, but with this much pumpkin, I'm sure I could use a few more."

"Coming right up."

She scooted to the back door, her steps so light as to make Ana think she wore wings on her boots.

"Say hello to Giles for me," Ana called teasingly. Laverne never missed an opportunity to visit with the hired handyman, today notwithstanding. Not that Ana minded being left alone to finish the dessert for tonight's meal. Truly she enjoyed her job at Mr. O'Bannon's candle shop, but working alongside Laverne in a warm, toasty kitchen with the scent of baking bread tickling her senses . . .

Ach, this indeed was heaven. And tucked away where no one could see, she need pay no heed to what others might think of her hands.

What Derry might think.

Ana frowned. As quickly as the name—and the face that accompanied it—rose in her thoughts, she shoved it away. Oh, but she wished she could as easily shake the feeling that something about him was familiar. Maybe then she could finally rid her thoughts of his wry grin and dancing, devilish eyes.

Devil, indeed, she huffed, giving the spoon a hearty tap against the side of the bowl. Who else but a devil could ensnare a woman's thoughts so?

"Anyone home?" Cara's merry greeting rang from the front hall. Her eager steps followed, and soon she popped into the kitchen, her eyes twinkling and her cheeks rosy from the fresh air outside. "Ah, there you are."

Rounding the table, Ana wiped her hands on her apron and enveloped Cara in a hug. "Why, Mrs. Turner," she teased, "you're early. We weren't expecting you until closer to dinner."

Cara sighed and pulled from Ana's arms. Taking a spare apron off a peg near the door, she draped it over her head and turned to allow Ana to fasten the buttons. "Rourke is working late. I thought I'd come by and help Laverne. Suits me better than sitting around the house waiting for my husband to come home."

"So, I take it he's thinking heavily on the offer to work for the mayor's office?" Finished, Ana gave the bow a pat.

Cara shrugged, but a frown pulled at her lips.

"You're not happy about his decision?" Ana asked.

Cara slowly lifted a pot from a shelf above the stove, fiddled with the handle, set it back, and chose another. "I just wish we knew more about this Alfred Smith—the man Rourke will be working with," she added.

Grabbing a pitcher of cream and a tin filled with sugar, Ana went back to her custard making. "He seems likable enough, from what I've heard around the city."

"Aye, that he does."

"Even heard it rumored he's got an eye on the assembly."

Cara bit her lip. "I've also been privy to that talk."

Ana held the cream midair over the pumpkin bowl. "Is that what has you so troubled? You think Rourke might be getting himself mixed up in all that Tammany mess?"

She sighed. "Politics are in Rourke's blood, Ana. I've known that all along. After all, he is his father's son." She carried the pots to the water bucket on the floor next to the sink and filled them, one by one. "Still, I thought—hoped, rather," she clarified softly, "that after his uncles left to go back to Ireland . . ."

"He'd put the politician's life behind him?"

Worry shadowed her expression as she nodded.

Ana spooned sugar into her bowl and framed her next question carefully. "Cara, is Rourke's involvement with city hall the only thing bothering you?"

Cara blinked. "Of course. Why do you ask?"

"Well, since last June . . . you and he . . . your brother . . ."
She fumbled to a stop.

"The search for my brother has not been affected by the demands of Rourke's job." A misty sheen filmed her deep green eyes. "He has been true to his promise. Tireless, in fact, so I'm confident we'll find Eoghan one day, when the time is right."

Ana frowned. "Then I'm not sure I understand, Cara. Why wouldn't you want your man to pursue something he loves?"

Cara ducked her head and turned to place the pots of water on the stove. When at last she spoke, her voice was low, heavy. "Rourke's father was a politician back in Ireland, Ana, remember? His involvement with Irish parliament is what killed him. I just worry . . . for our children, when we have them . . ."

Plunking the sugar bowl onto the table, Ana moved to clasp Cara's hands. "Sean Healy is what killed Daniel Turner, Cara—him and his turncoat friends. Not parliament."

"Aye, but if he'd never been in a position of power, if Sean and his bunch hadn't viewed Rourke's father as a means to accomplishing their ends—"

"Exactly." Ana squeezed Cara's trembling fingers. "They looked on him as a weapon, not a person. And don't you be forgetting that we still don't know for certain what their ends were. For all we know, it might have had nothing at all to do with Daniel's stand on home rule the way Deidre claimed."

At the mention of Sean Healy's wife, who earlier that summer had kidnapped Cara and attempted to kill her, she slid her fingers from Ana's grasp. Bending quickly, she picked up a bushel of potatoes, placed them on the counter, then brushed her hands free of dirt. Ana suspected she was brushing free of the conversation as well, for she snagged a paring knife and went to work with a vengeance.

"So? You never told me how your visit to Our Lady went," Cara said.

Ana sighed and reached for an egg to crack into the bowl with the pumpkin. Tillie's prodding about speaking with

Father Ed had indeed birthed a battle—not enough to change her mind about returning, but it did occupy far too many of her thoughts. "It was . . . interesting." Her thoughts flashed to Derry, and she blushed.

Cara peeked over her shoulder at her, then set down her knife and wiped her hands on her apron. "I'm sorry, Ana. I didn't mean to embarrass you."

Ana froze as her friend's contrite apology stirred a memory.

The back door swung open, sweeping in a gust of autumn air and Laverne's full figure, a basket of eggs slung over her arm. "Cara, dear! You're here. We weren't expecting you till this afternoon."

"I know. Hope you don't mind?"

"Don't be silly." She chuckled and bustled across the kitchen toward Cara. "You and that fine-looking husband of yours are always welcome. Where is he, by the way? He still hasn't made me that vegetable trellis he promised."

"Where he spends most of his time lately—at work, of course."

Holding the eggshell suspended over the bowl, Ana watched as Cara sauntered forward to accept Laverne's embrace.

"I didn't mean to embarrass you."

The same words. The same gait. Even their eyes and the color of their hair were similar—his a touch darker, but ruddy and tinged with a bit of gold.

Her breath catching in her throat, Ana set down the eggs, the bowl, and lowered her head to collect herself. It was no wonder everything about Derry had seemed so familiar.

He was Cara's missing brother.

— ❋ ❋ ❋ —

For the third time that morning, the razor in Eoghan's hand slipped and nicked his finger. Smothering a growl, he dropped the blade onto the top step of the ladder where he stood, then lifted his hand to inspect the damage.

The wound was painful and long, but not deep. He licked the index finger of his other hand and was starting to rub away the blood when Sister Mary's voice stopped him.

"Don't you dare. Do you want to die of infection?" She hurried across the sanctuary to the window where he was working and held up a towel she pulled from a basket slung over her arm. "Use this."

"Thanks."

In answer she humphed and propped her fists on her hips. Watching critically as he wound the cloth over and around his hand, she finally blew out a sigh and motioned for him to come down. "All right, let me have a peek at it."

"No need," Eoghan said hastily. "It's not bad really. Just looks worse than it is—"

Her stern glower stopped him. He lowered himself down the rungs and offered up his hand.

"See?" he said after she'd finished perusing the wound. "I've seen paper cuts worse than this. It's not even an inch long."

"An inch is a great deal in a man's nose," she retorted. "Besides, you haven't left that ladder since breakfast. Time for a rest." She waggled her brows as she reached into the basket. "I brought you one of Agnes's rolls."

Holding the bread high, she smiled and waved it back and forth under his nose. Enticed by the odor, Eoghan pinched the roll from her fingers and draped an arm over her shoulders. "You're a temptress, Sister Mary. I wonder if Father Ed has any idea."

She laughed and sat with him on the steps leading to the pulpit, her brows lifting in surprise when they didn't creak. "You fixed them?"

"'Twas an easy enough job. I replaced a few nails, added a couple of shims." He shrugged before stuffing his mouth.

Sister Mary gave the tread a pat, her fingers trailing the worn wood and coming to rest on the curved rail that stretched to the podium. "Ach, but I'm glad to see this place finally getting the attention it needs. I've told you before, but I'll say it again, we're fortunate to have you, Derry, me boy."

Something about the way she spoke the words this time stirred a warmth in his heart that felt suspiciously like affection. If he wasn't careful, he'd forget all about rejoining the Fenians. He studied the bread in his hands, tore off a piece, and shoved it into his mouth. He felt her watching him as she set aside the basket and then tucked her fingers into her wide sleeves.

"Derry, there's something that's been troubling me for a while now . . . since last we talked actually."

The affection fled, and he glanced longingly at the ladder. "Oh?"

Her head bobbed. From the corner of his eye, it looked like the motion of a great, black bird.

"I said something that upset you, I think, but upon my life I can't figure what it could be."

He sighed. Much as he would have liked to return to work and avoid her questions, he couldn't allow her to go on fretting. "It wasn't anything you said, Sister. 'Tis my own tangled history that's been nipping at my heels, making me irritable. Please, do not trouble yourself."

"Tangled history?" she repeated.

He could think of no other way to phrase it, so he nodded. She nudged him with her shoulder. "Care to tell me about it?"

Aye. Nay. Both desires warred inside him. But wouldn't it feel good to give vent to the bitterness of betrayal that had festered for so long?

He jumped to his feet and jammed his hands into the pockets of his trousers, regretting the action when his finger caught a seam and began to throb. Still, it was a welcome pain compared to the ache in his heart. He strode the width of the sanctuary, the angry pounding of his boots speaking for him.

"What troubles you, lad? Say it. You'll feel better for having done so."

"It's just . . ."

"Aye?"

"The boardinghouse where you said Miss Kavanagh lives . . ."

"What about it?"

He dragged to a stop and whirled to face her. "Years ago, I made a mistake, and when I tried to fix it, a man . . . two men . . . were killed. I fought to prevent it," he added hastily, hating the urge to defend himself, yet despairing over the look of dismay that washed across the nun's face. "I failed and was forced to flee in order to protect my family and . . . myself."

The last bit sounded self-serving, but it was the truth.

Sister Mary slipped one hand from her sleeve to clutch the crucifix that hung around her neck.

He forged on. "When I thought it was safe, I contacted my sister, told her to get on a ship and leave Ireland for America. I'd planned to meet her and then head west where no one knew us. Start a new life with new names and new identities."

Her eyes rounded. "You have a sister?"

He hardened his jaw. "Had."

"What happened to her?"

Bitterness—cold and biting—swept over him. "She betrayed me."

Sister Mary gripped the railing and rose, the fabric of her habit rustling. "Derry—"

"She ignored my warning," he interrupted, "and sided with

the very cur who sought to kill me. Worse, she claimed she'd fallen in love with the man and then . . . she married him."

He spat the foul-tasting words from his mouth and spun, searching for something to kick and seeing only pews. Instead he gritted his teeth and waited like a tightly coiled spring while Sister Mary crossed the sanctuary toward him.

"Your sister, she knew about your fight with this man before she married him?"

He nodded. "Aye, she knew. I even tried to warn her—"

She held up her hand, stopping him. "You know where she is now?"

Approximately. Again he nodded.

"Derry, lad"—she reached up to press both palms on either side of his face—"did it ever occur to you that maybe your sister knows something you don't?"

When he refused to answer, she pressed on. "You love her still or the feeling of betrayal would not pain you so." She said it matter-of-factly, with a confidence that did not question or leave room for discussion. "Go to her. Talk to her and find a way to forgive. Only then will you know peace."

Her touch fell away and, a moment later, her footsteps faded. But he remained fixed to the spot where he stood for several long minutes after she left. The sun, glinting through the window he'd been repairing, felt warm on his skin. How he wished it could reach deeper. A traitorous longing took root in his heart that although he tried, he could not force away. Maybe if he forgot all this and went back to work . . .

He started toward the ladder when he saw it through a misty haze—a vertical piece of wood that stretched from the sash to the highest, curved part of the window, and a second strip that dissected it three quarters of the way up.

His vision clearing, he glanced at the spot on the floor he'd just left, then back to the window. The streaming sunlight cast a distinctive pattern. Was it by accident? Slowly he swung his gaze to the crucifix that hung at the front of the sanctuary. There was a time, not long ago, when he would not have believed such a thing.

With the sun shining through the window, and the strips of wood that divided the panes blocking only partial light . . . he'd been standing in the shadow of a cross.

5

The bustle inside the barge office pressed on Brion from every side, clogging his throat and making him long for some fresh air. First and second class passengers had long since departed the ship, and after a cursory glance from medical personnel, they'd gone merrily on their way. He would have been among them, his job in America nearly finished, if not for that blasted Whitham.

Looking around the large open room, he singled out a skinny panic-stricken inspector and forged through the crowd toward him. "You there! I demand to know how much longer I'm to be detained."

Shouting only barely made him heard above the screaming mothers who wept for children they would be leaving behind due to illness. They'd have to leave them either to heal from some curious ailment or to bury later if they didn't survive, he thought grimly.

He motioned toward the inspector, who pointed at his own chest and widened his eyes.

"Aye, you," Brion growled. His path converged with the inspector's, and then Brion grasped him by the shoulder and dragged him to a corner partially protected from the crowd and confusion.

"Where are the doctors?" Brion asked. "I demand to see one."

"They're tending to the sick, sir." The inspector straightened his bony shoulders. "We've had a rash of cholera outbreaks in recent weeks. It'll be awhile before they can get to any disembarking patients."

Brion tugged a coin from his pocket and rolled it between his fingers. Speaking of something of which he was familiar renewed the inspector's confidence. Best to try a different tack.

Brion flipped the coin and then snatched it from the air. "Ach, but you see, lad, I'm not sick. And I'm not a steerage passenger. They sent me here to be examined because my cabin mate took ill, nothing more."

The inspector eyed him from head to foot. "You do look healthy enough."

"I'm healthy as an ox." Brion pulled out another coin and added it to the first. "And while I understand the need to prevent unwanted diseases from entering this country, I am a very busy man."

The inspector's gaze drifted to Brion's fingers, lingered there a moment, then returned slowly. "How busy?"

His thoughts winged to a raven-haired niece who, with one word, could strip him of everything he held dear. Indeed, his very life, if the truth be known. He removed a third coin. "I have business that cannot be delayed, you understand."

The inspector nodded, looked around him, then pressed closer, greed gleaming in his coal-black eyes. "Like I said, cholera outbreak. Wouldn't do to take chances. 'Course, if you really are healthy, I would hate to see you detained for no reason."

Brion's lips curled in a scowl. This was getting expensive.

He removed one last coin and held it aloft. "Aye, 'twould be a shame. I'm sure there are many here who would agree. Perhaps I should seek one of those?"

He dropped the bit of silver onto the pile in the man's palm. The inspector licked his thin lips, perhaps assessing exactly how much he could swindle before losing it all. Well, he'd let him know the answer, and quick. Brion closed up his fist and jammed it into his pocket.

"I've taken too much of your time, haven't I, lad? Never mind. I'm sure a doctor will be along eventually. Or perhaps another inspector—"

"No," the inspector said, lowering his voice. "Like you said, you're a busy man. There's no sense putting you through all that."

Ambition flared in Brion's chest. His ability to spot character flaws had served him well through the years, today being no exception. He pulled the coins free of his pocket. Soon he'd be rid of the troublesome gnat whose existence threatened his livelihood. That, and finishing the little task The Celt had given him, and then he could leave this disease-infested country and return home for good.

He dropped the money into the man's eager fingers. "Be careful while you're about it. Don't want to draw unwanted attention to myself. Just need to get through this process quickly, if you understand my meaning."

The coins disappeared inside the inspector's pocket. He leaned forward with a grin that made Brion's fingers itch for his knife. "I do, sir. Indeed, I do. Won't be no trouble. None at all." He motioned toward a set of double doors fitted with glass. "This way."

Brion followed the inspector to a stark but clean room, with a table and two stools. The fellow pointed to one of the stools. "Have a seat. Someone will be with you shortly."

Yet it was almost an hour after the man ducked out the door that Brion checked his pocket watch and then left the stool to pace up and down the cramped space. He'd even begun to think he'd been outsmarted.

His hands curled into fists. If he ever saw the cur again, he'd break his skinny neck, maybe crush his thieving fingers so he couldn't rob anyone of their hard-earned money ever again.

Sweat dotted Brion's brow, and he wiped it away with his sleeve. His chest constricted. He felt the same nagging tug in the pit of his stomach that had plagued him aboard the ship. Blast this infernal hospital. If he stayed here any longer, he really would get sick—probably die of some wasting disease that ate at his lungs. Where was that inspector?

He strode toward the exit, impatience burning his cheeks. He'd kill him, that's what, and the ship's captain as well, who'd ordered him detained instead of letting him pass into the city like most everyone save for those in steerage. Well, he'd not waste another minute on this crusted piece of rock the locals called New York.

He fought a rasping tickle at the back of his throat and threw open the door, surprising not only himself but a gray-haired, bespectacled figure on the other side, fist raised as though to knock.

"Are you a doctor?" Brion barked.

The man straightened and dropped his hand. "I understand you've urgent business you need to attend?"

Brion grimaced. Blast the inspector for repeating his private affairs. How much would this cost? He reached for his pocket. "Aye. Business."

The tickle increased in fervor, made his eyes water.

"It's important that I not be delayed." He swiped his finger over his eyes. "That I get to the city to find . . . to find . . ."

"To find?"

61

He could no longer resist the urge. Brion threw back his head and brought his palm up to cover his mouth.

It was a most unfortunate time to cough.

— ❋ ❋ ❋ —

Ana willed the hands on the clock hanging on Mr. O'Bannon's wall to creep forward the remaining few minutes before closing. Ach, but how the day working at the candle shop had dragged. Her back ached from lugging the heavy molds, her fingers throbbed where drops of hot wax had scalded, and she couldn't wait to get home and put her feet up.

The last bit would have to wait. When the bell chimed five, she grabbed the bonnet and cloak she had set alongside the door, bid the old chandler farewell, and then scurried outside into the brisk October evening.

The bite in the air toyed with the tip of her nose and the ends of her fingers. She fumbled with the top button on her woolen cloak before setting off down the street—not for home but for the church, Our Lady of Deliverance.

Her steps quickened in spite of the icy puddles swirling around her boots. She hoped her hunch about Cara's brother was right. Despite her initial resolve, she'd said nothing to Cara, choosing instead to know for a certainty that the man working for Father Ed was indeed Eoghan Hamilton before raising her friend's hopes.

As she neared the corner where her path would wind east, away from the harbor, she slowed and paused long enough to peer through the rows of brick-and-mortar buildings toward the glinting water. Unease had been building in her stomach all day, a feeling she'd attributed to her last visit to the church, but now . . .

Lights shone from the steamships teeming with new immigrants—dim flickering beacons she'd often thought pretty in their own hopeful way. But not tonight. Chased by foreboding, a shiver traveled her spine. She'd come on one of those ships herself, as a child, little though she remembered the voyage. She pushed her hands into the pockets of her cloak and continued down the sidewalk, oddly relieved when the spires of Our Lady came into view. She circled to the rear, passed through the kitchen entrance, and set off in search of Tillie.

"Ana? You came?"

Ana paused at the door to the dining hall. Tillie stared at her openmouthed, her palms braced on the plain cotton apron that hugged her waist.

Ana smiled and clasped her hands behind her back. "There you are. I thought I'd come by and offer my services, if you still be in need of an extra worker, that is."

Tillie gave a quizzical tilt of her head. "We can always use the help, but I thought—"

Ana shrugged out of her cloak and held it up by the collar. "Where should I put this?"

A twitch that looked suspiciously like the beginnings of a smile spread over Tillie's lips. Ana frowned. She'd put a stop to that, and quick. For certain she didn't want Tillie getting the wrong impression about her reasons for coming. She pressed her fingers to Tillie's forearm. "I'm still uncomfortable about being here, you understand."

Tillie's head bobbed. "But you've made the effort, and I'm proud of you. Would you like me to find Father Ed? I'm sure he'd be willing to sit down with you—"

Ana held up her hand, then slid the bonnet from her head, letting the strings dangle from her cold fingers. "Nothing to be proud of. I'm simply finishing something I've started. It doesn't mean I've changed my mind about baring my soul or attending services with you come Sunday."

"Not this Sunday, anyway."

"Any Sunday," Ana clarified strongly to Tillie's retreating back.

"All right, dear. Come along, there's plenty of work to be accomplished before supper."

Ana followed slowly, disappointed when a peek into the halls they passed failed to yield a glimpse of Cara's brother— the man she thought was Cara's brother, she corrected silently. But who else could he be, with that impish grin and easy manner?

To Ana's surprise, the dining hall was quite crowded with women and a number of small children. All of these people had traveled alone to America? She couldn't help but ponder the reasons as she hung her bonnet and cloak on a row of pegs that lined one wall before joining Tillie, Sister Mary, and Sister Agnes at the serving line. After a moment, Father Ed gave the blessing and supper began in earnest. Ana had no more time to look for Derry among the residents until the last ladleful of gravy was poured over the last bit of roast pork, and the dishes running the length of the table were all empty.

Except for one plate that Sister Agnes set aside and covered with a cloth napkin, Ana noted.

She rubbed her hands on a checkered towel and then pointed at the dish. "Is that for the hired man? For D-Derry?" She fumbled on the name.

Sister Agnes nodded. "I'm going to get one of the young ones to run it out to the stable to him."

Ana dropped the towel and extended her hands. "I'll take it. I don't mind. Is he working in the barn again?"

One fluffy brow lifted, making the sister's stern face rather comical. "Aye, that's right. Seeing to the livestock, he is, though I'd hoped he'd be finished by now."

"I'll check." Ana slipped into her cloak. She remembered to grab a fork this time before swinging for the back door leading from the kitchen to the barn. Light from several lanterns glowed from the windows, casting oblong shapes onto the frosty ground. Inside, a man's low voice spoke soothingly to the animals.

"There now, Boots. Make room for Bob. He's hungry too, you know. C'mon, Shirls. Best get your fill before old Boots makes a hog of himself. What's that? He *is* a hog? How could I have overlooked that?"

A low chuckle rumbled from a nearby pen. Ana wound toward it, then halted midstride at the sight that met her eyes. Derry stood in the center, shirtsleeves rolled to his elbows and a bucket dangling from his long, tanned fingers. Thick work boots encased his calves, and he stood with feet braced apart, a wily grin on his face. It slowly disappeared as he caught sight of her.

"Why, Miss Kavanagh. Hello."

Overcome with a sudden burst of shyness at having been caught staring, Ana felt her cheeks burn. "Hello." She swallowed and lifted the plate carefully wrapped in a napkin. "I've brought your supper. Sister Agnes sent it."

Derry scratched his head. "What time is it? I figured it was too early for them to have finished serving already."

"They just finished. We've not yet started cleaning the kitchen."

He crossed the pen toward the gate. "That explains it then. I'll go inside in a bit and collect the scraps. Old Boots will appreciate the addition to his supper of corncobs, won't you, Boots?"

The hog grunted and continued snuffling and scraping at the bottom of the food trough. Derry laughed as he let himself out of the pen. He took the plate from Ana. "Thank you."

She lowered her head—mostly to be spared another piercing glance from those hazel eyes.

Instead of standing, this time Derry carried the plate to a workbench that he quickly cleared for them both. He gestured to a stool.

Smoothing her skirts gave her the respite she needed to collect herself. When she finished, she looked at him. "Don't you ever eat with the others?"

He shrugged. "Sometimes. Depends on whether I have me chores finished or not." He grinned and picked up his fork. "Or if I feel like it. It's mostly women in there, you know. Can get a little loud, what with all the chatter."

A frown started until she caught sight of the twinkle dancing in the depths of his devilish eyes. He was teasing her—again.

Well, she'd not be baited. She sat silently and chewed the question aching to escape her lips while he ate his supper in peace. When at last he finished, she stood and jerked her hand out for the plate, wriggling her fingers with impatience when he only smiled, leaned back, and crossed his arms.

"Was it difficult?" he asked.

"Was what difficult?"

"Biting your tongue while I took my time with supper?"

Impertinent man! Thinking he knew her so well when they'd only met twice, and he not even honest then. Her suspicions about him being Cara's missing brother had to have been mistaken, for he was nothing at all like her sweet, mild-natured friend.

"Not all women idle away their days in mindless chatter, you know, just like not all men are lying scoundrels."

He grimaced and rubbed the top of his head. "Ouch. I assume by that remark you refer to me?"

She withdrew her hand and braced it on her hip with a smirk. "Not at all, but interesting that you would assume so."

Instead of the contrition she'd expected, he merely lifted a brow. "Interesting you would assume I thought most women spent their days in mindless chatter."

Her mouth dropped as she thought back on his words. "But you said—"

His lips curled in a most infuriating smile. "I said?"

Outrage built in her stomach. He wasn't handsome, or charming. He was smug, arrogant, and thieving as a fox's snout, just like . . .

She nipped the thought before it could fully form. It had been years since she'd reflected on *him*, and then only in her worst nightmares. She refused to be provoked into thinking about him now.

"Since it appears you are finished with your chores," she said, pronouncing each syllable with frosty precision, "perhaps you could be imposed upon to overlook your dislike of—how did you put it—oh yes, 'loud chatter' and return your own plate to Sister Agnes."

Grabbing her skirt, she spun on her heel and strode for the door, her thoughts, and her emotions, in a jumble. Before she reached the door, however, a strong hand caught her by the elbow.

"Ana, wait."

She whirled to stare at him. He'd learned her name?

"It appears I have vexed you again. Believe me, it was not intentional . . . at least not the vexing part. I admit, I've been known to enjoy a good teasing, and you, uh, you blush very prettily when you are flustered."

She narrowed her eyes at him. Cara had mentioned a time or two during their many conversations that her brother had enjoyed teasing her when they were children. Unfortunately, Derry's remarks could easily be taken for lighthearted banter, and that meant . . .

She sighed. For Cara's sake, she had to know the truth. "Fine."

At her nod, his hand fell from her elbow. Ana lifted her chin and formed her words carefully. "It appears you have me at a disadvantage."

"How so?"

"You've learned my name. I can only guess how. I, however, know you only by what the sisters call you, and they have reported readily that Derry is not your name."

The smile that appeared then was neither teasing nor arrogant. Indeed, if she pondered it for long, she might think he was pleased that she'd asked. Her breath caught as he nodded.

"Indeed, it is not."

She shifted impatiently, feeling the cold air that swept in from under the barn door on her ankles. "Well? Are you going to tell me, or will you be leaving me in the dark?"

Derry reached for a lantern, hoisted it aloft, and pushed open the door, stepping aside for her to precede him. "I would never deign to leave a lady in the dark," he replied, the teasing note returning to his voice. "My name, since you inquired so politely, is Eoghan. Eoghan Hamilton."

6

The Celt stared unblinking at the sweat-drenched figure lying prone on a thin, dingy pallet, arms and legs splayed, and an occasional groan rising from his throat. Pallor tainted the man's lips and forehead. Indeed, except for the twin patches of scarlet high on his cheekbones, he looked half dead already. And the stench! 'Twas quite evident he'd been sick for several days and stood in desperate need of a bath.

The man hovering at The Celt's elbow gave a snort of disgust. "That him?"

The Celt nodded. "Aye, that's him."

"He don't look so good."

The Celt resisted the urge to roll his eyes. Really, sometimes Kellen could be quite thick. "That would explain why he's still at the barge office, now, wouldn't it?"

He lowered to his haunches and examined McCleod from the top of his greasy head down to his gray-tinged fingernails, anger rippling through his midsection. The fact was, McCleod didn't look good, but explaining to someone like Kellen why that was a bad thing took more effort than he was willing to give.

Bracing his hands on his knees, he pushed to his feet and

turned for the door, barking orders as he went. "Find Mc-Dermott and get him over here. I want medical attention for this man immediately, understood?" He waited for Kellen's assent before continuing. "Then I want you to see where we are with the vote. Tell our men they may need to stall."

Fighting irritation at having to alter even a small part of his plan, he paused at the door and cast one last look at Mc-Cleod, then gestured at Kellen. "This is important. Make sure they understand they're to do whatever it takes to see that the seat remains empty until we're ready. And get a message to Kilarny. Tell him I want to see him."

"Aye, sir. I'll get on it right away."

"One more thing," The Celt said, stalling Kellen as he shuffled toward the door. "You remember the woman, the one I asked you to locate for me a few weeks back?" At the man's nod, he continued, "I want to know her whereabouts—where she goes and who she sees."

"Is that *all* you want?" Kellen replied, punctuating the question with the slightest narrowing of his eyes.

He glanced back at McCleod. Mayhap the man would recover and the plan could continue as intended. He grunted. "For now."

The excited gleam faded from Kellen's eyes and he gave an almost disappointed sniff. "All right. I'll see to it."

The Celt moved aside to let him pass. Ah, yes. Having a man like Kellen around did serve a purpose. For certain, his wick didn't burn the brightest, but he was devoted to the cause and that meant he attended The Celt's every whim without reservation or question—a crucial characteristic to possess in times like these. In fact, right now the only thing more crucial was saving McCleod's life. That, and making sure no one inside the Fenian organization ever found out about his connection to The Celt.

— ✳ ✳ ✳ —

Surprise flickered in Ana's somber, earthy-brown gaze. Surprise and something else. Regret? Reluctance of some sort? Eoghan raised the lantern and tilted his chin, angling for a closer look. He'd give anything to know what was going on inside her pretty head.

"Miss Kavanagh?"

"I h-heard you," she said, her bowlike lips trembling as she stumbled on the words.

His name upset her. Why?

He sucked in a breath as it struck him. She knew Cara. She lived at the same boardinghouse, spoke to the same people. She had to realize the connection, but if she knew who he was, why did the information trouble her so?

She shivered, and Eoghan gestured toward the church. "You're cold. I should get you inside."

She did not argue but merely allowed herself to be led into the night air, where a gentle snow had begun to fall, across the yard and up the steps to the rear door of the kitchen. With one firm push, the door swung open, spilling out warmth and the scent of Sister Agnes's cooking.

Inside, Eoghan shrugged from his coat and then waited while Ana slid from her cloak. Relieving her of it, he deposited them both onto waiting hooks.

Tillie, one of the regular volunteers, crossed the kitchen and clasped Ana's hands. "There you are. I wondered where you'd gone."

"Out to take—" she paused, two red splotches appearing on her cheeks—"Derry his dinner."

"And the plate?" Tillie wagged her finger at them both. "Sister Agnes is not going to be pleased."

"I'll fetch it," Ana and Eoghan said in unison, nearly colliding in the doorway in their haste.

Tillie chuckled and dismissed them with a wave. "Nonsense. I'll get it. You two go and warm yourselves by the fire. We're just about to begin the story hour."

At the questioning look on Ana's face, Eoghan held out his hand and moved toward the mammoth fireplace that heated the shelter and most of the church. "Every evening, Sister Mary reads to the children before they go to bed. The women also enjoy it, as it allows them time to catch up on their chores with no children underfoot."

The truth of his words was evidenced a short time later when a circle of children crowded around Sister Mary's feet, their upturned faces wholly enraptured by the story she read from the book laid across her lap.

All except for one child, Eoghan noticed, and her mother, who huddled with the young girl on the outskirts of the circle, their arms wrapped tightly around each other. Something about the picture they made tugged at his heart, and Ana's too, by the look of compassion that softened her features. He'd opened his mouth to suggest they move to stand beside them when Ana left his side and crossed the room. Eoghan followed along slowly, his curiosity piqued as to how she intended to handle them.

The little girl looked up, her blue eyes wide. Straightening, the weary mother pushed the child behind her back, her gaze darting between them.

"Who are you? What do you want?"

Ana blinked, retreated a step, and then stammered, "I . . . we . . . I'm Ana Kavanagh." She drew a breath and motioned toward Eoghan. "And this is Der . . . my friend."

So she was shrewd enough to recognize that he might prefer to make his own introduction. He bowed toward the girl and her mother. "Eoghan Hamilton, ma'am. It's a pleasure."

The woman acknowledged him with a curt nod.

"It's gotten quite chilly," Ana continued. "We thought you and your daughter might like to move nearer to the fire?"

The woman clutched a tattered shawl tighter about her frail shoulders. "We're fine," she said sternly, after which the child coughed and tugged on her finger.

"Please, Mama? My nose feels like an icicle. Feel." She stuck out her face, inviting her mother to test the proof of her claim.

Eoghan's heart clutched inside his chest. With her long braids and the smattering of freckles across her nose, the lass reminded him of a younger version of Cara. He waited while the woman sized both him and Ana up from top to bottom.

Finally, the woman said to Ana, "I've not seen you here before."

Eoghan clasped Ana's arm, cautioning her with a touch to avoid sudden movements that would cause the woman, like a small bird, to flit away.

Ana shook her head. "No. I'm a volunteer. Like my friend Tillie there."

She pointed to her friend, who reentered the shelter on a burst of frosty air. Spying them, Tillie held the plate high and motioned toward the kitchen. Ana nodded, then directed her gaze back to Eoghan expectantly as though waiting for him to do something. But what?

He eyed the woman's matted hair, the child's smudged, earnest face, and cleared his throat uncomfortably. "We . . . uh . . . could get you another blanket if you're cold."

After a moment, the woman gave a reluctant nod. "Aye, that would be a welcome kindness."

"Really?" Surprised, Eoghan glanced at Ana, warmth spreading over him at the look of approval he read on her face. "All right then." He clapped both hands together and gave them a rub. "We'll be right back. Ana?"

He waved for her to precede him. Smiling, she crossed to the linen closet and removed two gray woolen blankets, which she folded and laid in his outstretched arms.

"'Twas kind of you to offer to fetch these for them." Ana nodded toward the woman and her child.

Remembering the holes in the woman's shawl and the patches on the lass's dress, Eoghan shrugged. "They looked like they could use them."

"Mr. Hamilton . . . should I call you Mr. Hamilton or do you prefer Derry?"

He quirked an eyebrow. "I prefer Eoghan."

Her hand on the knob, Ana hesitated, her teeth worrying her bottom lip. She closed the linen closet and turned to him. "Mind you make no mention of your concern. 'Twould be unseemly to embarrass them, even with good intentions. Trust me," she continued when he opened his mouth to argue. "Well I remember the shame that accompanies a condescending look."

She ducked her head, but not before he saw the pained look that shadowed the cryptic words. He agreed and then returned with her to the woman and her child.

"Here you are," Ana said, her voice deceptively bright.

Eoghan could not help but watch in admiration as she tended to the mother, settling her in a chair near the fire, then dropped to her knees to speak with the child at her level. With her gentle manner, one might almost believe she was unlike others of her gender—

He speared the thought with an angry scowl. Only the sisters, in the short time he had known them, had proved worthy of his admiration—or his trust.

He watched in cynical silence as Ana spread one of the blankets, a smile budding on her face as the child stepped into it. She wrapped it around the lass's shoulders and tucked it snugly under her chin.

"There now. That should keep you toasty warm."

The girl sighed and looked to her mother, whose smile of gratitude nearly outshone the fire blazing from the hearth.

"Her name is Ellen. I'm Ione. We are indebted to you for your kindness."

"Nonsense," Ana replied gently. "It's why we're here." She appeared to catch herself as she cast Eoghan a glance. Collecting herself, she patted Ellen on the knee. "Be sure to let us know if there is anything you need. Either of you."

With a shy smile, Ione extended her thanks to Eoghan. "You're most kind. Both of you. 'Tis a blessing for sure that brought us to this place. I don't know what my Ellen and I would have done otherwise."

The words shamed him. He looked away as Ana bent and whispered something to her that he could not quite hear. When she straightened, Ione clasped her hand for a brief moment before resting against the chair.

Eoghan marveled at the change a kind word had wrought. Peace settled across Ione's face that had been absent before, and her hand rested easily against her daughter's arm instead of gripping her tight. It was with some reluctance that he accompanied Ana to the door a short time later to collect her bonnet and cloak as she and Tillie prepared to leave.

Outside, a thin layer of snow coated the streets and sidewalk. Gas lamps flickered merrily, casting shadows that might otherwise have been ominous if not for the moon glinting overhead. Eoghan accompanied the women to the gate and had opened his mouth to bid them good-night when Tillie groaned and grasped Ana's arm.

"I forgot my scarf. It's on the counter by the tables. Will you wait?"

Ana smiled as she tugged the strings of her bonnet into a bow beneath her chin. "Of course. Go and fetch it."

"I won't be long," Tillie called, her spry steps carrying her quickly up the stairs of the church and inside.

"The girl would forget her head if it weren't attached."

Ana's infectious grin urged Eoghan to laugh with her. Instead he lowered his gaze and turned up his collar. It was defensive—she'd already garnered a bit of his admiration. He'd not allow himself to be won by her smile.

Her smile faded. "You've no coat and it's starting to snow. You should go inside. I can wait for Tillie by myself."

"And what kind of gentleman would I be if I did that?" he replied, jamming his hands into the pockets of his trousers.

"A warm one."

Ach, but the twinkle in her eyes could prove downright irresistible if he was not careful. He studied the tops of his boots, then the blades of grass poking through the fresh snow, looking anywhere but at her—

Until she gasped.

Confused, he glanced up. She was staring at him . . . no, at something behind him, he realized. And by the look on her face, it was something terrible. He grabbed her hand and pulled her around behind him.

A split second later, a dark shadow fell over them both.

7

Though she wasn't tall enough to peer over Eoghan's shoulder, Ana still managed a glimpse of the shadowy figure that materialized from nowhere into their path. Misty breath plumed from his nostrils. Moonbeams bathed his face in pale light. On one cheek, a jagged scar snaked from his chin to his left earlobe. But his black eyes . . .

"Hamilton, Kilarny would like to speak with ya. Sends his apologies for the way the last meeting ended and says he has a matter he thinks you might find interesting. You coming?"

Ana shuddered and lowered her eyes. Only then did she realize that Eoghan was still clasping her fingers. And he stood defensively between her and the forbidding stranger, his broad back blocking her from sight.

"I'll come. I've got business to finish up here first," Eoghan said.

"Making your confession, are ya?"

"Not if Kil wants to speak with me tonight."

Ana glanced up sharply. The jest sounded forced to her ears, but the scarred man laughed.

"The pub. One hour. He'll be waiting."

"I'll be there."

Gradually the man's footsteps faded, freeing Ana to breathe normally. Eoghan released her fingers, but instead of moving away, he clasped her face in both hands.

"Are you all right?"

She shuddered. Not with him towering over her, his hazel eyes searing her soul and her heart pounding double inside her chest. "I'm fine," she croaked.

"I don't want you and Tillie walking home alone. When she gets back, I'll take you."

Ana's glance followed the direction the stranger had taken. How they got home was of little consequence under the circumstances. "Who . . . was that?" she stammered, a shiver that had nothing to do with the cooling temperature traveling her spine.

Eoghan's hands fell away, leaving behind a curious chill. He grimaced. "An old friend."

"He didn't look like a friend." Ana frowned. "And what was he doing prowling around like a cat after a canary?"

The church door swung wide and Tillie stepped out, her scarf looped gracefully around her neck. "Who was prowling? What'd I miss?"

"Nothing," he said before Ana could answer. His head dipped close and he whispered, "Don't be wandering around asking questions, Ana, especially when it comes to people and things you know nothing about. It isn't wise. Do you understand?"

She didn't, but she nodded and beckoned toward Tillie anyway. "C'mon. We'd best be getting home before Amelia starts to worry."

"I'll fetch my coat—" Eoghan began, but Ana cut him short with a wave.

"No need. Tillie and I are well acquainted with the way."

"Ana—"

"He's a friend, remember?" she interrupted. "Besides, by the sound of it, you'd best not keep him waiting."

Before he could respond, Ana grabbed Tillie's hand and almost dragged her down the path to the sidewalk. In three quick strides they'd slipped through the gate and were headed down the street.

Tillie craned her neck to look back. Certain Eoghan was still watching them, Ana kept her gaze trained directly ahead.

"What was that about?" Tillie said, skipping to match her gait. "Ana, slow down. What happened back there?"

Uncertain whether she was running from the stranger or from Eoghan, Ana reduced her steps to a more reasonable pace. "I'm not sure." At Tillie's frown, she struggled to explain further. "A man appeared from nowhere and said someone wanted to meet with Eo—Derry," she corrected quickly, though why she felt the need to keep the truth from Tillie was a mystery. "Derry claimed he was an old friend, but somehow I didn't believe him."

"And no wonder. What kind of friend would ask to meet at this hour? Did he say where he was going?"

Tillie stumbled on a crack in the sidewalk, sparing Ana from an immediate answer. She steadied her with a hand to her arm and then gave her a squeeze. "Are you all right?"

"Clumsy as ever." Tillie scowled at the mud that had splashed onto the hem of her skirt. "What a mess, and washing day not until Saturday."

"You can borrow one of mine," Ana said, urging her along with a tug. Despite her brave words to Eoghan, she couldn't help but check the shadowed street behind them and was glad when the lights from the boardinghouse came into view.

She scrambled up the steps, fumbled with the knob, and then finally managed to get both herself and Tillie inside and the door secured behind them.

The foreboding continued its tenacious hold much later when she kissed the pocket watch on her bedside table and climbed into bed. Not one given to prayer, she still couldn't resist breathing a simple request before turning down the lamp.

"Please . . . keep Eoghan safe," she whispered.

— ❀ ❀ ❀ —

The pub was crowded for a Monday evening, the faces of the patrons shadowed by a handful of greasy oil lamps that spewed more smoke than light. Eoghan swallowed the discomfort wrought by remembering his last visit and wound his way toward the back of the pub where he figured Kilarny was waiting.

"You're late."

Eoghan jumped at the unexpected voice, behind him and to his right. Ach, but he'd gotten careless working at the church. He hoped it wouldn't cost him.

Pasting on a wry grin, he turned and gave a brief nod to his onetime comrade. "Sorry, Kil. Couldn't be helped."

Kilarny measured him through guarded eyes and then tipped his head toward a seat at an empty table. A single candle burned at its center, a pool of wax collecting at the base. "Where ya been, Eoghan, me lad? We've missed ya." He yanked out a chair and sat heavily down.

"Where you left me," Eoghan replied, resisting the urge to scowl. "Bruised ribs take time to mend, especially with empty pockets. You could've at least left me enough to eat on."

Kilarny gave a bark of laughter that cut through the noise and brash music rising from a battered piano. "Ach, sorry about that. 'Twasn't my idea to work you over, ya know. Just doing what I'm told."

Told?

Eoghan narrowed his eyes and took the chair opposite Kilarny. "And? What are your orders now? Why'd you send for me?"

"Straight to the point, eh?" Kilarny motioned for a barmaid, who brought two large mugs of ale and set them down with a thud. When she left, he lifted one of the mugs, took a deep draught, then wiped his mouth on the sleeve of his tweed coat. Finished, he glanced at the other mug and then at Eoghan.

"None for me," he said firmly, jabbing the mug away with two fingers. "I'll be keeping a clear head tonight."

To Eoghan's amazement, he read a glimmer of appreciation in Kilarny's steely gaze. The man took another drink and then leaned his chair back to balance on two legs. "How long have you and I been knowing each other, do you reckon?"

The question was unexpected, perhaps designed to keep him off-kilter. Eoghan shrugged. "Since we were lads growing up in Derry."

"Long time."

"I guess so." Where was the man headed with these questions?

"And what year was it you took up the Fenian cause?"

His gut tightened as he sat forward to prop both elbows on the table. The room was no less crowded, but it had grown quiet. Too quiet. Eoghan lowered his voice. "I was eighteen, same as you. We joined the cause together, to fight for something we both believed in."

Kilarny nodded and rubbed his chin between thumb and forefinger. "You, me, and Sean Healy. Three of a kind, eh, Eoghan, me boy? Lofty dreams, all of us. Brothers committed one to another—or so I thought."

Recalling the events leading up to Sean's death, Eoghan tensed. "What's your point?"

"My point," Kilarny said, abandoning all pretense, dropping the chair to all four legs, with the resulting *thump* making those nearest their table flinch and look away, "is that you are no longer the only one who thinks Healy acted foolishly by taking matters into his own hands the night Daniel Turner was killed. He was rash, thinking he could force Turner's vote by threatening his life. The cause has suffered for his arrogance ever since."

"I've suffered some because of it myself," Eoghan said dryly. "Remember? Blamed for his murder, forced to go into hiding, hunted by the Fenians *and*, until recently, the Turners?"

Kilarny's thin lips parted in a smile. "Mayhap that explains why certain people are inclined to give you a second chance . . . let you prove yourself, so to speak. That is, if you're still interested."

Eoghan's heart rate quickened. What matter were a few bruised ribs if the Fenians were willing to take him back? He'd done nothing but try to prove himself since the day he left home to join the group ten years ago. Doing so again would be no different.

Curling his fingers into fists, Eoghan met Kilarny's gaze head-on. "All right, Kil, I'll bite. What do I have to do?"

8

The sharp wind whistling through Battery Park whipped tears into Eoghan's eyes. His cheeks and lips felt frozen, slurring his speech and making him sound weak-minded when he stopped to ask for directions. Hitching his shoulders up around his ears, he pushed south and then east.

He lengthened his strides, eating up the cobbled streets, until he reached a tall building with pale gray sides and a turret, or at least a cylindrical tower that resembled a turret, stretching up from the center.

Halting outside the door, he pulled a slip of paper from his pocket and checked the address. This was the place—the barge office, which was once again being used for immigrants since a fire had destroyed the station on Ellis Island last summer. June, to be exact. The same night his sister, his twin, had betrayed him and burned to the ground his hopes of starting a new life with her out West.

Jamming the paper back into his pocket, he checked his watch, then went inside and waited to be noticed, just as Kilarny had instructed him to do.

The man who eventually spoke to him was of frail build,

with sagging skin that gave him the look of a turtle, or perhaps a wizened old elf. "Can I help you?"

Eoghan dipped his head. "Kilarny sent me."

The man lifted an eyebrow. "You Hamilton?"

He nodded.

"This way." The man spun, his steps surprisingly spry as he led the way down one corridor and then another, to an office at the rear of the building. He shoved open the door and indicated with a tilt of his head that Eoghan should pass through.

Eoghan did, his hand inside his coat, clutching the packet Kilarny had given him to deliver. Then, aware of how the gesture might be construed, he pulled it out and allowed both hands to hang at his sides.

Tall, thin windows framed by heavy drapes cast rectangular patches of light onto the floor. In the middle of the room, a heavy oak desk with a paneled front and sides to match sat twixt two such patches of light. Behind the desk was a wooden chair with a long black coat slung over the arm. Eoghan turned to inquire as to the owner of the chair, but he was too late. The door closed with a click, leaving him alone and befuddled.

He hated waiting, especially since he was in the dark as to most of Kil's plan.

"Go to the barge office, wait just inside the door until someone comes to get you, then deliver this letter once they've escorted you inside. No name to ask for. Better if you didn't have one, if you get my meaning."

The skin on the back of his neck prickled, a sensation he'd learned to heed from his days with the Fenians. He got Kil's meaning, all right. He'd been sent to the slaughter. So much for his talk of second chances. Well, this was the last time he'd play the fool in a farce of Kil's making.

Relaxing his knees, he scoured the room a second time, and settled on the thick velvet curtains.

Someone was watching from beside the heavy drapes. He sensed it. Fortunately they weren't lying in wait to kill him or he'd have been dead already. Tensing, he thrust out his chin and called out. "Well? You gonna keep me waiting here all day?"

A figure detached itself from the shadows created by the gleaming windows—not far enough for Eoghan to make out his features, but enough that he saw it was a man of medium build and height.

"You have a package for me?" the man retorted, his high, reedy voice grating like sand across Eoghan's flesh.

He bobbed his head. "Aye."

"And the person you want moved through immigration—you have his name?"

Though he squinted, he saw nothing in the man's shadowed features that would lend insight into his intentions. Eoghan scowled. This was the errand that would ingratiate him to the Fenians? Just who was so important that they felt compelled to involve themselves?

He shrugged. "It's all in the package."

"I want to see the money."

The whole job was looking worse by the second. Eoghan lifted one hand, palm out, and slid it slowly into his breast pocket, removed the packet, and held it up so it was clearly visible.

"Open it."

"Look, why don't I just leave this with you," Eoghan began, stretching out his hand to drop the packet on the desk. The motion was interrupted by the unmistakable click of a pistol's hammer.

He froze, then slowly retracted the packet. "On second thought . . ."

Drawing the string that kept the envelope sealed, Eoghan released the knot and let the cord slip to the floor. Inside the crumpled brown wrapping was a significant amount of money—too much for him not to realize the importance of the man whose passage through customs the sum was meant to purchase.

A slip of paper fluttered off the stack of bills and settled right side up on the floor. On it was printed a name: *Brion McCleod*.

—⁂—

The church . . . again.

Ana stared up at the gleaming white steeple, a knot in her stomach so tight 'twould take the entire Continental army to unclench it. She sighed. Despite her apprehension, she had no other choice but to come by after she left the candle shop. Eoghan was Cara's brother, and he was obviously in trouble. What else could he have been doing with the scarred stranger the other night? The more she scoured her mind for possibilities, the more convinced she became—he needed help. Cara needed her brother.

And Ana was the only link between the two.

"Are you going inside?"

The small, angelic voice startled Ana from her reverie. Ellen peered up at her, eyes wide and curious. Dressed in a tattered coat, and stockings with more holes than fabric, the lass was a pitiful sight, except for the bonnie yellow ribbon that tied her brown locks in place.

Brown, so much like Brigid's, and indeed Ana's own hair.

She smiled and bent to prop her hands on her knees. "The thought had occurred to me, though I haven't quite made up my mind. What about you? What are you doing out on so chilly an afternoon?"

A dimple appeared on Ellen's cheek as she swung her arms to and fro. "It's washday. Mama says I'm too little to help, so she sent me outside to play." She flashed a bright smile. "I remember you. You're Miss Ana."

"That's right. And you are Ellen."

Looking pleased to have been recognized, the lass's smile widened and she nodded. "I am."

"Are you alone, Ellen?"

She shook her head and pointed up the street. A group of girls were squatting in a circle, drawing figures on the sidewalk with pieces of coal. "I'm supposed to be with them, but they don't want me. And they're mean. They called me names."

Ana frowned. "They did? Like what?"

"Like *bairn*. I told them I wasn't a baby and they told me to go away."

"I see," Ana said, hiding a grin as she straightened.

"What about you? Did you come to help with the washing?"

"Actually . . ." Ana fingered the pleats in her skirt. "I'm looking for someone."

"The man you were with the other night?"

For a moment, the lass's forthrightness took Ana aback. She really *was* like Brigid. "I . . . uh . . . have you seen him? That man, I mean?"

Ellen stopped swinging and tugged at one of her braids. "He left early this morning, before Mama and I ate our breakfast. I saw him go, but he didn't see me." She covered her mouth to stop a giggle. "I was hiding."

So Eoghan was gone. A twinge of disappointment pinched Ana's stomach, which she quickly pushed aside to concentrate on the child. "Oh well. No matter. I'd still like to go inside for a bit. Want to come with me?"

She held out her hand, which Ellen cupped in both of hers.

"Oh, your hands! What happened?" Eyes round, she ran the tip of her finger over Ana's scars.

How could she have forgotten? Ana's stomach sank. Even coming from a child, the questions were painful, but she wouldn't upset the lass by pulling from her grasp.

"I . . . was burned when I was a little girl," she explained woodenly.

Ellen's mouth dropped. "Little like me?"

"Aye, like you, though a tad older, I think."

"Did you get too near the cook fire?"

'Twas something she'd obviously been cautioned about. Ana shook her head. "Nothing like that."

"Oh." Ellen bent her head to examine Ana's scars more closely. "Do they hurt?"

"They stopped hurting long ago," Ana replied, squeezing Ellen's small fingers. "Shall we get you inside before you catch a chill?"

The giggle returned. Her eyes dancing, Ellen wrinkled her nose. "You can't 'catch' a chill. You only get chilled."

Rather than attempt an explanation, Ana matched her smile and gave a nod toward the church. "Right you are. Come on then. Show me to your mama."

"All right." Skirting the front steps, Ellen wound past a row of closely clipped evergreen shrubs, to the rear of the church. A cemetery stretched from the east corner, but the land directly behind the church remained open for gardening and other uses. Campfires for heating cauldrons of water still burned, most unattended except for a couple of stray dogs wandering about.

Ana's grip on the child's fingers tightened. No wonder Ione had sent her daughter away to play. They climbed the steps, and Ellen twisted the knob right, then left, then right and finally succeeded in forcing open the solid oak door after two pushes.

Inside the kitchen, preparations for supper had already begun. Sister Agnes peered at them over the rim of a large pot. "Ach, it's you, Ladybug. Got yourself a friend, I see."

Ellen craned her neck to look up at Ana. "She calls me Ladybug."

"So I heard."

She turned back to the sister. "Have you seen my mama?"

Sister Agnes pointed with a wooden spoon. "They're all in the wash room, finishing up with the day's laundering. Don't suspect they'll want you tottering underfoot, though."

"I'll keep a watch on her." Ana smiled down at the girl and squeezed her hand. "If that's all right with you, that is, Miss Ladybug."

Ellen mirrored her smile and gave a vehement nod, which tousled her curls. Ana led the way into a wide room that opened off the kitchen. A stone fireplace occupied one wall where a rack bearing several irons had been situated. Five of the shelter's residents manned ironing boards, while several more took the pressed linens and folded them before placing them into neat stacks.

Judging by the number of tables, wooden tubs, and built-in cupboards, the room had served a similar purpose for the nuns who had lived here before Father Ed converted the back of the church into a shelter. Off to one side and near the end of a row, Ana spied Ione, a checkered handkerchief holding back her hair, her head bent to the task.

"There she is," Ana said, pointing. Together, she and Ellen dodged in and out of the rows of working women until they reached the last one.

As they approached, Ione's head lifted and she frowned. The iron she'd been using clattered as she replaced it in a metal stand for heating. When she turned to give her daughter a hug, her face was a mix of worry and delight.

"Ellen, lassie, is everything all right? I told you to stay outside."

"It's cold outside, Mama. My toes are frost-nipped."

Ana stepped forward. "In truth, it's my fault, Ione. I met Ellen on the steps and she offered to show me inside."

"The big girls didn't like me, anyway," Ellen said, pushing her lips into a pout. "They're mean, and they didn't want to play with me, even when Sister Mary told them to."

"Now, lassie, you know that's just the way with girls some-times," Ione said, lowering to her haunches. "Doesn't mean they don't like you."

She lifted a corner of her apron to dab away the tears that rose to Ellen's eyes, cooing in just the same way Ana's own mother used to do whenever she or Brigid sought her with a scraped elbow or bruised knee.

"And it doesn't mean they aren't nice," Ione continued. "They just aren't interested in playing the same games you are. Now, tell me, were you able to finish up your reading lesson with Sister Mary before you went outside?"

Ellen nodded as she plopped onto her mother's bent knee. Though the tears had subsided, both arms twined around her mother's neck. "Aye, we finished. Sister Mary is nice, but I'd rather do my lessons with you, Mama. Like we used to."

Ione buried her face in her daughter's neck and took a deep whiff. "I know, dearie. I miss our time together too, but it's not to be helped when there's work to be done. Speaking of which, I'd best be about it. As for you—"

"Ana and I can help," Ellen interrupted, hopping to her feet. "Isn't that right, Ana? I know how to fold clothes."

"As do I," Ana said, reaching for Ellen's hand as Ione rose to stand. She leaned close and lowered her voice. "I don't mind keeping an eye on her, and there's more than enough work in here to keep us both busy—that is, if you don't mind."

Gratitude filled Ione's smile. "It'd be a relief actually. So long as you're sure? We don't want to burden anyone."

Ana winked at Ellen. "We're sure, eh, Ellen? Off to work instead of play?"

Ellen's giggle said she thought folding clothes with Ana an adventure rather than a chore. After locating a stool upon which Ellen could perch, Ana positioned herself between the child and the hot iron flashing so expertly in Ione's hand and got to work.

Ana tipped her head toward the skirt Ione was working on. "You're good at that."

"I was a laundress back home in Ireland," Ione said, in time to the rhythm of her iron. "My ma taught me when I was a girl. She and I managed a large household outside of Dublin."

Hard work, and usually reserved for the very poorest in society. Sympathy flooded Ana's heart, though she tried hard not to let the emotion show. She took a shirt that had already been pressed and showed Ellen how to make careful creases down one side and then the other before folding it into thirds and adding it to the stack Ione had started.

A stack that was already quite high.

Ana motioned toward it and the others like it around the room. "The clothes these women are working on, do they belong to people here at the shelter?"

Ione flashed a wry smile and sprinkled some water over the pleats on the skirt she was pressing. "Ach, no. These women kinna afford fine trappings such as these. This is all hired work Father Ed secured for us from a few of the wealthier families around town. Anyone who wants to can earn a small wage working here instead of looking for a job in the city. I figured it was best, what with me not wanting to leave Ellen to herself and all."

She shot a smile at her daughter, who waved and smiled back.

"The rest"—Ione gestured to the other women bent over washtubs and tables—"well, I figure it's all they're skilled at, like me."

So that explained it. Ana looked around at the careworn faces, some old and lined, others marred by fear and loss, and marveled at the ingenuity and kindness of the priest and nuns who ran the shelter. 'Twas evident that they cared for these women, even if the God they served did not. Was that why Tillie had urged her to share her burdens with Father Ed instead of seeking God?

"What about you?" Interest shone in Ione's bright gaze. "This makes the second time I've seen you at the shelter. Were you a resident here at one time?"

Ana shook her head. How to explain? "No, I . . . I work for a chandler during the day."

"And you volunteer here at night?"

Aye, thanks to Tillie.

Ana grinned. "I just started."

"Well, glad we are to have you, that's all I can say."

"I'm . . . glad to be here." Surprised to realize she meant it, Ana lowered her face and took extra care with the shirt she was folding.

"Look, Ana! I did it." Ellen proudly lifted a handkerchief that she'd folded into a neat square.

"Indeed, and a good job you've done, too," Ana said, giving Ellen's shoulder a pat.

Ione looked on as they chatted, a curious half smile on her

lips. When after some time Ellen skipped off to plead a glass of milk from Sister Agnes, she caught Ana's eye and then nodded toward her daughter. "You're good with her. She likes you."

A blush heated Ana's cheeks. "I like her, too. She's a sweet lassie. Reminds me so much of Brigid."

"Brigid?"

"My . . . sister."

Ione went still, her eyes agleam with curiosity. The heat in Ana's cheeks grew until her face felt aflame with it. Still, it felt good after so many years to speak her sister's name out loud. She mustered her courage and pressed on.

"She passed away when we were children."

Compassion mingled with the curiosity in Ione's eyes. "I'm sorry to hear it."

Ana dipped her head in thanks, though in truth it was partly to hide the hurt she felt. "I miss her. I can still remember how she smiled—with her eyes, like Ellen. And she skipped everywhere she went the way Ellen does, too." She smiled and lifted her head. "Ach, but Ma used to say Brigid was cursed with feet that refused to stay on the ground."

A knot rose in Ana's throat, so large it hurt to swallow, so deep the ache of it spread clear through her chest.

"I'm . . . sorry . . ." Ana began, but before she finished, Ione had skirted the table and clasped her trembling fingers.

"There there, now, lass. It's all right."

"But, I didn't mean—I'm supposed to be helping you."

Ione cocked her head, so much like a funny brown sparrow that Ana couldn't help but smile through the tears burning behind her eyes.

"Is that so?" Ione said. "And because you're the one volunteering, the rest of us aren't allowed to lend a listening ear?"

Chagrined, Ana went still. "I guess that is how it sounded, isn't it?"

Ione's gentle smile broadened.

"That's not what I meant."

"I know, lassie."

"I'm not even sure why I told you about Brigid. It's been years since I've spoken of her to anyone, even Tillie."

"Your friend?"

Ana nodded and rubbed her finger under her eyes. "She's the one who got me to come to the church in the first place."

"Ach, indeed she is a friend."

Ana quirked an eyebrow. "You say that? But . . . you're here. Alone. With Ellen."

The rest she left unspoken, but Ione's eyes shone with understanding.

"And where else would a woman without hope or another soul to call a friend run, might I ask, if not to a church?"

She said it with such confidence that for a moment Ana could think of no answer. Luckily she was spared having to find one, for at that instant the supper bell rang, sparking lively chatter as the women filed out of the laundry room toward the dining hall. Ione found Ellen, and the two of them claimed seats at the supper table while Ana set off in search of Tillie.

Instead she ran into Eoghan just entering the kitchen. His ears were red, and a light dusting of snow clung to his shoulders. Ana crossed to him as he stomped the mud from his boots and then hung his cap and scarf on a hook by the door.

Suddenly shy, she pushed her hands into the pockets of her apron while she waited for him to turn and see her. When at last he did, she had a smile ready.

"Hello."

For a fraction of a second, she thought she read a spark of gladness in his hazel eyes. It disappeared quickly as he looked past her into the dining room. "Miss Kavanagh."

"I was hoping I'd see you . . ."

The words died on her lips as she struggled for exactly the right way to approach him about Cara, about how she knew who he was, and how she wanted to help the two of them get past their differences. Then, realizing how she'd sounded, she blushed and began again. "What I mean is—"

Eoghan's strong jawline hardened, and his fingers combed his damp rusty locks. Bending slightly at the waist, he motioned toward the hall, then eased around her. "Your pardon, Miss Kavanagh, but I have pressing business I need to speak to Father Ed about. If you don't mind?"

She blinked once, twice. He was dismissing her? And quite curtly. "Of course. I only wanted—"

When at last he looked at her, his face was shuttered, his eyes hard and impatient. "What you and the other volunteers are doing at the shelter is a fine thing. I could almost be convinced to change my opinion of your gender."

He sounded almost surprised, but Ana focused more on his words than his tone.

What did he mean by that? "Excuse me?"

"I mean only to imply that you are . . . I've never seen anyone more . . ." He lifted his hand as though to reach for her, caught himself, and then dropped it. "My life is complicated. Too complicated . . . for you or any woman."

He thought to be gallant, but with his words, shame burned her. She crossed her arms and squeezed them to her chest. "I'm afraid there has been a misunderstanding—"

He gave her shoulder a most infuriating pat. "I'm sorry, Miss Kav—Ana. Truly. Perhaps in different circumstances . . . well . . . it's just . . . there are other things . . ."

Never before had she witnessed a man so lost for words. And all because he thought her attracted to him? No, more likely he pitied her and was struggling for a way to spare her feelings. Enraged that he dared be so condescending, she narrowed her eyes and stuck out her chin.

"By 'things,' I take it you mean the man who came to see you the other night?" She glared at him, daring him to deny it.

He stiffened and drew back his shoulders. "What do you know of him?"

"I know he's not a friend as you claimed. Not much of one, anyway."

He studied her, suddenly cool and with an air of anger about him that would've given her pause were she not so enraged herself.

"Well now, Miss Kavanagh, that's really none of your business, is it?" he said quietly.

She stomped her foot. "I didn't claim that it was, *Mr.* Hamilton."

"Then why did you bring him up?"

"You're the one who said you had 'other things' to attend—"

The conversation had begun to draw curious stares. Eoghan tossed a glance around the kitchen and then snagged her elbow and dragged her to the door. "I appreciate your coming by, but I'm afraid I don't have time—"

"What on earth makes you think I came to see *you*?" she asked coldly.

He blinked. "You mean you didn't?"

Nothing could have dragged the truth from her then. "No. I came to speak to Father Ed." Determined to leave Eoghan and Cara to their own devices—that was, *if* she even bothered to tell Cara that she'd found her arrogant, insensitive, hardheaded brother—Ana yanked from his grasp, jammed her arms to her sides, and whirled around.

Straight into a shocked, openmouthed Tillie. "Ana . . . Derry . . . is everything all right?"

"Fine," they chimed in unison, and then because Tillie appeared so concerned, Ana claimed her arm and lowered her voice. "A misunderstanding, is all."

"So it appears," Eoghan added.

Ana gritted her teeth and willed him to be quiet.

Tillie looked hesitantly from one to the other. "Well then, we're about to serve supper. Ana, we could use your help in the serving line, if you dinna mind. Meg was feeling a tad under the weather and went home straightway after work."

"Looks like that talk with Father Ed will have to wait," Eoghan said.

Tillie turned to Eoghan. "Speaking of Father Ed, he asked if you could fetch another table from the back. We're a bit full tonight. We could use both your help."

"Of course."

"Be glad to."

Their words overlapped, but Ana sensed as she bustled off to do Tillie's bidding that Eoghan was as glad as she was to part company.

Just as well. The nerve of him, accusing her of searching him out because he thought her attracted to him. What did he think she was—an addlepated schoolgirl? One could just as easily say he thought too highly of his handsome good looks. And then to feel sorry for her . . .

Her fists clenched. She'd have none of his pity—his or anyone else's. Cara could find her own way of mending fences with her brother if she chose. Ana intended to steer far clear of Eoghan Hamilton.

With that decided, she picked up a metal spoon and jabbed it deep into a bowl of buttered turnips, but slinging food did little to appease her anger. It stayed with her long after they'd cleaned up the kitchen and turned in their aprons.

Indeed, it nipped at her heels all the way home.

9

Long after Ana and Tillie left the shelter, the memory of Ana's flashing eyes, of her curled fists and upturned chin, burned Eoghan's conscience. He saw her face in the patterned walls of his bedchamber, and she stared accusingly at him from the cracked, mottled glass of his windows.

He'd insulted her.

All he'd been trying to do was spare her, keep from involving her or anyone else in his plans to rejoin the Fenians—which was downright admirable considering his past mistakes. Instead he'd made her angry. Made her think he found her unattractive.

Ridiculous.

Did she not see how beautiful she was every time she looked in the mirror? As if any man with air in his lungs could pass her by and not be affected by the depth of her sultry brown eyes, the tilt of her lips, the curve of her—

He cut the thought short. He'd never figure women. Never.

Jamming his feet into a pair of boots, he forced himself to consider his plans for the day. He could only assume the Fenians were pleased that he'd successfully delivered the packet to the barge office yesterday morn. Why then had there been no word?

Rising, he left the room and closed the door to his bedchamber. Father Ed would be in his study. Eoghan had meant to seek him out last night but instead found himself quarreling with a beautiful dark-haired woman.

Not today.

Today he'd sit down with someone he could trust—another man. Granted, he was a priest, but Eoghan wouldn't hold that against him.

Early morning light filtered through the windows of the empty rooms he passed. He met no one on his way to the study, but as he'd suspected, a dim glow escaped from under the closed door. He rapped lightly and waited.

The door opened a crack.

"Eoghan?" Father Ed pushed it open the rest of the way. "Come in, lad. You're up early." Fingers ruffling his hair, he ushered Eoghan past a bookshelf laden with heavy volumes, to a slender oak desk and two chairs.

A candelabrum with five candles burned to nubs lit the room, the wax pooling at the carved wooden base giving indication as to how long Father Ed had been awake. Why did the man not simply open the draperies? Eoghan smirked. Likely because he'd been there so long, night and day meant nothing to him.

He gestured to the ledgers open on the desk and a stack of scribbled notes. "Forgive me if I'm intruding on your study. I can come back another time, if you'd rather—"

"Eh, I've been at it for some time. I was ready for an interruption of any kind." Father Ed rubbed at his eyes, turning them red. He chuckled and motioned toward a pitcher dangling from a hook over a bed of hot coals. "There's warm milk there, if you'd like some. I can find an extra cup." He craned his neck, searching the study for a suitable container.

Eoghan lifted his hand and shook his head. "I appreciate

the offer, Father, but I've never been too keen on the stuff, warm or otherwise."

Father Ed laughed and settled into one of the chairs while Eoghan did the same. "Me either, though I've not been able to convince Sister Agnes. She insists warm milk is good for me bones, if not my taste buds." He grimaced as he laced both hands across his midsection. "Now, what is it I can do for you, laddie? I assume you have something you'd like to discuss?"

Ah, directness. Why couldn't women be the same? They always talked in circles, never saying what they meant, or meaning what they said. And to think he'd almost believed Ana different.

He frowned. Another reason why aiming all his time and attention at getting into the Fenians' good graces and helping in their cause made more sense. And yet . . .

He couldn't explain the unease in his gut. Leaning forward across the desk, he pinned Father Ed with his gaze. "I've not been to confession in a long time, Father. I suppose you know that."

He shrugged. "I'd assumed as much."

"I do remember, however, that the things shared in the confessional are made in confidence."

Father Ed pushed up in his chair. "Are you wanting to make your confession, lad? Is that what this is about?"

Eoghan snorted and sat back. "Not a confession, so much, though I would like your assurance that the things we speak of today . . ."

He lifted an eyebrow, waiting.

Father Ed tipped his head solemnly, and so, starting at the beginning, when Eoghan, Sean, and Kil first left Derry, he proceeded to tell the priest everything, ending with his meeting with Kilarny and the errand on which he'd been sent yesterday.

"Joining back up with the Fenians, it's important to you," Father Ed said gently when Eoghan at last fell silent.

He nodded slowly. "It was the one time in my life when I knew my purpose—when I believed in what I was fighting for."

"But your relationship with your sister is important, as well. Otherwise you'd not have risked everything, including your life, to send for her."

Eoghan thought back to the day he'd scribbled the hasty note, telling her that he lived and begging her to join him in America. He pressed his lips tight, swallowing back longing and bitterness.

"I know something of the Fenians," Father Ed said, a surprising touch of sorrow in his voice. "I've heard of their struggle to establish home rule in Ireland—by force, if necessary."

So ingrained was the need for secrecy, Eoghan barely even blinked.

Father Ed smiled. "How many of the women who come here do you think have found themselves widowed by this verra cause? I'm a priest, lad, but I'm not a fool. Even a few of my own brethren . . ." He sighed and bit his lip. "But that discussion is for another day." Bracing both hands on the desk, he pushed himself up and stood. "What you want to know is if I believe the Fenians right in what they do and how they do it."

Circling the desk, he came to a stop beside Eoghan, his hand heavy on his shoulder. "What I'd like to know is why you care what I think."

So great was the weight settling on Eoghan's chest, he found it hard to breathe, much less speak. "Because . . . you're a good man," he said with some difficulty.

"'There is none righteous, no, not one.'"

Somehow he managed to lift his head to stare at the priest.

Even by the fading light of the candles, he read compassion in the man's eyes.

He gave Eoghan's shoulder a squeeze. "No one, that is, except the Savior. Eoghan, me lad, I suspect 'tis His opinion you're really seeking. In fact, if one is honest, 'tis only His good favor that matters anything at all."

— ❋ ❋ ❋ —

The bell above the door to James O'Bannon's candle shop chimed merrily behind the last customer of the day. Ana waved them good-bye, then locked the door and sank against it wearily.

"Busy day." Cara exited the rear of the store, a stack of receipts in her hand. Though she no longer needed to earn a wage, she still stopped by on occasion to help the amiable old shopkeeper with his books, because as fine a candlemaker as he was, he couldn't add a column of figures if it meant saving his life. She waved the papers, inked documentation of the orders for the week. "Lots of customers."

Ana groaned and pushed off the door. "And I feel every one of them in my feet."

"Aye, and my back." Mr. O'Bannon rose from behind the counter, his hand at his waist. "Can't remember the last time we saw this many orders all at one time, and the month only October, to boot. Hoo-hoo! Imagine what the shorter days will bring."

"Word is getting out about the quality of your work." Ana joined him behind the counter and patted his stooped shoulder. "And fine time it is, too. There's not a better chandler in all of New York."

"The Lower East Side, anyway," he replied, chuckling. "But I'll not be deceiving myself or anyone else by taking the praise. Our success is thanks mainly to you. You've a way with those molds." He pointed to an array of wooden forms lining tall shelves, fastened to the wall on both sides of a large window. His hand lowered as he studied the deepening sky through the glass. "Oh dear. I'm afraid I've kept you long. Those clouds don't look friendly."

Cara joined him at the window, a matching concern on her upturned face. "Hmm . . . he's right. Those clouds are quite dark." Her eyes swept downward and she fell silent a moment, then whispered, "That's odd."

"What is?" Ana laid aside her apron and bent to remove her reticule and gloves from the same cupboard.

"That man outside the baker's door. I saw him earlier today. He's still there, almost like he is waiting for someone." She turned from the window to look at Ana. "Do you know him, Ana?"

She moved aside as Ana went to peer out the window. The streets were certainly crowded, yet she spotted nothing out of the ordinary. She glanced at Cara. "Which man are you talking about?"

Cara pointed. "Outside the bakery, by the window there. He's wearing a gray hat with a green feather on one side. Do you see him?"

Indeed, she did not, though she scanned both sides of the street and the bakery.

"Why, he's right there," Cara said. She moved to the window and looked again, then broke away with a shake of her head. "I don't understand. He *was* there."

Silence fell over the three of them, for even Mr. O'Bannon remembered the danger they'd faced last summer, Cara especially. "Did you recognize him, lass?" he asked with a worried pull to his collar.

She shook her head again and somehow managed a bright smile. "Perhaps we should take a carriage. It can drop us by

Rourke's office, and we can ride home with him from there. What do you think, Ana? We'll be happy to run you by the boardinghouse. Besides . . . there's something I've been wanting to share with Amelia and the others." She cleared her throat delicately. "Something I'd just as soon not see spoiled with talk of mysterious strangers, if you ken my meaning."

Ana did ken her meaning—she didn't want them to tell Rourke. She started to protest, thought better of it after a quick glance at Cara's pleading face, followed by a look at the brooding sky, and soon found herself ensconced across from Cara and Rourke in the carriage headed toward the boardinghouse.

"Tell me about your day," Cara said, leaning lightly against Rourke's shoulder. "Has there been any more talk about joining forces with Alfred Smith?"

Rourke's eyes fairly danced as he sought his wife's hand. "You must have truly missed me if indeed you're willing to be bored with talk of the office."

Cara shrugged a slim shoulder, the motion setting the plume in her bonnet to quivering. "Well . . . you have been staying later and later. Is it because you're trying to figure out where you stand?"

Rourke's eyes took on a troubled gleam, and then he nodded. "I'm learning my way. Things are different here from what they were in Ireland. More complicated. It's going to take some time before I feel confident enough to seek out Mr. Smith, to see if he'd be willing to take me under his wing."

Though they were thoroughly engrossed in one another, Ana did not feel ill at ease in Rourke and Cara's company. She enjoyed being privy to the companionship the two shared, the joy and love each one held for the other. Even so, she owed them a bit of privacy. So she turned her head to look out the window as Rourke began filling in the details of his new job.

The cheerful glow from half a dozen oil lamps shone merrily in the windows as the boardinghouse came into view. Rourke ordered the carriage around to the front and helped first Cara and then Ana alight.

"Will you come inside, Cara? Rourke? I'm sure Amelia and the others would love to see you."

After a glance at Rourke, who gave a slight nod, Cara clasped Ana's hand. "We'd love to."

Any thoughts of the stranger outside the candle shop flitted from her mind as Ana skipped up the steps. She pushed open the door, surprised when voices welcomed them from the library instead of the dining room. It was, after all, almost suppertime.

"Ana, is that you? Come in, come in," Amelia called, her cheerful voice ringing through the narrow hall. "We're in here."

Smiling, Ana put a finger to her lips before depositing her cloak along with Cara and Rourke's onto waiting hooks inside the hallway. At Cara's answering smile, she tiptoed to the library and poked her head inside.

Chaos was a fitting word to describe the state of the room. Boxes littered every inch of the floor, along with skirts of various color, blouses, shoes, even a bonnet that Ana swore she'd seen Meg wear on occasion.

Mindful of her own surprise lurking in the hallway, Ana lifted a brow and frowned. "What's all this?"

Meg jumped from behind the settee, her curls in comely disarray, a wide grin on her face. "Oh, Ana, there you are! Wait until you hear what we're doing. It's Tillie's idea."

"What? What's Tillie's idea?"

"The clothes," Amelia said, herself rising from a wing chair near the fireplace. "For the church. We've been collecting them from friends and neighbors all morning."

105

"They're for the shelter, actually, at Our Lady of Deliverance," Laverne added, her mobcap as askew as Meg's curls. She was surprisingly light on her feet as she picked her way through the field of boxes to Ana's side. "Tillie said some of the women there had a need for clothing—dresses and the like."

She pressed her cheek to Ana's in a welcoming hug, and then, spying Cara and Rourke, clapped both hands to the sides of her face and grinned. "Oh! What . . . ?"

Laughing, Ana grabbed Cara's hand and pulled her into the room. "Well, I thought to be the one with a surprise tonight, but it looks as though Tillie has surpassed me."

"Cara!" Amelia exclaimed, brushing aside a pile of coats and shoes to reach her. "And Rourke. This *is* a surprise. How wonderful to see you both. Come in and sit." She twisted to and fro, her hands fluttering at the clothes piled on the settee. "Well, I'm afraid we've got quite a mess—"

"All right, here's another load. Where do you want 'em?"

At the gruff voice, Laverne released Ana and spun to claim the handyman's arm. "Over by the fireplace, Giles, so's Amelia can sort them by size."

He grunted a greeting to Cara and Rourke as he moved to obey. Tillie tagged at his heels, her cheeks flushed a pretty pink above the linens and petticoats piled in her arms. Ana had to admit, she'd never seen her happier. Since she started working at the shelter, she seemed less careworn, more like a young lass than a grief-stricken widow. Gone were the lines of sadness that had once marred her countenance; or at least they had faded to dim shadows. Ana was glad. She didn't deserve the burden of sorrow she'd been forced to carry since losing Braedon and her unborn child.

"Hello," Tillie sang, eyes sparkling. "What a nice surprise. Are the two of you staying for supper?"

"I think so," Cara said, her hand darting up when the pile in Tillie's arms threatened to spill.

Suddenly, Ana realized her thoughts had blinded her to the threatening tilt of Tillie's armload.

"Whoa, best let me help with that," Cara said.

"I can do it," Ana said in the same moment, but before either of them could move, Rourke rushed between them, grabbed Cara's arm, then righted the stack of clothing.

"Cara, you shouldn't be lifting. I'll take them, Tillie. Where do you want these again?"

The room went silent in an instant. Rourke hefted the load, then swung his gaze from Tillie to Cara, to Ana, and back to Tillie.

"Tillie?"

"Aye?"

"The clothes?"

She cocked her head to one side, slowly. "What . . . what did you say?"

"Where do you want them?"

"Before that." Amelia stepped forward, a befuddled wrinkle forming between her brows. "What did you say before that?"

Suddenly sheepish, Rourke looked at Cara. "I . . . said . . ."

Suspicion formed in Ana's mind. "What's going on? What haven't you told us?"

A warm, happy smile melted across Cara's face. She motioned to Rourke, who dropped the clothes on the settee and moved to clasp her hand.

"Actually, Rourke and I have a surprise of our own," she began, drawing out each word with tantalizing slowness.

Tillie gasped, and both hands moved to cover her mouth.

Could it be? Ana's wondering gaze returned to Cara.

Twin spots of color appeared on her friend's cheeks before

she tipped her head up to peer lovingly at her husband. "I don't suppose there's any point delaying the news any longer, is there, my love? Secret's out."

All watched as her hand went to her midsection and lingered there.

"Cara . . ." Amelia said, clapping her hands together.

"You're expecting a wee one!" Laverne cried, after which an eruption of glad tidings filled the room.

Only Ana remained silent.

After the initial excitement, her thoughts immediately winged to Eoghan. What might his presence mean to Cara and her bairn? Would knowing that his sister was with child make a difference in his decision to renounce her? From what little she knew of him, he didn't seem the type of man who could turn his back on his sister *and* his niece or nephew.

More important, she alone knew where Eoghan lived. What if telling Eoghan about Cara's child was the balm needed to heal the rift between brother and sister?

Her stomach sank. She knew what she needed to do. Tomorrow she'd go back to Our Lady of Deliverance. She'd find Eoghan and tell him what she knew. Maybe then she could convince him to seek out his twin. Maybe then the bitterness that kept them apart would finally be erased.

10

A delighted squeal greeted Ana when she arrived at the shelter the next evening after work. In two quick winks, Ellen scurried to clasp her hand—two more and she found herself dragged to a long table where an assortment of paper dolls lay spread.

"You're just in time, Ana. I'm choosing an outfit for Lila." She held up one of the paper dolls. "You can pick one for Catherine."

Ellen's enthusiasm was contagious. Ana smiled and fingered the delicate doll that someone had taken obvious care to craft. The painted face was graceful and sweet, the lips upturned. In the place of hand-drawn hair, someone had fastened a few strands of brown string.

Ellen shoved the doll toward Ana. "See? She has dark hair, like you."

"And like you." Ana smiled and gave one of Ellen's locks a tug, which was instantly rewarded with a giggle that warmed the heart. Her grip tight on Ana's fingers, she tossed back her head and widened her eyes.

"Will you play with me, Ana? Mama has more ironin' to do before supper. I'm supposed to sit here until she comes for me."

What could it hurt? Ana pulled out a chair next to Ellen's. "'Twould be my honor, Ladybug."

"Ladybug?"

The deep voice caught both of them off guard. Ellen twisted in her seat while Ana soaked in the sight of Eoghan watching them from the doorway, one shoulder pressed against the frame. A full second later, she blinked and tore her eyes away.

Ellen scooted to a third chair and gave the one she'd vacated a pat. "We're playing dolls. Wanna sit with us, Derry?"

He chuckled. "You mean I'm allowed? I figured you girls would want to be alone."

Ana scowled.

As though he read her thoughts, he tipped his head in her direction. "Best check with your friend."

"She doesn't mind, do you, Ana?"

Ellen's sparkling gaze, so innocent and pleading, forced back the retort simmering on her tongue. "I don't mind a whit, but I'm pretty certain Mr. Hamilton has better—"

"Good. Then I'd love to join you."

He would? Ana narrowed her eyes, but if he noticed, he refused to show it.

He folded himself into the chair, his long legs crowding Ana's small space. Why, oh why, hadn't Ellen offered him the seat opposite instead of between them?

He scanned the row of dolls. "Which one is mine?"

"You pick," Ellen said, giggling as she dropped her chin into her palm.

Placing his finger to his jaw, he pretended to think. "Hmm . . . definitely one with brown hair. I'm rather partial to that color."

"Like mine and Ana's," Ellen said and clapped her hands.

"Exactly like yours and Ana's," he responded, chucking her lightly under the chin.

Ana refused to look at him. Only when Ellen became engrossed with choosing a dress for her doll did Ana hiss, "I am not appreciative of the game you be playing, Mr. Hamilton."

"And what game is that, Miss Kavanagh?"

Reminding herself of why she'd come, Ana took a deep breath and concentrated on calming her racing heart. Jaw clenched, she forced an apology through gritted teeth. "Forgive me. I suppose that was rather abrupt."

He lifted an eyebrow, a teasing glint in his eye that would quickly unravel her anger if she studied it overlong. She pressed on.

"And for the other day . . . I offer my apologies, as well."

"You're sorry?"

Did he want her to repeat it? Heat flooded her cheeks. She forced herself to think about Cara and the way her hand had lingered so lovingly over her midsection. "Aye. My words and manner were less than acceptable, and I apologize—"

Before she could finish, he grabbed hold of her fingers and gave a shake of his head. "No. You have nothing to be sorry for."

Scathingly aware of his touch against her skin, she flinched and pulled her hand away. "If you'll allow me to finish—"

He leaned toward her, so close she could see the flecks of gold dancing among the green of his hazel eyes. "But you don't understand—"

"Mama!" Jumping to her feet, Ellen scraped her chair back and flew to the door to throw her arms around her mother's legs.

Heart pounding, Ana rose and waited while Ione extricated herself from Ellen's grasp.

"You have playmates, I see." Her expression offered silent thanks to Ana and, behind her, Eoghan. She reached down to press her daughter to her side. "First the dolls, and now

111

your time and attention. Everyone here at the church has been more than kind. I kinna thank you all enough."

"Oh." Startled to realize she was still holding one of the dolls, and that it had become quite crumpled in her tight grasp, Ana dropped it on the table and smoothed the paper with her fingers. "No, we didn't bring the dolls."

Ione smiled. "Of course not. Tillie brought them by first thing this morning on her way to work. Ellen was so thrilled. Is she coming this evening to help with the meal?"

Ana's hand slowed over the pretty painted face. Tillie had crafted the dolls . . . undoubtedly for a daughter who hadn't lived to draw her first breath. Reminded of life's fleeting nature, all trace of anger ebbed from Ana's heart.

"I don't know if she's coming," she replied. Truthfully it had been nigh unto a week since she and Tillie had spent any time alone. Always it was with the others at the boarding-house or here at the church. She was inclined to rectify the situation as soon as she returned home later that evening.

"Well, if she doesn't, would you give her my thanks when next you see her? Mine and Ellen's."

"Of course," Ana said, nodding. "I'll tell her."

"Thank you." Ione bent down to her daughter. "We've finished with our chores for the day. Want to play a little before it's time to clean up for supper?"

Ellen happily agreed, and though they were but a few feet away at the table, Ana had never felt so alone. She held her breath and risked a peek at Eoghan.

He cleared his throat. "I . . . uh . . . suppose I should see about finishing up the list of chores Sister Mary left for me."

He hesitated a moment and then turned to leave. Ana pursed her lips. She'd not yet accomplished her task, so unless she was willing to brave another unsavory visit to the barn . . .

She spoke. Quickly. "Mr. Hamilton?"

He lifted a brow. "Aye, Miss Kavanagh?"

"If you've a moment, there's something I'd like to speak with you about."

Surprise flickered in his eyes, but he motioned to another table as far away from Ione and her daughter as propriety allowed.

Except . . .

It was very near to the fire crackling in the fireplace. Her heart fluttering, Ana forced her feet to move.

"Actually," Eoghan said before she quite reached her seat, "there's another table here, next to the door. Perhaps 'twould be better if we sat there, so I can hear should Sister Mary or Sister Agnes call."

The tension in her chest eased and she nodded. "All right."

Weak-kneed, she waited while he held out her chair, then circled to sit across from her. Aware that the fortitude she'd need to begin was fleeting at best, she lowered her gaze and plowed ahead.

"I have a confession to make. I've been keeping something . . . waiting for the right moment to reveal something," she corrected.

He said nothing, so she looked at him. Eoghan clenched his hands so tightly his knuckles shone white. So hard were his features, they looked as though they'd been carved from stone.

"Go on," he prompted at last.

His voice was tight, controlled—stirring a memory in Ana's brain that raised bumps on her flesh. She swallowed against a sudden knot in her throat. "Perhaps it might be better if I told you a little about myself first?"

To her relief, the hard mask slipped a bit and he nodded.

"I had a sister once, about Ellen's age." She glanced across the room at the little girl and then down at the bare stone floor. "Her name was Brigid. We grew up together on a farm outside of Dublin. She was younger than me by almost three years."

"What happened to her?"

Gone was the chill from Eoghan's voice. Ana looked up gratefully. "She died."

"In a fire?"

Tears sprang to her eyes as she nodded. "How did you know?"

His gaze dropped to her hands. She tucked them into her skirt.

"Family is . . . precious, Eoghan. I wish I'd realized it sooner, before Brigid and Mama . . ."

"Your mother died in the fire, too?"

"Aye." The lone word fell from her lips like a pebble.

"And your *daed* . . . have you no other family?"

Ana hesitated, a dim figure looming from her memory. "An uncle only. Da died a year before the fire."

"I'm sorry, Ana."

Not pity! Too many times she had encountered that tone and despised it. Ana tamped the bitter taste caused by his words and thrust out her chin. "I tell you this only because I . . . because . . ."

Why would speech not come? Ana cast frantically through her brain, relieved when Eoghan spoke for her.

"You know about . . . Cara. My sister."

Saddened by the anger in his voice, she nodded. "She's been looking for you a long time."

Jerking to his feet, Eoghan turned toward the fireplace, his broad back a wall no words could scale. "You do not understand the situation, Ana, and I . . . I prefer it that way."

His words cut deeper than she had imagined possible. Still, it was Cara's feelings she needed to think about now. Swallowing her own hurt, she circled to stand defiantly before him. "It's true, I don't know everything that happened to cause this rift between you. But neither do you know . . ."

Suddenly, Ana sensed it was not her place to tell Eoghan about Cara and Rourke's baby. But how would he ever learn the truth if he refused to even see his sister? Guilt washed over her, and a twinge of anger. She lifted her chin.

"Eoghan Hamilton, you owe it to your sister to at least speak with her. Let her tell you her side." She tapped her temple. "It may be you'll find out you're not as smart as you think."

His lips curled in an angry frown. "'Tis no use talking when the harm is done, Ana. What happened between Cara and me is over and done. Nothing will change that."

"Why, you stubborn—" She clipped the ire threatening to spill from her mouth, choosing instead to repeat something she'd heard her mother say long ago. "Unforgiveness is as bitter to the tongue as thick milk, Eoghan." And then more softly and with her eyes lowered, she added, "We'd both do good to remember that."

"Unforgiveness? You?" He snorted derisively. "I doubt that. I've seen how you are with Ione and Ellen. The women here at the shelter. Even Tillie and the other girl, what's her name?"

"Meg."

"Aye, her." He leaned back in his chair and crossed his arms. "You may suffer from a few of the other afflictions of your gender, but an unforgiving nature is not among your list of sins."

The warmth in his face as he spoke her praise robbed her of breath—tempered as it was with impertinence. For a moment, she was tempted to let him go on, however misguided his admiration. But then Father Ed's voice rang out, calling the shelter residents to the dining hall. She shook her head and lowered her voice as Ione and Ellen passed.

"You're wrong. I harbor as much bitterness as the next person. More. Why do you think I've been so reluctant to attend church services?" The admission formed with difficulty, spilling from a tongue that felt as dry and thick as a field of cotton. "'Tis a dreadful thing to turn your back on God."

"Is that what you've done?"

I've done only that which was done to me.

Though she thought the words, she did not give vent to them. Instead she fought to control her rising temper, to let go of the bitterness that had bound her for so long. So locked was she in the battle raging inside, she did not see when Eoghan stretched out his hand, and was startled when his warm fingers closed around hers.

"Your words are intended as a kindness. I bear you no ill will for having shared them." He pulled away, leaving her fingers burning where he'd touched her. "But the differences between Cara and I extend further than a mere apology can broach. She betrayed me, Ana, in a manner I can never forgive."

Despite his claim, pain darkened his eyes, turning them green. He loomed over her—all angular planes and sharp, hawkish features—yet with a vulnerability about him that tore her heart. Maybe she'd been wrong. He did need to know about the baby, and since he refused to speak with Cara . . .

Holding her breath, she reached up to boldly touch his shoulder. His muscles were taut beneath her fingers, like the string of a bow, drawn tight. She licked her lips and removed her hand. "Eoghan, the reason I came—"

A scuffle sounded in the hall, loud voices followed by pounding feet. Ana ignored them and pressed on.

"The reason I sought you out tonight—"

More shouting. She shot a glance at the hall, the revelation she'd been prepared to utter dying on her lips. Ione's cape lay puddled on the floor, and around it a handful of paper dolls were strewn.

A second later, a child's scream rent the air.

11

The initial scream was followed by a second more piercing cry. Eoghan knew the sound. He'd heard it during battle. It was pure, primal fear.

He launched himself into the hallway, jostling through a group that had gathered around the entrance to the kitchen. "What is it? What happened?"

"Ellen!" Ana shot past him, through the kitchen and out the gaping door to the backyard. Instinctively, Eoghan moved to follow.

Father Ed cut across his path, his hands cupped to his mouth as he shouted, "Someone fetch some cold water! And clean rags. We'll need plenty of them."

The floor rumbled as people darted off to obey.

Eoghan's heart thumped painfully. The child had been with them a second ago. She and her mother left what seemed like moments before he heard the scream.

Shouldering his way through the crowd to Sister Mary, he tapped her elbow and dipped his head to whisper, "What happened?"

Tears flooded the nun's eyes as she squinted up at him.

"The wee one . . . Ellen . . . Sister Agnes sent her out to fetch the milk pail."

"She wanted to go," Sister Agnes groaned from her spot near the door. "Why, oh why did I let her do it alone?"

"She hurt herself in the barn?" Eoghan urged, drawing Sister Mary's attention back.

Her face twisted in agony and she shook her head. "The fires we used for heating the laundering water, she got too near a cauldron and her dress . . ."

The fabric of her habit quivered as a shudder traveled her spine from head to toe. Sister Agnes wrapped her arms around her trembling form.

A hundred thoughts thrummed through Eoghan's brain, but one overruled them all.

Ana.

Ducking through the kitchen door, he ignored the steps and vaulted to the ground, covering the short distance to her side in a few long strides.

Ana knelt next to Ellen, her fingers shaking as she scraped frantically at the buttons on the child's sodden dress. Beside her, Ione clutched Father Ed, wild-eyed and panicked, her lips moving in a garbled plea.

"Is she all right? Is my bairn all right?" Over and over, like a mantra.

Ellen whimpered in answer. Her eyes were closed, her face was pale, and she trembled like a reed pummeled by a fierce wind.

"She'll be fine," Father Ed soothed, though he looked as white as the half-conscious child. "A-Ana, perhaps we should move her inside?"

"We've got to get her out of these c-clothes," Ana stammered. She jerked her head up. "Where's the water!"

"It's coming." Eoghan dropped to his haunches next to her. "What can I do?"

"Help m-me," Ana whispered. She motioned toward El-len's legs. "We can't let dirt or material from the d-dress . . . her burns . . . I'll need something to wrap her in."

Eoghan stripped off his shirt and shoved it into her hands. "Hold this." A moment later he carefully lifted Ellen's charred outer garment from her body. Though dirtied and wet, her underclothes and petticoat appeared relatively intact. Blisters and sections of raw flesh covered a portion of her right leg, but her left only looked angry and red.

He stuck out his hand. "The shirt."

She gave it back to him, but her gaze remained riveted to Ellen's legs. Eoghan carefully wrapped the shirt around the child's thin shoulders before lifting her into his arms and walking with her toward the church. Father Ed hurried ahead.

"Has someone called for a doctor?" Eoghan asked as he strode through the kitchen.

"Sister Agnes sent someone to fetch him," Sister Mary shot over her shoulder. Her hand flopped wildly as she mo-tioned for Eoghan to follow. They tramped down the long hall to the sleeping quarters, but instead of turning for the large room where the residents slept on rows of cots, she pushed open the door to her private chamber. "In here. The little one and her ma are going to need some privacy the next few days."

She looked questioningly at Father Ed, who dipped his head in agreement. Bustling inside, she drew back the covers on a neatly made bunk and gave the straw mattress a pat. "Here. Lay her down so we can get a better look at those burns."

A sallow-faced woman with graying hair popped through the entrance, a dripping bucket clutched in her hands. "Here's the water. It's clean. Drew it from the well meself."

Sister Mary took it from her hands. "And the rags?"

"They're a coming."

She nodded and gestured for Ione. Tears still streaked her cheeks, but at least a bit of the panic had disappeared from her eyes. Eoghan backed into the hall, confident that matters were well in hand, at least until the doctor arrived.

In the kitchen, troubled faces peered at him, but Ana's was not among them. His heart thumped. He assumed she'd followed them inside. Somehow he'd lost her in the action.

Two women stood at the door, looking out. Eoghan grabbed his coat and threw it on, then snatched another garment off the rack, one of the cloaks belonging to the nuns, and hurried outside.

As he suspected, Ana was still huddled on the ground, Ellen's sodden dress clutched in her fingers. Apparently, Ellen had bumped into the cauldron and knocked it from the stand suspended over the fire, for mud had formed around the hissing remnants of the flames.

Eoghan approached slowly, wishing he'd thought to close the kitchen door behind him as he became aware of the curious gazes following his progress. "Ana?"

Her head lifted . . . too slowly. She looked dazed. Like a soldier on the battlefield after a skirmish. Anguish snaked through him. He'd seen the outcome of that look too many times.

He draped the cloak gently over her shoulders and then crouched next to her, checking for signs of injury without touching—her hands, her face, her dress. "Are you all right, lass?"

She fixed him with a desperate stare. "Ellen?"

"Father Ed and the nuns are with her. They're waiting for the doctor."

She nodded, and Ellen's dress slid from her fingers. Eoghan sucked in a breath. Blisters covered her palms. Grabbing hold of her wrists, he did a quick examination, then sprang to his feet and sprinted to the well to fetch the water bucket. It was still half full. He yanked it from the hook, where it hung suspended, and brought it back to Ana.

"How did you burn yourself?" he asked, tight-lipped, as he set the pail between them and guided her hands into the cool water.

"The c-cauldron . . . her leg was trapped under it. I shoved it off."

By herself? He cursed himself for not having moved to help sooner. He inched around the pail to her side. "It's getting cold. We should get you inside before you get chilled."

She shivered and shook her head.

"Ana?"

"I can't, Eoghan."

"Why not?"

Grief filled her eyes, so deep it pained him to look.

He clasped her shoulders, willing the hurt away, wishing he could lift it from her as easily as he'd lifted Ellen. "What is it? Tell me."

A name spilled from her white lips. "Brigid."

"Ellen is not Brigid. She's going to be all right."

"I couldn't save her."

"You did save her. You moved the cauldron."

She shook her head. "Not talking about Ellen."

Understanding mixed with the concern seeping through him. "Brigid was not your fault, either. You were a child. You said so yourself."

"But she called to me . . ."

The rest ended on a pained sigh. He could bear it no longer. Mindful of her hands, he pulled her into his arms and squeezed her tight. "Ana, stop. Please. This was an accident, just as Brigid's death was an accident."

She sagged against him, no longer resisting but shivering, whether from the shock or cold he was not certain.

He gathered her close, his lips grazing her temple, then slid his hand to cup the back of her neck. "I'm taking you inside. Can you walk?"

She nodded, but swayed when she rose. Carrying her was easier. He didn't ask—just swept her into his arms the way he'd done Ellen. He almost wished she'd protest, hiss at him the way she did when she was angry. Instead she lay against him, melting his heart, robbing him of breath.

At the entrance, Sister Mary stood clutching a crucifix that hung about her neck. "The doctor's here. Father Ed and Ione are with him." Her gaze drifted to Ana. "How is she?"

"I'm fine—" Ana began, a tremor in her voice.

Eoghan cut in before she could finish. "She burned her hands."

Sister Mary snatched an oil lamp from a shelf near the door and turned the wick high. "Bring her to the table so I can see."

Eoghan gratefully complied. Ana would be fine with Sister Mary—or anyone besides himself—tending her. He set her gently in a chair, railing silently at the weakness that shook him at the sight of the pain twisting her features. Well he remembered how even a burnt finger made him squirm. His stomach churned at what she and Ellen must be feeling.

He whirled. "I'll get more water."

He didn't—couldn't—wait for Sister Mary's reply. Fortunately, by the time he'd refilled the water bucket and returned with it to the kitchen, most of his composure had been restored. Leastwise he could look at Ana without breaking into a sweat.

Sister Mary bent over Ana's hands, holding honey and a spoon. Spying Eoghan, she gestured him close. "Bring that towel over the sink. It's clean."

He did, watching curiously as Sister Mary drizzled a fine layer of honey over Ana's hands. He lifted an eyebrow.

"My ma taught me," she said before he could ask. "The honey will keep bacteria from growing. The cool water and rags will lessen the pain some."

Indeed, the grimace faded from Ana's face as Sister Mary dipped the towel in the water bucket and then wrapped it loosely around her hands.

"Keep it wrapped fifteen minutes at least." She jerked to her feet. "Stay with her, Derry. I'm going to check on Ellen."

She bustled off, leaving him no choice but to claim the seat she'd vacated. No choice? He groaned inwardly. If he were honest, she couldn't have dragged him from Ana's side.

He sat, so close their knees almost touched. "Are you all right, Ana?"

Her eyes were misty, and she still looked pale, but she nodded. "More worried about Ellen, actually."

Thankfully her voice was stronger. The tension in his chest slowly subsided. "She'll be fine now that the doctor is with her."

"I hope so."

She turned her face away. Oh, how his fingers ached to clasp her chin and draw her back. Instead he propped both elbows on his knees and clenched his hands in front of him. They waited in silence as the interminable minutes ticked past. Finally, Sister Mary returned with Sister Agnes at her side, and though the nuns appeared weary, their faces were devoid of worry.

"Doctor says she'll be fine," Sister Mary said.

Sister Agnes's head wagged in agreement. "Says we'll have to be on guard against infection, but none of the burns were as bad as we first thought. The little one is just going to be in some pain for a bit, bless her dear heart." She laid her hand over her chest and sighed.

"Now, Sister, you heard what the doctor said. He'll give her something to ease the hurt," Sister Mary said, patting the older nun on the back. She looked up. "And how is our other patient?"

Sister Agnes's head lifted. "Other patient?"

"Ana burned her hands helping Ellen."

"Oh no!" Sister Agnes scurried to the table as Ana rose. "How bad?"

"Not bad," she insisted, drawing her hands from under the towel and lifting them for her inspection.

Indeed, the blisters did not look nearly as angry as they had before. Welcome relief flooded through Eoghan as she turned her hands over and down.

"See?"

Despite her confident tone, she sought the towel quickly once Sister Agnes had finished her examination. Admiration flared in his chest. She didn't want the nuns to know that the burns still pained her. Good. That meant some of her spunk was returning.

The same woman who'd come to Ellen's aid with the water bucket poked her head into the kitchen. "How is the little one?"

"She'll be fine," Sister Mary said, then slapped both palms to her cheeks. "Good heavens! We forgot all about supper."

The woman shook her head and lifted her hand. "All taken care of. What few of us *could* eat after all that excitement, did. The rest of us are cleaning up now."

Eoghan looked around the kitchen, noticing for the first time that a couple of the shelter's residents had begun carrying mostly full bowls in from the dining hall. They hadn't

125

asked what needed to be done; they'd simply recognized the task and undertook it.

Cara was like that—always had been. He'd merely forgotten. His estimation of women rose.

"We saved the two of you a plate, too," the woman continued, tipping her head toward the nuns.

Sister Mary patted the older nun's bent shoulder. "You should eat."

"And you?" Sister Agnes peeked up from beneath her cowl.

"I'm going to see about getting Ana home," Sister Mary said. "It's late and cold, and I don't think she ought to be walking. I'll get Derry to hitch up the wagon."

"But that means you'll be riding back alone," Ana protested. "And there's no need since I can manage on my own."

"Absolutely not." Sister Mary stomped her foot and cocked her head like some giant angry bird Eoghan had seen only in books. "Never did approve of you lasses coming and going at all hours of the day. 'Tisn't seemly, no matter what those poster-carrying women outside city hall say. Ach, but I miss the good old days, when a pretty young lass wouldn't have dreamed of being seen without an escort."

"I believe they're called suffragettes, Sister," Sister Agnes said gently.

Sister Mary twisted about and planted her hands on her hips. "What?"

"The poster-carrying women. Suffragettes."

Sister Mary rolled her eyes, and Eoghan frowned. The conversation had taken a dour turn. He'd need to act fast or the nuns would lose control altogether. Clearing his throat, he stepped forward. "I'll take her."

Sister Mary lifted an eyebrow. "You?"

"No sense hitching the wagon and then waiting till you return so I can brush down the mare."

"That's true, Sister," Agnes said, her habit rustling with each agitated step across the kitchen. "Ana will be safer with him now that it's after dark. Besides, our young Derry is better acquainted with the streets—ain't it so, lad?"

He nodded. "Aye. I'll be back in half a wink."

Sister Mary pondered this a moment, her index finger scratching lightly at her temple beneath her wimple. At last, she sighed and looked to Ana for approval. "Well, lass? You won't mind going home with Derry?"

Strangely, Eoghan felt compelled to hold his breath while he waited for her answer. At her nod, he released the air from his lungs and slipped outside to ready the horse. In short order, Ana had joined him and the two of them sat side by side on the seat while the wagon rattled down the street.

Ana was the first to break the silence. "It's 1364 Ashberry Street."

He gave a one-shouldered shrug. "I know."

"Of course. Sorry. I forgot."

He tried not to notice the way her cheeks colored a pretty pink, or the way she bit her bottom lip whenever she was nervous or angry. He tapped the reins and urged the horse to quicken her pace.

Cold air nipped his own cheeks, a reminder that it was already November. He flipped up the collar on his coat, wishing he'd taken time to locate a scarf, thinking as he did that Ana too must feel the chill.

Switching the reins to one hand, he reached under the seat and pulled out a woolen throw. "Cold?"

A gentleman would have perhaps spread the blanket over a lady's knees. Eoghan didn't dare allow himself so close. As it was, his flesh tingled where her fingers brushed his as she accepted the blanket.

"How are your hands?" he said, for something to say and

to keep from thinking overmuch about what his reaction to her touch meant.

Though she likely couldn't see them in the deepening gloom, she turned her palms up a moment before slipping them into the folds of the blanket.

"Better. I'm sure by morning I'll be fine to go to work."

"Work!" Eoghan checked himself and hunched his shoulders. "Nonsense. You should take a day off to rest."

"You don't even know what I do."

Teasing? Eoghan shot her a sidelong glance. Sure enough, a smile accompanied her words. "All right," he said, grinning. "Where do you work?"

"A candle shop."

"Really?"

She nodded, then bit her lip. "Cara used to work there, too. She kept the books."

"Oh." He ducked back inside his coat.

"She's good with numbers."

"Ana . . ." He sighed and rolled his shoulders. "Look, I know you and my sister were friends."

"Still are."

"Fine."

The wagon rumbled over a hole in the cobbled street, but before he could reach out to steady her, she righted herself, caught the end of the blanket, and smoothed it back into place. He studied her, swaying so gracefully on the seat next to him. The way she moved, they could have been riding in a phaeton or paddling gently along a lake instead of bumping along in a rickety old wagon. He couldn't be harsh—not when she looked like a faerie sitting there next to him.

"You and Cara are friends," he began again, softer, "and what you do, you do out of concern for her."

"And for you."

Did she have to keep on interrupting him? He stifled a groan. Ach, but the girl had a way of confounding his thoughts.

"I appreciate that, Ana. Truly. But—"

"May I ask you something?"

They were passing beneath the glow of a streetlamp. Bathed in its light, she looked more ethereal than ever. Swallowing, he gave a silent nod.

"If I knew something . . . about Cara . . . and I thought it would affect you . . . would you want me to tell you?"

A loaded question. Likely he wouldn't approve of the answer. His fingers tightened on the reins. "That depends."

"On what?"

"Whether or not you were trying to convince me to reconcile with my sister."

She fell silent, her teeth working on her bottom lip. Almost to Ashberry Street. If he could just keep her quiet a few more minutes . . .

In the lull that followed, he thought he heard the clopping of another horse's hooves, yet a glance over his shoulder revealed nothing. Why then did icy fingers scrape at the back of his neck?

He'd hoped it was the chill, but now he wasn't so certain. He chirped to the mare, urging her faster with a light snap of the reins.

"All right, then," Ana continued, leaning toward him earnestly, "what if I told you that this news might make you angry at first, but over time it would most certainly make you happy?"

"You kinna know what will make me happy," he said, squinting into the shadows but trying to appear as though he wasn't looking.

"That's true, I suppose, but from what I've learned about you—"

"And what is that?" Eoghan interrupted, turning his head to her, when in fact he was watching the progress of a shadowy figure on horseback in the side streets running parallel to theirs over her shoulder.

Her brows lowered in a frown. "Well, I know that you aren't nearly as prickly as you first appeared, even though you try verra hard to make people think so."

He attempted a smile that he feared looked more like a grimace. No help for it—it was all he could manage under the circumstances. Whoever was following them kept to the shadows and rode low in the saddle. In the gaps between buildings, he saw the rider was keeping pace with the wagon— never slowing, never drawing even.

It was most certainly him the man followed, but with no clue as to who he was or what he wanted, he couldn't risk pulling over and putting Ana in danger. Maybe he could get her to the boardinghouse before the rider made his move.

"Glad to hear it—" he began, but froze when her hand slipped from the blanket to rest against his cheek.

"And you have a gentle streak inside you. I saw it today in the way you tended to Ellen and then to my burns. I don't think I said thank-you for that. Did I?"

Her eyes were bottomless pools. Her lips, tantalizing petals whose softness he could only imagine.

But her touch . . .

Her touch blazed a path to his soul, snaring him so that he couldn't have freed himself even if he'd wanted to—which, of course, he did not. Except that he had no choice, because at that moment the rider who'd been dogging their trail hunched his shoulders, kicked his heels, and veered into a side street.

A horse's sharp whinny cut the air, followed by the clatter of hooves against the cobbled street. Eoghan yanked back on the reins, sensing what was coming but knowing it was too late to prevent it.

Horse and rider streaked through the alley formed by two tall buildings. A second later, they shot out of the gap and wheeled, skittering and screaming, directly into the wagon's path.

12

For a split second, all Ana could remember was flashing
hooves pawing at the night sky, a horse's wide, frightened
eyes, and Eoghan grabbing her wrist and yanking her to
safety.

At least that was what it felt like cradled against his chest,
with his strong arms clamped tightly about her shoulders.
His wool coat rubbed against her cheek, rough yet strangely
intoxicating. Her eyes fluttered closed as she inhaled long and
deep. Never had she been this close to a man, felt so loved
and protected by anyone . . . except her da, and that had been
so many years ago.

His warm breath fanned across her face. "Are you all right?"

Unable to find her voice, she nodded and struggled upright. Just that quickly he vaulted from the wagon, circled
to the front to calm the frightened mare, and snarled at
the rider, who had somehow come through the entire mess
unscathed.

"What do you think you're doing? You could've gotten
yourself killed. Or us, for that matter—"

The man threw back the hood of his cape. Eoghan fell
silent, glanced back at Ana, and then again at the rider.

"What do you want?"

"Got a delivery for you." He pulled an envelope from his cape and handed it down to Eoghan. The moment his fingers closed around it, the rider wheeled and disappeared as quickly and mysteriously as he'd come.

Ana watched him go, her heart thrumming inside her chest. When the sound of the horse's hooves faded, she turned to Eoghan. "Who w-was that?"

"No one," he replied, jamming the envelope into a pocket of his coat. He took a couple more seconds to croon softly to the mare, and when her eyes no longer looked so wide and her nostrils no longer flared, he climbed back into the wagon and took up the reins. "Giddap."

Despite the pain caused by her blisters, Ana gripped the side of the seat, scarcely able to control her trembling. Who were these people that sought Eoghan in the dead of night and materialized from the shadows like specters? More to the point, why was he dealing with them? What did they have that he wanted?

Fear for him tightened her throat the rest of the way home. Even the lights shining from the boardinghouse windows failed to alleviate her alarm. He must have sensed her disquiet, for after rolling to a stop he set the brake but made no move to disembark.

"I'm sorry, Ana."

He stared glumly at the reins clutched in his hands. Was he unwilling—or unable—to look her in the eye?

She raised her chin and forced her voice to remain steady. "Eoghan, who was that man?"

Finally his head lifted. Lines creased his brow, tugged at the sides of his mouth. Sorrow in its rawest form stole her breath. She leaned toward him and laid her hand over his arm. "Eoghan?"

"He's a Fenian." His voice was tight. Strangled. "That is all I can tell you."

"You know him?"

He nodded.

"And the note he gave you . . ."

His piercing gaze cut her to the heart. "Do not ask me."

She bit her tongue and waded through her memory for anything she knew about the Fenians. It wasn't much. What little information she had was gleaned from her conversations with Tillie. But maybe there was more she could uncover if she asked.

While she debated the possibility, Eoghan jumped from the wagon and circled to her side. Arms upraised, he waited to help her down.

Ana shivered. The last thing she wanted was to feel the warmth of his arms around her again, but with her fingers and palms already throbbing, and she barely able to clasp the edges of her cloak, she was left with little choice.

She sighed and reached down, letting her hands rest lightly against his broad shoulders, pulling away the moment her feet touched the ground. Even with that fleeting contact, she felt the shudder that rippled through him. Was she so repulsive to him, then? She snatched her hands back, dismayed by the sinking of her heart.

Tears burned her eyes, but she refused to give in to them. She stiffened her spine and battled them down. "I will send word to Mr. O'Bannon at the candle shop of my injury so he will not expect me in tomorrow—"

"I will come check on you," he interrupted quietly. "We can finish our talk then."

"Our talk?"

"From the boardinghouse. You said there was something you wanted to tell me."

She gave a stiff nod, all she could manage with the ache in her chest growing. He stepped toward her, and then not even breath was left to her, stolen by the look of warmth that shone from his eyes.

"You saved Ellen's life tonight. It was a brave thing to do."

She swallowed and studied the tops of her shoes. "I did nothing. Any person faced with the same situation would have acted the same."

He shook his head and gently lifted her chin. "I'm not so sure." His lips moved, as though he struggled to say more. Instead he touched his fingers to his brow and gave a slight bow. "Good night, Ana."

"Good night," she whispered, though it was doubtful that he heard.

He climbed into the wagon, clucked to the mare, and rumbled off down the street, leaving her alone on the boarding-house steps, with only the glow from a single streetlamp to keep her from plunging into total darkness.

— ※ ※ ※ —

Fury locked Eoghan in its clutches, growing in strength and intensity the farther he drove from the boardinghouse. Ana could have been hurt tonight, killed even, and it would've been his fault.

His, and Kilarny's.

Thinking the man's name brought a snarl to Eoghan's lips. One of these days, Kil was going to push him too far, and then both he and the Fenians be hanged.

He reached into his coat and yanked the envelope the rider had delivered from his pocket. Outside were scrawled two simple directions. Take the envelope to 24 Wharf Drive. Leave it with a man named Brion McCleod.

McCleod.

He'd seen the name before, inadvertently, but he remembered it. He flipped the envelope over. Too thin to be cash. Sealed and stamped with wax. He jammed it back into his pocket.

Fine, he'd deliver the message, whatever it was, to McCleod. But afterward he'd have a few words to share with Kilarny. Giving the reins a light snap, he turned and set off for the harbor.

Wharf Drive was easy enough to find, twenty-four a little more difficult given the number of tightly packed warehouses that crowded the place. At last, he reached a ramshackle building with a sagging roof and dirty, broken windows, sadly boasting the number over a rotted gray door. He stiffened at the sight of the rusted hinges, and the faded paint, falling in curls to the ground. The door he approached reminded him of the place where he'd recovered from a gunshot wound last winter—a bullet delivered by a member of his sworn enemies, the Turners.

He rechecked the number against the envelope before climbing from the wagon and landing on the dirt street with a thump. No time now to think of the Turners or his sister's betrayal. He raised his fist and knocked.

At first, no one answered. Indeed, the place looked deserted. Certainly not the nicest part of town. Eyes peered at him from darkened alleys—those that weren't illuminated by campfires.

He rapped again, the sound created by his knuckles hollow and loud, reinforcing the notion that the place was deserted. Still, there was one thing he knew about his old friend. Kilarny was seldom wrong, which meant the choice of building was intentional, and there was more than likely a gun trained on his chest.

After a moment, the door scraped back, a solitary candle split the gloom, and Eoghan stared into the blackest eyes he'd ever seen. He tensed. "Brion McCleod?"

No words. Just raspy, labored breathing, and then the man nodded.

Eoghan slipped the envelope through the crack. The man snatched it and immediately slammed the door in his face.

His errand done, Eoghan jumped back into the wagon and set off for the one place he was certain to find Kilarny—a pub on the east side of town.

— ❋ ❋ ❋ —

Brion watched through a grimy, cracked pane as the wagon carrying Eoghan Hamilton rumbled out of sight. Shoving his pistol back into the waistband of his trousers, he limped from the window, chuckled, then regretted the action when a bout of coughing took him.

So that was the man The Celt wanted dead. Handsome-looking fellow. And lucky. He couldn't kill him until he'd gleaned the information he needed. He'd lose the only high card in his hand otherwise. No doubt, The Celt realized that, and bravely played the game anyway.

His admiration melted into a sneer. He might have liked The Celt under different circumstances. The two of them had much in common.

Brion shuddered as he set the candle on a high shelf. Fie on The Celt, anyway, and America, and the cholera running rampant through the barge office. Thanks to them, he'd almost died . . . still might. He crowded close to the fireplace and ripped open the envelope Hamilton had been sent to deliver. Few words were scribbled across the single slip of paper, but they were enough. After a moment, he dipped the end of the note into the candle's flame and watched as it shriveled and disappeared on a wisp of smoke before tossing it onto the hearth.

The envelope had not contained a name as he'd hoped, but the message was clear enough: 1364 Ashberry Street.

He was one step closer to finding his niece.

13

The air turned chilly as the night grew older. By the time Eoghan reached Shanahan's Pub, in a seedy corner of the Lower East Side, a light snow had begun to fall and ice was forming on the puddles nestled between the cobbles along the street.

Eoghan blew on his hands, then jumped from the wagon and looped the reins quickly over a hitching post. His carnal side screamed for action, urged him to storm up to Kilarny's table and drag the lout outside. Aye, and he'd deliver him a sound beating for putting Ana in danger. His more rational side realized with the Fenians packing the place, he probably wouldn't make it past the bar.

The heavy pub door formed a protective barrier from the enthusiastic fiddling and raucous laughter throbbing inside. Giving it a shove, Eoghan squared his shoulders and sauntered through, pausing on the threshold to give his eyes time to adjust to the low light. Near the back, a big fellow in a dark tweed coat stood watch over a group of men playing a noisy game of cards. In their midst sat Kilarny. Eoghan moved toward them. As expected, the ogre shifted to block his path.

"Help you?"

Behind him, the card game ceased. With a sweeping glance, Eoghan sought and found the beast's weaknesses—a slight limp in his gait on the left side, turning his body instead of coming at his target head-on. A puckered scar wound down his neck and disappeared into the collar of his shirt.

An old injury, one he compensated for by displaying slightly to the right.

Feigning nonchalance, Eoghan tucked the information away and lifted his hands, palms out. "Easy now. Just here to share an ale with a friend."

The man lifted an eyebrow. "This friend expecting you?"

Eoghan shrugged. "Maybe. He sent me a message earlier today that was clear enough."

"Your name?"

"Eoghan Hamilton." A chair scraped the floor and Kilarny stood. A crooked leer on his lips, he leaned forward and clapped his hand to the beast's shoulder. "Relax, Rob. He's with me."

The beast's gaze remained locked on Eoghan. Reluctantly he backed up until he'd reclaimed his spot next to the table.

Kil stuck out his hand. "You're late. I expected you much earlier."

Eoghan gripped it and gave it a shake. "Then maybe you should have sent word instead of nearly having me killed."

The men around the table chuckled. With their laughter, the music and the card game resumed, and Kil retook his seat.

"Deal you in?" He shoved the moist end of a cigar between his teeth and held up a card.

Barely keeping himself in check, Eoghan leaned forward and propped both fists on the table. "Later. First, we need to talk."

Kil's eyes gleamed. "*First* . . . cards." He looked around the table at each of the men. "Eh, lads?"

Four heads bobbed in agreement, four mouths curled in smirks. The beast crossed his arms, flexing his massive biceps.

Forcing his anger down a tight throat, Eoghan pulled out a chair and sat.

"There's a good lad," Kilarny said, puffing cheerfully on his cigar.

He dealt five cards to each of the men around the table, none of whom Eoghan recognized. Eoghan reached for his cards. Kil beat him to it. His hand shot out, blocking Eoghan's.

"Not so fast, old friend. Before we get started, we need to be sure you're good for the game."

Eoghan bristled. "I'm good for it, Kil."

He nodded, eyes slitted. "For certain I know that, but me friends here, well, they not be knowing you like I do. Ain't that right, fellas?"

Eoghan spared them a fleeting glance. This wasn't about the others. Kil had a reason for calling him out in front of them, no doubt, but what it was . . .

Reaching into the breast pocket of his coat, he withdrew several bills and dropped them onto the table. What Sister Mary would think of him gambling away his wages, he didn't care to ponder. In fact, he took no pleasure in the game himself.

Had to be because of what had happened earlier, Eoghan told himself, picking up his hand after a satisfied nod from Kilarny. His reluctance couldn't be because the sister's holy way of life and Father Ed's solid preaching had begun to take root.

A round of betting followed, after which Eoghan discarded two cards from his hand and drew two more.

That put three kings in his hand.

Father Ed had preached on three kings the Sunday before

last. Guilt crept over Eoghan, starting somewhere in the center of his chest and radiating outward.

"Eoghan?"

Startled, he looked up to see Kil and the other players staring at him through narrowed lids.

"You in, lad?" Kil said softly.

Eoghan folded his hand and laid the cards facedown on the table. He'd lose the ante, but at least he'd be able to look Sister Mary in the eye. He leaned back in his chair and crossed his arms. "I fold."

Kilarny's eyes gleamed speculatively, but he went on with the game. At the end of the hand, the bounty in front of him had grown a sizable amount. Eoghan pushed back from the table and rose.

"Forgive me, lads. I shouldn't have interrupted your night, especially since I have somewhere else I need to be."

"One hand?" Kilarny said. "That's all?"

"'Fraid so," Eoghan replied, fixing Kil with a steady glare. Getting out of the pub wasn't going to be easy, but neither was explaining what had driven him to come in the first place. "We'll talk another time."

Kilarny watched him, silently measuring. At last, he scooped his earnings from the table and stood, as well. "Actually, there is a matter I need to discuss with you, old friend. Now's as good a time as any."

Protests rose from the other players, but Kil merely tipped his cap at them. He circled the table and clapped his arm about Eoghan's shoulders. "Sorry, lads. Business calls."

If any of them had a mind to do more than protest, one glance at Rob was enough to discourage them.

Kilarny led the way outside, but then shoved his hand against the big man's chest at the door. "Give us a minute, will you, lad?"

Rob grunted, and the door closed on his scowling face.

"Who's your friend?" Eoghan asked, jamming his hands into his pockets to protect them from the cold.

"Nobody important." A grin spread over Kilarny's face as he lifted the collar of his coat around his ears. "Wasn't kidding earlier. I figured you'd be coming by. Got my message, did you?"

"I got it."

"Not too subtle?"

"Almost got me killed."

"Aye, well, that was the point."

A chill gripped the back of Eoghan's neck. Kilarny had a habit of telling the truth like it was a joke. Something told him this was one of those times. He flicked a glance over his shoulder.

"Calm down, lad. If I'd wanted you dead, the deed would have been accomplished easily enough earlier today."

Then what exactly was going on? Eoghan swept his arm toward the snow-dusted street. "Care to walk?"

Kilarny narrowed his eyes, but nodded after a bit and swung off the sidewalk, his boots crunching on the cobbled street.

They passed through the glow of one streetlamp and left it behind for the shadows that huddled along the sidewalk until the next circle of light—light and dark, over and over. The trek was made in silence, even the sound of their footsteps muffled by the gloom.

Finally, Kilarny cut through a side street and popped into an abandoned alley. Eoghan scanned both sides of the narrow corridor. No lamplight here, and with the absence of a full moon, he had to squint to read Kilarny's face, though he stood mere feet away.

"What are we doing here, Kil?"

"Didn't want to risk being overheard."

"By who? I thought those men at the pub were your friends."

Kil's ragged breath was a ghostly specter on the cool night air. "How bad do you want back in the Fenians?"

Eoghan paused. The question was surprisingly difficult to answer. "I've done everything you asked, everything the Fenians asked."

"True." Kil braced his back against an old brick building lined on both sides with plain wood doors. "But that wasn't my question."

"Then *my* question would be why you need to ask." His dry tone matched the withered feeling inside his chest. "If I didn't want back in, would I have bothered being your lackey these past few weeks?"

Reasonable enough, but even as he spoke the words, Eoghan found himself hard-pressed to believe them. Where was the fire that had once consumed him? The passion that had once occupied every waking moment?

He slumped against the wall next to Kil, matching his posture.

"What are we fighting for, Kil?" he rasped. "What are the Fenians fighting for? I thought I knew once."

"As did I," Kil said, his voice echoing quietly along the alley. After a moment, he turned, and though Eoghan could not read his face, he sensed the urgency in his voice. "You and I were close growing up, ain't that so, Hammy me boy?"

Eoghan suddenly found it hard to swallow. "Aye, that's so."

"And on the sake of that, were I to tell you something, you'd believe it, even with the mistrust between us now?"

Eoghan lowered his voice to a growl. "What are you about, Jacob Kilarny?"

Kil pivoted until he stood in front of Eoghan, a hairsbreadth away. His hot breath razed across Eoghan's cheek, past his ear, down his neck. "There's some who want you dead. Powerful men. Not the Turners."

He scrutinized the area, up one side of the alley and down the other, before he continued. "You messed up, laddie boy, but good when you crossed old Sean."

"The man was as rabid as a dog, Kil! His plan could have cost us everything—did cost us everything," Eoghan corrected sharply. "We were lucky to get out of Ireland with our lives after Daniel Turner was killed."

"Aye, I reckon that's true enough, the way you and I see it."

Eoghan grabbed Kil by the collar and yanked him even closer. "What are you saying? You know who sees it different?"

The clouds overhead parted, letting feeble light trickle into the alley. Though he couldn't see his eyes, there was no mistaking the drawn brows and worried scowl on Kilarny's face. He shrugged free of Eoghan's grasp.

"The message you carried tonight, did you deliver it?"

"I did."

Kilarny nodded. "That's good. But you see, I didn't send it."

Eoghan shoved free of the wall and sent Kilarny stumbling backward. "What are you talking about? You admitted it just an hour ago."

Kil shook his head. "I admitted to choosing the messenger who took it to ya. And I gave him orders to do it in such a way as to be sure to draw your attention because I knew it would light a fire under ya, get you to seek me out. But the note itself—" he checked the alley again and lowered his voice—"that came from someone else. Someone important."

"So what?" Eoghan sneered. "We've known all along that someone higher up pulled the strings. You and I carry out orders like good little soldiers. That's how it has been, how it always will be."

Even by the light of the half-moon, Kil looked pale. His Adam's apple bobbed as he swallowed. "You're wrong, Hammy. It's different this time."

"Different, how?"

"Because this time, old friend . . . this time the order was to finish you off."

14

Eoghan's throat went dry. "Who issued the order?" he rasped.

Kil lifted both hands, palms out. "I swear to ya, I don't know. 'Tis only because of our history that I'm talking to ya at all."

"The message I delivered tonight, was I carrying my own death sentence?"

"I have no idea what was inside that note."

"And the man I gave the message to, is he the one assigned to kill me?"

Kil stared blankly.

"Who is he, Kil? What is he doing here?"

"Hammy, if I knew—"

Eoghan grabbed him by the collar and shook him. "What *do* you know? Why should I even trust you? You turned tail quick enough when Sean went rogue and threatened to murder Turner and I tried to stop him."

Kil's face darkened as he thrust Eoghan's hands from his coat. "Don't push your luck. I've done you a favor telling you what I know. Risked me own neck!"

His words echoed and bounced along the cobbles in the alley. He drew a breath and shoved his face into Eoghan's. "Can't tell you how I know, only that I do."

Reining in his rampant emotions, Eoghan nodded. "Fine. I'm beholden to you."

His response sparked a kind of satisfaction. Kil withdrew to his side of the alley, half of his face and his gleaming eyes hidden by shadow. "I'm not asking for ya to be beholden."

Ach, so that was it. Kil wanted a favor and this was his way of getting it. Eoghan jammed his fists into the pockets of his coat, afraid that if he didn't, he'd use them to pummel his "old friend."

"What do you want, Kil?"

"It isn't like that, Hammy—"

"What. Do. You. Want?"

Kilarny flinched with each clipped word. A moment later, the last trace of feigned benevolence melted from his features. What was left was naked ambition.

"I want to know everything you have on Daniel Turner's death," he hissed.

The words snaked up Eoghan's spine, left him tingling. He mimicked Kil's action and withdrew into the shadows. "You know all there is to know."

Kil shook his head. "I don't think so. There's more, even if you are too thick to realize it. The bit about being a pawn?" He leaned into the moonlight. A leer became visible on his lips. "You may be content to play that role, but I'm not. I intend to change all that."

"How?"

He hesitated, his gaze measuring. "Let's keep moving."

He spun and headed down the alley. Eoghan fell in step beside him. "So?" he said when they'd covered a considerable distance.

They veered out onto a wide street lined with carts and vendor stands. Eoghan kept to Kil's heels as they loped down the sidewalk, until they reached a long row of squat buildings.

An apothecary, Eoghan noted, and a dressmaker's shop huddled next to it. Farther down, a clockmaker. Kil seemed to show no preference. He zigzagged through them all, then darted into another darkened alley.

The old wound below Eoghan's right shoulder throbbed in protest to the strain caused by running. Even his breath was slow in returning.

Kil noticed the weakness and sneered at it. "Still not recovered, eh?"

"Getting there," Eoghan said. "Just who do you think is following us, anyway?"

"If I knew, I wouldn't need you," he retorted.

"Right. And what is it you want me to do again?"

Now that the tension in his lungs had lessened, Eoghan straightened and sucked in a couple of deep breaths. Kilarny, however, couldn't seem to keep still. He paced up and down the alley, leaving muddy footprints in the thin layer of snow. By morning, both would have melted into the cobbles.

"All right," he grunted at last. "I'm going to give it to you straight, but mark my words, Hammy, a word of this gets out and I'll kill you myself."

"Go on."

A gas lamp situated at the mouth of the alley made seeing easier. Eoghan read apprehension in the tight lines of Kilarny's face and the bunched muscles of his jaw. He stopped pacing.

"I have reason to believe Sean Healy wasn't working alone. Someone wanted or needed Turner dead."

"You think the plan was to murder him all along?"

Kil nodded. "I need to know who was behind that plot and why."

"What makes you think I can ferret out the information? Who would I even ask?" He froze as he read the motive in Kil's eyes. "You want me to ask my sister."

His lips thinned. "She be a Turner now herself."

"So what? I've had nothing to do with her since . . . Even if I did what you ask . . ."

"Not suggesting you have to deceive your own flesh and blood."

A chill crept over Eoghan's flesh. "But Rourke Turner, now he's another matter, is that it?"

Kil returned only silence. Eoghan spun away—it was his turn to pace. "If I do this"—he cut a glare at Kil—"and I'm not saying I will, what do I get out of it?"

"A fair question." He smiled, as though he'd already sensed what Eoghan's reaction would be. "You help me get the information I'm after and I'll see to it that you are accepted back into the Fenians."

"One of whom wants to kill me."

Kil shrugged. "I have a feeling the two are likely linked together. We flush the one—"

"You'll get the answers you want, and I may avoid winding up dead," Eoghan finished for him.

He nodded.

Kil had always possessed a keen sense of exactly what was going on inside a person's head. It was what made him so skilled at poker. Eoghan turned his back to think and caught sight of the flickering gas lamp. Eyeing the flame, his thoughts winged to Ana.

She was haunted by the fire that had consumed her entire family. Not her entire family, he realized with a start. She mentioned an uncle. If he were to have access to resources, to his old contacts inside the Fenians . . .

He swept clean his features of emotion and turned. "You're right, Kil. This little arrangement could be beneficial to us both."

His brows drew in a frown. "I don't like that look on

your face, Hammy. Why do I think you've something else in mind?"

Eoghan allowed the comment to pass and lowered his voice. "What matters, old friend, is that you *do* have something I want, something I might even be pressed to bargain with you for."

Interest flared in his eyes.

Eoghan waited, crossing his arms and leaning against the wall. "Well? Do you want to hear my idea or not?"

He watched as Kilarny debated, doubt flickering across his features. For a split second, he even thought his offer would be refused before he could give it voice, but then a smile spread across his friend's face.

"All right, then. Let's hear it. What is it you want?"

Eoghan licked his lips. He needed to frame his words carefully, keep Ana's name out of Kilarny's hearing if he could help it.

As for the rest, he'd worry about his part of the bargain later, when he'd had time to think about exactly how he'd go about betraying his sister. Only it wouldn't be betrayal, because by revealing the truth about the Turner clan to her, he'd in fact be saving her.

He repeated the thought to himself later, after he and Kilarny had parted ways, and again when the wagon rumbled up the street in front of the church. It made no difference. Even multiple reprisals failed to give him the peace he sought.

He scowled at the one portion of the church visible in the deepening gloom—the ghostly steeple piercing the night sky like a sword.

Fie. If the church didn't offer what he wanted, he'd find it somewhere else. Instead of circling the wagon around to the back, he clucked to the horse and kept driving.

Never, not even after he'd fled Ireland and pretended to be dead, had Eoghan ever wanted a drink so badly.

— ✳ ✳ ✳ —

A low whistle drifted on the night air, a haunting melody that raised bumps on Ana's flesh. She craned her neck to see, first one way and then the other. Farther up the street, against one of the lampposts, leaned a man of average height and build. Atop his head—she squinted—aye, atop his head he wore a cap with a jaunty green feather sticking out from one side.

The same man Cara had seen outside the candle shop? Her pulse quickened as she stumbled on the steps and felt behind her for the knob. What was he doing here? Perhaps he'd followed them the night Cara and Rourke brought her home and now mistakenly thought to find Cara here, unless . . .

She shivered as the man straightened and with slow, measured steps closed the gap between them. What was wrong with the knob? Why wouldn't it turn?

Though it meant taking her eyes from the man, Ana twisted and grasped the knob with both hands. It refused to budge. The hour? Her stomach sank as she realized it was after eight, and Amelia had no doubt locked the door.

She fumbled in her reticule for her key. After what seemed an eternity, she found it, though it took an extra half second to yank the thing free once it became entangled in the fringes that lined her cloak.

The whistling was louder now, closer than before. Ana's heart beat harder, and her breathing came in shallow spurts that formed wispy clouds on the cold night air and made it nearly impossible to see the keyhole. Perhaps she should knock.

Ana lifted her fist and pounded once, twice, then looked

over her shoulder at the approaching man. He was close enough to see his face, to see the gleam in his narrowed eyes and the half smile on his full, whistling lips.

She shrugged closer to the door and knocked again. "Amelia? Laverne?"

There was panic in her voice, a shrill edge no bluster could hide, but she didn't care. The man stared steadily at her now. There was no denying his intended path. She tried the lock again, but instead of fitting the key into the hole, it slipped from her fingers and clattered onto the steps.

"Evening, miss."

Ana whirled and pressed her back against the door. There was no weapon here, no hiding place she could seek.

The man peered up at her from the bottom of the steps, half his face shadowed by the brim of his gray tweed cap. He gestured at the key lying at her feet. "Locked yourself out, have you?"

So dry was her mouth, she found she couldn't answer. Instead she simply shook her head.

"Perhaps I should help you."

He moved as if to reach for the key. Ana stooped and snatched it up before he could get to it.

"N-no, thank you. I have it."

"Ah, well, all right then." Laying his finger alongside his cap, he gave a smart salute. "Good evening, Miss Kavanagh. Was a pleasure meeting you."

His eyes remained fixed to her, his gaze as unyielding as a snare, holding her captive. Only when he'd moved a significant distance away was she finally able to slide the key into the lock and give it a half turn. She grappled with the door, wresting it open and shoving her way inside, then slamming it closed behind her. One thought swirled through her brain, one mind-gripping, terror-wrought idea.

His words, his manner, they were benign, even benevolent. He'd offered to help, after all. Still, she'd never seen him before, of that much she was certain. And yet . . .

He'd known her name.

— ✳ ✳ ✳ —

It was intoxicating, holding another's life in one's hands, seeing fear spark in a person's eyes, knowing that with just a swipe of his knife . . .

Kellen sighed and tucked the blade in his palm back up into the sleeve of his coat. Too bad The Celt had been explicit in his directions. Otherwise he might have given in to his instincts—those which made him a born killer—which fed the empty, hollow place inside that gnawed at his guts until it forced him to move or go mad.

Giving a jerk, he shook the thought free. Killing wasn't the only thing that satisfied him. Power was an adequate substitute. Being near power, seizing it when he could.

The Celt had power—imparted bits of it to Kellen now and again, which was why he stayed by his side. And this . . .

He smiled.

McCleod would fail, and then the job would fall to him. Power over life. Power over death. He would claim it. And then . . .

He rubbed the ragged scars that snaked up both wrists. Killing the girl wouldn't be enough to scrub away the memory of what had been done to him, to remove the childhood fears that haunted him to this day. But at least the gnawing, aching hole would be filled . . . temporarily.

15

Outside Ana's window, a sharp wind rattled the limbs of a bare oak tree, seeped through the cracks in the sill, and chilled her nose. Unwilling to leave her warm bed, she snuggled deeper into the covers. The day was dreary and overcast—perfect for napping. She was tempted to lie abed until midday, except . . .

Her eyes snapped open.

Tillie. If she wanted information on the Fenians, she'd have to catch her before she left for the milliner where she worked. Shrugging off the blankets, Ana climbed from her bed and scurried to the washbasin. The icy water splashed away the last vestiges of sleep. By the time she had finished with her toiletries, she was more than ready to don a warm woolen dress and join the others for breakfast.

She hesitated as a gleam from the nightstand caught her eye. Her father's pocket watch. The gold chain it hung from had been her mother's. She'd taken to wearing it like a locket after he died. For some reason, Ana had never been ready to do the same. She brought the watch to her lips, then laid it gently back on the nightstand and left the room.

The inviting scent of frying bacon and fresh biscuits greeted her on the stairs. From the dining room, Tillie's laughter mingled with Meg's and one with a lower register that had to belong to Giles. Ana slowed her pace. She hadn't missed her, then.

"There she is," Meg said, chuckling and pointing as Ana entered the dining room. "We thought you meant to hide under your covers all day."

Ana pulled a chair from her place at the table. "I overslept." She cast an apologetic glance at the owner of the boarding-house. "I'm afraid I didn't have time to tidy my room, Amelia. I'll see to it first thing this afternoon."

Amelia smiled at them all from her seat at the head of the table. "Posh. You girls are such a help to me, always seeing to your chores and then helping Laverne with hers. Don't give it a second thought."

Relieved, Ana sank into her chair. A pot of coffee waited at her elbow. She poured a cup and let a sip chase away the chill from her morning ministrations. A moment later, Laverne carried in a fresh platter of eggs and plunked it onto the sideboard.

"All right, that's the last of it." She eyed Giles's near-empty plate before grabbing the platter of biscuits and presenting him with one. "Anyone else care for another biscuit?"

"Ana," Tillie said, nodding.

"Ach, there she is." Laverne planted one fist on her ample hip. "What kept ya? Not still hurting from those burns, I hope?"

Ana studied her hands. The redness had gone and only a few blisters remained. She shook her head. "Just didn't want to leave me bed, is all."

Laverne humphed and deposited a biscuit onto her plate. "I still think three days off isn't near enough time. Why, you're barely healed."

"I can't afford to lose any more work," Ana reminded her gently. "Besides, Mr. O'Bannon is as bad as you when it comes to watching over me."

"Always knew I liked him," Laverne replied, breaking into a smile.

Giles's head lifted. "Not as much as you like me, I hope."

Color immediately flooded Laverne's round cheeks. She swished her apron at him, tsking as she grabbed Ana's plate and filled it with eggs. Next to the eggs she laid three thick slices of bacon.

Ana sighed. She'd never eat everything Laverne had piled on her plate, but as the surly housekeeper set it down in front of her, she obediently picked up her fork.

Tillie drained her coffee cup, then replaced it on the saucer. "Well, I'd best be off or I'll be running late, too." She pushed back her chair before clearing her place of empty dishes.

"Wait, and I'll go with you," Meg said, rising.

"Take the wagon," Amelia said. "It's quite cold and will likely be snowing by this afternoon."

Ana hastily swallowed the bite of eggs in her mouth and stood. "Tillie, before you go, might I have a moment?"

She hesitated at the door. "Of course."

Ana grabbed her plate and moved to follow.

"But you haven't finished your breakfast," Laverne protested.

Ana took another swallow of coffee before adding the cup to the dishes in her hands. "No time, but thank you," she said, bending to press a light kiss to the mobcap on Laverne's head.

"Fie, go on with you, then." Laverne raised both hands. "Don't know why I even bother making breakfast for all you girls. Always flitting off like you do. Giles is the only one who rises early enough to appreciate my cooking."

"Now, Laverne," Amelia said, smiling and waving them

out as she picked up her morning newspaper. "You know very well that there is no one more thankful for your skill in the kitchen than I—"

The rest of her words were cut short by the shutting of the swinging dining room door. Ana fell into step beside Tillie, and Meg led the way to the kitchen. In minutes they'd washed away all traces of the meal, donned their bonnets and cloaks, and set off in the wagon to deliver Meg to her place of employment—a seamstress shop where she handled all the repairs while the owner took on new orders. It was first on their list of stops. The chandler where Ana worked was second.

"So?" Tillie said, deftly handling the reins as they set off down Ashberry Street once more. "What's on your mind that you didn't want to say in front of Meg?"

Ana frowned. "It was obvious, eh?"

"Only to me," Tillie said, bumping her shoulder against Ana's. "So?"

How to ask? Since bringing her home the night Ellen's dress caught fire, Ana had seen no hint of Eoghan, not even to ask how the girl and her mother were faring.

The girl and her mother . . .

Ana peeked sidelong at Tillie from under the brim of her bonnet. "You've been to the church since the accident, aye?"

Tillie nodded. "Ellen's doing much better now. Her burns are healing and she's sitting up some." She lifted an eyebrow. "And that, you couldn't ask in front of Meg?"

Ana sighed. Her friend was entirely too intuitive. "Actually, I was wondering if . . ." She bit her lip. She'd not told Tillie about the stranger who'd nearly collided with them outside the boardinghouse, or of the mysterious message he'd given Eoghan to deliver, or of the man with the gray cap and feather waiting outside their door.

158

"Tillie, something happened the night Eo—Derry brought me home."

If Tillie noticed her slip, she didn't show it. "Oh? What?"

"A man stopped us and passed Derry a note with instructions to deliver it."

"What's strange about that?"

"It's just the way the man approached us—nigh ran us off the street. He frightened me."

Tillie slowed the wagon. "Have you asked Derry about it?"

Ana shook her head. "I've not seen him."

Furrows creased her forehead. "Hmm, come to think of it, neither have I."

"He hasn't been at the church?"

"I don't think so." She shook her head. "No. I'm sure of it."

Ana bit her lips in consternation, and a touch of fear. "Where do you think he could be?"

"Why don't you ask the sisters?" Tillie said. "Maybe he's on an errand for them or had to go out of town."

"A three-day errand?"

"You never know. Could be they sent him off somewhere for supplies."

Ana fell silent for a moment. Feeling Tillie's gaze, she looked up at her friend. "What?"

"Are you worried that you haven't seen him, or upset that he hasn't come by the boardinghouse to check on you?"

"Tillie!"

"Well?" She narrowed her eyes. "I've seen the way he watches you. And you be known to cast a glance in his direction, as well." Her grin widened. "Tell me I'm wrong."

Ana opened her mouth, but the treacherous words refused to come. After a while she snapped it shut, sparking a giggle from Tillie.

"I thought so."

"Fine," Ana said, crossing her arms. "I'll ask the sisters this afternoon after I leave off work."

"I'll pick you up," Tillie said. "Been meaning to head that way myself."

Ana nodded, a bit of her unease disappearing as the wagon rolled to a stop outside the candle shop. By midafternoon, however, it had returned full force, thanks to her preoccupation with Eoghan. By the time she and Tillie arrived at the church, gnats were fluttering in her stomach.

The church façade was inviting as always. Smoke curled from the chimneys, and the evening candles had been lit. Ana climbed from the wagon, mindful of her remaining blisters, and waited, stamping her feet to keep warm while Tillie tied the horse to a hitching post. Inside, the normal preparations for supper were being made, the same chatter of the residents rang through the halls, and Sister Agnes barked directions while Sister Mary and Father Ed did their best to stay out of her way.

Tillie nudged Ana with her elbow. "There's Sister Mary. Go on with you now. You've got me as curious as you."

"In a moment," Ana replied, unwinding her scarf from around her neck. "First, I want to check on Ellen."

Tillie's teasing immediately melted into a contrite grimace. "Of course. Let me know if there's anything she or Ione needs."

Ana nodded and hung up her cloak before heading down the hall. She tapped lightly on the door and waited until Ione's quiet voice bid her enter before twisting the knob.

Ellen's face brightened the moment she laid eyes on her. "Ana, you're here! I've missed you."

"Shush now," Ione begged, struggling to keep the covers over her daughter's wriggling form. "Don't be getting yourself all riled up."

Ellen ignored her and scooted sideways to pat the edge of the bed. "Come sit with me. Sister Mary said 'twas you who pushed the cauldron off of me. Did you, Ana?"

Overcome with a sudden rush of shyness, Ana nodded.

"Grateful we are that you done it, too," Ione said quietly. "Sister Mary said you burned your hands?"

Ana held them out for her and Ellen to see. "They're better now," she assured them when Ione clucked sadly.

"I'm better, too." Ellen reached for a corner of her blanket. "Wanna see?"

"Absolutely not," Ione said. "You heard what the doctor said. We're to keep your burns clean and covered at all times."

Ellen's hopeful smile drooped into a pout. "Mama, how much longer am I going to have to stay in the bed?"

"Until the doctor says you're well enough to be out of it," Ione said, rising from her chair to stretch her back. Her gaze shifted to the clock above the mantel. "It's late. Guess I should see about helping with supper." She bent and pressed a kiss to her daughter's forehead. "Will you be all right, me darling?"

"I'll sit with her," Ana volunteered. She crossed the room to the extensive stack of books on Sister Mary's desk. "Maybe Ellen would like me to read her a story?"

At Ellen's nod, Ione released a smile. "Verra well, then. I'll be back shortly with a tray for you both." She gave another kiss to Ellen, then wrapped Ana in a firm hug.

"I truly am grateful to you, Ana. I'll never forget what you done for my daughter." She glanced at Ellen and back. "Mind she doesn't talk you into getting out of the bed. She feels all right at the moment, but the medicine the doctor left for her will be wearing off soon. I don't want her taxing herself." She wagged her finger and made Ellen laugh by making a funny bunched face before exiting the room.

So, Ellen's bright smile was coaxed in part by the pain

reliever the doctor had left. Choked with emotion and unwilling that the child should see, Ana turned to Sister Mary's desk. Exactly what kinds of books did one find in a nun's bedchamber? She ran her finger down the spines. Amidst the many prayer books and missals was a rather large volume on the rite of penance—hardly fit reading for a child.

Ana frowned.

"Never mind the book, Ana," Ellen said with a cheery wave. "I'd rather you told me a story, anyway."

Relieved, she turned. Indeed, a story might be easier. "You would?"

Ellen patted the bed once more, and this time Ana gladly claimed the spot she indicated.

"Well, let's see . . . I think I can remember a tale or two that my mother told me when I was a wee one."

Frowning, Ellen shook her head. "Not that kind. I want to hear about how you were burned when you were a girl."

Ana's breath caught. "What?"

Ellen rounded her eyes and lightly touched the scars on Ana's hands. "Please?"

There was more to Ellen's earnest expression than mere curiosity. Ana sensed a craving for kinship, knowledge that someone else understood her suffering.

She shifted gently, moving the bed only a little, until she sat facing Ellen. "I will tell you, but only if you promise to keep the story between us."

She could almost see the lass's ears perk. "Like a secret?"

Ana pursed her lips, thinking. "More like a story I'm entrusting only to you. Do you promise?"

At Ellen's somber nod, Ana folded her hands in her lap and began, "It happened when I was a little girl, around nine years old."

Ellen sat up from her pillows. "I'm seven."

"I know," she said, smoothing the blankets and gently pressing the girl back at the same time. "I had a sister almost the same age."

"What was her name?"

Her child's mind didn't even question the use of past tense. Ana swallowed the momentary sadness and forged on. "Her name was Brigid. She was a sweet lass, just like you."

With each word she tapped Ellen's nose until she drew a giggle. But then Ellen forgot about her burns and wiggled, which drew a wince, and Ana remembered why she was telling her about her sister.

Her smile fading, she clasped Ellen's hand. "One night, many years ago, our house caught fire while we were sleeping. I don't know what caused it. I only know I woke to flames at the windows and along the ceiling."

Ellen's eyes grew large and she stopped fidgeting. "Were you scared, Ana?"

Mindful of the age of her audience, Ana left out the details of her horror, of the thick smoke and the steaming hiss of charred wood. Simply remembering the panic that had consumed her brought a chill to her bones, which she somehow managed to hide with a smile.

"Aye. I was scared. I went looking for my ma, but when I found her, I couldn't wake her, so I went looking for my sister instead."

"And did you find her?"

A door engulfed in flames. Smoke so thick and black, it scorched the eyes. Brigid's terrified screams.

Ana wrapped her arms around her middle and looked away—at the door, the floor, anywhere but at Ellen, whose earnest face reminded her sharply of Brigid's at the moment. "Not in time, I'm afraid," she managed to croak past a raw, burning throat.

Suddenly a small warm hand covered hers. Ana opened her eyes to see tears brimming in Ellen's.

"Is that how you burned your hands? Trying to save your sister?"

Sighing, Ana braced her elbows on her knees and dropped her chin into her hands. "Sometimes, Ellen . . . sometimes we just aren't strong enough to do the things we want to do, even though we try. I think the day that you went out into the yard, you were trying to help Sister Agnes, isn't that right?"

Ellen gave a solemn nod.

"And even though you didn't mean to bump the cauldron, you did."

Again the girl nodded.

"That is what you and I call an accident. It's terrible, and we didn't mean for it to happen, but sometimes it just does."

"The fire that burned your house was an accident, too."

Deep inside, guilt and doubt pricked Ana's heart. She bit her lip, troubled. "Aye, I suppose that's true," she said slowly.

Ellen gave her hand a pat, like a little old woman in a pint-sized body. "I'm verra sorry about your sister, Ana, but I'm so glad you're my friend."

The beginnings of a real smile tilted the corners of Ana's mouth. "I'm glad too, Ladybug."

"And so am I."

The masculine voice startled Ana from the edge of the bed. She gripped the sides of her skirt as she turned. Eoghan leaned in the doorway, his face covered in stubble, his eyes red-rimmed and weary.

"Derry! You're back," Ellen exclaimed.

"So I am." He left the door and came to stand next to Ellen at the bed. "How are you feeling?"

"Better. Ana is too." She studied him up and down, her lips drooping into a frown. "You look terrible."

He chuckled, but Ellen was right. Up close, he looked even more worn than Ana first thought. Worse, the stench of liquor and stale tobacco smoke clung to his clothing.

Her back rigid, she circled the bed and came to a stop beside him. "May I speak with you in the hall?"

"Now?"

The last thing she wanted was his foul self hovering over Ellen. Steeling herself against his rakish grin, she nodded. "If you please. Ellen, lass, we'll be right outside the door if you need anything."

The little girl nodded, but her face was troubled, and no wonder. She had to sense the tension sparking between the two of them. Feigning her brightest smile, Ana gave her shoulder a pat and then snagged Eoghan's elbow and led him to the door.

"Where have you been?" she hissed the moment they stepped into the hall. "And what were you thinking showing up in Ellen's room looking . . . and smelling"—she waved in disgust at his disheveled clothing—"like that."

"Actually, it wasn't Ellen I was searching for."

"I should hope not." The more she spoke, the more she seethed. The man had obviously been drinking. In his current state, he had no business seeking out a little girl. She crossed her arms, little though the action did to hide her shaking. "And you still haven't answered my question. Do you have any idea how worried we've all been?"

He had the gall to smile. "You were worried?"

Fury took over and Ana stomped her foot. "You . . . you think this is funny? Are you so thickheaded that you actually don't realize the concern you've caused or—" she narrowed her eyes, barely able to keep from spitting out her anger— "are you just so selfish that you dinna care?"

The smile slipped from his face, and he reached out to touch her.

She jerked away. "Don't."

"Ana—"

"Everything the nuns have done, what Father Ed has done, and this is how you repay them?"

"What are you talking about?" Drawing back his hand, he crossed his arms and stared at her, glowering.

With one sweep she indicated his muddy boots, wrinkled trousers, and half-tucked shirt. "This . . . this is what I mean. You've obviously not been taking care of yourself."

Dragging his fingers through his hair, he nodded. "Aye, that much is true, I reckon."

The admission only fueled her rage. "And you've been drinking!"

His eyes widened. "What?"

"Don't bother denying it. I can smell it all over you. Most likely Ellen could, too. What do you suppose she makes of all this?"

"I have no idea."

Ione rounded the corner, a tray in her hands. By the concern on her face, it was apparent she'd overheard at least part of their conversation. She hurried to them. "Everything all right?"

Regret washed over Ana. "I'm sorry, Ione. We were just talking, and . . ." Unable to finish, she bunched her fists, despite the searing pain caused by her blisters, and hid them in the folds of her skirt.

Ione looked from Ana to Eoghan. "The room next to the dining hall is open if you'd like to finish this conversation in private. Mind you leave the door open and let one of the sisters know where you are."

Ana gave a stubborn shake of her head. "That won't be necessary—"

"Thank you," Eoghan cut in, grabbing hold of Ana's arm. "Come with me."

He left her little choice but to obey. Her feet barely touched the floor as he dragged her to the dining hall. Keeping his fingers firmly clamped on her elbow, he ducked his head inside to let the sisters know where they'd be . . . talking.

"Now," he said when he'd finally pulled her into the office and released her arm, "what exactly is it you think I've been doing?"

"Isn't it obvious?" She cast a long, scathing look at his clothing. "Just when Sister Mary and Sister Agnes could use the extra help too, what with Ellen still recovering and Ione having to tend her. I wager Father Ed has been at his wits' end without the use of his wagon—"

"You wager, but you haven't asked?"

She fumbled to a halt. "What?"

"I returned the wagon to Father Ed the night I took you home." He strode the length of the office, which only took three steps, thanks to its diminutive size and his long legs.

Refusing to relent, Ana clenched her jaw and crossed her arms. "Fine. I admit, 'twas more than I gave you credit for."

He lingered at the window, his shoulders bent and haggard lines crisscrossing his face. Suddenly she was forced to consider that it might perhaps be weariness that made his eyes look red, and not the effects of too much drink.

His brow lifted. "So, it occurs to you that you might be wrong. That perhaps there is another explanation as to why I look and smell as I do."

The anger slipped, and a horrible, creeping remorse took its place. Swallowing, she dropped her gaze and reached for a straight-back chair with molded arms and clawed feet. "You're saying I was wrong, then?" she said, sitting. In truth, she already suspected that to be the case.

Sighing, he grabbed the match to the chair Ana occupied and swung it around so they sat facing each other. "I will explain," he said at last, "but you must promise to hear it all. Do I have your word?"

If he needed a vow, it had to mean she wasn't about to like what he said. She nodded apprehensively, then wished she could draw her agreement back when he grimaced, took a deep breath, and slowly blew it out.

"Good. Then I'll tell you everything."

Again, his fingers tore his hair. The motion alone was enough to tug at Ana's heart, but the agony on his face . . .

There was resolve in his face when he looked up, and something else—something that set her nerves to tingling and birthed a knot of dread in her stomach.

"I'm doing it, Ana. I've decided to seek out my sister. I'm going to talk to Cara."

16

The words lashed Eoghan's already ragged conscience. For three days he'd wrestled the beast and thought at last he'd won. But confronted with Ana's outrage, he wasn't so sure.

Her brown eyes widened. Unable to meet them, he rose and turned away.

"That's wonderful," she whispered. "Cara will be so happy."

On the wall above a small desk, a painting of the Savior condemned him. Kindness shone from His face, and His pierced hands were spread in an attitude of mercy. Biting back an inward groan, Eoghan turned toward the easier of the two: Ana's hopeful gaze.

"I didn't do it for Cara," he said, glad to speak at least a mite of truth. When the hope on her face faltered, he resumed his seat and gently clasped her hands. "Will you tell me something? The story I overheard you sharing with Ellen . . . it is true?"

At her nod, a bit of the tension squeezing his chest eased. A part of him detested the duplicity he'd engaged in with Kilarny—despised the deception it would take to ferret the information for the Fenians from Cara. But another part . . .

He stroked the back of her hand with his thumb. "But there was more you didn't tell Ellen."

With the tremor that shook her hands, all remaining doubt he'd had about deceiving Cara fled.

He could help Ana.

He'd focus on that. Ignoring his own sin wouldn't be easy, but he'd never claimed to be innocent, anyway. It was Ana who deserved better. Not him. Not Cara. And especially not Rourke Turner.

"Will you tell me the rest?" he asked softly, reluctantly letting go when Ana pulled free.

"Why? What good can come from reliving painful memories?"

Her voice quivered, and it was all he could do to keep from sweeping her into his arms.

Looking down at the bare wood floor, he shrugged. "Perhaps you're right. It's just . . . I want to help you, Ana."

"How?"

He couldn't tell her about his deal with Kilarny, but some of it—the part about him looking for her uncle—that he could share.

If he were standing.

He couldn't bear to sit still. Rising, he paced the cramped room, stopping when he reached the desk, where he turned and repeated the three-step journey.

To tell Ana how he used his contacts within the Fenians to find out what he could about her missing uncle, he'd have to tell her about his past. Every last, ugly detail.

"When I was eighteen," he began, studying the walls, the floor, everything but her, "I joined a revolutionary society called the Fenians. You've heard of them?"

She nodded. "They were created to establish home rule in Ireland."

He shrugged. "Aye . . . and nay. Depends who you ask. Those who started the organization were shopkeepers mostly, or local people discontented with English rule. The idea was to achieve Irish independence, not cripple her people—at least that was what I believed when I joined." He swallowed a sudden swell of bitterness. "But then something happened. I was forced out and branded a traitor."

"Daniel Turner."

He shot her a glance. "You know about him?"

She shook her head. "Only what Cara has told me."

His bitterness grew. "Then let me give you my side." He waited until she gave indication before forging ahead. "The plan was to kidnap a member of Irish parliament, force them to change their stance on home rule. Daniel Turner was the most outspoken."

"Which was why they chose him."

"Exactly."

"What happened?"

He drew a deep breath. He'd been asking himself the same question for years. "I don't know. Truly. One minute he was arguing about the way we were handling matters—pleading, in fact, for us to allow parliament a chance to work things out democratically, and then . . ."

Sean's pistol, pointed at Turner's head. Eoghan stepping between them, demanding that he see reason. The struggle for the gun. An ear-splitting report. His knife, pulled from the waistband of his trousers by Sean's grasping fingers. Blood.

He closed his eyes against the onslaught of memories. "We fought. When it was over, both Turner and one of the Fenians were dead."

"Sean Healy, Deidre's husband."

He lifted a brow.

"She tried to kill Cara . . . and you . . . last summer, out of revenge for his death."

"She wasn't the only one who wanted me dead." Fresh pain over his sister's betrayal washed over him. "The Turners, too. And Rourke Turner, Daniel's son."

She leaned forward in her chair. "Because he blamed you for his father's death. But when he and his kinsmen found out the truth—"

He shook his head, a part of him unwilling to listen, unwilling to experience the same deep disappointment he'd experienced from Cara with Ana. "After Cara betrayed me, I went back to the Fenians, tried to convince them to let me prove myself. The man who almost charged into us the other night was one of them."

She shuddered and rubbed her hands over her arms. "He wanted you to deliver a message."

He nodded.

"And did that message have anything to do with your decision to see Cara?"

Here was the tricky part. He gave a slow nod. "In a roundabout way, I suppose so."

"What do you mean?"

He crossed to the chair and sat. "Ana, do you remember our conversation about healing the rift between Cara and me?"

A bit of hope returned and flickered in her gaze. "Aye?"

"I've thought some on your words. In fact, they've plagued me."

Her touch on his arm seared his flesh. "Go on."

"You were right."

"Oh, Eoghan . . ."

"'Twasn't easy. I wrestled with my decision for days."

"Which is where you've been this week."

He looked down. "Holed up in a pub, trying to make up my mind . . . tempted to wash away my guilt with drink."

Her grasp on his arm tightened. "But you didn't?"

"No."

She breathed a gentle sigh. "So? What happened?"

"I agreed to do as the Fenians asked, but not because I wanted back in. I agreed only if they would do something for me."

A look of horror flashed across her face and she recoiled. "Eoghan, this task . . . was it to spy on Cara?"

His breath caught. "Why would you ask that?"

She hesitated, her teeth working at her lip. "I don't know. I just thought . . ."

He shook his head, his throat thick. "No. My decision to see Cara, I made for you."

Half true.

A bit of the fear melted from her face. "Then what?"

"I agreed to continue doing their bidding in exchange for information, Ana." His heart lightened with anticipation of her joy, her gratitude. If nothing else, at least he could find some justification in knowing she would thank him for reuniting her with the only family she had left.

"Eoghan, what . . . ?"

He covered her hand with his own, hardly able to contain himself as he squeezed. "I asked them to help me, Ana. I asked them to help me find your uncle."

— ❊ ❊ ❊ —

It was as if someone had pulled a plug and allowed all the blood to drain from Ana's body, out of her feet. Her mouth went dry. Her tongue felt thick. She moved her lips and yet no sound emerged.

"Ana? Are you all right?"

173

Eoghan's voice pulled her from the brink of hysteria.

"Y-you . . . did . . . what?"

The mangled words rasped from a throat tight with panic. Rising, she walked on weak legs to grip the edge of the desk. It could not be. She'd traveled a continent away, changed her name . . .

Whirling, she pinned him with a glower. "You had no right."

Confusion marred his face as he stood. "I don't understand. I thought you'd be happy—"

"You're right! You don't understand," she yelled, then clasped her head in her hands and forced her breathing to calm. "You do not understand what it is you've done."

He crossed to her, not touching, yet reaching out in a way she sensed hurt him. "Then explain it to me."

And give him even more of her heart than she had already? She shook her head. "It won't help."

"Ana . . ."

Desperate to escape the pleading in his voice, she darted around him and made for the door.

"Where are you going?"

"Home."

"Let me walk you."

"No!" If she slowed, she'd burst into tears. Unwilling to let him witness such a display, she hurried through the dining hall to the kitchen door, where she'd hung her cloak. Buttoning it would take too long. She threw it over her shoulders and lunged into the falling darkness.

"Ana!"

His voice called to her from the door. Ignoring him, she willed her feet to move faster over the cobbled street. Away from him. Away from the church.

Away from the fear that he had given birth to with a few simple words.

"I asked them to help me find your uncle."

Fury shook her limbs so that she stumbled and nearly fell. *How dare he do such a thing? How did he even know to look?*

She slowed beneath the glow of a streetlamp. She'd told him, that was how. Covering her face, she released the tears that had been building since hearing his words. The night she'd burned her hands and he asked about her family. She'd told him then, only she never dreamed . . .

She forged onward past a row of squat buildings with hanging hand-lettered signs, but there was no escaping the ragged memories hounding her steps. She felt them creeping nearer, threatening to overtake her. If she could make it home . . .

At last, the shadowy line of the boardinghouse roof came into view. Tears blurred the sidewalk beneath her feet. Never had the row of shrubs on either side of the steps leading up to the door given her pause. Neither had the shadows cast by the buildings crouching alongside ever caused her to tremble. Yet fear took hold as she threw herself up the stairs and through the front door. She slammed it behind her and fell against it, her trembling knees no longer able to give support.

Home. Safe. At last.

After several long moments, her breathing slowed and her heart rate returned to normal. Only then did she realize the stillness of the boardinghouse, the absolute quiet that so rarely favored its halls. She pushed off the door and moved toward the parlor. In the fireplace, the coals from the evening fire cast the only light. Ana crossed to the hearth, lifted a candle from the mantel, and using a long, slender piece of kindling she brought flame to the wick.

The gentle circle of light brought immediate comfort. At least now it wasn't so dark. Dusk had been falling earlier and earlier as the fall progressed. Never before had the progression of the seasons bothered her as much as it did now—now that her uncle knew she was alive.

She shuddered and rubbed her hand over her arm. Where were Amelia and Meg? And Laverne? Surely they hadn't gone to bed. Despite the darkness, it wasn't that late.

Leaving the parlor, Ana wound down the hall to the library. Here too she was met by a shadowed room and the coals of a dying fire.

"They must have gone out," she mumbled quietly to herself. 'Twas the only explanation as to why the fires would have been allowed to go out so early. Strangely, the thought brought a mixture of sorrow and relief. She would have liked to have sought Tillie's company tonight, rather than facing her fears alone, but at least now she'd be spared a lengthy discourse on why she never intended to speak to Eoghan Hamilton again.

Thinking his name brought a stab of angry, bitter disappointment. Refusing to dwell on him further, she gently slid the library door closed, as though slamming it might disturb the boardinghouse, and sprinted up the stairs toward her room.

Sleep. That's what she needed. Several hours of uninterrupted rest to ponder what she should do next.

At the landing, the candle sputtered and nearly went out. Ana shielded the flame with one hand and slowed her pace. Inside her bedroom, a fire had been laid and waited for a spark to be set alight. She hunkered at the hearth and brought the candle near. It would be nice to have the boardinghouse to herself. It happened so rarely, and tonight of all nights . . .

A sound behind her stiffened her spine. She strained her ears. It sounded like . . . for just a moment, she thought she'd heard . . .

It came again, louder this time. And closer. Harsh, ragged breathing.

She bolted to her feet and whirled. At the sight that met her eyes, a scream rose to her throat. She had no time to release it, for just a split second later, a hard, heavy hand clapped over her mouth.

— ❋ ❋ ❋ —

How could he have been so stupid?

Eoghan slowed and nearly stopped dead in the street. Arrogant, that's what he was, and rash as ever. Why else would he have acted without consulting Ana first? Remembering the shocked look that had crossed her face, he gave himself a mental kick.

And now? What was he doing but acting exactly the same? Following her home. Intending to demand that she speak with him—allow him to explain. And what could he say? He thought she'd be happy with the news.

He resumed walking, his steps slower and less certain. What if she didn't want to see him? She was angry, she'd made that plain enough.

Aye, and she had every right to be.

He bit back a groan. The other choice was to let her go on thinking him a cad, or worse. Oddly he found the idea reprehensible. No, he'd seek her out and beg her forgiveness. Whether she gave it or not, at least she'd know that he hadn't meant to hurt her. Never that.

His mind made up, he forged ahead until the roof of the boardinghouse came into view. The windows were dim, the chimneys quiet. Had the household retired for the night?

At the top of the stairs, he hesitated. Perhaps this was his answer. He lowered his hand without knocking. He should go home, leave Ana in peace and hope that someday she'd overcome her anger.

He backed up a step.

After all, wasn't this what he'd hoped to accomplish? If she was angry, she'd not be close enough to him to be affected by his dealings with the Fenians.

He took another step back.

Of course, keeping his end of the bargain with Kilarny meant he'd have to see her sooner or later.

He clenched his jaw. Later would be better, after he'd had a chance to add some distance between them, both physically and emotionally.

He drew in a sharp breath. Emotionally? Aye, if he were honest. He whirled, prepared to leave the boardinghouse and his growing feelings for Ana far behind. On the first step, however, a sound from inside the boardinghouse drew his attention.

A muffled scream?

He frowned and turned back. "Ana?"

Brick and mortar. Blank, staring windows. The boarding-house was quiet, and then—

Another scream. Louder.

"Ana!"

Eoghan vaulted across the landing. Though he'd been prepared to rip the door open, the knob turned easily in his hand. He flung the door open, a chill traveling his flesh as Ana's terrified scream was abruptly cut short.

A roar tore from his throat—desperate. Primal. He pounded through the boardinghouse, the stairs beneath his feet a shad-owy blur.

"Ana, where are you! Ana!"

Halfway up, a dark figure materialized in the hall. Instinct took over. Eoghan froze, half-crouched, his hand reaching for the blade in the waistband of his trousers at his back. The man too froze, but only for a second, and then he was pressing his advantage, barreling down the stairs straight for him.

The strict confines made maneuvering difficult. Eoghan narrowly missed being shoved headlong down the stairs. He ducked, sideways and down, caught the intruder with the heel of his hand under the chin.

They wrestled. Eoghan fell—landed heavily with a stair tread hard in the center of his back. The force drove the air from his lungs. He kicked, dislodging his attacker and sending him scudding down the stairs.

Gagging, Eoghan struggled to draw air into his lungs. In the same moment he yanked his knife free, but the attacker was already on his feet and heading for the door. And Ana—

Eyes and lungs burning, he spun and staggered up the stairs.

"Ana!" he croaked, jerking to his right as a sound met his ears. Midway down, a door stood partially open—a black, gaping cavern in the dimly lit hall. He wove toward it. Only when he pushed it open and spied her by the light of the moon spilling from the window did the air return fully to his lungs.

She sat in a crumpled heap on the floor. Panting heavily, he crossed to kneel beside her. "Ana, are you hurt?"

Tears streamed down her pale cheeks. Twice now, he'd seen the same terrified look gleaming in her eyes. It was too much. Folding her gently into his arms, he drew her close, comforting and shielding her with his body, knowing it was not enough.

"Shush now," he soothed as he tucked her head into the crook of his shoulder. "It's all right. You're safe."

"Who . . . who was that?"

"I don't know. Did he hurt you?"

179

A tremor, followed by the slightest whimper. Dismayed, he squeezed her tighter. "I'm so sorry, Ana."

"No . . . I'm all right." Her voice cracked and she began again. "You saved me. If you hadn't come . . ."

She shuddered and buried her face in the folds of his shirt. Holding her this way, he didn't want to think about what might have happened if he hadn't come.

"I'm here," he said instead, breathing deep of the fragrance of her hair.

Thank God.

The idea startled him. Pulling back gently, he rose and then lifted her to her feet. "A candle?"

"On . . . on the mantel."

He found one and lit it, then used it to light an oil lamp on the bedside table. Soon a soft glow bathed the room in golden light. Ana stood slightly apart from him, her arms wrapped around her middle, but she looked no less frightened.

He cleared his throat. "Perhaps we should go downstairs. Try to figure this out."

She nodded.

"Can you walk?"

The worried frown cleared from her face and a ghost of a smile flitted across her lips. "Do I look that bad?"

Relief swept through him. She was going to be all right. He fought a grin. "Well, I was sort of hoping you'd let me carry you."

Her smile faded and her eyes widened.

She remembered.

Her uncle. The Fenians. His bargain with Kilarny. Regret roiled in Eoghan's belly. "That man who attacked you . . . did you know him?"

She shook her head. Downstairs, something stirred and then voices drifted up the hall.

"We're home, Ana. Are you here?"

Eoghan glanced back at her. This time, there was no doubting the source of her tears. He steeled himself against the sight. "I'm sorry, Ana. For everything."

More voices, closer now.

He eased toward her, hand outstretched, dismayed when she took a wooden step back. His hand fell.

"You should go," she whispered.

He nodded, pausing at the door for one last glimpse of her ashen face. "I'll find out who did this," he vowed, though in his mind he suspected already. She said nothing, a slight nod the only indication that she'd heard.

He angled his chin toward the stairs. "Will you tell them?"

She shrugged. "Tell them what? I don't know who the man was or why he was here. It would only frighten them."

He had no right to argue, and doing so might push her further away. His heart heavy, he slipped into the hall and made for the stairs, but deep down . . .

Deep down he sensed he was leaving a part of himself behind.

— ❋ ❋ ❋ —

The moment Eoghan slid from view, trembling returned to Ana's limbs. She wobbled on the threshold, soaking in the deep timbre of his voice as he explained to Amelia and the others how she had returned to the boardinghouse early because she wasn't feeling well, and he had followed her there to make sure she made it safely.

Not exactly a lie.

Not completely the truth.

Sadness filled her at the predicament. She'd felt protected in his arms. How then could a man who made her feel so safe be the same man who'd taken away her safety?

A knock sounded on her door, and then Meg poked her head inside. "Ana? Are you all right? Derry said you weren't feeling well."

The muscles in Ana's hands and face were like stone, tight and cold. She could barely speak. "I'll be fine. I'm tired, is all. Think I'll turn in early."

She could manage no more. She trailed off, relieved when Meg nodded and offered a smile instead of demanding an explanation.

"All right, then. I'll check on you in the morning. Good night."

"Good night."

The door closed quietly. Only then did Ana realize that she'd been standing with her fists clenched and her arms wrapped around her middle. And . . . there was something in her hand.

She lowered her gaze and uncurled her fingers, one by one. Horrified by what she saw, she gasped and flung her hand out, shaking the offensive thing away. It fluttered gently to the floor.

A green feather. She'd grabbed it during the scuffle and had been clutching it the entire time.

Desperate to hold something of comfort, Ana scurried to the nightstand in search of her father's pocket watch. Except for the oil lamp, the table was empty. Had it gotten knocked to the floor in the scuffle?

She ripped back the blankets and searched the floor under and around the bed. Nothing. Fighting panic, she scoured the drawers of her nightstand and dresser, then pulled all the blankets from the bed and shook them out one by one. Finally she had no choice but to accept the hard, bitter truth.

The watch was gone.

But why? What could the intruder have wanted with a trinket whose only real value came from what it meant to her?

Overcome by tears, Ana climbed into the bed and burrowed under the blankets.

But no warmth would reach her. Even with her eyes closed, she sensed it. Warmth and safety went hand in hand, and now . . .

She doubted she would ever feel either one of them again.

17

"Ana, please. You must come down. It's been two days."

Ana burrowed deeper into the bed covers. Tillie's pleas early that morning had gone unanswered; she had no intention of heeding Amelia's now.

"Won't you at least tell me what's wrong? How will I ever be able to help you if—"

"You can't help," Ana interrupted, poking her head out from under the covers. Her beloved watch was gone, and with it her last link to her family. "No one can."

"You don't know that. Maybe if you would talk to me, tell me what happened." More knocking. "Ana?"

Sighing, Ana slid from under the covers and padded to the door and drew back the lock. She didn't wait for it to open, however. She trudged back to the bed and climbed up in. Behind her, the door creaked long and low.

"There you are. I've been so worried."

Guilt compounded the weight burdening Ana's shoulders. "I'm sorry, Amelia. I never meant to cause you or anyone else here any worry."

"It's not just us here at the boardinghouse, dear," Amelia said. Her feet swished softly across the rug until she reached the corner of Ana's bed. "That poor young man from the church has been simply beside himself."

At first, Ana thought she meant Father Ed, but quickly righted her thinking. "Derry has been here?"

"Oh yes. Twice, in fact. And when we told him that you refused to come downstairs . . ." A frown marred her pretty brow as she sat. "Oh, Ana, won't you tell me what happened?"

Tears sprang to her eyes at the concern in Amelia's voice—and just when she thought she'd exhausted them all. At her sniff, Amelia pulled a handkerchief from her sleeve and pressed it into her hand.

"Thank you," Ana said, unable to look at Amelia for fear that she'd erupt in an onslaught of fresh weeping.

The bed dipped and rocked as Amelia rose. A moment later, water wrung from a towel into the washbasin, dribbled and splashed. Amelia returned and dabbed the cloth to Ana's forehead and eyes.

"There now. You're bound to feel better after you've washed your face."

If only her cares *could* be vanquished with the swipe of a cloth. Still, she mumbled her thanks and then waited while Amelia fetched a ribbon for her hair. Surprisingly she did feel better with her tangled locks drawn back from her cheeks. Enough so that she could meet Amelia's gaze without fear of breaking.

Amelia smiled and gave her knee a satisfied pat. "There. Told you so." She lifted a slender brow. "Well? Can you talk?"

She pushed up in the bed. She owed it to Amelia to tell her a part of what had happened. Beginning with the day Ellen had been burned by the cauldron, she proceeded to fill her in on her conversations with Eoghan, up to and including his relationship to Cara, but leaving out the part about the intruder. That was still too raw. Too personal.

When she finished, Amelia shook her head. "But I don't understand, dear. Why did his trying to help you find your uncle upset you so?"

She clenched her jaw. "My uncle hated my family, Amelia. He and Ma had some terrible rows after Da died. I remember them arguing once, and him threatening to kick us all off the farm."

Her eyes widened. "Could he do that?"

Ana shook her head. "I have no idea. I only know that I dreaded seeing him come around after that. I was always afraid he'd come to take our home."

"And now Derry's actions . . . I mean, Eoghan," she corrected, "his actions have nigh posted a sign above your head telling your uncle how to find you." Her hand fluttered to her throat. "No wonder he was beside himself."

Compassion soaked her eyes when she again looked at Ana. "I can't blame you for being so angry, dear, but have you stopped to consider his side?"

"His side!"

She quickly reached out to cover Ana's fisted hands. "You said he wrestled with the decision for several days. It must have cost him a great deal to make such a concession, especially since, in his mind, Cara betrayed him."

"So you're saying what he did was a good thing?" Ana asked.

Her lips twisted in a wry smile. "I'm saying, dear girl, that you must mean an awful lot to that young man for him to heed your advice—or did you not tell him he should seek to reconcile with his sister?"

Wary of the gleam in Amelia's eyes, Ana drew back her hand. "Aye, that was my intent. But it's different with my uncle and me. He is a harsh, angry man. Cara is nothing like that, and she loves her brother, if he would just give her a chance to prove it."

"Give her a chance, hmm?" Her gaze lowered. "Ana, could it be that the same might be said for your uncle?"

A shiver traveled Ana's spine. "I was terrified of my uncle."

"You were a child," she replied gently. "Perhaps you had reason to be afraid, but perhaps"—she leaned close and lowered her voice to a whisper—"your fear was composed mostly of fantasies created in a little girl's mind."

Ana turned her face away. The memories, the nightmares— she refused to believe they were a figment of her imagination.

"Regardless, dear," Amelia continued, her warm hand covering Ana's knee, "don't you think you at least owe it to your uncle to see if he's changed? After all, what harm could he do?"

What harm could he do?

Though she repeated the words inwardly, they brought no calm or sense of assurance. Instead, a chill crept over Ana.

— ❈ ❈ ❈ —

Eoghan paced the floor in front of the fireplace in the boardinghouse's parlor. Waiting had never been his strongest virtue. Waiting *patiently* was absent altogether. Every creak of the door had him turning expectantly, every footfall, craning until he thought his head would snap off.

"Ain't no good to go on pacing like that, ya know," Laverne said, her plump fingers working a needle through the sock she was darning. "Amelia said she would talk to her and let you know."

Framed in the light streaming from the window, she might have made a pleasing enough picture were she not the object of Eoghan's current frustration.

"Perhaps if you had just let me speak to Ana myself, none of this pacing would have been necessary."

"What, give you leave to burst into a lady's bedchamber,

unannounced and unwelcome?" Her lips puckered in a frown. "I think not. Besides, whatever ya done to make Miss Ana so cross with ya, well, I'm thinking trespassing where ya wasn't wanted may not have been the best way to go about fixing the situation."

Another argumentative female. Seemed everywhere he turned of late, he encountered another one. Eoghan threw his hands into the air and resumed pacing, but not for long. A light step sounded on the stair and then Amelia entered, followed by a somewhat pale Ana.

Eoghan's heart lurched in his chest.

"There, ya see?" Laverne left her seat by the window and crossed to wrap a plump arm around Ana's slender shoulders. "I knew Amelia would be able to sort things out."

"Laverne, would you be so kind as to fetch these two some tea? They have a few things that still need to be worked out."

"Just the two, ma'am?"

Amelia nodded. "I'll take mine in the library."

She ducked her head and then scurried out to do Amelia's bidding, her brows drawn in a puzzled frown.

"Now," Amelia said, fixing them both with a stern look, "you two have a lot to discuss. I'll leave you to it, though I trust"—here she doubled the intensity of her glower—"that you'll each share openly with the other."

At their mumbled agreement, she smiled, gave Eoghan's arm a pat and Ana's cheek a kiss, and then slipped out the doors.

Not only was Ana pale, she had dark smudges beneath her eyes. And she looked thin. Though she met his gaze, she moved no farther into the room. It took a moment for him to realize it was the fire and not his presence that kept her rooted to her spot near the door.

"Ana, I'm sorry—"

He broke off as Laverne's heavy tread thumped down the hall. Laden with a tray bearing a flowered teapot and two cups, she swung into the parlor, deposited the tray onto the table in front of the settee, then peered back and forth at them both.

"There now, that should do it. If there's anything else you need—"

"We'll let you know," Ana said.

Still, Laverne hesitated. Finally, she gave a stiff nod that nearly dislodged the mobcap on her head and backed out of the room. "All right then. I'll leave you two to your business. Holler if you need anything."

The doors slid closed with a snap, leaving Eoghan alone with Ana for the first time in days.

It was not an entirely comfortable feeling.

He moved to the fireplace, scooted one of the chairs away from its fiery warmth, and placed it so that it sat catty-corner to the one Laverne had occupied at the window. Motioning toward it, he invited Ana to join him.

Once she was seated, he claimed the other chair, neither one breaking the silence that stretched between them. Finally, he cleared his throat and finished the apology Laverne had interrupted with her entrance.

"Ana, you have every right to be angry. I should never have gone meddling in your business. Maybe if I'd left things alone, you wouldn't have been attacked. I'm sorry."

His heart lurched at the sudden tears that sprang to her already reddened eyes. She reached out her hand and laid it lightly over his arm. "I don't think so, Eoghan. The intruder in my room—I think he was after something specific."

"What do you mean?"

Her jaw worked and she ground out, "My father's pocket watch. It's missing. I didn't notice until after you left."

His mind whirled. Could the intruder simply have been a thief? "The watch . . . was it valuable?"

"Only to me."

His stomach sank. So, Ana *was* the target. A part of him had hoped the entire incident an unhappy coincidence.

"You mustn't blame yourself, Eoghan. Were it not for you, that night could have resulted in far worse—" She broke off and, after a moment, opened her hand. In her palm lay a green feather.

He quirked an eyebrow. "What's that?"

"I snatched it from the intruder's cap when we fought. I thought it might help you find him."

He nodded and slid the feather into a pocket of his coat. "Still doesn't excuse the other thing," he mumbled, reluctant to even voice it.

"You were only trying to help."

He'd pondered for the last two days what he would say once he saw Ana again, and determined to speak the words, he gave a stubborn shake of his head. "Aye, and quite a mess I made of that, now, didn't I?"

Instead of agreeing with him, she smiled, robbing the next words right off his tongue. He covered her small, delicate hand, still lying so gently on his arm, and gave it a squeeze. He had to know . . .

"What happened, Ana? To your ma and Brigid . . . the fire . . . There's more you haven't told anyone. Isn't that so?"

A shadow fell over her, followed by swift, fleeting sorrow. She bowed her head, her long hair tumbling forward over her shoulder. "It was so long ago."

"But it haunts you still?"

"Sometimes," she admitted.

Though he longed to brush the tendrils from her forehead,

he resisted. She'd tell him if she could, and if not, he'd not repeat the mistake of pressing too hard, too soon.

"My uncle was my father's half brother. Unmarried. No children."

He watched, still and silent, as she was drawn into the memories. Her face, normally so expressive, went blank, and pain filled her soft brown eyes.

"We never saw much of him when Da was alive. Only after he was killed did he dare come around. I think it was because he was always a little intimidated by my da."

"How did your daed die?" Eoghan asked gently.

"A farming accident. That's all Ma would ever say, though I remember some men carrying him in, and one of them going out to put down one of the horses after." A shudder shook her. "My uncle started showing up a lot after that, always carrying on about the farm being too big for Ma to run by herself, and how women shouldn't be allowed to own land. She never budged, but he kept coming by. Eventually I think Ma got to where she was afraid of him."

"Why?"

"I don't know. Just a feeling I had, maybe? I couldn't put my finger on it then and certainly wouldn't try now, so many years later. It's just . . ." Her pretty features twisted. "I wasn't the only one who didn't trust him."

Eoghan leaned forward in the chair. "What do you mean?"

She stared at him, her eyes deep wells, beckoning to him. "I managed to get out of the house the night of the fire, but Ma and Brigid . . ." Her eyes fluttered shut. "I don't even remember going to the church on the outskirts of our village. I was burned, and in shock, yet something drew me. The priest there found me, tended to my wounds, and when I was well enough to travel . . ."

191

She fell silent, and he sensed she was reliving those child-hood moments. Helpless, he waited, afraid to speak for fear of startling her.

"Father Joseph changed my name and bought me passage on a ship bound to America."

He drew a sharp breath. "Changed your name? Why?"

"At the time, he said it was to keep me safe. I didn't un-derstand then, but now I think it was because he didn't trust my uncle."

"So he sent you to America? A child, alone, in a foreign country?"

"Not alone," Ana said. "He contacted a friend, some man I had never met. He traveled with me to an orphanage run by another Irish priest here in New York."

"Who was this man? Do you remember?"

She gave a slow nod. "But Father Joseph, he bade me never to tell who it was that helped me. To this day, I've never breathed his name to another living soul."

Frustrated, Eoghan dragged his fingers through his hair. "Your uncle, then. You remember his name?"

The muscles along her jaw bunched. This time, her nod was stiffer. "Aye. I remember him."

"Well?" he prompted, though his chest tightened even be-fore she opened her mouth to speak.

"McCleod. My uncle's name is Brion McCleod."

Eoghan's stomach sank. The Fenians had paid to have a man by that name delivered from the barge office. He'd seen the note. Worse, he had personally delivered the message.

And that meant that he, and he alone, had set loose upon the city—and the woman he'd grown to love—the one man who still haunted her dreams.

18

Ana's heart melted at the agony twisting Eoghan's handsome face, as though he sensed her despair and shared the weight of it with her. Of their own volition her fingers sought the rugged planes of his face and smoothed the worried lines from his forehead.

His breathing hitched. "Ana, there is something I must tell you," he began in a ragged whisper.

She shook her head. "Whatever it is, it doesn't matter. You were trying to help me, that's all."

"Aye, that much is true, but I was also helping myself."

She considered this for a moment, then raised her chin. "All right, and should I blame you for that? Anyone in your position would do the same—"

"E-Eoghan?"

Both she and Eoghan turned at the sudden voice drifting from the door. Ana looked back at him. His face had gone ashen, and no wonder. Cara stood framed in the entrance, her eyes glistening with a painful mix of hope and disbelief.

She took a faltering step across the threshold. "It *is* you. What are you doing here?"

Ana stood to her feet in the same moment as Eoghan, but

instead of moving toward the door, he remained rooted in place, his features frozen, hands clenched at his sides.

Her mouth dry, Ana swallowed and turned to look at Cara. "How did you know?"

"Laverne. Laverne sent for me."

Never mind how the wily old housekeeper had found out who Eoghan was. The fact was, she had, and now here the two stood, face-to-face. Ana held out her hand. Cara slowly crossed to take it, her tear-filled gaze fixed on her brother. But instead of welcoming her with an embrace as Ana had hoped, he only nodded stiffly.

"I . . . should let the two of you talk," she said. When neither one moved or spoke, Ana slipped from between them and glided silently toward the door. With just a nudge she slid it closed, then stood in the empty hall thinking. Whether she approved of his methods or not, she had no doubt Eoghan had intended to help, and she couldn't fault him for that. Indeed, her own meddling was not all that different. Hadn't she hoped for the very outcome with which she'd just been presented?

Sighing, Ana pushed from the hallway and grabbed her cloak off a peg near the front door. It was evening, and the sun had long ago cast its final rays across the city, but the air was pleasant enough. A brisk walk would clear her head, sharpen her thinking. She hesitated as she opened the door and stared out at the street.

What if *he* were still out there? The intruder. She still had no idea who he was or what he'd wanted, yet something inside her refused to allow him or her uncle to keep her trapped in her room any longer.

Her boots made a sharp sound as she skittered down the steps, made even keener since Ashberry Street was quiet this time of day. The vending carts that lined the sidewalk were empty. The merchants had stored their wares, and what shoppers once crowded the street were home in front of their evening fires.

To the south lay James O'Bannon's candle shop. Ana turned north.

So, her uncle now knew she was alive, or soon would, if the men Eoghan had confided in did their jobs properly. She replayed Amelia's words. *"Don't you think you at least owe it to your uncle to see if he's changed? After all, what harm could he do?"*

A picture of her uncle's sharp eyes and hard, ruthless features flashed before her eyes. Could a man like that change? Was such a transformation even possible?

She shuddered and hugged her cloak tighter to her body. At one time, she hadn't thought so, and yet hadn't she herself undergone at least the beginnings of change? She was no longer the same bitter woman she'd been just a couple months ago, afraid to set foot inside a church. True, she still felt anger when she thought of her mother and sister, but was it solely God whom she blamed?

On the sidewalk, a thin dusting of snow crunched beneath her feet. She slowed her steps, listening to the sound, pulling deep draughts of crisp November air into her lungs . . .

And fighting the feeling that someone was watching her.

Ana shivered. That was her imagination taking hold, trying to drag her back into the fear of two men—one she'd only glimpsed, and the other she barely remembered. Still, she couldn't resist casting a glance over her shoulder, down the street in the direction she'd come.

Her feet faltered.

A shadowy figure *was* lounging in the narrow space between the boardinghouse and the building next door. He straightened at the sight of her, and even stared after her for a moment, his face illuminated by the hard yellow glow of a streetlamp.

In that one glimpse, terror bloomed inside Ana's chest. She knew that dark, menacing scowl, those flintlike eyes. The man who'd been standing outside the boardinghouse, who whirled and disappeared into the shadows when she caught sight of him . . .

That man was her uncle.

— ※ ※ ※ —

A low whistle trilled from Brion's lips as he retraced his steps to the tenement where he'd set up temporary shelter. It was neglected and dirty, and he'd thought it would most likely collapse around his ears the first time he caught sight of it, but it drew little attention and hid him well.

He'd been given no key. There was no need for one—nothing to steal inside. Jamming his shoulder against the door, he gave it a shove until it swung open with a groan. Inside was a rickety table, two chairs with broken slats, a dusty pallet, and a wardrobe with only one door. Brion dropped his coat and cap on the table and sat down to remove his boots.

The Celt's information was sound. Three women of proper age, size, and build occupied the boardinghouse on Ashberry Street. None of them bore the name McCleod, however. Obviously the old priest who'd rescued his niece had taken pains to hide her. Why? And why had the girl gone along with the charade? Unless the priest knew something. Or she did.

He scowled and flung one of his boots against the wall next to the pallet. Exactly how much did she remember?

Determining which of the women was his niece would prove an easy enough task—a few aptly placed questions. But that wasn't what mattered. What mattered was the nature of the game The Celt was playing. Why provide an address and nothing more? Surely the man realized he wouldn't wait for permission, but would act accordingly with a woman who threatened his very existence.

He drew in a breath and cut it off mid-whistle. 'Twould take a bit of time and planning to make the girl's demise look like an accident, but in a city this size? Aye, he could accomplish it easy enough.

The stub of a candle sat in a flat wooden holder at the center of the table. Brion struck a match and lit it. By tomorrow he'd have to purchase another or go without light, and by the look of things, the cramped American city would play host to him far longer than he'd intended.

His thoughts winged to Hamilton. Finishing him off, now that would require a bit of strategy. The man had a way about him—like a wolf maybe or a cornered dog. Either way, battling him could be dangerous, and Brion couldn't afford to be careless.

Waving out the match, he realized what it was that slowed The Celt's hand.

It was Hamilton.

The Celt wanted him dead, for sure and for certain, but he was afraid of moving too quickly, which explained why he fed the information to Brion in bits. So then, the real question remained. What hold did Hamilton have over The Celt?

He pondered the question as he stood and shrugged out of his suspenders. 'Twas a tricky puzzle, and he hadn't near the pieces required to solve it.

Realizing he'd gained the curious stare of a passerby outside his window, Brion winked and even added a jaunty tip of his head to the stooped old woman who gaped and hurried on.

Meddlesome fool, he thought as he flicked the tattered drape covering the window shut. Curiosity like that could prove disastrous. He had to give the people of this neighborhood time to get used to seeing him, until by his very acceptance he became invisible.

He cursed and nearly stumbled on a sudden irksome thought. What if the girl talked before he'd had time to silence her? If that were the case, he'd have more than just her and Hamilton to worry about.

Unfortunately, he wasn't known for his patience, but in this instance the prize was definitely worth the price. After all, he'd waited this long.

The whistle returning to his lips, Brion scrounged through the crumbs leftover from a roll he'd purchased for his lunch.

Aye, he'd wait. And he'd listen. And when he returned to his beloved Ireland, he'd never have to think about The Celt, or Hamilton, or his infernal niece ever again.

19

For several long seconds, Eoghan merely stared at his sister. Her eyes were wide and tear filled, her lips slightly parted and trembling as she breathed his name. How easy it would be to believe her innocent, to think that she'd never betrayed him.

Her hand lifted, beseeching him. "We've searched so long, tried so hard to find you . . ."

"We?"

"Rourke and I."

His mind slammed shut on the notion of her innocence. "It seems you have found me."

"Eoghan—"

His gaze flitted past her to the door. "Where *is* your charming husband, anyway? I assume here at least, with bystanders in the way, he'd be inclined to forestall any attacks he has planned?"

She flinched, as if each of the bitter words were a physical blow. "That's hardly fair, Eoghan. You dinna even know my husband."

His anger strengthened, spewing from his lips like lava. "I know I spent two years running from his kinsmen. I know one of them shot me in the back and left me for dead. I know

I risked everything, *everything*, to find you and bring you to America. Even after all that . . ." He stopped short of accusing her of betrayal.

"But all of that was a misunderstanding. If you would just let me explain—"

"A misunderstanding, Cara? Really?" He whirled, shutting out the sight of the pain on his sister's face. It only made him angrier, and he had to remain calm or she'd never believe that he wanted to reconcile.

"You're right," she whispered. "*Misunderstanding* is not a strong enough word for what happened between us. I'm sorry." Her heels tapped lightly across the floor and came to a stop behind him. "Eoghan, you are my brother, the only family I have left apart from Rourke, and . . . you have to know that I love you, and that I would never intentionally hurt you."

He blew out a breath, steadying himself and reinforcing his resolve with the simple act. "Aye, Cara. I do believe that."

He turned, taking in the planes of her face, so similar to his own, in one sweeping glance. There was no guile in her eyes, no duplicity in her expression. On her wrist was the twisted leather bracelet their father had given to them years ago. Eoghan had owned one like it—worn it up until the day he'd been shot. It disappeared that night, but now, seeing Cara with hers . . .

His breath caught with the realization that he'd been wrong all along. She hadn't betrayed him. She'd been deceived— fooled into thinking the Turners guiltless by her conniving husband. And as her brother, it was his duty to make her see the truth, but he'd have to be careful. Cara fancied herself in love, which meant getting her to accept facts would not be easy or quick. He had to keep reminding himself of that if he hoped to free her from the Turner clan's wicked clutches.

Lowering his gaze, he studied the swirling patterns in the rug beneath his feet. "I agree that things have passed between us that neither have understood. But you *are* my sister, Cara, despite all that has happened. Perhaps, if you are willing, we could try to put some of that behind us?" Shame flooded him at the look of joy that blossomed on her face. He put up his hand quickly. "Understand me, Cara, I still do not trust that husband of yours and likely never will."

Her expression faltered. "Not now, perhaps, but who knows what the future will bring. I ask only . . . Eoghan, you will try?"

The deception he'd been forced to play left a bitter taste in his mouth. Instead of speaking, he gave a slow, grudging nod.

It seemed enough to satisfy her. She grasped his arm, her smile bright, if a bit wobbly. "Thank you. Oh, my dear, we have so much to discuss, and it's been so long. I can hardly wait to tell you—"

In the hall, a door smashed open, followed by a burst of cold air. Both his and Cara's heads turned toward the sound, but it was he who moved when, a moment later, Ana appeared at the entrance. Her face was pale, her eyes wide as saucers.

He reached her side in four long strides and gently took hold of her arm. She trembled beneath her cloak. "Ana? Are you all right? What happened?"

Tears soaked her eyes as she looked up at him, but it wasn't sorrow that caused them. Sweat dotted her forehead, and her teeth clattered even with the muscles in her jaw bunched. She was terrified. He looked past her toward the door.

"I saw him," she whispered.

Cara hastened toward them, her brow furrowed in concern. "Saw who?"

"The man with the feathered cap?" Eoghan added.

Ana's focus remained fixed on Eoghan. "Not him. Outside,

on the street. He was standing in the shadows, watching the house."

His grip on her tightened. "Who did you see?" he prompted, though deep down he feared he already knew.

"My uncle," Ana said, leaning more heavily against him with each word she uttered. "I saw my uncle."

A second later she collapsed, unconscious, into his arms.

— ※ ※ ※ —

Noise like the hissing of a serpent dragged Ana from sleep. She opened her eyes, blinked, and immediately felt them begin to itch. And it hurt to breathe.

Drawing her pretty, flowered blanket to her chin, she sat up in the bed, frightened. "Momma?"

Smoke filled her small bedchamber. Instead of the soft glow of the lamp her mother used to read by, a harsh orange glare danced through the crack under her door. It looked like . . .

Fire.

"Momma!" The scream cut from her throat. Ana threw back the covers and ran barefoot to yank open the door. The curtains over the windows blazed and swung as though pushed by a breeze. All around her, a wall of heat and flames loomed. Ana instinctively clasped both hands to her chest. Where was her mother? And Brigid?

Momma first. She would know what to do. Ana veered toward her mother's room, dropping to her hands and knees when the smoke got so thick it stung her eyes. Reaching her mother's door, she groped for the knob and gave it a turn.

Inside, the chamber was cool and dark. The black smoke had not yet reached here. She slammed the door and scrambled to her feet.

"Momma?"

Light from the moon splashed through the window onto

her mother's sleeping face. Relief brought tears to Ana's eyes. She hurried to her side and gave her shoulder a shake. "Momma, wake up! The house is on fire."

Her mother slept on.

"Momma! Wake up!" She shook her again, harder. Her mother's head flopped sideways off the pillow.

Ana stared. Outside the door, the hissing fire had become a screaming beast, clawing and snarling, louder and closer. Her chest felt like someone had reached inside and squeezed, yet she could not move. Something was wrong. The way her mother slept . . . so still and quiet.

She backed away from the bed, one step and then two, and finally she whirled and ran for the door.

She had to get Brigid and then figure out how to wake up her mother. She flung open the door. No time to crawl this time. She'd never make it past the stairs.

Hitching up the sides of her nightdress, she drew a quivering breath, closed her eyes, and jumped headlong into the fire.

20

Ana's skin burned with fever. Eoghan shifted in the chair next to her bed, attentive to every sound that escaped her lips. Laverne swore it wasn't a natural sickness that had taken hold, but something else. He knew what that "something else" was—fear. No, that was too gentle a word. It was horror. The way she tossed, as if she were searching for something, ripped at his heart.

Groaning, she flung her hand out. He caught it and pressed it tightly to his chest. He'd done this. 'Twas his foolish action that brought Brion McCleod to her door. And now she lay, wrestling demons she alone could see.

"I'm sorry, Ana," he whispered as he brought her hand to his lips. "I will not let him hurt you. I swear it."

Soft rustling sounded behind him, and Tillie entered, a tray in her hands. She set it on the bedside table and bent to rest her palm on Ana's brow. "How is she?"

He shook his head. "The same. What's wrong with her, Tillie? Why won't she wake up?"

Compassion softened Tillie's face. "Likely the shock of seeing her uncle has stirred up old memories. Bad ones, I fear." She reached across the bed to squeeze Eoghan's shoulder. "She'll be better once she's rested." Her face brightened with a hopeful smile. "Cara is still downstairs. I told her I would fetch you. Will you see her?"

Eoghan's gaze drifted to Ana. She still looked flushed, and between her perfect brows was a troubled crease that he longed to smooth away, but she no longer tossed. He sighed and rose.

"I'll call if she wakes," Tillie said, giving his arm a soothing pat, then waved him toward the door.

Helpless to do naught but obey, he slipped quietly into the hall and made his way downstairs to the parlor. A light glowed from the door. Low voices, one of them familiar, drifted loud and then soft as he drew near.

Ach, Cara. Seeing her again had affected him more deeply than he'd expected. If not for Ana's sudden appearance, they might have forged a sort of peace. Still could. But first he had to convince her that the man she'd married still wanted him dead.

He drew a breath and strode across the threshold, prepared to do whatever he had to in order to persuade his sister to listen—to drive the truth home by force, if need be. Instead he froze two steps into the parlor. Cara was perched on a slender chair. At her side stood the man he'd once sworn to protect her from at all cost—Rourke Turner.

Her husband.

Eoghan gritted his teeth, then forced his muscles to relax, one by one. Confident he'd hidden the anger seething deep inside, he lifted his chin and strolled into the room.

Cara stood. "How is she?"

"Sleeping still. Tillie insists it was just the shock of seeing her uncle."

"Well, Tillie is absolutely right," Laverne said from her spot near the window.

Eoghan's awareness of the room broadened. He'd been so fixated on Turner, he hadn't even seen Amelia and the others. He doubted the man would try anything with so many women present. Still, he watched Turner warily from the corner of his eye.

Amelia seconded the notion with a nod. Rising from her seat, she accepted the arm Meg offered and left the warmth of the fireplace. "She'll be fine once the surprise—and disbelief too, I suppose—wears off. What about you? Are you all right? None of us here ever imagined that the friend Ana spoke of . . . that you and Cara . . ." She trailed off and turned her gaze to his sister. "Do you suppose she knew who he was?"

"We were all a bit surprised by Eoghan's appearance," Cara said, laughing weakly. "But it will all be worked out once Ana wakes."

Dark smudges beneath her eyes became visible as she looked up at her husband. He wrapped his arm about her waist and pulled her close. Unable to watch, Eoghan looked away.

"You still have much to discuss," Amelia said. She motioned toward the hall. "Shall I have Giles stoke the fire in the library?"

Turner opened his mouth, but Eoghan cut him off with a shake of his head. "Not tonight. I'd prefer to wait until Ana wakes, if you do not mind. I'm sure Cara understands."

He tensed as Turner walked toward him, though without his knife he'd be forced to rely on his fists to defend himself. But if it was a fight he wanted . . .

The man stopped a few feet shy of him and extended his hand. Eoghan eyed it suspiciously.

"We're just happy to have found you, Eoghan. We'll talk when you're ready."

The man was smooth, no doubt. He'd probably anticipated this moment and arranged it to look as though he meant no harm. Well, enough hot lead had been dug from Eoghan's back for him to know that a Turner couldn't be trusted. Reluctantly, Eoghan accepted his hand and gave it a shake.

"We've waited so long—two years, in fact." Cara moved to him, her head tilted pleadingly. "My dear brother, I have so much to tell you."

Turner placed a gentle touch on her shoulder. "Cara."

She looked questioningly at him.

"'Tis been a long day, and you're tired. There is time now, sweetheart. Do not worry. This can wait till morning."

He'd never seen his sister so obedient. Her gaze fell, but she nodded and tucked herself into her husband's side.

"Of course. You're right."

It was all Eoghan could do to keep from grabbing her wrist and yanking her from Turner's arms as they turned and moved for the door.

Wait. Bide your time, he reminded himself as they said their good-byes with a promise to return in the morning. Even so, it festered like a canker as he sat and waited for word from Tillie on Ana's condition. Finally, feeling as though he might erupt, he grabbed his coat and went in search of Amelia. Though he would have liked to stay until Ana woke, he knew what he really needed was to learn what he could about the man with the feathered cap, and what Brion McCleod was doing in New York.

He found both Amelia and Laverne in the kitchen, sipping cups of tea. He didn't tell them where he was going, only that it was urgent he go. After vowing to return, he headed out into the cold night air.

This time of the evening, hiring a hack was easy enough. He gave curt instructions to the driver, then sat back for the brisk ride to Kilarny's house on the outskirts of town. Lights glowed from the cottage windows. On the roof, a tendril of smoke curled from the chimney. He paid the driver and then hurried up the walk past a row of leaded-glass windows to a wreath on the door. It was all quite inviting. The cold metal of a pistol barrel against his ear was not.

"What are you doing here, Hammy? I didn't send for ya."

"You always greet your guests this way?"

"Uninvited ones, I do." He pulled the gun away from Eoghan's head and jammed it into the waistband of his trousers. "Lucky for you, I saw ya coming."

Eoghan held out his hand. In it was the dagger he'd slipped from a sheath at Kilarny's side. Flipping it to grip the blade, he smirked and said, "Lucky for you, I saw you, too."

Kil's answering chuckle set them both at ease. "Still got reflexes like a cat, I see. Glad to know no one will be sneaking up on you anytime soon." He reclaimed his knife and gestured with the tip of it toward a barn set back from the house. "Let's go in there. The wife and kids are still up."

"Kids? I thought it was just the one."

Kil wound behind the house and stepped back to allow Eoghan to enter the barn. "You've been gone a long time, Hammy, me boy. I've got three now." He grabbed a lantern from a hook next to the door. Striking a match, he watched it hiss and flare to life, then held it to the wick until it glowed softly. Satisfied, he straightened and waved the match out. "I assume you have something you'd like to talk about?"

"Who is he, Kil?"

Kilarny took his time replacing the lantern on the hook. When he turned, his face was blank. "Not sure who you're talking about."

Eoghan pulled the feather from his coat pocket and held it up. "He was wearing this in his cap."

Kilarny studied the feather and shrugged. "Lots of people wear feathers. Nothing special about that one."

Much as he disliked the answer, he knew it to be true. Eoghan replaced the feather angrily. "Fine. What about Brion McCleod? The Fenians paid a lot of money to move him through immigration."

Interest sparked in Kilarny's eyes. Could it be he'd been unaware of the contents of the packet Eoghan had been asked to deliver? But then that meant . . .

Eoghan crossed his arms and leaned back against the nearest stall. "Those orders didn't come from you, either. Someone is doing an awful lot of work behind your back, old friend."

Kil's eyes narrowed, but he made no protest.

"Who was it from, then? Who sent the package and how did they know to give it to me?"

"The money changed hands several times. I have no idea where it started. Giving it to you to deliver, well, that *was* my idea."

He'd known Kilarny a long time, but that didn't mean Eoghan trusted him. He studied the man for hints that would indicate he was lying.

One side of his mouth twitched. "Look, Hammy—"

"You never answered my question," Eoghan interrupted, his voice low. Though he maintained his relaxed posture, every muscle was tensed, and he sensed Kilarny was no different.

"I knew *what* the money was for, I didn't know for who."

"Now you do. The name mean anything to you?"

Kilarny looked up, then shook his head. "Never heard of him."

"But you've contacts back home that could do some checking."

"Aye, it would be easy enough."

Eoghan waited, measuring the silence stretching between them by the rustle of hay and stomping of hooves in the stall behind him. "What's going on here, Kil?" he asked at last.

For a moment he doubted Kilarny would answer, but then he pushed up from the door, away from the lantern, and crossed to stand at Eoghan's side.

"A while back, I asked if you remembered when we joined the Fenians."

"So?"

"Things have changed, Hammy, and not for the better."

"What kinds of things?"

"McCleod, for example. How does getting him through immigration help Ireland?"

"That the only thing that has you concerned?"

Kilarny shrugged. "All right, so it's more of a feeling. You saying my instincts are wrong?"

Eoghan grunted.

"Right. So what are we going to do about it?"

"We?"

The two men stared at each other in silence.

"Why are you asking me this, Kil? Why not someone else?"

A wry grin split Kilarny's lips. "Someone who hasn't been branded a traitor, you mean?"

"Aye, someone like that," Eoghan retorted.

"Your being an outsider makes you the perfect choice—no leaks, no chance of my moves being noticed by the wrong person." The smile slowly faded. "All right, so that's not the only reason. I may not have always agreed with your ideas or your methods," he admitted, "but I never doubted your motives. Not for a second."

"Is that right."

"Why do you think I brought you back in by having you be the one to deliver the money?"

"Why don't you tell me?"

Kilarny sighed and rubbed his hand wearily over his face. "Used to be, I knew exactly what I was doing and why I was asked to do it. Now I'm never sure who I can trust. I question every intent, every order that comes my way." He paused, and when he next spoke, his gaze was fixed and steady. "There's only ever been one person I trusted implicitly, one person I thought joined the Fenians for exactly the same reason as me, which was to do what was best for Ireland. That man was you, Hammy, me boy."

He gave a bark of laughter that echoed in the broad confines of the barn. "We're idealists, you and me. There's no changing our minds when we get something stuck in here." He rapped his knuckle against the side of his head. "Am I right?"

Choosing to ignore his last remark, Eoghan squared his jaw and jutted out his chin. "I appreciate the compliment—"

"'Tweren't no compliment. I'm calling you a stubborn Irishman, same as me."

Eoghan snorted, and just as quickly found he no longer felt tense around his former compatriot. "Whatever you say, Kil."

They watched the flame flickering in the lantern in silence a moment, and then Kilarny spoke, so softly that Eoghan strained to hear.

"What are we going to do, Hammy?"

Without having to ask, Eoghan knew exactly what he meant. He gave himself a shake, then jammed his hands into the pockets of his coat and made for the door. When he reached it, he turned and looked back at his old friend. "Kil, me boy, you and I are going to find out who brought Brion McCleod to America and why. And then we're going to find out what any of that has to do with the Fenians."

21

A soft knock on her bedroom door pulled Ana away from the curtain hanging over her window. Sensing it wasn't one of the boardinghouse residents who awaited her in the hall, she paused at the mirror to steel herself before moving to answer. Eoghan stood on the other side of the door, his broad shoulders nearly filling the frame.

"You're awake."

She let her hand fall from the knob and moved back to the window. "Aye."

"Where's Tillie?"

"I got tired of her fussing, so I sent her downstairs."

The floor creaked behind her. Ana motioned to the teeming city outside her window. The workday was in full swing, with vendors busily hawking their wares and shoppers swarming both sides of the street.

"Out there somewhere is the man from whom I've spent most of my life running," she said quietly.

Eoghan stopped behind her, close enough that she could feel the warmth from his body, not so close that they touched. "Why? What did the priest tell you to make you think you had reason to fear Brion McCleod?"

"I feared him long before the priest told me I should."

His fingers closed around her shoulder, and he gently turned her to face him. "Why is that, Ana? What had he done? What do you remember?"

Though she tried, she failed to suppress a shudder. The vestiges of her dream were still fresh, the icy claws still real and biting into her flesh. Eoghan's face became a watery silhouette as tears burned her eyes. She shook her head. "I can't . . ."

"You can. Tell me, Ana."

The pull of his voice, so warm and insistent, proved too strong to resist. She drew a quivering breath and released it, along with all the pent-up dread she'd been harboring from the moment she'd opened her eyes. "Brion McCleod murdered my mother."

Eoghan went perfectly still. A second later, his hand fell from her shoulder. "What?"

Shivering, she drew her hands up and down her arms. "At least, I think he did."

He took a deep breath before crossing to the vanity and pulling out the chair. He waved her toward it, but Ana shook her head. At this moment she preferred to remain standing.

When she failed to sit, Eoghan took the chair himself. Lines of worry marred his handsome face, or was it disbelief? Afraid to scrutinize his expression too deeply, she wrapped her arms protectively about herself.

Propping his elbows on his knees, he steepled his fingers and fixed her with a steady gaze. "Ana, are you telling me that you remember something about the night your mother died that you didn't before?"

She nodded, her chest tight.

"And that was?"

If she told him and he doubted her, or worse, mocked

her . . . She swallowed against the knot lodged in her throat. "The night of the fire, my uncle came to see my mother. She sent us to bed, but I hid around the corner, listening. I remember them arguing about the house."

"What were they saying?"

"My uncle accused my mother of wantonness, saying it wasn't right for a woman to live alone, especially with two young daughters in the house. He said even the church . . ." Ana shuddered as a new memory sprang forth. Was this why she'd always felt the church condemned her? She forced herself to go on. "He said even the church frowned upon her single state—that the women of the congregation had begun to talk, and that he was only looking out for our reputations."

She fell silent. After a moment, he prompted, "And then what happened?"

"I woke up to a house filled with smoke."

"You didn't hear any more of the conversation between your mother and McCleod?"

She shook her head. "I crawled back to my room and pulled the covers over my head. After a while, I guess I must have fallen asleep."

"Go on."

She read nothing on his face. Suddenly she was uncertain. He could at least act like he believed her, though why it was so important that he should was unclear to her. She pressed her hands to her stomach and lifted her chin.

"I went to my mother's room to wake her." Her temples began to throb as details of that night came flooding back. "She was so quiet and . . . still. Unnaturally so. My mother was always a light sleeper, but that night, nothing I did roused her."

Sweat dotted her lip and forehead, but she forged on, faster and faster. "Seeing my uncle again, after so many years, it stirred up all those old memories. Things I thought I had forgotten."

"Such as?"

"My mother's dress," she blurted, sweat dampening her palms. "Eoghan, why would she have gone to bed fully clothed?"

One eyebrow lifted. "Maybe she lay down to rest and just fell asleep."

Ana paused, thinking. "No. The lantern was out. And her hair—it was still braided."

He rose and walked to her, his steps slow and measured. It took an interminable amount of time for him to reach her, as though he were crossing a great expanse. Her heart beat faster, her breaths grew shorter. The tears fell freely now, and while she wanted to flee, her feet refused to budge.

"Why else wouldn't she wake, Eoghan? Why couldn't I wake her?"

He reached out to her. At first she resisted, but before long, giving in to the tug of his arms became easier.

She fell against him with a sob. "It was my fault."

Eoghan gently stroked her hair. She closed her eyes against the pleasure his touch wrought, refusing to allow herself to be comforted by the strength of his fingers or the solid length of his body. "It w-was all my fault."

"No, Ana, it wasn't."

She cried harder now, and found words more difficult to form. "The f-fire. Losing Momma. And Brigid . . . Why didn't I just go for help? Someone stronger, more capable, might have reached them in time."

She beat her fists against his chest in an utterly futile gesture that brought no satisfaction and only compounded her feelings of guilt.

"Ana!"

Eoghan shook her, harder and harder, until finally she snapped her head up to look at him.

His face was grim, every muscle chiseled and tense. "Your mother's death was not your fault."

She blinked, hardly daring to believe his words. "What?"

"It wasn't your fault, and neither was the fire."

"How can you say that? You weren't there."

His lips thinned to a stern line. "It doesn't matter. I know."

Already the brief hope sparked by his confidence was fading. "How? How can you know?"

He paused to suck in a breath and blow it slowly out. "Because I do think your uncle killed your mother. And then I think he set that fire to cover up her murder."

— ❈ ❈ ❈ —

Eoghan tightened his grip on Ana's slender frame. For several long seconds, she merely stared at him, her mouth slightly parted and her eyes wide and filled with tears.

When at last she managed to speak, it was one halting word. "What?"

"I had my suspicions, but tonight, the things you remembered from the fire, they only confirmed what I thought all along."

"Then . . . you don't think I'm mad? That I'm not just making things up to try and deal with my own guilt?"

Fresh tears rolled down her pale cheeks. He shook his head and drew her, unresisting, into his arms. "You're not mad, Ana, though by all rights you should be, given the things you've seen and endured."

He felt protective of her and couldn't imagine the fright she must have experienced as a child, and still lived with as an adult. "I'm so sorry, Ana. I'd give anything to be able to go back and shield you from the things that happened that night." Placing his finger beneath her chin, he tilted her face up toward his. "But I'm here now, and I swear to you, I'll never let anything like that happen to you ever again."

Her lashes fluttered down to cover her eyes. Heeding the urge that laid claim to him, he pressed a kiss to first one eyelid and then the other. Her resulting sigh sent a shudder through him.

"It's all right, sweetheart. You're safe now."

She bent her head back to look at him. "My uncle?"

"I've already started asking questions. I'll find out what he's doing in New York—and what he's looking for."

"And the man who attacked me?"

"The same. Eventually we'll know something about them both." He waited. After a moment, she agreed with a nod. "In the meantime," he continued, "I think it's best that you stick close to the boardinghouse."

She stiffened and would have pulled free of his arms if he'd allowed her. "But Mr. O'Bannon and the church—"

"I'll take care of speaking with your employer," he insisted firmly, "and I'm sure the sisters at the church will understand, as well."

She pressed her hand to his chest. "No, Eoghan, you mustn't tell them."

Taken aback by the stubborn tilt of her chin, he slackened his hold. "Why not?"

She bit her lip, troubled by something she found difficult to give voice to. This time when she pulled away, he let his arms fall.

"Eoghan, there is so much more I have not told you."

A part of him knew she had secrets she kept buried, but another part feared feeling again the pain and loss he'd suffered at Cara's betrayal. He crossed his arms instinctively. "Such as?"

"My name. It isn't Ana Kavanagh."

He lowered his gaze, pondering. "It's McCleod?"

When he looked up, she nodded. "Lucy McCleod."

"And the priest who helped you after the fire . . . he told you to change it?"

She gave the barest tip of her head.

"Why? What did he know? And why didn't he tell anyone? Why send a child, all alone, to a foreign country?" He dragged his fingers through his hair. "It just doesn't make any sense."

"Unless . . ." She paused and paced the floor. "He must have known, or at least suspected foul play, something he realized that a child of nine would never understand. But if that's true, there can only be one reason why Brion McCleod would come to America." She shivered and her eyes widened. "I'm still a threat."

"What?"

She stepped closer to him and clutched his arm. "Think on it. Why else would he travel so far? He must believe that I know something that could prove damaging to him."

"Ana—"

"It's true!" Her voice quivered and then cracked. "He's here, looking for me."

"You were only nine," Eoghan said, fighting his own rising panic. "Even if you did remember something, you have no proof. What harm could you have possibly done—then or now?"

The silence between them stretched to a razor's edge. Finally she blew out a sigh and turned away. "I have to go to him."

"What?"

"I have to find out what he wants from me."

Eoghan could no more resist sweeping her into his arms than he could stop breathing. "No. I won't let you do that, not so long as there's even a hint of danger."

"But *you're* in danger. Didn't you say you'd already started asking questions around the city?"

"That's different. I can take care of myself."

"And I can't?"

"You misunderstand, Ana. It would be too easy for Mc-Cleod to catch you unaware."

"He'd do the same to you, Eoghan."

"No, he wouldn't."

"Why not?"

"Because I'm trained in battle. I'll have my guard up."

"So will I . . . now."

"Ana, I said no. I think it's best—"

"It's not up to you, Eoghan."

"Aye, it is!"

"Why?"

"Because—"

Because I can't bear the thought of you coming to harm. Because you've come to mean more to me than I ever intended. Because if I'm honest with myself, truly honest . . .

"Eoghan?"

He sucked in a breath. Her eyes, her hair, the delicate scent of her skin—all combined into a temptation too great to resist. He lowered his head.

Instantly he found himself swept into the shocking sweetness of her lips. His senses swirled into a maelstrom of conflicting desires—end her touch and free himself from her spell, or linger in the enthralling trance that was her kiss.

His arms tightened. Only when he felt her tremble did he have the strength to let her go. She stared up at him, her eyes no longer shadowed by fear, but wide and questioning. Her fingers, when she lifted them to touch her mouth, shook slightly.

"I'm sorry, Ana," he began, though in truth he was already fighting the urge to take her back into his arms.

Again she turned from him, but not before he witnessed a flash of pain across her face. "I want you to go."

"Ana—"

"Now. I think it's best."

Indeed, if his raging emotions were any indication, it certainly was best that he leave. He crossed to the door, pausing with his hand on the jamb. He stared at her rigid back, determination warring with doubt inside his chest. "I'll go, but not before I have your word that you won't seek out your uncle alone. I'll find him, find out what he wants from you, but I must have your promise that you'll keep to the boardinghouse while I search him out."

Her reflection was a ghostly shadow in the window, her eyes dark wells that no amount of optimism could fill.

Though he wanted more, her barely visible nod would have to be enough. For now.

Swinging through the door to the hall, Eoghan strode down the stairs and out of the boardinghouse. He could count on Ana to keep her promise, but not for long. Not forever. He had to find out what he could about Brion McCleod before she was tempted to take matters into her own hands—or if his hunch was right, before McCleod could get his hooks into her.

Either way, it boiled down to one thing. Eoghan couldn't afford to fail, because doing so might mean losing Ana. And if the kiss they'd shared proved anything, it was that he wasn't ready to do that.

Ever.

22

A light snow had begun falling, trickling down through the towering buildings and settling in the cracks of the cobbled street. Not at all like Ireland. Not like the playful wind that whistled along the moors that Brion called home.

And it *was* his home. His. No one could take it from him.

He quickened his steps, muttering as one oblivious traveler brushed against his shoulder as he passed.

Though he kept his head lowered, the man tipped his gray cap and muttered, "Beg yer pardon."

Brion ignored him. Shanahan's Pub loomed on the next corner. 'Twas a seedy place, but one he'd been told was often frequented by one Jacob Kilarny. Heavy doors guarded the structure—a hard spot to drive a hare out of, especially if the pub proved to be a bush Kilarny wasn't in.

Sharp glances measured him as he stepped inside, out of the cold. Shrugging the snowflakes from his shoulders, he cast a sweeping look around the pub before making his way to the bar.

"Help you?"

The barkeep was a short, fat man with pudgy fingers and bulging wide-set eyes. Brion ordered a drink and then watched while the man poured it into a greasy mug.

"That it?" the barkeep asked, plunking the mug onto the bar in front of Brion.

"Aye, that's it," he growled, flipping a coin into the man's hand and settling onto a stool.

Few patrons occupied the place at this hour of the afternoon. Now that their curiosity had waned, most had gone back to their business of drinking and playing cards. Except for one, Brion noted. A thin stranger with sandy-brown hair who watched him through narrowed blue eyes.

Swallowing his distaste at the grime that was sure to be bobbing in his drink, Brion lifted his mug and took a hearty draught. The action seemed to satisfy the barkeep, who gave a low huff and shuffled off to tend another customer. Sliding off the stool, Brion hefted the mug and moved across the pub to the stranger's table.

He waved the mug toward an empty chair. "Mind if I sit?"

The stranger inclined his head. His fingers were laced across his midsection, his posture relaxed and comfortable, but Brion wasn't fooled. The man was anything but relaxed.

Brion sat and shot a quick glance around the room. "Nice place," he said, knocking back another swig from his mug.

The stranger grinned wryly. "You new here?"

"You could say that."

"Haven't seen you around before."

"Just arrived."

"And you made Shanahan's your first stop?"

Brion sneered at him over the top of his mug. "Heard the food was good."

The stranger gave a sharp laugh and leaned forward in his chair. "What can I do for you, friend? I don't think you're here for the beer, or the food."

Brion gave a shake of his head. "Looking for someone."

"Oh?"

He nodded. "A man by the name of Jacob Kilarny. Someone told me I might find him here."

The man quirked an eyebrow. "What business have you with him?"

Resisting the urge to smile, Brion set his mug on the table and braced both elbows on the arms of his chair. The man's face was too bland, too disinterested. Unless he was mistaken, he'd just found Kilarny. "He's supposed to help me with a job."

"Is that right."

The man's voice had dropped to a dangerous level. Brion shifted his fingers closer to the knife sheathed at his side. "Uh-huh. I was told he might have some information that would prove useful to me."

"What kind of information?"

Mistakes were the one thing Brion could not afford. He leaned forward and stabbed the man with a steely glare. "Are you Kilarny or not?"

The man took his time answering. Finally he nodded. "You found him. Who are you?"

"That doesn't matter."

"It does if you want my help."

Fie. The last thing he needed was to have his name bandied about. Brion cast a glance around the pub, which was growing more crowded by the moment. "The name's McCleod." He lowered his voice. "I'm on business for The Celt."

If he'd thought to jar the impassive look from Kilarny's face by dropping The Celt's name, he was mistaken. The man simply stared at him, as bland as before.

"Well? Did you hear me?"

Kilarny grunted. "I heard you. Just wondering what you having business with someone named The Celt has to do with me."

223

He slumped back in his chair, truly befuddled. "So then, you're not . . ."

"What I am not," Kilarny hissed as he planted both hands, palms down, on the table, "is comfortable airing my business—any business—in a public place."

Brion narrowed his eyes and snarled, "Where then?"

Kilarny scoured one side of the pub and then the other. Finally his eyes settled back on Brion. "The wharf. One hour."

He leaned forward and ducked his head. "I'm not familiar with the wharf."

Kilarny studied him in silence as he lifted a small glass to his lips. "Well then, friend, I suggest you get familiar. Quick."

Rage filtered from the top of Brion's head to the tips of his fingers. He'd just as soon kill this troublesome rat as do business with him, but The Celt had hardly left him a choice. He shoved back from the table and stood. "Fine. I'll be there."

Not waiting for an answer, he spun and strode out the way he'd come. This affair with Hamilton was going to be more trouble than he'd bargained for, but if there was one thing he enjoyed, it was a challenge. And maybe a diversion. He knocked open the door and stomped outside.

Aye, that was how he would look at it—a diversion from his own troubles. And it would last right up until the moment he put a bullet in Hamilton's forehead.

— ❈ ❈ ❈ —

Eoghan rubbed wearily at his eyes. For the last hour, he'd been standing outside the house where Rourke Turner lived with his sister, wrestling with the nagging doubt that perhaps his suspicions were wrong and Turner wasn't the devil he thought him to be.

He reached back and rubbed the old wound on his shoulder, just below the bone. It still ached if he pressed it. A

Turner was responsible for that. Could he possibly entrust his sister, his twin, to a man whose family had hunted him so mercilessly? Even if Cara was right about Turner, what of the rest of his clan? What if one of them still wanted revenge and picked his sister as his target?

He couldn't risk it.

Sighing, he moved past the row of trimmed boxwood to a painted front door fitted with a heavy brass knocker. The housekeeper answered after the second knock.

"I'm here to see Cara Ham . . . er, Turner," he corrected with a scowl.

The woman dipped her head, and after taking his coat and escorting him to an elaborate sitting room with a plush-covered round table in the center, bid him wait and swished away. A moment later, she returned with Cara in the lead.

She approached him, a smile on her lips and her arms partially outstretched. "Eoghan, what a surprise."

Indeed, 'twas a look of surprise on his sister's face. She appeared uncertain as to whether or not to embrace him and so ended up raising and lowering her arms in a way that reminded him of a chicken.

He ended both of their misery by wrapping her in an awkward hug. When he let go, she turned to the housekeeper. "That will be all. Thank you, Louise."

Louise gave a nod and scooted out, closing the wide double doors behind her.

Cara motioned toward a set of overstuffed chairs with doily-covered arms. "Will you sit awhile?"

Since the only other option was pacing a hole in the floral carpet, Eoghan moved to the chair and sat. "You have a beautiful home," he said, unwilling to allow the silence to linger too long between them. "Quite different from our tiny cottage back in Derry, eh?"

A pleased grin curved her lips. "Aye, quite different. Never did I imagine when I left Ireland that I'd live anywhere so grand, or be nearly so happy." Both hands fluttered to her lap and she clasped them tight. "I-I'm glad you like it." She leaned forward. "Oh, Eoghan, I've longed for this moment. To have you here—"

"I've come on business, Cara," he interrupted before she could finish. The topic of her conversation was sure to lead to uncomfortable questions. Better if he got to the point quickly.

She lowered her eyes. "I see."

"What I mean is," he rectified quietly, "it may take me awhile to get past the differences between us. I am, however, willing to try."

"Of course." Her face, and her tone, brightened. "So, tell me how you met Ana."

A safe enough topic. In short order, he told of his coming to live and work at the church and subsequently befriending Ana. "She was a resident when you lived at the boarding-house?" he ended by asking.

The earnestness returned to Cara's face as she nodded. "She has proved a loyal friend. I don't know what I'd have done without her back when . . ."

She paused and bit her lip, a gesture he'd seen often in their younger days when she was nervous or uncertain. This might be his chance, tempered with bias toward the Turners though her tale was likely to be.

He braced both elbows on his knees and studied the patterned carpet beneath his feet. "Tell me, Cara."

It was all the encouragement she needed. Beginning with his letter, she relayed the details of her arrival in America, including the day she'd met Rourke and how he'd protected and helped her, even though she'd lied about her search for her brother. She spoke of meeting a businessman named Douglas

Healy, who told her about the boardinghouse, and who in fact turned out to be Sean Healy's father. Tears filled her eyes when she talked about her battle with Deidre, Sean's widow, and how it ended with her kidnapping and then Rourke arriving to save her.

"He killed his cousin in order to rescue me, Eoghan," Cara said, her voice filled with pleading. "When he found out that Hugh had betrayed his family, that he'd helped to kidnap me, Rourke didn't hesitate to come to my aid. He risked his own life to save mine."

Eoghan gritted his teeth. "I didn't come to be convinced of your husband's noble nature, Cara. You can speak all you want about his valor, but he is a Turner. I'll never be persuaded that he is anything more than the blackguard I've thought him and the rest of his clan to be."

He drew a breath and blew it out. Easy, lad, he reminded himself. Convincing her of the truth would take time, not insults hurled willy-nilly.

Her lips thinning, she pressed her hands to her stomach, then rose and paced the room. "If that's true, then why did you come? Was it only to slander the man I married?" She whirled, her eyes flashing green fire.

Just like when we were children. Eoghan resisted a chuckle. He'd seen that look often enough to know that to laugh would only earn him a book—or one of the ornately shaded lamps on the table next to the door—upside his head.

"Because if that is the case," she snapped, "I must warn you, I won't stand for it. Not from you or anyone else."

"Not to fear, sister dear. That's not why I've come." At least not the only reason.

A bit of tension seeped from her shoulders and she held them less rigid. "Then why?"

Suddenly he was reluctant to deliver the practiced speech

he'd prepared. His mouth went dry, his tongue felt thick, and worst of all, shame burned his cheeks.

And what have I to be ashamed of? he thought, running his damp palms over his thighs. *It's not like I'm the one who hunted an innocent man for two years and drove him clear off the continent.*

He thrust out his chin. Cara would see the kind of man she married, and it would start by making her question the things she thought she knew. Regret at the pain she'd endure when she finally saw Turner for who he was washed over him, but it was not to be helped. Not if he hoped to save his sister from the Turners and their wiles. He'd not allow the sweet, kind Cara he remembered to be swept away, leaving a cruel and vengeful shell in her place. For that was surely what would happen if she stayed married to a Turner for any length of time. If she lived long enough.

He lifted his head and looked her in the eyes. "You said he helped you when you first arrived in America, but were his motives truly as selfless as you remember?"

The storm clouds returned to her gaze. "What do you mean?"

"Wasn't there a part of him that thought he could use you to get to me? Tell me the truth, Cara. Once he found out that you were my sister, did he admit to who he was or did he go on lying?"

She paled. "That's not fair, Eoghan."

"Why? Because I'm right? When are you going to stop making excuses for him and listen to reason?"

"He thought you murdered his father," she cried, her cheeks reddening. "Would you have not done the same? And when he found out the truth, he tried to help me . . . to help you!" She lifted pleading hands. "What do you think he's been doing ever since the night you disappeared? Trying to find you, that's what, and not because he still thought you guilty, but because I asked him to. Because he knew how much it meant to me to find you.

"Eoghan—" she crossed to him and knelt to grip his hands—"if you only knew the lengths to which he's gone, I know you'd feel differently about him. He's spent months scouring the city, hired men to aid in the search, even enlisted his contacts in Ireland to listen for a hint of your where-abouts."

With each word she became more vehement, more con-vinced that what she said was true. For a brief moment, he was tempted to believe her himself . . .

Fie. Who was he fooling? A part of him did believe her. He'd seen the Turner tenacity firsthand, had he not? And if that dogged determination were turned to his advantage . . . nay, to Ana's advantage . . .

An idea took shape in his head.

"Eoghan?" Cara stared up at him, her eyes hopeful.

He stood, waiting while she rose with him. "You claim that he wanted to help me. Fine. Would he be willing to prove it?"

She frowned. "What?"

"If I asked him to do something, would he do it?" He paced the floor as he spoke, his steps falling faster and faster.

She blinked in confusion. "I . . . don't know. I suppose it would depend on what you needed him to do."

"It's not for me. It's for Ana."

Her eyes widened in alarm. "Ana's in trouble?"

He nodded and drew to a halt before the hearth. "You could say that."

Sparing any details he thought might embarrass her, he proceeded to tell Cara about Ana's uncle and their suspicions regarding the fire. He left out that by working with Rourke to track down information on Brion McCleod, he also hoped to uncover something that might be useful to the Fenians' cause. Learning who his contacts were, what relationships he still maintained in Ireland—those were the things Kilarny had specified were important.

"Well?" he asked. "Do you think Turner's cohorts in Ireland might be able to uncover something on McCleod?"

Lines of worry marred her brow as she shrugged. "It's possible, but . . ."

"What?"

"You do not think that involving more people will put her in further danger?"

He shook his head. "We don't have a choice, Cara. If it's true that McCleod came here to silence his niece, then time is a luxury we do not have. I need answers and I need them quickly."

"You're right. I'll speak to him when he gets home." Her jaw hardened and she gave a curt tip of her head. "I know my husband, Eoghan. He'll do what he can."

For a split second, her confidence gave him pause. He nodded his thanks and turned for the door. "I'll wait for word. You can reach me at the church—"

"Eoghan, wait."

He paused as she moved toward him, her hand outstretched. He grasped it and squeezed, transported for one brief instant to their childhood when his greatest task was looking after his sister.

"If you don't mind, I'd like to pray with you for Ana's safety—and for peace between the two of us and Rourke."

He jerked free. "What?"

Sorrow creased her face. "I hoped that God would bring you back to me, Eoghan, and now He has. Perhaps if you and I were to seek His help—"

"I have no need of God's help," Eoghan snapped, anger

building in his belly. Who was Cara to speak of seeking God when she herself was so blinded by the Turner clan's deceit? "Have you forgotten? 'Twas my faith that got me banished from Ireland in the first place. Without faith, I never would have gotten involved with the Fenians, or Daniel Turner, or . . ."

He trailed into silence.

"My dear braw lad," Cara whispered, "your faith was never in God. It was in the church you followed, and the Fenians, not the Savior."

"Stop, Cara."

"It's true, dearest, even if you won't admit it. My own mistakes have led me to realize that without Him, I am nothing. Why do you think the Scriptures say that Jesus is the way—?"

"I said stop!"

Cut short by the sharpness of his tone, she peered up at him, her eyes awash with tears.

Steeling himself against the sight of them, he took two steps back and thrust out his chin. "I've asked for your help, but I'm not prepared to listen to your ramblings about God in order to get it."

She wrapped her arms about her waist and said nothing.

"Well?" he demanded. "Are we agreed? You'll help me watch over Ana, but leave any talk of God out of it?"

With her shoulders slumped and her head hanging low, she looked to have had her heart broken.

"As much as I am able," she replied sadly. "I'll not force you to listen to my beliefs about God."

It was as much as he could hope for. Striding into the hall, he called for his coat and then waited impatiently while Louise delivered it.

God. The church. As though either one had ever been there for him—had ever cared one whit for his well-being or his safety.

Which wasn't exactly true, he admitted as he swung onto the sidewalk and turned his feet toward home. He did have a roof over his head, but that was thanks to Father Ed and the nuns, not God. Not the church.

And most certainly, definitely not Jesus.

Still, a quiet voice haunted him as he wound his way toward the shelter and then fished a key from the pocket of his coat to let himself in through the back door. Why then was Father Ed compelled to do the work of running the shelter? Why were Sister Mary and Sister Agnes willing to spend hours of backbreaking labor feeding and caring for the residents? The truth was undeniable.

He had no answer.

23

Ana peered out her bedroom window at the gray day. Snow had begun falling before dawn and continued past lunch, and now fluffy banks lined Ashberry Street, which though pretty to her, caused much chagrin to a host of unhappy vendors. Accustomed to regularly hawking their wares along its length, they shoveled furiously to clear the street and sidewalks with little result. Few people braved the snow and chilly temperatures for necessities like meat or bread, much less a chance at a pretty bauble.

She sighed. While the snow had slowed, thick clouds warned of more to come. At least the weather had given her cause to avoid the candle shop. She hated to think of poor Mr. O'Bannon struggling to run the place alone. But Eoghan's instructions had been quite clear.

Eoghan.

She blew out a breath that left a frosty imprint on the glass, then traced his initial in the icy crystals. He'd scarce left her thoughts since coming by the other day, and that wasn't good, especially since she had no idea if he suffered from the same affliction. At the notion that he did not, her heart gave a painful thump and she scratched out the letter with her fingernails.

Giving a toss of her head, Ana left the window, skirting the wide fireplace on her way out of the room. Enough inactivity. She might not be able to return to work, but she could sure enough drop by the church and offer her services.

Wrapping herself in her warmest wool cloak, she grabbed a scarf and mittens and headed for the front door.

"Amelia, I'm going out," she called as she passed the parlor. "Tell Laverne not to hold dinner. I'll eat at the shelter."

Afraid Amelia would argue if she delayed, Ana swung open the door and drew up short at the figure she found hovering on her doorstep. "Eoghan!"

Seeing him made her heart jump. Snow covered his thick auburn hair and dusted his shoulders, but it was his mouth that drew her attention. Immediately the memory of his kiss came flooding back.

Lowering his hand, he narrowed his eyes and scowled at her. "Where do you think you're going?"

"What?"

"I thought we agreed you'd stay here."

That was all he had to say? Nothing about what had happened between the two of them? Ana set her chin stubbornly. Well, she could be as dispassionate as he. "I'm going to the church. I've sat idle long enough."

"I don't think so. We talked about this."

"You talked." She shoved her way onto the steps and slammed the door. "I pretended to listen."

"Ana—"

"What am I supposed to do?" Angered by the tears suddenly burning her eyes, she stamped her foot on the icy steps and propped both hands on her hips. "Hide out in the boardinghouse forever? Stop living until my uncle either forgets about me or goes away? I don't think either of those is going to happen anytime soon. Do you?"

"No."

"Well? Then what is it you suggest I do?"

To her surprise, he reached out to claim both of her shoulders. Even through the thick wool of her cloak, his touch warmed her to the bone. "Ana, I realize this situation is by no means fair to you. I'm sorry about that. It's just, I haven't been able to stop thinking about you—worrying about your safety," he clarified, his cheeks coloring a dull red. "Especially since most of this is my fault."

At his admission of her place in his thoughts, Ana had stopped listening. "You . . . were worried about me?"

His brows drew in a puzzled frown. "Of course."

Of course hardly sounded encouraging. She stiffened and turned to march down the steps. "Well, you needn't have. I'm perfectly capable of taking care of myself. Besides," she added when he caught up and fell in stride beside her, "I haven't seen hide nor hair of my uncle since the other day. Maybe wishing he'd go away isn't so farfetched."

"Maybe," he said, though his tone sounded anything but certain.

She eyed him swinging alongside her critically. "What were you doing at the boardinghouse, anyway?"

He quirked an eyebrow. "What?"

She jerked her chin back the way they'd come. "When I opened the door, you were about to knock."

"Oh, that." He looked down, but too late to avoid stepping into a snowbank. Scowling at the sticky flakes clinging to his pant leg, he stomped his foot against the sidewalk, the resulting hollow crunching sound muffled by layers of packed ice.

"I came to see you." One corner of his mouth lifted. "I figured you were getting antsy."

Though her anger ebbed, she refused to return his smile. "And you thought to keep me company?"

"Actually, no," he said, slowing to tip his hat toward a row of disgruntled vendors whose full carts gave evidence to the dismal day. "I thought to tell you about my visit with Cara."

She halted in her tracks and turned round to stare at him. "You went to see her? When?"

"Day before last." He jammed his hands into the pockets of his coat and shifted from foot to foot. "I thought maybe she and Rourke could help me find out something about your uncle."

"And?"

"They agreed to help. Turner has already sent word via telegraph. It'll likely be two weeks or longer before we hear anything."

Two weeks.

She smothered a sigh and resumed walking. "Do they even know what they're searching for?"

"Anything that will tell them who he is, what his business dealings are, and how they might be tied to you."

She glanced at him in alarm, but he shook his head quickly. "Don't worry. They'll be looking for information on someone named Lucy McCleod."

The knowledge was only slightly comforting. Inside her mittens, she curled her fingers into fists. "I didn't ask for this, you know. I'd have been content to live out my days here"—her mittened hand sliced through the air—"in total anonymity."

Eoghan hunched his shoulders. "What about Amelia's claim that your uncle may have changed?"

"You know about that?"

"She told me last time I stopped by."

Ana wagged her head and pushed on. "No secrets at the boardinghouse, I suppose."

Before she'd gone two paces, he caught her by the arm and pulled her to a stop. "Don't be angry. Amelia cares for you, that's all. She knew I was trying to help . . . that I just wanted to help you."

Though he fumbled to a stop, his hold on her arm continued, even intensified when he edged closer, and Ana shivered at his nearness. Ach, but laying her head upon his broad chest was a temptation almost too great to bear, especially when he gazed at her with such concern in his hazel eyes.

He lifted his finger to caress her cheek, adding fire to the warmth spreading through her belly. "You're cold. I should get you to the shelter."

He'd mistaken her shiver for cold, but she wasn't about to argue—not when the real reason for her discomfort was standing right in front of her. Still, her heart gladdened when he kept hold of her arm and tucked it neatly into the crook of his elbow.

"Tell me more about your mother's farm," he said as they resumed walking. "How big was it? Did you raise animals?"

"Not big," she said smiling, "but large enough to support our small family, and Brigid did have a goat and several chickens. She named the goat Anabelle." She laid her hand over her chest. "After me. Anabelle is my middle name."

Eoghan laughed, and she soon joined him. Chatting in this way about her family made the trip to the shelter pass quickly. It was nice, for once, to speak of them without tears. Her smile remained fixed when they shed their outer garments to a chorus of welcome greetings. She especially received with joy the one delivered by a grinning Ellen. She walked with a limp and her leg was still bandaged, but her spirits were bright as she wrapped her arms around Ana's neck in a lengthy hug.

"We've missed you," she whispered into Ana's ear.

"I've missed you, too," she whispered back. "Shall I walk you to your mother to say hello?"

Ellen nodded gaily, and after shooting a questioning glance at Eoghan, who nodded his agreement and shooed them off with a wave, they left, Ana slowing her gait to match the little girl's hobbled pace. Like Ellen, Ione greeted her with a smile and a hug. Ana wanted to stay and chat, but then prompted by a small, secret desire unfurling in her stomach, she asked if either of them had any idea as to Sister Mary's whereabouts.

"It's about time for her morning prayers," Ione said. "Have you checked the sanctuary?"

Ana said no, and after delivering a promise to return shortly, she gave Ellen's fingers a squeeze and then set off in search of the nun. As Ione had suggested, she found her in the sanctuary, but rather than wait for her to emerge as she might once have done, she slipped inside and joined her on her knees at the altar.

Sister Mary paused in her prayers to shoot Ana a sidelong glance. One corner of her mouth lifted in a smile, and no wonder. Ana would never have dreamed of assuming such a humble posture a few short weeks ago. Saying nothing, Sister Mary closed her eyes and went back to her devotions.

Calm filled Ana as she folded her hands and looked up at the gleaming crucifix hanging above their heads.

The worst had happened. Her uncle had found her, yet here she was, surrounded by friends and completely at peace. Perhaps Amelia was right. Perhaps he'd changed. Even were he the same man she remembered from her childhood, what harm could he possibly do? She owned nothing of value, possessed no proof of any youthful recollections. She was no threat to him whatsoever, and it was only a matter of time before he saw that.

Bowing her head, Ana did something she had not dared in years.

She breathed a prayer of thanks.

— ❆ ❆ ❆ —

Brion squinted against the driving snow lashing him in the eyes. So, Kilarny was right—Hamilton was living and working at the church. And the woman with him, that was Lucy. He sensed it.

He'd been a trifle surprised to see her walking with Hamilton, though perhaps he shouldn't have been. It certainly explained why The Celt had sought him out. The man was as wily as a fox.

Shrugging deeper into his coat, Brion whirled and strode back up the street the way he'd come. It had taken some careful maneuvering to satisfy Kilarny's questions—who he was working for and what he wanted with Hamilton. Only after much haggling had he managed to pry any information as to where he could locate the man, and he'd had to give up details on his meeting with The Celt just to secure that.

It was all worth it now, however.

He smiled at the thought of how quickly this business with his niece and Hamilton might be over. A day or two. Possibly more, but he doubted it would take that long.

Ach, but it would be good to be home before any real snow hit. He lengthened his strides, suddenly in a hurry to get out of the cold and into the relative warmth of the hovel where he'd set up camp. Despite the chill, he puckered his lips and began to whistle.

Still, he admitted as he rounded a corner and ducked into an alley, it might have been nice to witness for himself the holiday these Americans called Thanksgiving.

It gave him a taste for turkey.

24

Brion slowed as he neared the door of his tenement. The snow around the entrance had been disturbed, and recently, if the lack of buildup inside the footprints was any indication. Had he been followed?

Unlikely.

Flipping up one side of his coat, he withdrew his dagger from the waistband of his trousers and eased to the door. It was ajar, but in this part of town, anyone could have broken in. If they were unlucky enough to still be inside, however . . .

He shoved the door wide with his foot and waited. Nothing.

"Who's there?" he barked.

"Brion McCleod."

Brion flinched and scanned the gloomy corners of the room for the source of the voice. To his left, a figure dislodged from the shadows.

"You Brion McCleod?"

Suspicion narrowed Brion's eyes. The traveler in the gray cap who'd bumped his shoulder? Not that he was remarkable in form or fashion, but given his current situation, Brion was inclined to remember everything down to the smallest detail.

He lowered his voice to a snarl. "Who are you and what do you want with me?"

The man's lips stretched into a half smile. "I've instructions for ya."

"From who?"

His smile widened.

"Fine. What does The Celt want now?"

"What do you think? To remind you that he's in charge and to tell you no more varying from the plan." He then slid something from his pocket and dropped it into Brion's waiting hand.

Brion studied the glittering object, shiny by the light of the rising moon streaming in from the window. "What's this?"

"Proof. He could just as easily be helping her."

Brion curled his fingers around the chain, squeezing until his hand went numb. "Is that a threat?"

The man shrugged. "Take it how you like. Only remember, he's the one giving the orders."

Aye, for now, Brion thought, sliding the watch into his pocket, but all that was going to change. Soon.

As if reading his thoughts, the man snorted and moved for the door, pausing when he reached it to drive a knife and small scrap of paper into the wall. He gave one last backward glance and then ducked outside.

Barely keeping his rage in check, Brion strode to the door and snatched the note from the wall. Scribbled inside was the name of a pub and an address, plus two words: *one hour*.

He balled the paper and tossed it to the floor, then grabbed the knife and stowed it in his pocket. Blast that Celt. What did he want now that couldn't have been said earlier? And who was he to be ordered about like a lackey? If he had the time or inclination, he'd teach the whelp some respect.

Returning to the foul temperatures outside with a growl,

Brion jogged a couple of streets to a more reputable neighborhood and hailed a hack. To his surprise, the driver did not take him to another seedy establishment as he'd expected. Instead he drove some distance and pulled to a halt outside a large tavern frequented by upper-class types and businessmen, if the gentlemen in long coats strolling inside were any indication.

Brion withdrew the fare and tossed it up to the man, who tipped his hat and drove away. Grumbling, Brion stepped inside.

"You McCleod?"

He started at the large Irishman who appeared at his elbow. "I'm him."

"This way."

The bloke spun on his heel and lumbered past the bar, where several patrons balanced on barstools, then down a dim hallway to a narrow door. He rapped once, turned the knob, and stepped back.

Brion stared at the open door and then back at the bloke. "What's going on? What am I doing here?"

The man crossed his arms and nodded at the entrance.

Fine. Squeezing past him, Brion stepped inside a darkened room lit only by a single lamp on a small writing desk, behind which sat the man he'd only had opportunity to meet once in his life.

The Celt.

"I'm here," Brion hissed. "What is it you want from me?"

The Celt seemed to take pleasure in Brion's discomfort. He leaned back in his chair, folded his hands over his belly, and smiled. "Hello to you too, Mr. McCleod. What do you think of the city?"

"I'll be glad to be shed of it, and you haven't answered my question."

243

The Celt rose, circled the polished desk, and gestured toward a couple of chairs situated near the fireplace, where a cheery blaze crackled and snapped. "Why, I'm here checking on your progress, of course. Shall we sit?"

To deny the invitation would only make the situation more awkward. Brion claimed one of the plush leather chairs, The Celt, the other.

Spanning the gap between the arms of his chair, The Celt clasped his hands and studied Brion over the top of his laced fingers. "So? What can you tell me? What have you found?"

"What have you given me?" Brion snapped. "An address only. Any one of the women living there could be my niece."

"Ach, but you're a sharp man. I think you've figured out which one you want. And that, me dear fellow, is why I had you come here today."

"Fine then, get on with it. What is it you want now?"

The Celt's lips spread in a sneer. "Just your patience, McCleod. That's all."

"My patience! What is that supposed to mean?"

Lifting the lapel of his gray suit, The Celt pulled out a sheet of paper, folded in thirds, and laid it on the table between them.

"Did I ever tell you the story of a young lass who came to the parsonage of a friend of mine—a man who happened to be a priest?"

Impatience flared in Brion's gut. He thrust out his chin. "Get on with ya. What does any of that have to do with me?"

The Celt continued studying him, his eyes glittering slits in the glow of the fire. "Have you never wondered how it came to be that I not only knew your niece was alive, but how to locate her? That priest friend came to me for help, confessed, if you will, his suspicions regarding the death of her parents." He paused and lifted an eyebrow. "Both of them."

Brion's heart raced as The Celt leaned forward and pushed the paper across the table at him.

"What's that?"

"Read it."

Brion snatched up the paper and opened it with a flick of his wrist. With each line he read, the tension in his gut grew. Finished, he refolded the paper and slid it back across the table. His hands didn't shake, but it was by sheer force of will that he kept from launching himself at The Celt in black rage.

"So that's how this is going to be?" he snarled, his nails digging into the arms of the chair. "You plan to blackmail me with the scribbled babblings of a senile old priest?"

"Blackmail would imply I intended to keep you at my service. No, this is more like an assurance that you stay to my timetable and not your own."

He cut through the air with his hand. "Assurance? Bah! That letter is no proof." He leaned forward to glare at The Celt eye to eye. "Especially if the priest who signed it wound up dead. Then it would just be your word against mine."

The Celt scratched his chin thoughtfully. "Aye, that's true enough, I suppose, if you were truly willing to risk such a battle."

Brion paused. The threat was real enough. Suddenly he felt as if it were a chess match he played with the Irishman sitting across from him . . . and he despised chess. "What is your timetable, then?" he asked, voice low. "When do I get this business over and done with?"

The Celt gave a nod that was entirely too satisfied and replaced the letter in his pocket. "Hamilton has reached out to the Fenians. We've reached back in exchange for information. It's a tidy arrangement, one I think will benefit us greatly. When we're through with him, I will let you know."

Brion's mind whirled. What could the Fenians—and The Celt—glean from Hamilton? Or from him? He startled as the thought struck him. Obviously he was of some use or they wouldn't be having this meeting. *What does the man want?*

He narrowed his eyes. "That letter, my brother's pocket watch, even my niece's word—they're nothing in a court of law. No jury would convict me based solely on those. If, however, I were to continue with this plan, do what you ask and kill both Hamilton and my niece, then you would have something, wouldn't you? I'd not be able to back out then."

Cold, dark fury stole across The Celt's features. "Careful, lad. You'll not be wanting to cross me now."

"I'll certainly not be able to later."

"You're a fool if you think it's not already too late."

Anger roiled in Brion's belly. "You could have gotten anyone to carry out this business for you, and yet you chose me. Why? There has to be a reason, so how about we do away with the games and come right out with what it is you really want?"

"Which is?"

"You tell me."

The Celt leaned back in his chair, at ease it seemed, despite the dire circumstances. "Well, well . . . I'm surprised it took you this long." He slid open a desk drawer and removed a worn satchel, cracked and stained.

"What is that?"

A grin curved The Celt's lips. "Letters. Your letters. To her. Very incriminating, some of them."

Brion didn't bother to ask if they were real. They were. "How did you get them?"

"I have them. That's all that matters."

Perhaps he'd been wrong to overlook the man. Up until now, he'd viewed him only as one might a roe deer—as prey.

Now he knew. He'd been looking at it wrong. *He* was the deer; The Celt was the hunter.

"Good," The Celt said, as though reading his thoughts. "We understand each other. Now I think it's only fair that I tell you what it is I'm after."

Helpless to do more, Brion clenched the arms of his chair. "And that is?"

"Your land, your wealth, they've made you somewhat important, aye? But I can make you truly powerful. Isn't that what you want? All I ask for in return is your vote. Your influence with the people of Derry. Your unmitigated support when it comes time for filling the chair vacated by Daniel Turner and his temporary successor."

So that was it? He wanted a place in parliament? Disbelief crowded Brion's mind. Why? What did he and the Fenians have planned?

"Until then," The Celt continued, "your instructions are to sit back and wait for my orders. Are we clear?"

"Aye, we're clear," Brion said, wiping his face of expression as he rose.

It took two to play chess. He'd wait, but not idly. He'd use the time to find out what he could about Hamilton, and thereby discover exactly what it was The Celt hoped to gain from him. Then he'd use that information to turn the tables.

"I take it we're finished?" he asked calmly.

The Celt nodded. "Aye, we're finished."

"Good. You know where to find me." Whirling, he strode for the door, pausing when he reached it to remove from his pocket the knife he'd pulled from his wall. "Oh, and I think this belongs to you."

Flicking the handle so that he gripped the knife by its blade, he drew back his arm and threw it squarely in the direction of The Celt. It stuck, quivering, in the table next to the man's elbow.

Check.

With a grin, Brion jerked open the door and walked out. It was the first time he'd seen the man jump. It felt good to have the upper hand, even if it was just for a moment.

25

Ana rose before dawn and dressed quickly, anxious to return to her job at the candle shop and a semblance of normalcy. After fastening the small pearl buttons on her collar and cuffs, she crossed to the vanity, surprised to feel no sorrow, no remorse, for the first time in many years.

"Thank you, God."

Her eyes snapped to her reflection. She'd said the words aloud . . . without thinking. But she meant them. She repeated the line slowly, staring into her own eyes. When she finished, she lowered her hands to her sides in amazement.

Somewhere in *there*, that lass had changed—accepted her past—made a conscious decision to proceed with her future, uncle or no.

She drew a deep breath and moved from the mirror. Her shoulders felt light, her steps lighter. She skipped down the stairs, grabbed her wool cloak from the hooks in the hall, and slid into it without giving a thought to breakfast. Outside, the snow had ceased to fall, but much of it remained banked along the sidewalks. Hitching her skirts high, she strolled down Ashberry Street toward Mr. O'Bannon's shop.

"Ana, wait!"

Her heart leaped in her chest as Eoghan's familiar voice rang across the morning air. She turned and saw him striding toward her, his cheeks flushed from running, and a lock of unruly hair falling gently over one brow.

"You weren't at the boardinghouse," he panted.

A smile she was helpless to repress rose to her mouth. "That's because I decided it was time for me to get back to work. It's been nigh unto a week, and business this time of year is fierce with Thanksgiving only a week away. Mr. O'Bannon needs me."

Bracing his hands on his hips, he drew back his head and frowned. "You seem different. Is everything all right?"

His eyes gleamed quizzically, and why not? She'd only discovered the change in herself this morning.

"Everything is . . ." She paused, thinking. The sky was still gray, the street crowded and dirty, yet nothing was the same. Her lips parted in a slow smile. "Everything is as it was, but you are right. I am different. Thanks to God." She added the last as an afterthought, then nodded at the appropriateness of the statement. "Aye, that's it."

She waited to see how he would react, surprised when he said nothing, but turned with her to continue toward the candle shop.

She laid her hand on his arm. "Eoghan, you didn't tell me what you were doing at the boardinghouse this morning."

"I went to meet you. I knew you'd reached the point where you wouldn't be content to stay buried in the boardinghouse much longer."

She chewed her lip, pondering the confidence with which he'd voiced his knowledge of her thoughts. Not thoughts, she amended. It was deeper than that. He knew *her*.

Her smile broadened as they strolled past a row of hedges dusted with snow. Never had she considered what it might feel like to have another person with whom to share her innermost hopes and fears. It was . . . safe.

Aye, Eoghan made her feel safe, and not because of his size or the catlike grace with which he'd moved to defend her when the man from the Fenians appeared so suddenly. It was because she knew he truly cared for her.

"I'll be coming by the candle shop to walk you home. What time should I collect you?"

She blushed at the direction her thoughts had taken her, barely able to risk shooting him a peek for the warmth blazing in her cheeks. "You don't have to. The weather is fine and—"

He caught her hand and gave it a squeeze. "You know it's not the weather that concerns me. I'm going to see to it that you're safe, and if that means walking you back and forth from the shop, so be it."

She gulped and managed a shaky "All right."

Ach, but what he could do to her senses with just a touch or a glance, she thought as he slanted his hazel eyes in her direction. He pulled her to a stop, and she held her breath.

"Ana?"

She swallowed, wishing her mouth weren't suddenly so dry. "Aye?"

"We're here."

"What?"

He angled his head toward the familiar red door. "The shop. Mr. O'Bannon?"

"Oh . . . of course. Thank you," she said, reaching for the knob.

He grabbed hold of her hand. "You didn't tell me what time to be back."

She blinked. "Five. I leave off at five."

He lowered his head until she felt the warmth of his breath

against her cheek. "I'll be here. Promise you will not leave without me?"

Unable to speak, she nodded.

"Good. I will see you at five, then."

He gave a merry wink and went on his way, leaving Ana to ponder throughout the day the strange feelings her walk with him had stirred. As five o'clock approached, she found she'd been watching the time, and when at last the minute hand struck the hour, her eyes shifted to the door. True to his word, he breezed through at exactly that moment, a smile on his face and a twinkle in his eye.

"I have a surprise for you," he whispered as he helped her into her cloak.

"For me?"

He nodded and then tipped his hat in greeting to Mr. O'Bannon, who watched them with a cheerful grin.

"Good night, then," the old chandler called, shooing them off with a wave of his apron. "Go on with you. I wouldn't want you to keep your young man waiting."

Ana debated a moment, then crossed to him and pressed a kiss to the old man's wrinkled cheek. Like the candles, he smelled of honey and beeswax. "Good night, Mr. O'Bannon. 'Twas good to be back here at the shop."

He gave her hand a pat. "'Twas good to have you back. This old shop was lonely without your cheerful company. And, Ana?"

She lifted an eyebrow.

He dipped his head to whisper in her ear. "'Twas good to see your smile back, as well."

Her heart melted at the look of genuine affection in his kind gray eyes. She squeezed his fingers, then went to join Eoghan at the door.

"Ready?"

"Ready," she said. This time when he took her arm, she wasn't surprised or even embarrassed. She snuggled closer to his side and let him lead the way.

The stars overhead sparkled like gems once they left the streetlamps of Ashberry Street behind. Only once did Ana catch herself checking the shadows for signs of a forbidding figure. She quickly tore her gaze away and concentrated on the handsome escort by her side.

"Where are we going?" she asked when she could resist the temptation no longer.

"You'll see. Almost there." He nodded toward a circle of trees, limbs dark against the night sky.

"The park?"

He gave her a broad smile that made her heart do flip-flops. Once they reached the trees, excited chatter filled the air and Ana realized that quite a large group already occupied the area. One of them straightened and shot a hand into the air.

"Eoghan! Ana! Over here."

Ana squinted for a better look. "Is that Tillie?"

"And Meg. And the people from the church. Even Father Ed, if I'm not mistaken."

His pace quickened as he led her to a large campfire, where most of the residents from the shelter had gathered to warm their hands.

"'Bout time the two of you showed up," Sister Agnes scolded, though her lips curved in a merry smile. She pressed a mug of hot cider into Ana's hands and then filled a second cup for Eoghan. "Better drink up. The skating is about to start."

"Skating?"

Ana shot Eoghan a look. He couldn't have looked more pleased with himself. Even without the glow of the fire or the few scattered streetlamps, his face would have lit the nearby pond.

She smiled back and elbowed him in the ribs. "You knew about this?"

"I did."

"And you didn't tell me?"

"I thought you'd enjoy the surprise. Besides," he said, lowering his head to her ear, "you've been entirely too serious of late. I thought you could use the distraction."

Ana shook her head helplessly. "But I don't skate."

"Well then, I'll have to teach you." He lifted his mug and saluted her with it before taking a swallow.

Even with the butterflies chasing around in her stomach, Ana managed a sip, the warm cinnamon brew slipping over her tongue in the most delicious, savory manner. A second later, Meg danced over to her and added a molasses cookie to the treat in her hand.

"Glad you could come, Ana," she said, then winked before skipping off to deliver more cookies.

"Meg knew about the surprise, didn't she?" Ana asked, narrowing her eyes at Eoghan.

He merely laughed and drained the contents of his mug before plunking it down on a bench and confiscating hers.

"Enough dawdling. Come with me."

"But my cookie." Ana nibbled a corner of the molasses cookie and smiled. "I haven't finished it yet."

Not to be dissuaded, he leaned over and snatched the cookie with his teeth.

"That was mine!" Ana said, though in truth, having his mouth graze her fingers had nearly robbed her of breath.

"I'll fetch you another. Later," he said, still chewing.

Giving her hand a tug, he led her to the pond, where several large logs had been rolled along the bank for seating.

Tillie and Sister Mary were busily handing out skates, but the moment they approached, the two women looked up and waved them over.

"I take it these will do?" Tillie asked. She held up two pairs for Eoghan's inspection.

"Tillie, you too?" Ana propped both hands on her hips, but her feigned anger didn't affect the lass in the least. She giggled and pointed innocently at Eoghan.

"His idea."

Ana snatched the smaller of the two pairs of clamp-on skates and then looked at Eoghan. "Don't say I didn't warn you when your backside hurts from falling on it."

Moving to an empty spot on one of the logs, she plopped down to examine the skates. Tricky as it was to lace up her boots, it proved easier than clamping on the skates. Eoghan had finished with his and knelt to help before she'd finished with her first skate.

Ana flashed a glance in the direction of the nuns. Behind them, Father Ed's tall frame was outlined by the fire. She grabbed for the hem of her dress and clutched it tight against her calves, blushing as the heat from Eoghan's fingers traveled across the bridge of her foot. She leaned forward to whisper, "A lady never shows her ankles in public."

Eoghan glanced at her, then at her foot, then back at her. "Really? What if it's inside your boot? It's not really seen then, is it?"

"That is not the point and you know it," she snapped. "Now, let go of my foot before someone notices."

Her discomfort merely added to his mirth. He released her, but only after an exaggerated sigh that all but rustled the branches over their heads. Standing, he turned his back to her and crossed his arms, his fingers thrumming the tweed fabric of his overcoat.

"Well?" he drawled after a moment. "Can I look now?"

Ana snugged the clamp on the sides of the skates and frowned. Now that she had them attached . . . what? Attempting to stand on her own would likely reveal far more than her ankle. She smoothed her skirt over her knees and sighed. "All right, you can look."

He smiled and reached out his hands to her. "Ready?"

With his skates already on, he was taller than ever. Ana sucked in a breath and placed her shaking fingers in his. "You'll not let me fall?"

His clasp on her tightened and the smile fled his lips. "Never."

Her knees weakened at the intensity of his gaze. Any trembling she could blame on the skating, she thought as she struggled to her feet. Except for a slight tilt of her right ankle, she felt quite stable and glanced at Eoghan in surprise. "Oh . . . I can do this."

"Just wait," he said, smiling. "We aren't on the ice yet."

Indeed, stepping off the bank onto the frozen pond proved far more difficult than simply standing on the narrow blades. Ana clutched Eoghan's arm all the tighter, afraid that if she let go or relaxed her stance even an inch, her legs would fly in opposite directions.

"Eoghan, wait!" she said just as he took one long stride that sent them gliding away from the bank. Behind them, a cheer rose from the onlookers.

His arm slipped lower around her waist, and he pulled her tight to his side. "Just lean against me, Ana. I won't let go."

If the feel of his strong arms was any indication, she could most likely lift her feet and not touch the pond at all and he'd still glide as effortlessly as he did now. A bit of the tension drained from her shoulders.

Round and round they went, joined by most of the children

from the shelter, and a few of the women. Even Sister Agnes glided by, making Ana stare openmouthed at the grace with which she moved. After a bit, she even dared to imitate the side-to-side strokes she saw her take.

"Good, Ana," Eoghan said, beaming down at her.

Her heart thumped. "'Twould be a different tale indeed if I didn't have you to lean against," she admitted, but he only smiled and slackened his hold.

"Eoghan . . ."

"You can do it, Ana."

"No, I—"

A second later, she was gliding along, the wind tugging at her hair, her hands grasping for an arm she could no longer see. Stopping was impossible, and the bank was approaching faster than she found comfortable. She flailed her arms, but only for a second and then Eoghan was at her side again, laughing as he caught her to his chest and brought them whirling to a stop.

"You . . . you said you wouldn't let go," she accused, breathless.

"And you said you couldn't do it, yet you did fine until you lost your confidence and started flailing like a bird."

"Aye, and what a sight that must have been." Suddenly picturing it made her laugh. "I bet I looked like one of Sister Agnes's chickens."

"Much prettier than a chicken." His eyes gleamed and he lifted the edge of her gray cloak. "More like a pigeon."

She gave an unladylike snort and slapped his shoulder, realizing too late that neither of them was prepared for the sudden motion. Her feet slipped out from beneath her. A look of surprise flashed across Eoghan's face, followed by determination as he grabbed her and swung her around so that he lay beneath her when they both crashed to the ice.

Her landing was much softer than his. Eoghan gave an "oomph," as if all the air had rushed from his lungs, but still he held her cradled on top of him. Brushing a lock of hair from her eyes, Ana scrambled to her knees.

"I'm so sorry! Eoghan, are you all right?" She ripped off her mitten and laid her palm to his cheek. "Did I hurt you?"

He was looking at her in a way that truly concerned her. His hazel eyes were slightly narrowed, almost dazed.

"Eoghan?"

"Aye," he whispered. "You hurt me."

Her stomach plummeted. She scanned the length of him for sign of a broken bone. "Where?"

Her hands fluttered uselessly for a moment, and then he grabbed her unmittened hand and held it to his chest. "Here. I wasn't ready to let go of you yet."

Heat raged across her face as his meaning became clear. "Eoghan Hamilton!"

For all her embarrassment, she was helpless to tear her gaze away. He sat up, bringing her slowly with him as he stood. "Are you all right?"

"I'm fine except . . . you're making it hard to breathe," she admitted, shocking herself.

And for him, or so it seemed. His eyes gleamed and dropped to her mouth. "You are so beautiful," he whispered, in a ragged voice that raised goose bumps on her flesh. "I could kiss you now except . . ."

"You'd shock the sisters and Father Ed," she whispered back.

"Aye, likely I would."

They fell silent, the air from their lungs mingling in a smoky cloud Ana had never found so intoxicating.

"You should let me go," she managed at last, though in truth she longed for him to go on holding her in exactly the same way.

To her disappointment, his hold loosened and he nudged himself away. The thrill returned full force, however, when he leaned forward to whisper, "I believe it's too late for that, Ana. I can't let go of you now . . . or ever."

She hadn't fully absorbed the thought before he reached down, grabbed her mitten, and held it up for her to put on. She slid her hand in, too timid to look at him for the thumping of her heart. Only when he'd taken both her hands and pulled her to the shore did she realize their brief encounter had gone entirely unnoticed by those gathered on the bank.

She stepped off the ice, glad to once again have solid footing beneath her, or somewhat solid. With Eoghan's words dancing through her head, she doubted anything would ever feel quite the same to her again.

More wondrous still, she doubted she'd ever want to.

26

The week leading up to Thanksgiving flew by, with the anxiety Ana had felt regarding her uncle only a distant memory. Perhaps it had been her imagination that made her think she'd seen him, prompted by the discovery of Eoghan's attempt to locate him.

Eoghan.

Her heart thrilled at the thought of him. He would be joining them for Thanksgiving dinner, along with Cara and Rourke.

Laying aside her comb, Ana felt a momentary tinge of sorrow. Cara had yet to tell her brother about the babe she was carrying, but when asked why, she would sadden and say it wasn't yet time.

Time for what? Hadn't the two of them put their differences behind them? Hadn't Eoghan gone several times to visit Cara in her home? He'd even started calling her husband "Rourke" and only occasionally referred to him by his surname.

Fully dressed, Ana left her chamber and went downstairs to help with the decorations. A fine scent met her nose once she reached the parlor. Amelia favored the holidays, Thanksgiving especially, and went to great lengths to see a fine feast prepared and the boardinghouse decorated. As anticipated, when Ana entered the dining room, a variety of gourds, Indian corn, and bundles of wheat lay scattered across the table.

"Ana, just in time," Amelia said, holding up a wreath fashioned of twisted stalks of wheat. "What do you think?"

She fingered the feathered edges. "It's beautiful, like a golden crown."

Amelia's smile widened at her praise. "It's for the front door. Will you hang it?"

"Of course." Ana took it from her and pointed to a fat pumpkin. "What about that?"

"The steps. But it's quite heavy, dear."

Ana smiled. A perfect job for Eoghan when he arrived. "I'll take care of this and come back for the pumpkin later."

"Before you go . . ." Amelia held up a sprig of dried berries she had dusted with glitter to look like ice. "For your hair. Turn around."

Ana had pulled her long dark hair into a neat braid, twisted into a bun at the nape of her neck, with ringlets that framed her face. Amelia inserted the sprig into the top of the bun, then gave her head a pat.

"Beautiful, and so perfect with that ginger-colored dress. You are quite stunning, my dear."

Blushing, Ana smoothed her hands over the crushed velvet of her skirt. The underskirt was a striped accent of matching color. The material had been an extravagant purchase, to be sure, but the color flattered her hair and skin, and she hadn't been able to resist the thought of Eoghan seeing her in it.

"Do you think so? I wasn't sure when I bought it," she said shyly.

Amelia circled to press her palms to Ana's warm cheeks. "It's divine. Guaranteed to catch a man's eye, although I think there's only one man whose eyes you hope to catch. Am I right?" She chuckled and pressed a kiss to Ana's forehead. "I've seen the way he looks at you, new dress or no. I'm happy for you both, dear."

"Eoghan has not . . . There is no arrangement between us," Ana felt compelled to admit. She hugged the wreath close to hide the trembling of her fingers. "His kindness is likely just out of concern for me because of my uncle."

Amelia grabbed a carved wooden bowl and began filling it with a variety of gourds. "Posh. I know lovesick when I see it, and that man is as smitten as they come." She waved a yellow squash in Ana's direction. "And if I'm not mistaken, the same can be said for you, young lady."

Rather than wage an argument she had no desire to win, Ana fled with her wreath to the front door. A knock sounded as she approached, and her smile only widened when she opened it to find the subject of their conversation lounging on the other side.

Her hand fell from the knob and she tipped her head in greeting. "Hello, Mr. Hamilton. You're early—dinner's not for another couple of hours."

She'd hoped to surprise him with her appearance, but his reaction far surpassed her expectations. He stared quietly a moment, then brought his hand to his waist and gave a slight bow.

The bow alone was enough to flatter, but after which he blew out a long breath. "Ana, you . . ."

Heat rose from her neck to the top of her head. She handed him the wreath, then turned slightly, giving him the full effect of her dress and the berries that Amelia had tucked into her hair. Except for them, she wore no other adornment.

"Do you like it?" Her voice emerged an airy squeak.

"It's . . . you . . ." He smiled and bent toward her, his lips brushing her cheek. "Now you're making it hard for *me* to breathe."

Never in her life had she so wanted to swoon as in that moment. She caught her lip in her teeth, then reached for the wreath. "Give me that before you crush it to bits," she said, though a trifle too breathlessly to appear harsh.

His low chuckle nearly undid what little reserve she had left. Instead of letting go of the wreath, he stood behind her and helped her lift it onto a hook fashioned for that purpose, then pulled her back against him and wrapped his arms around her middle while they admired their handiwork.

"Nice."

"Amelia made it."

He laughed and pressed his lips to her hair. "I was talking about you."

Flushing deeper, Ana smacked his hands and pulled away. "Enough of that. Amelia has plenty of chores for us to do before the guests arrive." She waved him in and closed the door. "You'll regret coming by so early before long."

Eoghan shook his head. "Actually not. You'll be surprised to learn that I promised Giles I'd help him get the boarding-house ready nearly a week ago. Is he here? And what is that heavenly aroma?"

Ana laughed. "That aroma is dinner, and Giles is in the kitchen with Laverne. She's had him running errands since before dawn."

He gave her an exaggerated frown. "Maybe I should see what Amelia needs."

Ana laughed and grabbed his arm. "This way."

Before long, Amelia had them both sorting leaves to sprinkle across the table in a random pattern. Candles glowed down the center, and the boardinghouse's best china and crystal waited on the sideboard. They were Amelia's own set, brought with her from England and passed down from her mother. Ana took extra care polishing each piece before placing it on the table in front of each chair.

Laverne emerged from the kitchen, muttering, "That Giles, always underfoot, he is. 'Tis a wonder I get any work done at all."

Ana set the last knife down alongside the last plate. "Now what's he done?"

"Nibbling at my corn-bread dressing, he was. Had to slap his hands and send him out the back door." She untied her apron and slung it over the arm of one of the chairs. "Good thing I made plenty."

"You always do," Ana said, rounding the table to give her a hug.

When she pulled away, Laverne stuck both hands on her hips and eyed Ana from top to bottom. "Well, just look at you. Aren't you a sight for the likes of us. Never seen you look prettier."

"It's the dress," Ana said, cheeks flaming. "It's new. I made it with some fabric I purchased from Mr. Southby last week."

Someone pounded the knocker on the front door, but Laverne ignored it and shook her head. "The dress is fine, to be sure, but I think it's more the gleam in your eyes what has you looking so lovely today." She dipped her head and winked conspiratorially.

"I'll get the door," Eoghan called out, poking his head into the dining room before heading down the hall.

"And that," Laverne said, motioning to the hall where Eoghan had disappeared, "is the reason for the gleam."

Exasperated by all the teasing, Ana threw her hands into the air and whirled for the kitchen. "Our guests have arrived. What say we get started putting supper on the table?"

"Not you," Laverne said, catching her by the shoulders. "I

won't have you sullying that dress. My gravy is good, but it won't go with ginger. You go sit with your young man. Giles and I can get dinner 'round."

Giles appeared at that moment, his cheeks ruddy and his gray hair wild from the wind outside. "What? What are we doing?"

"Come with me," Laverne said, then grabbed his arm. "You're in charge of carving the turkey. Wash your hands first. I won't have you flavoring my cooking with sawdust from that firewood you was chopping."

Ana couldn't help but smile as they went on their way, muttering to each other. Laverne could be accused of having a gleam in her own eye, and Ana could just as easily guess who put it there.

She left the dining room and followed the trail of voices to the parlor, where Amelia was serving from a bowl of spiced apple cider. Cara was there, and she'd been joined by Tillie and Meg, but Rourke was absent, and so was Eoghan.

"Oh, Ana." Cara set her cup down and crossed to grasp her hands. "You look lovely."

"So do you," Ana said, admiring the deep forest green of Cara's dress against her auburn hair. She leaned forward and whispered, "And might I add, you have a most becoming glow about you?"

Cara's hand went to her midsection. Her giggle melted into a sigh. "It won't be long before the reason is evident to everyone."

"You'll tell Eoghan before then?" Tillie asked quietly.

She nodded. "Aye. It wouldn't be fair to him otherwise."

"And speaking of Eoghan," Amelia said, bearing a cup of cider over to deposit with Ana, "where have he and Rourke disappeared to?"

Cara glanced at Ana in a disconcerting way that left her

with a peculiar feeling in her stomach. "They went to the library. He and Rourke have something they need to discuss."

Ana's grip tightened on her cup. Though it wasn't said, she sensed the topic Eoghan and Rourke were discussing had something to do with her.

— ※ ※ ※ —

"Tell me again what you know about Ana's parents," Rourke said. He was seated behind the large desk, his jacket removed and slung over the back of his chair and a folder open in front of him. At his elbow, a jeweled lamp cast rosy light on a stack of papers he'd pulled from the folder.

Eoghan paced the length of the library from the window to the door. He didn't like being beholden to anyone—a Turner, especially—but he couldn't deny that Rourke was going out of his way to find out what he could about Ana's family, which was more than he could say for Kilarny.

He frowned. Despite their deal, the man had yet to deliver anything of interest.

"What little I know is what she's told me," he began, pausing at the window to stare out at the falling snow. "Her father was killed in a farming accident, and her mother and sister died a year later, the night of the fire."

Rourke pulled a second stack of papers from a leather case on the floor at his feet. "And it is your understanding that Brion McCleod is Ana's only living relative?"

Eoghan gave a puzzled shrug and paced back across the rug to the desk. "Aye, but what—?"

Rourke motioned him closer. "Take a look at these."

Taking the papers from his hand, Eoghan scanned them slowly, then looked up with a frown. "What are these?"

"Information I dug up at the office where I work. It's called the Guardianship of Infants Act."

"Which is?"

Rourke sat at the desk and gestured for Eoghan to do the same. "You said Ana believes McCleod may have murdered her mother and used the fire to cover his crime."

Eoghan nodded and slid into the chair next to Rourke. Obviously the man was leading somewhere, but so far he couldn't see where.

Rourke picked up a quill and used the tip to scratch his head. "That didn't make sense to me. There was no need for McCleod to commit murder since, according to Irish law, the land and even the children should have become his after his brother died. So I did some searching and came up with that." He pointed at the paper still clutched in Eoghan's hand.

"They were half brothers," Eoghan said, suddenly remembering something else Ana had told him.

"Half brothers," Rourke repeated slowly.

Eoghan eyed him quizzically. "That means something?"

He straightened and shook his head. "Not for Ana, but maybe in the overall scheme . . ." He looked Eoghan directly in the eyes. "This is conjecture only. I have no proof of wrongdoing on McCleod's part, or any other."

He tensed. "Go on."

Rourke took the paper from Eoghan and pointed at something he'd underlined. "See here? Before 1886, any children born in a marriage became the legal property of the husband and father. If he died, the children went to the closest male guardian. In this case, that would have been McCleod."

He raised a brow. "And after 1886?"

"The Guardianship of Infants Act. It allowed women to become the guardians of their own children, but only if her husband died."

"Which explains why Ana's mother was raising her daughters on her own."

Rourke nodded. "McCleod couldn't get his hands on them."

Sensing there was more, he leaned forward across the desk. "And the land?"

Rourke removed a second sheet of paper and passed it across to him. "The Married Woman's Property Act. Ana's mother was legally able to keep any money she earned on her own, which meant the farm and any land she bought and paid for all belonged to her, not her husband."

"What if they bought the land together?"

"Already checked. Ana's mother came with a sizable dowry when she married, but according to the records, most of that was put away for Ana and her sister. The land was paid for after Shamus McCleod's death with funds Adele earned while they were married."

"So if McCleod were only to become aware of this after his brother died . . ." Eoghan sucked in a breath.

"It could have been an unpleasant surprise for someone thinking to inherit."

Eoghan left his chair, his thoughts whirling. "McCleod killed his half brother, thinking no one could stop him from legally claiming his land."

"Conjecture only," Rourke cautioned, raising one hand.

Eoghan paused and stared his brother-in-law in the eyes. "But you believe it?"

He said nothing, but his jaw clenched and he did not look away.

Gratitude for his help and a sort of grudging admiration wormed into Eoghan's heart. He still didn't like the man, and wasn't totally convinced he could trust him, but he was forced to admit to the possibility he'd been wrong about him.

Turning his back to the fireplace, he leaned against the mantel and crossed his arms. "You've done a lot of digging.

More than I expected." He swallowed and ground the words out, "Thank you."

Rourke dismissed his thanks with a curt shake of his head. "There's still much we don't know. I've asked my uncle to locate the priest we think helped Ana escape to America. Maybe he can fill in some of the missing details. I'll let you know when I hear."

Eoghan nodded, then cleared his throat as Rourke stood and scooped up the paper work and prepared to stash it inside the leather case.

"Can I ask you something?"

Pausing, Rourke looked at him and then sank back into the chair. With a wave, he motioned for him to continue.

"I have no misconceptions about why you're helping Ana. She and Cara are friends. It has nothing to do with me. What I don't understand, what I just can't get my mind around, is why you're still here, in New York." Eoghan left the fireplace and moved back to the desk, his eyes sharp as he watched Rourke for his answer. "Why didn't you just go back to Ireland when you had the chance? Was it Cara?"

Rourke's brows lowered in a glower Eoghan had seen only once before—on his father's face. "Still can't trust a Turner, eh?"

"Still don't know if I can."

"Fair enough." He paused, took a deep breath. "My father loved Ireland. He had faith in her people and wanted to see her free as much as any man. He just . . . *we* just had different beliefs about how to accomplish that. But he was a good man, and he devoted his life to helping others. When I thought you'd killed him"—he looked up, his sharp blue eyes making Eoghan's fingers itch for his knife—"I wanted nothing more than to see you brought to justice."

"And now?" Eoghan asked.

"It took me a long time to realize I'd been wrong." He gave a shake of his head and sighed.

"That's it? After two years of searching, you just accepted that your father's death was an accident and moved on?"

"It was no accident," Rourke said. "I still believe someone besides Sean Healy was behind my father's death. I just . . . my family and I stole a lot from you in our quest for vengeance. From Cara. I owed it to her to try and find you."

"So you stayed in New York."

"Aye."

Eoghan narrowed his eyes. "Will you go back to Ireland now? Resume the search for information regarding your father's death?" His heart pounded against his ribs. He'd promised Kilarny he'd get the information, but was surprised to realize he wasn't only asking because the Fenians wanted to know. *He* wanted to know. He clenched his fists and waited.

Uncertainty flashed across Rourke's face and then he shrugged. "For now, I'll do what I can from here. In the future, who knows? I won't rule it out, but unless God calls me back, my home is here, with Cara and . . ."

You.

He didn't say it, but Eoghan felt his meaning as clearly as if he'd spoken, as if he'd finished the thought. Unable to bring himself to fully accept the possibility that he'd been dead wrong about Rourke, or that maybe the man was speaking the truth, he simply dipped his head in acknowledgment.

Rourke gave a slow nod. "One last thing. If we're right about McCleod, there can only be one reason why he's here, and that's to find Ana. I think it would be best if you kept a close eye on her for a while, maybe make arrangements to see her safely to and from work."

"Already thought of that. I'll speak to Father Ed in the morning."

"Good. If you need help, let me know. I'll send one of the hired men around, to make sure she's not alone."

"Thanks."

"Of course. And, Eoghan, have a care for yourself. No sense taking chances, aye?"

Eoghan nodded. His throat tight, he turned and strode for the library door. Rather than figure out where he stood with his new brother-in-law, he'd focus on protecting Ana.

Starting today.

27

The hammer in Eoghan's hand felt unusually heavy, the motion of swinging it unwieldy. Still, he attacked the woodbox he was repairing with a vengeance.

For several days, ever since he and Rourke spoke, he'd been unable to get his warning out of his head.

"I think it would be best if you kept a close eye on Ana for a while."

But how to accomplish that without frightening her half to death?

He cursed a knot in the wood that made securing a nail to it nearly impossible. Seeing Ana to and from the candle shop where she worked wasn't enough. He wanted her by his side every minute.

Muttering in frustration, he lifted the hammer and drove it down with a resounding bang.

"Easy, lad. You'll likely take off a finger swinging like that."

Kilarny leaned in the open barn door, his crooked grin setting Eoghan's already raw nerves on edge.

Giving Kilarny his back, Eoghan set the hammer down and wiped his hands on a towel draped over his waistband. "What are you doing here, Kil?"

"Looking for you. Haven't seen you around for a while. Figured something happened to ya."

Turning, Eoghan drew the towel over the sweat on his face. Kilarny watched him, a speculative gleam in his eyes.

"And why would you figure that?" he asked, voice low.

Kilarny shrugged and shoved off of the door. "If you aren't too busy"—he sneered and pointed at the woodbox—"I have a matter I'd like to discuss with ya."

Eoghan slung the towel over a bench and followed him through the door, grabbing his coat on the way out. "Where are we going?" he asked, mindful of the time he had left before he needed to meet Ana at the chandler's.

"Just walk," Kilarny said, peering over his shoulder as they left the churchyard and swung onto the sidewalk.

Eoghan fell silent as he buttoned his coat. The day had grown cold, the sky overhead gray and overcast. As they walked, he kicked at the piles of snow along the street. Finally, when he could stand the silence no longer, he looked sidelong at his friend. "What's going on, Kil?"

"I could ask you the same question." With his thumb, Kilarny pushed back the tweed cap on his head. "Exactly what kind of mess have you gotten yourself into now, Eoghan, me boy?"

"What do you mean?"

Kilarny grabbed his arm and swung him down a narrow alley. At the end he withdrew a long key and jabbed it into a door with a rusted lock. Inside, the only light filtered through a frost-covered window high on the wall.

Eoghan scanned the place. Except for a rat or two, they were alone. "Where are we?" he asked, resisting the urge to whisper.

Kilarny poked his head through several doorways leading off the main room where they stood. Satisfied, he circled back to the entrance and Eoghan. "Somewhere we can talk."

273

"We couldn't do that at the church, or even the pub?"

He shrugged. "Too many ears for my liking."

Eoghan hunched his shoulders. This conversation reeked of danger and he didn't relish it, not with Ana already in so much trouble. "All right. So let's talk."

"Why haven't you been by the pub? The more Fenians who see you about, the better your chances of winning their trust, which is why I suggested we meet there in the first place."

"I haven't been by because I had nothing to tell." He jammed his hands into the pockets of his trousers, his conversation with Rourke fresh on his mind.

"Nothing? Are you sure? Not even that you and your long-lost sister are back to being friends?"

Anger pricked him, raised the hair on his skin. "How did you know that?"

"It's my business to know."

By sheer force of will, he managed to keep his voice even. "So, spying on me is your business now, is it? When did that happen?"

Kilarny launched himself across the vacant room, his face flushed beneath the cap. "Listen here, Hammy, did we or did we not have a bargain? I get you the information you want, and you fill me in on anything there is to know about Daniel Turner's death."

Eoghan thrust out his chin. "So?"

"So you've had plenty of time to ask questions. I'm beginning to think you ain't telling me everything."

"And you haven't given me anything from back home, so I guess we're even."

Kilarny's eyes narrowed, and then he blew out a breath and stepped away. "All right, then. You have a point." His jaw worked a moment, as though he were mulling an idea like a piece of wheat. Finally he looked up and sniffed. "How 'bout we strike a new bargain?"

Eoghan pulled his hands from his pockets and crossed his arms. Even when they were lads, he'd always been a tad suspicious of Kil and his wily ways. "Like what?"

Kilarny paced the room, his boots raising dusty clouds on the weathered floor. He stopped in the patch of light coming through the lone window. "You tell me what you know about McCleod, and I'll tell you . . ." He paused, like an actor with an audience, Eoghan thought with a scowl. "I'll tell you who it is that's looking for information on the Turners."

Eoghan's breath caught in his chest. "The Fenians, who else?"

"You sure about that?"

"What do you mean, Kil?"

He ducked his head, his eyes glittering and cold beneath the brim of his cap. "Do we have a deal?"

Indecision tore at his gut. He wouldn't risk putting Ana in further danger, but the way Kilarny spoke . . .

He gave a curt nod and then swept his hand toward Kilarny's chest. "You first."

A wry grin curled his lips. "Don't trust me?"

"Never."

At that, he chuckled outright. "Always said you was as smart as they come."

"Fine. Out with it," Eoghan said with a snort. "What do you know?"

"Someone's pushing, Hammy. Hard. They want to know if Rourke Turner has any intention of filling the parliament seat vacated by his father."

"That was two years ago," Eoghan retorted, his anger rising. "The seat's been filled."

"Not permanently," Kilarny said. "Not if another Turner

were to claim it for his own. A move like that could change the tide for the Fenians and home rule."

"So it is the Fenians who are asking about the Turners."

He shook his head. "Not the Fenians. One Fenian." He licked his lips, only this time it wasn't for effect. "The Celt."

Eoghan scratched his temple. "Are you telling me The Celt is acting alone in this? That he's digging for information outside of the organization's wishes?"

Straightening his shoulders, Kilarny nodded. "Your turn. What do you know about McCleod?"

Suspicion gathered in the back of Eoghan's mind. He smiled. "I'm starting to think you may know far more about McCleod than I do."

The gleam in his friend's eye only added to the idea. Eoghan shook his head and then proceeded to fill Kilarny in on everything he knew about Brion McCleod.

— ❈ ❈ ❈ —

Ana glanced at the clock on the wall above Mr. O'Bannon's desk. Five minutes past the hour.

Outside the large window on the back wall of his office, the sky was overcast, threatening snow since early that morn. The foul temperatures didn't explain Eoghan's absence, however. It wasn't like him to keep her waiting. In fact, the past few days he'd arrived early and kept Mr. O'Bannon in stitches with his quick wit while she finished up her duties for the day.

She fastened the last button on her coat and took her time snugging the bonnet ribbon beneath her chin before casting one final glance at the clock.

Mr. O'Bannon circled the counter, the apron he wore while fashioning his candles bunched tight in his fist. "Time to go already, eh? Where is that young man of yours? Not like him to be late."

"No . . . perhaps he got caught up at the church. Sister Mary has been keeping him busy since he started working there." Tucking her scarf into the collar of her cloak, she moved to the door and turned to give him a wave. "I'd best not wait. He may not even be coming, after all."

Mr. O'Bannon frowned and peered outside at the gathering gloom. "I don't know, me dear. One would think the lad would have told you if he weren't coming."

Though deep down she agreed with him, she smiled and patted his shoulder. "I'm sure it's nothing. He'll probably swing by the boardinghouse later and apologize for not meeting me."

At least, she hoped so.

Stepping from the candle shop, she hurried to join the throng of people winding through the streets toward their homes. There was comfort in the number of people still about, though she tried not to think about it as she turned onto Ashberry Street.

The boardinghouse was a welcome sight in the gloomy neighborhood. She hastened up the stairs, half expecting to see Eoghan waiting for her there, and was disappointed when she met only Tillie instead.

Tillie's cheeks were red and the hem of her gown damp, as if she had just recently returned to the boardinghouse herself. "Ana, you're alone? I figured Eoghan would be with you."

She shook her head and shrugged from her cloak. "No, he didn't meet me today. He must still be at the church."

"I just came from there," Tillie said, taking the cloak from her and giving it a shake to release the moisture clinging to its folds. "No one has seen him since just after lunch. Sister Mary was a little worried when he didn't come in for one of Sister Agnes's rolls. It's Thursday. She said he'd know."

Ana unwound the scarf from about her neck slowly, and Tillie crossed to put her hand on her shoulder.

"Are you all right?"

Ana forced a smile. "I'm a little disappointed, is all. I expected he'd leave word here or at the church."

Tillie's face brightened. "Let's ask Amelia. Perhaps she or Laverne know something. They're in the dining room getting the table ready for supper."

Despite her optimism, neither of them had seen nor heard a thing from Eoghan. The unease in Ana's belly grew.

She clasped Tillie's fingers. "After dinner, what do you say we take a ride, you and I, and see how Cara be faring? I'll ask Giles to hitch the mare."

"Oh, would you?" Amelia said, clapping her hands together. "I have the most beautiful layette I've been meaning to take to her. I just haven't found the time."

Tillie glanced at her and then Ana. "We'd be glad to, Amelia." To Ana she whispered, "This isn't about Cara, is it?"

Ana waited until Amelia had departed in search of the layette before crossing to the hutch and removing the dishes for the evening meal. "I can't explain it, Tillie. It's just"—she set the plates down on the table with a thump—"a feeling that all is not right."

Tillie paused with the napkins clutched in her hands. "Perhaps we shouldn't wait. If you want, I can ask Giles—"

"No." She grabbed a handful of silverware and shook her head. "Leaving before supper would only cause alarm. It can wait."

Ana ate quickly and said little throughout the meal. The food sat like a stone in her stomach, and with every passing minute her desire to be gone intensified. Tillie seemed to sense her unease and elected to skip dessert in exchange for a hasty cup of tea. When they finished clearing the table, she fetched their cloaks and bonnets while Ana took the bag of clothes for the baby from Amelia.

Outside, the snow had finally begun to fall. Amelia hugged her shawl tightly about her shoulders and peered up at the night sky. "Are you certain you want to do this, dear? It can always wait for another day. Or I can ask Giles to go along?"

Ana gathered the reins and gave a determined shake of her head. "Nonsense. We'll be back before the snow even has a chance to collect."

Amelia rubbed her hands over her arms nervously. "All right, but don't venture out if the weather gets too bad. I'm sure Cara wouldn't mind putting the two of you up for the night."

Ana nodded and glanced at Tillie, whose white lips and tense posture must have matched her own. "Ready?"

She nodded and clutched the edge of the wagon seat as Ana gave a chirp. They set off, neither one speaking, both of them sighing with some relief when the wide, sloping roof of Rourke and Cara's home came into view. By the time they pulled up the bricked drive, the snow had indeed worsened, making visibility difficult. Even the copper warming pan that Giles had heated and wrapped in cloth to warm their feet failed to chase away the chill. Ana handed the reins to the liveryman and then scurried up the walk after Tillie.

Cara welcomed them at the door alongside the house-keeper. "Ana, Tillie, this is a surprise. Come inside before you catch your death."

She waited while the housekeeper took their outerwear before leading them to the library. 'Twas evident by the curiosity on her face that she questioned the hour of their visit, but she said nothing, only casting an occasional glance over her shoulder at them.

In the library, a hearty fire blazed in the fireplace. Rourke rose from behind a large walnut desk to welcome them, and then ushered them to the warmth of the hearth.

Ana held out the bag from Amelia. "These are for the baby. Amelia sent them. She said she's been meaning to stop by, but hasn't found the time."

Cara took them, a puzzled smile on her face as she sat to examine the contents of the bag. One by one, she lifted out the tiny dresses, all with embroidered details, and admired them by the light of a lamp with a jeweled shade. "They're beautiful, Ana, but surely delivering them could have waited for a finer day?"

Behind her chair, Rourke placed his hand on her shoulder, his gaze steady on Ana and Tillie. "Is everything all right at the boardinghouse?"

"Actually . . ." Ana glanced at Tillie, who urged her on with a tip of her head. She drew a deep breath and resumed. "Cara, have either you or Rourke seen Eoghan this evening?"

Seeing the pallor that washed over Cara's face, Ana immediately regretted her rash words. "It's just . . . he didn't meet me after work, so I was wondering . . . I thought perhaps he'd come to see you, and possibly you shared your news with him, which kept him late."

"He's not been by," Cara said, her hand going to her midsection. She looked to Rourke, her eyes wide.

He turned to Tillie. "He wasn't at the church?"

She shook her head. "But we haven't spoken to Father Ed or the sisters. It may be they sent him on an errand that he forgot to tell us about."

His jaw hardened. "We should ask them. I'll send one of the men."

Ana stepped closer to him, her palms damp. "What is it?" His aversion to meeting her eyes caused her heart to race. "Rourke?"

"It's just . . ."

Cara rose as he cleared his throat. "What is it?"

His brows drawn in concern, he took her hands in his. "Eoghan and I talked. We both agreed it would be wise to keep Ana close for a while."

Ana's mouth went dry. "Close . . . You mean keep an eye on me? Why?"

"Is she in danger?" For a moment, the rustling of Tillie's dress as she crossed to Ana and clasped her fingers was the only sound in the room. "Is she?"

"Possibly," Rourke said, his voice thick. His gaze flew to Cara and he pulled her close. "Maybe you should lie down."

"You're worried."

"Of course I am. All this excitement isn't good for the bairn."

"I mean about Eoghan."

"Cara—"

"Send someone to the church. See if you can find out if one of them knows something."

He hesitated, then nodded and moved to the door. Ana barely heard as he gave the orders to his men. When he returned, she tugged free of Tillie's grasp and went to him.

"You said you and Eoghan talked. What about?" When he didn't answer, she clutched his arm. "Please."

Finally he took her hand and led her to one of the chairs near the fireplace. Once they were all seated, he began. "You understand, Ana, most of what Eoghan and I discussed was speculation only. We didn't tell you because . . . well, we had no proof of wrongdoing or of intent to do wrong."

Unable to speak, she nodded.

"Very well." He cleared his throat and then slowly detailed everything he'd found while they waited for word from Ireland, ending with his admonishment to Eoghan to keep a close watch on Ana.

When he finished, she felt as if a vise had been placed around her chest. Tears burned the back of her eyes as she gazed first at Tillie and Cara, then Rourke. "You don't think he went on an errand, do you? You sent your man to the church to check, but deep down you're worried that something has happened to him."

He didn't answer, or need to.

Ana rose and walked on trembling legs to peer out the window at the worsening storm. "Something's happened to him." In the reflection on the glass, a circle of pale faces watched her with worried eyes. The roiling in her stomach increased. She swallowed and clutched the sill. "We *all* think something's happened to Eoghan."

When no one spoke, Ana turned and said, "Cara, I'm so sorry. Eoghan is missing . . . again, and it's all my fault."

28

Brion braced his legs against the pitching of the deck below his feet and stared across the table at the large Irishman with the brown derby tugged low over his brow. A smile pulled at his lips, and why not? He'd finally discovered the man's true identity, and when the time was right . . . well, he'd play his cards carefully.

"Well?" He pushed his cap back with his thumb, then propped both hands on his hips. "What's your next move, or do you even have one?"

The Celt withdrew a piece of paper from a leather satchel slung over the back of his chair and laid it on the table next to an inkpot and quill. "Sit. I've some work for you." Leaning forward, he turned up the wick on a battered oil lamp.

Brion shrugged, then sank onto one of the chairs fastened to the floor. He rested his elbows against the table. "What's the matter with ya? Not feeling well?"

The Celt, for all his arrogance, looked a bit ragged about the edges. His eyes were dull and red, and his skin bore an unhealthy pallor.

A quiet click cut the air. Brion flinched and pushed back in his chair. Lifting a weapon from under the table, The Celt's lips parted in an unholy smile before he laid the gun gently on its side. He waited, indicating the gun with a sweep of his hand. "If you think that's the case, you are quite welcome to try and disarm me."

Debating the odds was tempting, but Brion was no fool. The Celt wouldn't have risked putting the gun within reach if he didn't think he could wield it. Whatever it was that ailed him, it wasn't physical.

He raised his hands, palms out. "Just asking, is all. Didn't mean to offend."

The Celt's smile spread, baring his teeth in a wolflike grin that Brion found unnerving. His voice lowered to a growl. "If that's so, then perhaps you oughtn't be making inquiries you've no right to ask."

The two men stared at each other, both refusing to blink, neither giving ground.

Finally, The Celt broke the standoff. "If you're that set on knowing who I am, perhaps you should just ask me. Nicely. I might tell you. Then again, I might just kill you, or see you killed. Is that what you want?"

He spoke in such a jovial manner, it sent a shiver down Brion's spine. He'd uncovered the man's identity, but what good was that knowledge if it cost him his life? For the first time it occurred to him that perhaps he'd underestimated The Celt—something he wasn't often wont to do.

He narrowed his eyes. "I'm a businessman, like you. It pays to know who I'm climbing into bed with, if you ken my meaning."

"Any more digging," The Celt said, "and it'll be a grave you're climbing into, if you ken *my* meaning."

Brion clenched his jaw so tightly his teeth hurt. With great effort he forced himself to stick to his plan and wait until he had The Celt by the throat before revealing everything he knew.

Thinking of the fragile old woman with a loose tongue and empty pockets residing in a hovel in the Lower East Side eased the tension from his muscles. He even managed a smile. "Easy now. Your fight's not with me, is it? It's with one Eoghan Hamilton."

He feigned indifference with a casual wave of his hand. "You asked me to kill him. It's only logical that I should want to know why."

"Logical?" The Celt barked a laugh that echoed against the rusted crossbeams of the old freight ship's hold. "What care you about that?" His glare sharpened. "You're looking for something to hold over me, and that's for certain. Watch out, Brion McCleod. If you're not careful, you just might loose a whole box of secrets you'd rather see kept hid."

"Secrets?" Brion hissed, straightening against the back of his chair.

"Like a late-night fire that spread through a small cottage with no apparent cause and killed a woman and her two children." He paused and raised one finger in the air. "Make that one child. The other lived, ain't that so? And the mother? Well, who knows what secrets the surviving child could tell."

Lacing both hands in a gesture reminiscent of prayer, his expression turned pious. "Or the priest who saved her, now there's a man with the power to make people listen." He lowered his hands, his eyes gleaming in the greasy light of the oil lamp. "Or an unfortunate stranger who happens upon a small church and finds, much to his surprise, a priest in need of help. Who confides his troubles and offers to give the man anything—" he paused and leaned across the table— "*anything* in exchange for his services."

"You have me," Brion said with disgust. "What more do you want?"

The Celt pushed the paper across the table to him. "Just to finish this job, that's all. Finish this job and stop poking around in places you oughtn't."

Brion grabbed the paper and snatched up the quill. "Who's the letter to, and what do you want me to say?"

The Celt's tense posture eased. "You're going to write a message to your niece. Don't worry, I'll have one of my men deliver it for you," he continued as Brion opened his mouth to protest.

"How will she know it's really from me?"

"I'm sure you'll think of a way."

The pocket watch. So that was why he'd taken it. He couldn't help but marvel at the lengths to which The Celt had gone.

"Besides, do you honestly think she doesn't know you're in town?" He wagged his finger in Brion's face. "You haven't exactly been discreet, now, have you? Bandying about, letting everyone and their cousin get a look at you." He snorted. "Lucky for you, I've a plan that will cover your tracks, and mine." He nodded at the paper. "Now write."

Brion jabbed the quill into the inkpot, splattering dots of blue along the table and onto the paper.

The Celt clucked his tongue and pulled a fresh sheet from the satchel at his back. "There now. Try and be more careful with this one, won't you?"

It was all Brion could do to keep from snapping the quill in two. Line by line, he took down the words that spilled from The Celt's mouth, then signed just his initial with a flourish. "Is that all?"

The Celt turned the paper, took his time reading over the message, and blew gently across the page to dry the ink. "Aye, that'll do."

Brion tossed down the quill and wiped his fingers across

his trousers, leaving behind blue streaks that were likely permanent. "Good. Now what?"

After folding the letter into thirds, The Celt slid the paper into a pocket of his coat and rose. "Now you wait for word from your niece and leave the rest to me."

The boat pitched just then, making Brion claw for the edge of the table. The Celt, however, took the motion in stride as he crossed the hold and threw open the door.

"He was your son, wasn't he?" Brion called, catching him on the threshold. "The man Eoghan Hamilton killed. And the woman who tried to take her revenge and wound up dead—that was your daughter-in-law?"

With his back to him, the expression on The Celt's face remained hidden, but his shoulders stiffened, and his breath rasped against the ship's rusted steel walls.

"That's why you're doing this, why you want Hamilton dead?" Brion continued, willing the man to turn around, and disappointed when he didn't.

"Wait for word," The Celt said before disappearing out the door.

Brion grimaced. He was right, he sensed it, but while the deaths explained The Celt's quest for revenge, they didn't answer another more pressing question. What exactly did the man want from the Turners? What did they have that even Hamilton's death couldn't give? The man had put off murdering his son's killer because he thought he had something to gain, and when Hamilton failed to provide that link, he'd given the order to finish him off. But what was it? What piece of the puzzle did Brion lack?

For a moment he was tempted to leave the boat and go on searching, to risk nosing about to uncover what it was that a man as powerful as The Celt would set aside everything in order to attain, but then a noise caught his attention, a quiet groan that rose from the corner.

He cut his eyes in that direction. "You're awake? Good."

Rising from the table, he picked up a piece of pipe, broken and discarded long ago. The weight of it was good, the feel of it solid. He slapped the thin end in his open palm and smiled. "I'm going to enjoy this."

29

The storm outside Rourke and Cara's house lashed with a fury that set Ana's nerves on edge. The wind howled and scraped at the windows, snow drifted and piled against the door, and the meager fire in the fireplace struggled to give heat.

She bunched the borrowed shawl at her throat and tried not to think of Eoghan struggling alone against the icy night.

"No word?"

She turned to the door, where Tillie waited and shook her head. "Rourke said his man made it back before the storm really hit. No one at the church has seen Eoghan since before lunch."

Tillie glided across the rug on the library floor to envelop her in a hug. "He's fine, Ana. I'm sure he's simply holed up somewhere waiting out this storm."

She forced a smile, then held out one edge of her shawl. Tillie moved into it and the two stood wrapped in its warmth.

"We've not spoken in a while," Tillie prompted gently. "Do you want to talk?"

Tears flooded Ana's eyes at the concern in her voice. "I've not meant to neglect . . ." She broke off, a catch in her voice. "Oh, Tillie, I'm so worried."

"There, there," she said with a pat to Ana's shoulder. "Let's sit down. All this standing around and fretting would give anyone fits." She led Ana to a settee. "Just what is it you're so afraid of?"

The house was quiet now that Cara and Rourke had retired. At Rourke's insistence, Cara had agreed to lie down and at least attempt rest, but the look on her face as she left the library said she was as worried as the others.

Ana sank onto the settee's cushions. Indeed, her uncle's arrival had given her many sleepless nights, but it was Eoghan's disappearance that had her pacing holes in the carpet tonight.

"Ever since my uncle found out I was alive," she began, "Eoghan has been so determined to keep me safe, and now . . . Tillie, what if something's happened to him?"

Like water pouring from a dam, the emotions came spewing out—her growing attraction for Eoghan, her unresolved feelings of guilt, and her fear that the recent happenings involved a kind of holy retribution for her years of rejecting God.

Tillie grasped her by the shoulders. "Ana, that's not how the Lord works and you know it."

Sniffing, she looked up through a haze of tears. "But what if I'm supposed to prove something to God?"

"Like what?"

"I don't know . . . my faithfulness or something. He's asked it before, isn't that so? Of others? Why should I be any different? I just don't think I can . . ."

She bowed her head and gave in to a fresh bout of tears. Tillie's arms slipped around her, and she gratefully leaned into them, glad, even if just for a moment, to let her friend shoulder her burdens.

Her breath rustled the hair on Ana's head as she sighed. "If there's one thing of which I've learned to be certain, it's this—if God allows our faith to be tested, it is not to punish us, and it's not to show Him that we be trustworthy." She pulled back and smoothed the hair from Ana's brow. "Dear one, it's to prove himself faithful to us."

Sorrow tugged the corners of her eyes, and deep lines creased her face, but there was peace there as well, and Ana found her spirits lifted.

Wiping away her tears with the tip of her finger, she said, "Tillie, may I ask you a question?"

"Of course."

She drew a slow breath. "Your babe, and Braedon . . . have you never felt anger toward God for their loss?"

Tillie's gaze fell and color flared in her cheeks. "I've carried anger and bitterness enough." Sighing heavily, she raised her eyes. "But the carrying of it was never sufficient to make me feel any better. 'Twas easier just to let it go."

She grasped Ana's hand. "The scars we bear are proof that God has never left us to face our trials alone. Think on it. Your priest, the one who rescued you and sent you to America, and my captain, who carried me here off the ship when I was heartsick and barely alive . . . do you truly believe it was by accident that they appeared when they did?"

She leaned forward, her gaze burning with an intensity Ana had never before seen.

"If God is calling you to a trial, rest assured, He does not intend for you to walk through it alone."

A lump rose in Ana's throat. Deep down she sensed that God *was* calling her to a trial. Her fear was not that she would walk it alone, but that she would walk it without God . . .

Or Eoghan.

— ❅ ❅ ❅ —

Brion left the deck of the freight ship, the sweat on his face cold in the onslaught of wind and snow sweeping off the harbor. At least he no longer felt the same tension, the same nagging need for action as before.

Muttering to himself, he turned and secured the lock on the cargo bay doors—a heavy rusted thing he'd be lucky to get open again.

Part one of The Celt's plan was accomplished. Satisfying as it was, it wouldn't compare to part two.

Striding toward the rail, he lifted the metal pipe, now stained red, and dropped it over the side. It landed with a splash and quickly disappeared under the icy waves. Brion ducked his head against the blinding snow and moved toward the gangplank and land.

The pipe and its scarlet evidence were gone, washed away by the waters of New York Harbor. Not that he'd need it anymore. He had a much different fate in mind for his long-lost niece, like finishing what he'd started nearly ten years ago.

Whistling a tune, he snugged the collar of his coat up around his ears and tread the narrow bridge from the boat to the dock.

Aye, he'd finish, and then his thorn of a niece would be gone forever and he would have his land, his home, everything that should have rightfully been his from the beginning but for a greedy half brother and their dim-witted father.

His steps quickened as the driving snow swirled about his legs and feet. The hard part would be the waiting. Even he had to admit, he'd never been particularly good at it. But this time . . .

This time he could almost smell the wisps of smoke, and see the conclusion of this final devastating chapter. It wouldn't be long now.

Not long at all.

30

Ana woke to a light tapping. Prying her eyes open, she scoured the room for the source of the sound before finally realizing it came from the library door.

And she was in Cara and Rourke's house.

And Eoghan was missing.

More tapping. "Ana, dear? I have a message for you."

Fully awake from her nap now, she slid from the camelback settee and opened the door. She'd not fallen asleep till the wee hours, and exhaustion had again overtaken her late in the morning.

Cara waited in the hall, holding out a fat envelope, folded and sealed, bearing Ana's name in bold ink. "It arrived by messenger while you were napping."

"For me?" Ana asked. "Maybe it's from Eoghan."

Snatching the letter, she hurried to the desk to open it. At the door, Cara wrung her hands and waited, her expression hopeful.

The moment Ana peeled open the envelope, something heavy and gold dropped into her palm. She stared at it in disbelief, then at the signature at the bottom of the letter.

"Well? Is it from him?"

"No," Ana said, "it's . . . the letter . . . it's from . . ."

Cara crossed to touch her shoulder. "Are you all right? Should I send for Tillie?"

Closing her shaking fingers around the pocket watch, Ana drew a breath and shook her head. "The letter is from my uncle."

Her eyes widened. "What?"

She nodded and held up the note. "You said a messenger delivered this?"

"Yes." She eyed the paper as if it were a roach, then looked back at Ana. "What does it say? And what is that inside?"

Licking her dry lips, Ana grasped the letter in both hands and read the first line.

"'My dearest Lucy.'" She peered up at Cara. "That's my name . . . my real name. Lucy. Lucy McCleod." Strange how she stumbled on the syllables of her own name, once so familiar and now completely foreign. "I changed it when I came to America."

Cara's grasp on her shoulder tightened. "I'll give you a minute alone. But I'll be right outside the door if you need me."

Ana offered a weak smile, what little she could muster with her heart pounding so. A second later, the library door closed with a soft click, leaving Ana alone once more. Her gaze drifted to the incredible words scrawled across the page in her hands.

My dearest Lucy,

What unbelievable chance, what indescribable joy is mine to have found you alive after so many years! To know that I have been blessed to have a piece of my brother with me, I can only say that I am shocked, as I know you must be.

Shocked? She grimaced. *Terrified* was a more fitting description of what she'd felt upon seeing her uncle for the first time. The paper rustled as she set it aside and rose from her chair, her father's watch still clutched in her hand. After a moment, she grasped one end of the chain and let the rest dangle. Her father's watch, and her mother's. She never thought to see it again.

She slipped it around her neck and pressed the gold against her skin. Perhaps she'd been wrong to deny Tillie's presence. Having her friend nearby would certainly ease a bit of the doubt gnawing at her mind. Biting her lip, she looked back at the letter, sitting on the desk half open.

Pray, Ana.

Father Ed's voice echoed through her head. Pray—that's what he'd tell her to do. Tillie too, most likely. And Sister Mary. She listened harder.

Pray!

Not Father Ed's voice or any of those others. It was her mother's gentle tone that whispered inside her head.

Lowering her gaze, she breathed in halting words the one prayer she could remember from her childhood. "Our Father . . . who art in heaven . . ."

The rest of the prayer sped to her memory, flooding her with strength and peace. Finished, she moved back to the desk and picked up the letter.

"All right, Lord, I'm listening. Whatever is in this letter, I look to you for guidance." Drawing a deep breath, she opened the page and resumed reading.

How I have regretted the mistakes I made where your mother was concerned. I pray that you will allow me to explain, as much as I am able, the things that led me to do all the things I did. Nothing I say can

*ever make up for the harshness with which I dealt
with your mother, but I can at least hope to atone, in
some small measure, by dealing differently with you,
her offspring. My niece.*

*Lucy, it does not escape me that you have no reason
whatsoever to believe that I have changed. The man
you remember was hard and, I am ashamed to admit,
cruel in both speech and manner. I am not proud of the
judgmental attitude that once was mine. I can only say
that I have changed, and that I hope you will give me
a chance to prove myself different. I return this watch
to you, your father's watch, toward that end, and pray
that the lengths to which I've gone to reclaim it will
somehow help convince you of my goodwill.*

*When I learned that you lived, I boarded the first
ship I could find to America. It is my hope that you will
allow me to help restore to you all of the things that
are rightfully yours—your home, your mother's land,
and ultimately one sad, broken member of your family.*

*You and I are all that remain, dearest Lucy. Come to
the harbor near Liberty Pier. I have taken up residence
in a tenement there. If instead you would rather send
a representative, or even respond by way of writ, I will
understand. My messenger has instructions to return
this evening. I await your reply.*

> *Humbly,*
> *B.*

The initial, so stark against the white page, burned like
a brand.

Single. Solitary.

That one letter more than anything else tugged at her heart.

Could it be true? Was Amelia right? Had her uncle come to America hoping to prove that he'd changed?

She read again the line about her home and her mother's land. What did he mean by saying they rightfully belonged to her? Her home had burned to the ground, and the land . . .

She shook her head and laid the letter on Rourke's desk. Her home was in America, not Ireland. But the rest . . .

The rest of his words beat against her mind and spirit, battering her will until she felt nigh unto tears. Slipping her parents' watch from around her neck, she flipped open the lid and stared at the picture pressed inside.

Shamus McCleod, so tall and handsome as he gazed down at his wife, Adele. Her mother, locked arm in arm with her father. On the opposite side, a lock of her mother's hair. As a child, Ana used to bring it to her nose and pretend she could still smell the fragrant heather that billowed from her skirts and scented her braid.

Her eyes returned to her father's dark locks, the raven brows. If drawn in a frown, she could imagine they belonged to his half brother—her uncle. Surely they could not be so different. They had the same father, after all. Would she ever truly know the truth behind what happened the night her mother and sister died unless she met with Brion McCleod? And what if he *had* changed? The only way to know for sure was to see him face-to-face, to talk with him and at least offer him the chance to explain.

In the meantime, could she set aside her fear for Eoghan? He was still missing, and if she left now, and word came that he'd met with harm . . .

She shivered and buried her face in her hands, the pocket watch slipping between her fingers and landing on the floor with a thump. How much easier it would be to cling to her old fears and insecurities and forget all about Brion's letter.

Reminded of her promise, she closed her eyes tight and begged God for an answer. What to do? And if He said go, would she have the strength?

"If God is calling you to a trial, rest assured, He does not intend for you to walk through it alone."

Tillie's words wound like mist through her mind. Ana caught her breath as their meaning came into focus. 'Twas not her own strength she need rely on . . . it was God's!

A second later, doubt snatched her fleeting confidence. What if she couldn't trust Him? She'd only recently returned to Him, after all. Yet she'd learned to trust Eoghan and Father Ed. Sisters Mary and Agnes. Was not God greater than all of those?

She jumped to her feet and went to the window to stare out at the frozen landscape. Even at midday, gloom made the house, the street, even the sky dark. "Eoghan, where are you!"

Her voice rang hollowly against the glass. Despairing, she rested her forehead against the cold pane to think.

If her uncle was telling the truth and he wanted to prove that he'd changed, perhaps he could help in the search for Eoghan. If he wasn't . . .

She jerked upright. If he was lying, he could at this moment be holding Eoghan prisoner.

She lifted her chin and blinked back tears. She wanted the truth. She wanted freedom from her past. If ever she were to be rid of the nightmares, it would have to be now. This was the path. Her trial, and hers alone. She sensed it.

Limbs shaking, Ana turned and headed for the door.

31

Pain ripped through Eoghan's shoulders, down his arms, to his fingers. Try as he might, he couldn't wrest from the ropes that bound his wrists, and struggling only seemed to tighten the knots.

He took a tentative breath. If he was careful, he could keep the searing agony in his ribs at bay. He inched backward on his side until his shoulders and hips touched the steel wall of the freight ship's hold. Light trickled in from the portholes that rimmed the wall and through cracks in the metal. Maybe with a little maneuvering he could sit up, out of the icy water sloshing about his chin.

He grimaced. It was the water that had pulled him from unconsciousness, brought him sputtering and coughing to aching awareness. The bitter storm must be more than the rusted old tub could handle. He shivered, then groaned as the movement brought a fresh wave of torture.

McCleod had been skillful with the pipe. Luckily he'd broken no bones except possibly some ribs. Still, he'd caused enough damage to make movement distasteful.

Eoghan spat the blood from his mouth and then eased farther up the wall, sighing in relief when at last he rested upright. The steel hull provided little warmth, but at least he was out of the stinging salt water. Now if he could only see . . .

He squinted in the dimly lit hold, and spied a desk or table of some sort, chairs that were no doubt bolted to the floor and would therefore prove useless, and a lamp.

He inhaled sharply, winced, then squinted harder. The lamp would contain glass. If he could break it and use the shards to loosen his bindings, he might be able to break free. His legs weren't bound. Once he got his knees under him, he could navigate the rocking deck to the table. Why hadn't McCleod finished him and been done with it?

The answer inspired a wave of dizziness and desperation. He paused to let it pass, then took several shallow breaths, bracing for the pain that was sure to come. He pushed against the wall, gritting his teeth to muffle his groan.

He was bait for Ana. He had to get free before McCleod could lure her to the ship. Or was he already too late? How long had he been unconscious? Panic drove his feet. He plowed through the shallow water and made it to the table. Now what? With his hands tied behind him, he couldn't reach for the handle.

Bending forward, he knocked the lamp to its side with his shoulder, but instead of shattering, it rolled off the edge and landed in the water with a splash and then bobbed gently away.

"Aargh!"

His angry cry echoed against the metal walls. He debated a split second, then lowered to his knees and reached for the lamp with his teeth. Straightening again would be agony, but Ana was all that mattered now.

He plunged his face into the water, came up empty, spit out a mouthful of salt water, then dove back in. The second time he felt the thin metal handle that looped from the top of the lamp. Securing it in his teeth, he brought the lamp up and rested it on his knees, gasping for a moment before shoving to his feet and stumbling to the hold's wall.

He swung the lamp as hard as he could, nearly passing out when the motion jarred his ribs. The lamp banged hard against the wall, but didn't break. He tried again. And again. Each time, his vision narrowed and dimmed, but he screwed his eyes tight, waited for the pain to pass, and then swung the lamp.

Futile.

Eoghan fell with his back to the wall. His knees were weak, his mouth cut and bleeding. He had strength for one more swing, and that was all.

Please, God. Help me. The words resounded over and over in his head. *Help me!*

Shoving off the wall, he braced his feet wide and swung with all his might. The lamp shattered, sending pieces of metal and glass cascading into the shallow waves.

Eoghan sagged against the hold in relief. He was cold and wet and probably on the verge of hypothermia, but if he could get free, he might stand a chance of reaching Ana in time to save her from McCleod.

He slid to his knees and then edged sideways as far as he could stand, until his fingers grazed the bottom. At last, he felt it—a thin piece of glass about three inches long and jagged. He wrangled it up between his tightly bound wrists and began sawing, heedless of his own flesh, of everything except getting free and warning Ana.

She was in danger . . . and he didn't have much time.

— ❈ ❈ ❈ —

Ana bent low and gave a chirp to the mare, urging her onward through the wind and snow. The biting cold whipped her cheeks and brought tears to her eyes, and she couldn't feel her hands, even with Rourke's gloves as protection, but she was glad she hadn't bothered with the wagon. Asking for it to be hitched would have raised too many questions—ones she didn't care to answer.

She hunched lower against the mare's neck, trying to keep the wind from slashing against her face. At least she could outrun her doubts, or try to.

She nudged her heels into the mare's sides. "C'mon, girl. Almost there."

The horse's head dipped and her hooves became a blur. Ana held on for dear life. Finally the harbor came into view. She pulled back on the reins to slow the mare and came to a stop altogether when she reached the wharf.

Whitecaps rolled in the distance, the only marker between a gray sea and a grayer sky. She'd only been to the wharf on a few occasions, but she knew the general location of Liberty Pier.

Activity along the pier had crawled to a halt. The boats that bobbed at anchor were lifeless and dark. The warehouses lining the opposite side of the road were locked up tight. Ana shivered and tightened her grasp on the reins. Obviously the storm had driven everyone to their homes—everyone except her . . . and her uncle.

The buildings to her left were long and box shaped, with narrow windows mounted high on the walls, and oversized doors. None of these looked like a tenement, yet her uncle had said this was where they were to meet. She cleared her throat, then craned her neck to scan the street.

"Hello?" The wind and snow muffled her voice so that it thrummed dully along the deserted street. She swallowed hard and tried again. "Hel—"

"You there! What's a lass like you doing out alone? You lost?"

Ana flinched and twisted in the saddle to see who spoke. A smallish man with stooped shoulders and a wrinkled face peered at her from the deck of one of the ships—a sleek wooden thing with naked masts that pierced the sky.

She turned to him. "I'm looking for my uncle, a man by the name of Brion McCleod. Do you know him?"

The man scratched his temple. "What's he look like?"

"Tall . . . dark hair . . ." Ana brightened with sudden inspiration. She could show the man a picture of someone similar. Slipping her hand under her cloak, she felt for her father's pocket watch. Gone! She'd left it at Rourke and Cara's. She frowned. "Um, he probably scowls a lot?"

The man gave a snort of laughter. "You just described most of the blokes what work this here dock." He slapped his hand against the boat rail and then turned to go. "Sorry, lass, I can't help ya, 'cept to say you'd best get out of this storm."

"Wait!" Ana slid from the mare's back and scurried the short distance to the water's edge. "He said he lives in a tenement near Liberty Pier. Are you familiar with any such place?"

The man narrowed his eyes. "Aye, I know a likely spot for a building like that. Not a nice place, though, 'specially for the likes of you. Sure you want to be looking for it?"

She nodded.

He grunted and pointed toward the far end of the wharf. "All right then. It's down that way. Take the side street and turn left. Ain't nobody lived there in quite some time," he warned as she moved away. "It's mostly just drunkards and ne'er-do-wells what live there now."

"That's all right. I'll find it. Thank you," Ana said, giving a tug on the reins and leading the mare up the street.

But her heart thumped against her chest as she left the glow of the gas lamps for the less populated side of the wharf. There were no warehouses here, only broken-down ships in need of repair, and vacant buildings with staring windows for eyes.

Shuddering, she drew closer to the mare's side, though it was little protection should someone try to accost her. Why hadn't she asked Tillie to accompany her? Or Rourke? Or . . .

She shook the thoughts free. No sense deriding her decision now. She'd come alone because she had to, because the fears of her past belonged to her, and breaking free of them was her task to accomplish. She refused to put anyone else she loved in danger.

Still, she longed for Eoghan's solid strength. Ach, but his braw face and ready smile would be a comfort in this moment. She cast a nervous glance about her. No Eoghan here, just an empty street, the choppy waves, a rusted boat, and in the distance the gleaming, hopeful figure of Lady Liberty.

She drew a breath to calm her nerves and continued walking. Tracks crisscrossed the snow. In several of the prints, flecks of bright red stood out against the blinding white. At least one person here had braved the storm.

She squinted harder, her grip on the mare tensing. The spots looked like blood. She lifted her head and followed the path of the tracks to a rusted boat. On its side was a name she could barely read, and below it, more faded letters.

Emerald . . . something.

Emerald Isle? Where did she know that name? Her heart lurched. *Emerald Isle Freight.* The man who owned it was Deidre Healy's father-in-law. Earlier that year, Deidre had tried to murder Eoghan and Cara inside one of his warehouses because she blamed them for her husband's death.

Her attention returned to the spots of red in the snow. With fluffy drifts nearly filling the tracks, they were barely visible. Her stomach sank to think how much blood had already been covered. Indeed, on closer study, it appeared as if someone had aided the wind and snow. Broad strokes eliminated many of the prints. Here and there, clots of mud testified to the ferocity with which the work had been done.

Her breathing quickened as she stared at the boat bobbing low on the waves. Inside her chest, something drew her, like the tug of a thread, too powerful to resist.

The reins slipped from her fingers as she took one step, then two. Her cloak flapped when she started running, her focus locked onto the rusted metal hull and its faded warning.

Eoghan was on that boat. She was certain of it, but she also knew . . .

She was running out of time.

32

Eoghan tensed as hollow footsteps echoed against the deck above his head. Someone was up there. As the sound drew closer to the hatch, he sawed more frantically against the ropes on his wrists. Warmth trickled down his skin, making the glass harder to hold. A little . . . more . . .

He held his breath as the person walking across the deck thumped down a flight of metal stairs and then halted outside the hatch. He wasn't free, but he could fight. If it was Mc-Cleod, he might not expect him to be alert. Struggling to his haunches, he mustered his strength and prepared to launch himself at the intruder.

"Hello? Is anybody in there?"

"Ana?" Hardly daring to believe his ears, he lifted his head and stared. "Ana, get out of here!"

"Eoghan, thank God! I'm going to get you out." The rusted hatch groaned as she beat upon it.

"No!" He shoved to his feet, sloshing through water that had risen to mid-thigh. "Ana, go get help. Tell Rourke. It's a trap!"

She fell silent. Panicked, he thrust his shoulder against the hatch. "Did you hear me? You can't be here alone. It's not safe."

"I'm not leaving you."

His knees weakened at the determination in her quiet voice. Did she not realize the danger she was in? He dropped his head against the cold metal hatch and closed his eyes. "Ana, listen to me. If you'll just—"

The rusted metal bolt securing the hatch scraped loudly, stopped, then scraped some more. "I can't . . ." She grunted and then the bolt gave way with a clang.

Frantic now, Eoghan wrestled the bindings on his wrists like a madman, ignoring the pain that shot from his ribs, his chest, even his battered fingers and legs. "McCleod brought me here. Look around. Do you see him?"

"I can't get the door open. You have to help me push!"

She refused to listen! He shouted at her in desperation. "McCleod kidnapped me to draw you here. Do you hear me? He may be close."

"Why won't it move? Is something blocking it?"

"There's water in here." He kicked at the hatch in frustration. "Ana, you've got to get out. Get Rourke . . . or Giles . . . anyone. I'll be all right."

Sweat mingled with the splashing salt water to form a stinging haze. Eoghan blinked and tossed his head to fling his hair from his eyes.

"I'm going to look for a stick or something to help me get the door open. Don't worry. I'll be right back."

She wasn't leaving. Terrified as the thought made him, his heart swelled to think of the danger she was willing to face.

"Be careful!" His shout rang against the ship's walls, bouncing back on his head over and over. "McCleod is still out there. Do you hear me? Ana!"

She'd already gone, but the ropes were loosening now. He could move his wrists. In just a moment more . . . He wiggled his shoulders and used the slickness of his own blood to inch one hand higher than the other. Higher.

He sagged against the wall as fatigue and cold gripped his muscles. Much longer and he'd be unable to control the chattering of his teeth.

The hatch squealed open. He looked up, blinking through streams of trickling water and sweat. Ana stood in the entrance, a pipe in her hands. Beautiful Ana. So brave and pale, only . . . she was here because of him, and McCleod had to be nearby. He shoved toward her.

"Eoghan!" Ana climbed through the hatch, then dropped the pipe with a plunk, gasping as she jumped into the frigid water.

"Don't come in here. Get out, back the way you came. Now, Ana!"

Despite his plea, she forged toward him, tears streaming down her cheeks. The water he'd fought to escape tore at her skirts and she stumbled.

He couldn't catch her. "Ana, be careful. There's glass—"

Two steps from him, she fell against his chest, and together they sagged against the hull. Pain shot through his ribs, but he'd never been so happy to see anyone in his life.

"You're . . . all right," he panted, using the wall to keep himself upright. "I was so afraid I wouldn't get to you in time . . . that McCleod . . . Ana, we've got to get you out of here."

She tore the gloves from her hands and ran her fingers over the swelling on his cheek and eyes. "What happened to you? Are you all right?"

"There's no time to explain. McCleod could return any minute."

Her examination of his wounds came to a sudden halt. "Eoghan, are you certain it was him?"

"It was him."

"But why would he do this?"

He hesitated. "He used me as bait . . . to lure you here?" The confusion on her face gave him pause so that his voice lifted in question.

"No, you were missing. I had no idea you were here."

"Then how did you find me? Are you saying McCleod didn't contact you?"

"He did, but he said it was to reconcile. He wanted me to meet him at some tenement or . . . something, so I came to the wharf. But then there was blood in the snow and I thought . . . I thought . . ."

She broke off. He strained against the ropes, wishing with every fiber of his being that he could wrap his arms around her and pull her close.

Her hands returned to his face. "He did this?"

Eoghan nodded.

"Why?"

"I thought it was to trap you," he groaned. He shifted to show her his hands. "We'll figure it out later. I need you to help me get free of these ropes."

"You're bleeding!"

"It's the glass. Can you see it?"

"Aye . . ." Her voice wavered.

"All right, grab it and—"

The rusted hatch groaned, cutting the words from Eoghan's mouth, and then McCleod's tall frame filled the opening. Ducking his head, he stepped inside and fixed them both with a steely glare. "My dear niece. What a surprise. I didn't expect to find you here. Actually I didn't expect to find you alive at all, so I guess that makes you full of surprises."

"Ana, get behind me," Eoghan growled through clenched teeth. "Now!"

The water churned as she struggled to obey.

"How verra noble. Ever the protector, eh, Hamilton?"

309

Despite his injuries, Eoghan threw his shoulders back. "I'll protect her from *you*. Try and touch her! I'll—"

"You'll what?" Brion reached behind him and withdrew a pistol from the waistband of his trousers, then pointed it directly at Eoghan's chest.

"No!" Ana twisted to put herself between him and her uncle. "I beg you, don't shoot him."

His heart lurched. If McCleod were to fire now, he wouldn't be able to move in time to save her. "Ana—"

"Don't hurt him. Please!" Her ragged cry echoed against the cold, metal walls. "It's me you want."

Eoghan jerked against the ropes. "No! Ana, don't—"

"I won't let him hurt you!" She whirled and stared at her uncle. "Please, let him go."

The pistol in Brion's hand dipped, and he looked back and forth between them. "He was right." His derisive laugh echoed off the wall, the ceiling, then faded. "How rich."

Turning, Ana brought both hands to Eoghan's face. "I'm so sorry. If only I'd come sooner."

Agony ripped through his heart. "Would that you hadn't come at all." He shifted to rest his head against hers. "The glass in my hand. Take it," he whispered urgently.

She slid her arms through his, pretended to hug him close while he placed the glass into her shaking fingers and up her sleeve. And then she was holding him . . . clinging to him . . . and he knew he'd never be able to let her go.

He shivered, and she pulled back to peer into his eyes. "You're freezing."

"Ana, listen to me."

"Back away from him!" Brion's voice pierced like a knife.

"Don't . . ." Eoghan whispered, but slowly her arms fell from his waist.

"Now come to me," Brion ordered.

"She stays with me!" he shouted, then dipped his head to stare at her. "You cannot go with him. Do you hear me?"

The gun hammer gave an ominous click. "Come, or watch him die," Brion said.

Her eyes widened as she backed up, water swirling around her skirt.

His pulse soared. "Ana, he'll kill you."

"And if I don't, he'll kill you," she whispered. Her eyes were somber pools, so desperate and deep . . . If he could only reach her! Her hands curled into fists and she lifted her chin. "My fate is in God's hands, not his."

He shook his head and plunged toward her, only stopping when Brion shifted and pointed the gun at her.

"We'll find another way," Eoghan said, his voice hoarse.

She backed away, widening the distance between them. "There isn't time."

She was almost to the door. He searched the hold frantically. The pipe! He staggered toward the spot where she'd dropped it, but before he reached the entrance, she whirled and stepped through the hatch.

"I'm not alone, Eoghan," she said, one hand reaching out to him a second before the door slammed shut. Still, he heard her cries. "He can't kill me if God doesn't want me dead."

With the scraping of the bolt, Eoghan fell forward—succumbed to the dark and cold and icy water.

A moment later, she was gone.

33

Ana watched stiffly as Brion yanked the bolt she'd struggled with earlier into place. Inside the hold, Eoghan's strangled cries tore at her heart. She stared at her uncle, beyond caring if he killed her now. She had to know.

"Why are you doing this? Why not just kill us both?" She jabbed her finger toward the hatch. "In there? The wharf is deserted. No one would hear."

Brion McCleod's mouth stretched in a wicked grin. Slicked by the wind and snow, his hair clung to his skull like a cap. She shuddered. How could she have ever thought he resembled her father?

"Far too risky, my dear niece. Can't have your death tied to his in any way."

"His . . ." She stared at the bolted hatch. Inside, the water was rising. Eventually it would fill the hold. "He's going to drown."

"Aye. Verra likely. You, however, have a much different fate in store." He motioned with the gun. "The gangplank. Move."

The cold eye of the gun's barrel propelled her toward the long, narrow bridge spanning the distance from deck to dock.

Far below, the waters of the harbor churned up a frothy mixture of ice and snow. The freezing air squeezed her in its cold grasp. Her teeth chattered. She could jump, but she wasn't a strong swimmer and she'd already felt the pull of the waves against her skirts. Running was not an option either, for she had no doubt that her uncle's long legs would devour any distance in half her strides.

He poked her between the shoulders with the gun. "Ever seen anyone drown? Not pretty, and that water . . ." She flinched as he brought his mouth to her ear. "You'll freeze before you ever make it to shore. I'll see to that. Now move."

She jerked her feet forward, down the gangplank, across the dock and onto the frozen shore. Once again he motioned with the end of the pistol. "Over there, to that buggy."

It was a black rig with a black horse hitched to it. It looked as dark and forbidding as the man standing behind her. She plowed through the blowing drifts. Gone were the tracks that had led her to the boat where Eoghan was being held captive. Even if someone came looking, she doubted they'd find him, or her, in time.

She glanced over her shoulder at her uncle. "Where are we going?"

"You'll know soon enough." He jabbed her with the gun. "Get in."

Dragging her heavy, wet skirts, Ana climbed into the buggy, glad despite her uncle's terrifying presence to be out of the biting wind. But it was more than the cold that made her shake. She grasped the edges of her cloak, drawing its scant protection tight, then paused when something pricked her wrist.

The shard of glass Eoghan had placed there before she left . . . if she could get close enough to use it as a weapon, she might be able to break free.

Her uncle climbed into the buggy. He would have to use one hand to handle the reins. Even if he kept the gun trained on her, it was the most vulnerable he was likely to be, and she might be able to slow him down. Ana fumbled with her sleeve, fearing at any moment that her uncle would see and realize what she was doing. Instead he tucked the gun between him and the side of the buggy, then grabbed the reins.

"No tricks now. Sit there like a good lass, you hear?"

Her fingers tightened on the glass. It was now or never.

Flipping the edge of her cloak back with one hand, she closed her eyes and thrust the shard out and down as hard as she could.

Her uncle's enraged roar filled the buggy. Frightened by the sound, the horse snorted and gave a jerk, tossing Ana sideways. Her uncle reached for her, his fingers curled into claws, murder in his glare.

Ana scrambled backward, away from him, as far as the buggy allowed, and then farther until she tipped and plunged to the hard, frozen ground.

Aware of the horse's stomping hooves and the buggy's rocking wheels, Ana rolled hard and fast, then grabbed her skirts, leaped to her feet and ran—up the street the way she'd come. Remembering the old man who'd offered directions, she veered in the direction of his boat.

"Help! Help me!" The wind snatched her screams and carried them away. Snow, which seemed to fall horizontally, stung her eyes. Behind her came a familiar rumbling.

The buggy!

Ana pumped her legs harder, through the ice and drifts that made her feet feel like lead. "Help!" she screamed again, the wind burning her lungs. "Somebody help me!"

She was almost to the boat. She stuck her hand out, reaching for something or someone, but it was too late. The horse's shrill neigh and hot breath stirred the hair on her neck. She spun and saw the black beast, and the buggy behind it bearing down.

She had just enough time to throw her arms up over her face before the animal's hooves flashed and then . . .

Everything went dark.

34

The second piece of glass did the trick. Eoghan groaned as the rope slipped from his wrists and his hands fell free. Even so, he could barely move. He had long since lost feeling in his legs and had very little control of his fingers, both stolen by the frigid temperature and icy waves.

His ragged breathing loud in the confines of the hold, he pushed through the water along the floor. The pipe was here. It would be of little use against the hatch, but perhaps one of the rusty portholes would prove weaker.

He grimaced. The portholes were too small to squeeze through. The most he could hope for was to force one free and yell for help, a possibility that would sink quickly enough if the icy water hugging his chest was any indication. At least he no longer felt the sharp ache in his ribs.

A low clunk rumbled from the ship's bottom. The pipe . . . he must have kicked it. Drawing a tremulous breath, he dove into the freezing depths and felt along the floor until his fingers closed around the pipe. Twice, he lost his grip and had to try again. Finally he came sputtering out of the water, hugging the pipe to his chest.

Now what? He could barely hold it. He forced one leg to move toward the nearest porthole, then the other.

"God, p-please keep Ana s-safe." His lips were so cold, he stumbled over the prayer, yet it helped to have something break the silence in the dark, deadly hold. "Protect her and h-help me to reach her"—he strained to hoist the pipe higher—"in time."

Somehow he managed to wrap his fingers around the pipe. His target indeed bore rust around the outer edges. He aimed for what looked like the weakest spot and drew the pipe back.

"Give me strength," he whispered, concentrating every ounce of energy on the small porthole.

One blow and the metal around the rim erupted in a shower of rusty flakes. Another blow and a bolt broke loose and plopped into the water. He struck three more times before the porthole itself cocked outward, away from the hull—not completely loose, but enough that he could put his mouth to the gap and yell.

"Help! Someone . . . anyone!" He drew the pipe back and hit the rusted metal around the porthole again. "Is anyone out there? I need help!"

He screamed until he was hoarse, but the storm outside had intensified to a raging mass of white. No figures braved the swirling snow. No hope penetrated the deepening gloom inside the hold.

Ana's words thrummed through his brain.

"He can't kill me if God doesn't want me dead."

Eoghan sagged against the wall and allowed the pipe to slip from his fingers. The freighter listed badly now, battered by the howling wind and condition of the hull. Eventually the waters of the harbor would overtake the ship, and it would sink to the bottom, taking him along with it.

So this was the end, then. Eoghan looked around him at

the metal confines that would form his coffin. Likely, Cara, Sisters Mary and Agnes, Father Ed—they would never know what had become of him. He closed his eyes. Worse, he'd never know if Ana lived or died.

Regret squeezed his heart. "I'm so sorry, Ana." He drew a shuddering breath and directed his gaze upward. "All right. If th-this is the end, then . . . your will be done." Burning gathered behind his eyes, but it was joined by an overwhelming peace. "I've never really given you much of anything, have I? Except blame. I'm sorry for that. I wish . . ." He shook his head. No time for that. "Cara was right. I haven't followed you. It was the church, the Fenians . . . never you. But I'm following now, and if this is the way you want it to end, I accept your right to decide my fate. It's in your hands."

The tremors shaking him grew stronger. He wrapped his arms around himself in a futile attempt to preserve warmth.

"Ana kn-knew that, d-didn't she? She w-went with her uncle, trusting you for the outcome." He blew out a shuddering breath. "I'm glad she believes in you."

The bones of the ship groaned. It shifted again, and the water inside the hold splashed against his chin.

Not long now. He would drown long before he froze to death. Neither thought was very pleasant. At least he could say he'd fought to the end . . . though how much that would matter, he'd probably never know.

"Please don't let Ana suffer. If he's going to kill her . . ." A surge of protectiveness roared through him and then ebbed away. "I just don't want her to suffer. Let it be me. Let me stay here for however long it takes. I'll do anything, endure anything, but don't let her—"

"Eoghan!"

He went still, hardly daring to believe he'd actually heard a voice. Summoning the last of his strength, he pushed away from the porthole and half walked, half swam toward the hatch. "H-Hello?" His voice was a raspy whisper. He cleared his throat and tried again. "Is someone out there?"

"Eoghan, thank God! It's Rourke. Hold on, do you hear me? Hold on! I'm going to get you out."

Rourke.

For the first time since McCleod dragged Ana away, Eoghan felt a spark of hope. That it was inspired by his brother-in-law did not escape him. So when he finally broke down enough to pray, God sent a Turner?

It was almost enough to make him laugh—wildly—except that he'd probably sound mad and Rourke might think twice about setting him free.

"The b-bolt," he stammered instead. "Halfway down the hatch. You have t-to slide it back before you c-can open the door."

"I see it."

Instead of scraping back, the bolt made a low groan. It was underwater, too? How far had the freighter sunk?

Slowly . . . unbearably so . . . the hatch swung open, spilling more water and ice into the hold. Rourke leaned in and stuck out his hand. "Come on. We don't have much time!"

Somehow, Eoghan managed to hold on as Rourke yanked him up and out.

"Can you walk?"

He tried to answer, ended up shuddering uncontrollably, and then simply leaned on Rourke as he tossed his arm about his shoulders and dragged him up the metal stairs and across the half-submerged deck. The gangplank hung precariously to the dock. It wouldn't last long, and Eoghan's legs were almost useless.

He glanced sidelong at his brother-in-law. He cupped a hand to his mouth, forced to yell to be heard above the howling wind. "If we don't make it, I won't be able to swim far. Tell Cara—"

"We'll make it!" Rourke's grip on his wrist tightened. "Let's go."

The distance across the gangplank seemed to stretch for miles. Eoghan kept his eyes fixed on the shore, certain that at any moment they'd feel the wood give way. Instead they stumbled onto the shore, both of them breathing hard. A few feet away, a carriage waited, Ana's mare tethered to the back. Rourke dragged him toward it, then practically threw him inside.

For several seconds, neither of them could speak. Both lay gasping against the carriage seat. Finally, Eoghan pushed himself upright.

"The mare. Where d-did you find the mare?"

Rourke gestured up the wharf. "An old man found it wandering the road and remembered having seen Ana riding it."

"He t-told you how to find me?"

Rourke shook his head and reached under the carriage seat to pull out a blanket. "No. You did that. I heard you calling." He tossed Eoghan the blanket, then stripped out of his coat and shirt. "Take your shirt off before you freeze. Mine's drier."

Somehow, Eoghan managed the buttons on his sodden coat. He yanked it off, then pulled his shirt over his head. "What about Ana? Did he say anything about her?"

"Just that she was looking for someone. McCleod?"

Eoghan nodded. "How did you know?"

"We found his letter."

"What lett—? Never mind. We have to find her." He struggled into Rourke's shirt, still warm from his body, and groaned. With the return of feeling came pain.

Rourke lifted an eyebrow at the purple and black bruises that covered his ribs and chest. "You all right?"

"I will be." He yanked the shirt down the rest of the way. "I think I know where McCleod might have taken Ana."

"Where?"

"A tenement near here. I've been there before. I think I can find it again."

Rourke grabbed his arm. "Hold on a minute—"

He shrugged free of his grasp. "We don't have a minute. He's going to kill her, Rourke. Said he was going to finish what he started."

"You're hurt. You can barely move."

"I'm going!" He winced as the force of yelling tore at his ribs. He swallowed and clutched one arm to his chest. "Turner, there's not enough time to go for help. We have to find her before it's too late. Please, I . . . I'm begging you."

Rourke only hesitated a moment, then grabbed the reins and directed a sharp glance at the blanket on the floor. "Put that around you and hold on."

The latter proved difficult with the carriage swaying wildly. Eoghan gritted his teeth as the jarring ride sent spasms of pain shooting through his midsection. It faded into horror as the buggy swung around.

"Which way?" Rourke barked.

Eoghan stared at the buildings on the horizon, what blood he had left draining from his face.

"That way," he said, then lifted his finger to point shakily at a ghostly plume of smoke billowing into the sky.

35

Before Ana was fully awake, she became aware of a throbbing pain in her head, her hands, everywhere really. She moaned and then, remembering where she was, sucked in a breath and bit her lip to stifle a cry of pain.

"No sense trying to hide. I know you're awake."

Ana cracked an eyelid. She was warm. Too warm. She bolted upright and immediately regretted the move when her vision swirled and dimmed. Forcing herself to breathe slowly, she waited while everything came into focus—the wooden floors, dank gray walls, barred windows, and . . .

Her uncle's broad back.

Ana slipped her tongue over her dry, cracked lips. "What . . . what are you doing?"

He turned slowly, favoring the leg she'd stabbed with the glass. A bright red scrap from his shirt bound the wound. In his hand was a makeshift torch, but behind him . . .

Her eyes widened in horror. "What is that?"

"Some would call it a pyre." He chuckled and scratched his brow. "Aye, the word is appropriate, for upon it I will be purging all that remains of the ghosts from my past." He reached out and tossed the torch onto the stack of burning furniture and wood.

Ana moved backward until her shoulders bumped the wall. "So this is what you meant by 'finishing what you started.' You murdered my mother and my sister, and now you intend to kill me."

"Your mother's death was an accident, girl!" he shouted, jabbing his finger at her. He drew a deep breath and squared his shoulders. "I never intended for Adele to die. She just . . . wouldn't . . ."

Ana stared openmouthed. Was it . . . could it be sorrow she read on her uncle's face? She laid her palms flat against the wall and inched upward onto her haunches. "You . . . loved . . ." The word stuck like tar in her throat. "You *loved* my mother?"

His face grew hard. "I met her first, long before my half brother. Did you know that? You and your sister, you could have been my bairns." He thumped his chest. "But Adele wouldn't hear of it, not after Shamus stole her heart. And even after he died . . ."

He whirled, removed his coat, and used it to fan the flames. She could feel the heat now, the pain of old scars coming to life as the smoke and ashes began to rise and waft toward the cracks in the plaster. Except for the barred windows, the only exit remained the door, and her uncle effectively blocked it. Before long, the room would be a furnace.

Ana pulled her cloak over her hands and up to her mouth. "What happened to my father? 'Twas no accident that claimed him, was it?"

He peered at her, his eyes narrowed against the smoke that was quickly filling the room.

"I deserve to know!" Ana shouted, jerking her bunched

fists down. "You've taken everything from me. Give me this much!"

His gaze lowered, then returned slowly to her. "I rigged the wagon to fail. He'd filled it too full, and when it got stuck, I found him pinned underneath. I might have saved him, but it was at that moment I realized it could all be mine."

"Only my mother didn't want you."

His lips curled in a sneer. "She reviled me and we fought. She fell and hit her head. I had to cover up her death."

He spoke calmly, as if the problem and its solution were simple enough things to understand. Ana shuddered. He was mad, yet he didn't realize his madness. Until now she'd only thought him wicked.

"I am sorry for you," she said softly.

He shifted on his heel to face her fully. "What did you say?"

She lifted her chin. "You heard me. You are to be pitied, with your deranged logic and selfish ambitions." Over her uncle's shoulder, a shadow fell, but she kept her focus pinned to his face and willed him to look into her eyes. "It is no wonder that my mother chose my father instead of you."

"Quiet, girl."

There was a *whoosh*, followed by an eruption of sparks. The walls had caught fire. Flames licked the ceiling. His eyes followed their path across the room, and he began backing toward the door. "She should have listened to me, your mother. 'Twas her fault things happened as they did. And this." He motioned to the growing blaze. "This too is her doing."

"And Eoghan?" Ana yelled, rising to her feet. "What about him? Are you going to blame my mother for his death, as well? Why kill him if not to draw me to you?"

The fire had its own voice now. It screamed and hissed at them both. Wood from the pyre popped, and her uncle flinched, then reached for the gun at his waist. "Hamilton's death is not my doing."

He's afraid, Ana realized. He looked from the growing fire to the windows to her.

And she was not afraid.

God truly was with her, giving her strength. Brion McCleod would never know such peace. He'd get what he wanted, her death would see to that, but he'd remember this day. It would trouble his dreams, and upon his own death . . . she shuddered to think of the fire he would face.

"You will never be free of this." The smoke stinging her eyes brought tears. She blinked them away and stepped toward him. "If you do this, it will haunt you."

He pointed the gun at her chest. "I hardly think so. This is justice. Do you hear me? Justice! Shamus McCleod stole everything from me, and now . . . now I take it all back. All of it! I'll never allow his foul offspring to claim what should always have belonged to me." His hand shook as he drew the hammer on the gun. "But I will show you mercy—"

The door crashed open. The gun in his hand fired. Ana clapped her hands over her ears at the sudden explosion of motion and sound. And then something hit her, drove her back against the wall and knocked the breath from her.

"Are you shot? Ana!"

She blinked in confusion. "Eoghan?"

"I have to get you out of here. Can you walk?"

What is happening? The question rattling in her head found its way to her mouth. "What's happening?"

"Move, Ana. Now!"

He dragged her to her feet. In the center of the room, Rourke and her uncle were locked in a struggle for the gun.

Eoghan spun her to look at him. "The whole building's on fire, not just this room. We have to get out."

She struggled to free herself from his grasp. "But Rourke and my uncle, they'll die here!"

"He—"

Another explosion sheared the words from his mouth. He ducked and grabbed her arm to pull her down with him.

It was the windows. A second eruption of glass followed the first. Ana screamed and used her cloak to shield her eyes. This time, Eoghan didn't bother to ask if she could walk. He picked her up and carried her to the door, into a narrow hall, and down a flight of stairs.

The smoke and fire downstairs was thicker than the room above. She couldn't talk, could barely breathe. Even if Eoghan got her out, how would Rourke or her uncle ever escape?

Eoghan turned one way, stopped and then backed up. A wall of flames blocked the exit.

"Eoghan . . ."

He ignored her and turned down another hall, breathing heavily. Sweat poured down his face and neck.

Ana beat against his chest. "I can walk, Eoghan. Put me down. I can walk!"

Either he heard her or his arms gave way. She landed on her feet, grabbed his hand, and tugged. "This way. There's light over there."

At least she prayed the ghostly square shimmering through the smoke and flames was light. She covered her mouth with the edge of her cloak and struggled toward it, stumbling as the feeble beacon danced in and out of sight. Midway there, the roaring heat and smoke became too much. She dropped to her knees and attempted to crawl, then tripped by her skirt, she fell forward.

"C'mon, Ana!" Eoghan's hand closed around hers. He dove forward, pulling her along with him. "Almost there."

It was a door. And the small square of light was a window.

Ana coughed and gasped as he reared back to kick the door, again and again. Finally it burst open. Whirling to grab her by the arms, he dragged her through and half pulled, half carried her to a snowbank a safe distance away.

"Stay here."

"Where are you going?"

"To get Rourke."

No time to argue. No time to soak in the sight of his face or even say that she loved him. He spun and ran back into the blazing tenement.

Nausea rolled through her stomach. She'd seen this before. She drew her knees to her chest. "No . . ."

The building groaned and held its breath.

"No," Ana said louder. Hot tears traced down her face. The building was going to collapse with Eoghan and Rourke still inside.

She scrambled to her feet, but it was too late. With one final gasp, the old building crumpled, sending ash and sparks and flames shooting into the sky.

She couldn't move. Couldn't scream.

Grabbing her middle, Ana turned away from the horrible sight and fell in a heap onto the hard, frozen ground.

36

"Can you move?" Eoghan clawed through a pile of smoldering rubble toward Rourke. "Turner!"

"I can move." Rourke rolled onto his side and choked out a cough. "What about you?"

"I'm all right."

"And McCleod?"

They scanned the remains of the first-floor tenement. Eoghan had met Rourke on the stairs carrying an unconscious McCleod and run to help, but halfway down, the stairs had begun to give way. At the bottom step, Eoghan had tackled Rourke into one of the adjoining halls. It saved their lives. The narrow hall was all that had kept burning timbers from piling onto their heads. They'd managed to crawl free before the entire building collapsed, but McCleod . . .

Eoghan spied his broken body among the blazing ruins of the second floor. "Too late," he said, pointing. "Let's get out of here."

Hoisting his brother-in-law by the shoulders, Rourke helped Eoghan limp out the same door Eoghan had brought Ana through. A few feet away, she lay in the snow, a sobbing, shaking heap.

Eoghan staggered toward her. "Ana?"

She lifted her head. Her tears had washed pale streaks through the blackened soot on her face, but as she drew her arm across her mouth and half rose to her knees, she had never looked more beautiful.

"Eoghan?" She grabbed her skirt and struggled the rest of the way to her feet. "Eoghan!"

She dashed the short distance to him. Pain flashed through his ribs when she crashed against his chest, but disappeared just as quickly when he wound his arms around her waist and squeezed her tight. She was all right. McCleod was dead and Ana was safe in his arms.

Eoghan closed his eyes and dipped his head to soak in the feel of her skin and the softness of her hair. "It's over, sweetheart. You're safe."

She burrowed closer, fresh tears washing his neck. "I thought I lost you. You walked into that building and all I could see was the fire at the cottage."

His heart aching, he tucked his finger under her chin and lifted her face so she could look at him. "I am so verra sorry that you had to go through that. Through all of this. I swear to you, Ana, I will never let anyone hurt you again."

"You may not have a choice." Both of them turned their heads to watch Rourke limp toward them. "Not if we stick around here much longer." He gestured toward the billowing smoke and jumping flames. "The fire is going to draw attention. We need to go. Now. Before the authorities get here."

"Authorities?" Ana's glance bounced from one to the other.

Eoghan gathered her safely under his arm. "What difference does it make if the authorities come? We've done nothing wrong."

Rourke shook his head and met Eoghan's eyes. "I'll explain

on the way back to the house." He nodded at Ana. "Help her into the carriage. Hurry, we've no time to waste."

Apprehension wormed through Eoghan's gut. Rourke knew something. Eoghan had no idea what it was, but he trusted him. He marveled at the revelation as he led Ana to the carriage and helped her inside. How had he managed to go from despising his brother-in-law to trusting him?

On the carriage ride home, Rourke explained how they'd found Ana's pocket watch and the letter, and how it had led him to the wharf. Eoghan told them of the ambush after departing Kilarny's house, leaving nothing out, not even the details of the plan to use his renewed tie to Cara to glean information on the Turners.

"I don't understand," Ana said. "Who would want information on Rourke's family, and why?"

Rourke said nothing, just shot them a glance and kept driving. So that was it. The secret Rourke was keeping had something to do with his family. Eoghan said nothing and tightened his hold on Ana.

"Inside," Rourke instructed as the carriage rumbled to a stop outside the house. "We'll talk there, and I'll tell you everything I know."

Stepping from the carriage, he handed the reins to a stable boy, waited while Eoghan helped Ana dismount, and then followed them into the house.

Cara and Tillie met them in the foyer. Cara ran to Rourke first, then turned and stretched out her arm to include Eoghan in her hug.

"We've been so worried. Tillie and I haven't stopped praying since you left." She pressed a kiss to Eoghan's cheek. "And you disappeared. What happened?"

Holding his wife, Rourke gave a heavy sigh. "Let's go to the library. I'll explain everything there."

Ana shivered, and Tillie crossed to wrap her arms around her shoulders. "But first we need to get all of you out of your wet clothes. We'll meet again in a few minutes. Cara, help me with Ana."

Though they all agreed, Eoghan hated to be parted from Ana for even a second. He hurried to wash the sweat and grime from his face and neck, dressed in a set of clothes borrowed from Rourke, and then went with haste to wait in the library.

Rourke met him there. Upon entering, he tipped his head at Eoghan's chest. "How are the ribs?"

He ran his hand over one side. "Sore, but not broken actually. At least I don't think so."

"I've sent John for a doctor. We'll get you checked out and know for sure."

Eoghan nodded his thanks and moved farther into the library. A crackling fire drew him toward the fireplace. He stood before it and warmed his hands.

"Still a little chilled?" Rourke walked to him, holding two steaming cups of coffee, and handed one to him.

He accepted it gratefully. "A little. Listen, I don't think I thanked you for coming to look for me back there."

Rourke shrugged and took a sip from his cup. "There wasn't exactly time."

"No, I guess not. In fact, any later and I'd have probably died in that ship—and Ana in the fire."

Rourke studied him over the rim of his cup, then turned and set it down. "I dinna blame you for what you did. You had no reason to trust me, no reason to believe I wouldn't hurt your sister, or you."

Eoghan waited silently.

"I hope that has changed now that you realize how much I love Cara. I would do anything . . . anything to keep her from harm."

He gave a nod, copying Rourke's motion and setting down his cup. When he straightened, he looked Rourke in the eye and lowered his voice. "What is this about?"

Rourke glanced at the door, then back at him. "I need to ask a favor of you, Eoghan."

He gave a snort. "Aye, well, you saved my life. I figure I owe you."

Instead of smiling, Rourke gripped the fireplace mantel with both hands and lowered his head. "I need . . ."

He tensed. Whatever he was about to say, he was having a hard time saying it. Eoghan shifted and clapped his hand to Rourke's shoulder. Surprised, Rourke looked first at Eoghan's hand and then at him.

"This is about Cara, isn't it?"

Rourke shook his head.

"What do you need me to do?"

He let out a long sigh. "I need you to take Ana and Cara . . . and leave the city." Pain shadowed his gaze as he turned to face Eoghan head-on. "I need you to take the women and leave New York. Tonight."

37

Ana sat on the same settee where she'd slept the night before, Cara beside her on the cushion, and Tillie behind them at her shoulder. The settee was drawn up close to the fire, for Ana found she no longer feared the flames and the heat felt good on her face. The look in Eoghan's eyes, however, troubled her deeply.

"I don't understand. We're leaving? Why? I thought you said my uncle died in the fire."

He dropped to one knee beside her and claimed both of her hands. "It's not McCleod that is the threat now, Ana. It's something . . . someone else."

He glanced at Rourke, who nodded and turned with an apologetic look to his wife. "I'm sorry, Cara. I should have told you sooner what I suspected. I just thought it would be safer for you and the baby this way."

Cara's gaze flew to her brother. "He told you?"

Eoghan clenched his jaw and nodded. "He had to in order to convince me to take you with me."

Tears filled Cara's eyes. "I'm sorry," she whispered. "I wanted to tell you earlier, but the time was never right."

"I'm to blame for that," Eoghan replied. "Not you."

A tear rolled down her cheek. She wiped it away and then looked up at her husband. "What have you learned?"

He cleared his throat and looked at Eoghan, who rose to stand with his arm about Ana's shoulders. Bracing herself for whatever Rourke had to say, Ana lifted her chin and leaned against his side.

"After we realized it wasn't Eoghan who was to blame for my father's death," Rourke began, "my uncles and I set out to discover what had really happened the night he died."

Ana glanced at Cara. "But . . . I thought all of that had been settled. It was Sean Healy who murdered Daniel Turner."

Cara nodded and tilted her head at Rourke.

"He wasn't working alone," Rourke said. "We knew someone gave him the information about where my father would be the night Sean kidnapped my father, and that person was a traitor to my family."

"Your cousin," Tillie said. She cast a glance around the room and fell silent.

Rourke nodded. "Aye, my cousin. Hugh O'Hurly."

"But we found out about that last summer," Cara said. "I don't understand what it has to do with us now, or why we have to leave New York."

Rourke stepped away from the fireplace. "Because, Cara, someone paid Hugh for the information on my father, and it wasn't Sean."

Her eyes widened. "You know this for a fact?"

He nodded. "It's what my uncles and I have been working on—not city hall, as I allowed you to believe."

She drew a slow breath and lowered her head. Rourke moved to her and covered her hands with his own. "I'm sorry, Cara."

Though her lips trembled, she squared her shoulders and lifted her chin. "What did you find out?"

"About the man who paid Hugh for the information?"
She nodded.

Rourke's gaze flitted to Eoghan, and both men circled to stand in front of the settee.

"We think it was an Irishman in charge of the Fenians. So far, all we've been able to uncover is that he's known as The Celt."

Tillie's head jerked up. "You think the Fenians are involved in this?"

Rourke lifted his hand quickly. "Not the Fenians—the man leading them. As far as we've been able to determine, he worked alone."

"Why would he want your father dead?" Ana asked. "And what does any of that have to do with me?"

Eoghan cleared his throat. "It was never about you, Ana. Not this, anyway. McCleod was just a means of accomplishing an end."

"You mean . . . my uncle and this man were working together?"

"We think so. He was probably blackmailing your uncle into doing his dirty work. In exchange, he gave McCleod information on where to find you. That's why our deaths couldn't be linked together—because mine had to look like an accident."

Ana shook her head. "But the boat sinking . . . my uncle couldn't have arranged that. It was the storm—"

"Not the storm," Rourke interrupted. "It was scuttled purposely and made to look as though the storm finished it off."

Ana scrambled to remember everything she knew, everything her uncle had said. "On board the ship, my uncle said he was right." Her chest tightened. "Who did he mean?"

Lips white, Eoghan admitted to his part in helping to buy Brion's passage into America, how he'd delivered the envelope with the money to the barge office, but how Kilarny had been surprised to learn of its purpose.

"The Fenians didn't know, Ana," Eoghan said, "but someone else did."

She blew out a sigh. "The Celt."

He nodded.

No longer able to sit still, Ana rose and paced the room. "So, who is he then, this Celt man, and why hasn't anyone stopped him before now?"

"We have no proof," Rourke said. "We aren't even certain of his involvement. But we think that may be why he wanted Eoghan killed, because something he knows could prove dangerous."

Ana held her breath. Though she was afraid to ask, she had to know. "Such as . . . ?"

Eoghan balled both fists at his sides. "All these years, we thought Daniel's death was an accident, that Sean was stupid and crazy, and the plan to force Daniel into voting with the Fenians simply went terribly wrong."

"You don't think so anymore?" Cara whispered, her eyes widening.

Rourke shook his head. "No."

Suddenly, Ana knew what Daniel had that someone else could have wanted. "They killed him and made it look like an accident so they could take his seat in parliament. That's right, isn't it?"

The room fell silent, the occupants exchanging uneasy glances.

Ana swallowed a lump in her throat and crossed to stand before Eoghan. "What if you're wrong? What if this Celt and my uncle weren't working together?"

"We aren't wrong, Ana," he said softly. "Rourke's men have already checked out his theory. And there's something else."

336

Something in his eyes turned the blood in Ana's veins cold. Instinctively she wrapped her arms around herself. "What is it?"

He clenched his jaw. When at last he met her gaze, his expression was hard. "McCleod perished in the fire. Whatever knowledge he had burned with him. I supposedly drowned on the ship. So long as the freighter stays on the bottom of the harbor, The Celt thinks his secret is safe."

"And me?" Ana asked.

Eoghan winced and reached out to grasp her shoulders. "You were never a threat to him, remember?"

She swallowed and shook her head. "What are you saying, Eoghan? What is it you're trying to tell me?"

Slowly, his hands fell from her shoulders. "I'm saying, Rourke is right. I have to go and I'm taking Cara with me. It's the only way to keep her safe while Rourke and his uncles try to figure out the identity of the man behind all of this. But you . . ." He gave a weak smile. "You're free, Ana. Your uncle is dead, and your mother's farm, the land, it's yours now. All of it. You can go back to Ireland and never have to deal with any of this again."

Leave America and . . . him? Her breath caught.

Rising from the settee, Cara took Rourke's hand and led him to the door. "We'll leave you two alone. Tillie?"

Tillie joined them at the door, but before slipping out, she shot one last glance at Ana. In her eyes was everything Ana felt—sorrow, regret, but most of all, heartache.

Unable to bear the tears she saw rolling down Tillie's cheeks, Ana turned to stare into the fire.

It was the heartache that hurt most of all.

38

Eoghan forced himself to maintain his distance from Ana, though his arms ached to hold her, and he felt as if a void had opened inside his chest. To touch her would only make her decision harder, something he refused to do.

He jammed his fists into his pockets. "Ana . . ."

Her head lifted. "You want me to leave?"

At the look of anguish that twisted her features, pain hit him with the force of a sledgehammer. "No."

Abandoning his earlier resolve, he cut the span that separated them and pulled her fiercely into his arms. "No, I don't want you to go."

He pressed his lips to her hair, her temple, but stopped short of her mouth.

Breathe, Eoghan, he told himself. *Remember what you promised.*

"Ana, the thought of you going away, of never seeing you again—" he swallowed and forged on—"I love you more than I ever thought possible. The idea of losing you now fills me with fear—more than I felt when I was trapped on the freighter, more than when Rourke and I were caught in the tenement and for a second I thought we might die in the fire." Drawing back, he brought his hands to her face. "But I swore something when I was on that ship, Ana. I swore that I would do anything, endure anything, if it meant sparing you.

"Ana . . ." he said, bending to whisper against her forehead, "you are the most important person in this world to me. I would die before I'd let harm come to you. And if letting you go back to Ireland is what it takes to see that happen, then I will endure being apart from you. I'll see to it that you are settled, and safe, and—"

She lifted her hand and laid her fingers over his mouth. "No, Eoghan."

"Ana—"

She shook her head, her beautiful brown eyes soft and shining with love. "I didn't leave you on the ship except to save your life, and I will not leave you now."

"But this battle isn't about you, or your family. You don't have to face any of it." He gripped her by the arms, ashamed of how much her words thrilled him, yet all the more driven to see her removed from harm's way. "I couldn't bear to see you hurt again, and if I thought I were to blame should something happen, it would destroy me. Do you understand?"

Incredibly, she smiled and pressed her palms to his cheeks. "Eoghan, my sweet, braw lad, tell me again why I went willingly with my uncle. When I knew he intended to kill me, why did I leave you to go with him?"

He hesitated, then let his eyes drift closed as the realization hit him. She had done the same thing he was trying to do, only she'd done it first. Then his eyes flew open as something warm and astonishingly sweet touched his lips.

She was kissing him.

The moment he realized it, instinct took over. Sliding his arms around her, he drew her close and returned the kiss—

ardently, possessively. What a fool he'd been to think he could live without her.

Regret filled him when at last she pulled away. He could have gone on kissing her forever, wanted to go on kissing her forever, but only if she was his. Completely.

"Ana?" he rasped.

She was breathless, her voice a throaty whisper that set his nerves on fire. "Aye?"

"I'll take you with us. Somehow I'll find a way to keep both you and my sister safe, but first . . . I have to know. Will you marry me?"

A bright smile blossomed on her face, filling him with more hope than he'd felt in a year.

"Aye," she said, tucking her head into the crook of his neck. "I will marry you. And, Eoghan?"

He managed a nod. "Aye?"

"It's about time."

Acknowledgments

With each new book, I am amazed at the wonderful people God has put into my life to encourage, uplift, and pray for me. These are but a few:

To my awesome critique partners, Jessica Dotta, Michelle Griep, Ane Mulligan, and Janelle Mowery, thank you for your expertise and patient teaching. I love you all so much.

To my editors, David Long and Luke Hinrichs, I am so grateful to be working with you. Thank you for your faith in this series and for your many hours of careful editing to make these stories the best they can be. And to the rest of the remarkable team at Bethany House, y'all are amazing! Words cannot express my gratitude for your many efforts. Please accept my humble thank you.

Lastly, to my husband, Lee, my children Ben and Mandy Ludwig, and Derrick and Abby Cole, I love you all so much. This writing journey hasn't always been easy. Thank you for loving and supporting me through all the ups and downs.

Elizabeth Ludwig is the award-winning author of *No Safe Harbor*, Book One in the EDGE OF FREEDOM series. Her work has also been featured on Novel Journey, the Christian Authors Network, and the Christian Pulse. Elizabeth's debut novel, *Where the Truth Lies* (coauthored with Janelle Mowery), earned her the IWA Writer of the Year Award. Her first historical novel, *Love Finds You in Calico, California*, was given four stars from *Romantic Times*. And her popular literary blog, The Borrowed Book, enjoys a wide readership.

Elizabeth is an accomplished speaker and teacher, often attending conferences and seminars where she lectures on editing for fiction writers, crafting effective novel proposals, and conducting successful editor/agent interviews. Along with her husband and two grown children, she makes her home in the great state of Texas. To learn more, visit Elizabeth Ludwig.com.

If you enjoyed *Dark Road Home*, you may also like...

More Historical Fiction From Bethany House

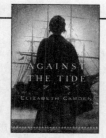

When Lydia's translation skills land her in the middle of a secret campaign against dangerous criminals, who can she trust when both her life and her heart are in jeopardy?

Against the Tide by Elizabeth Camden
elizabethcamden.com

She's never questioned her Quaker beliefs, but as lives hang in the balance, must she choose between forsaking the man she loves and abandoning the bedrock of her faith?

The Messenger by Siri Mitchell
sirimitchell.com

Masquerading as a governess, Lady Sumner is on a mission to find the man who ran off with her fortune and reclaim what's rightfully hers. But does God have something—or someone—better in mind?

A Change of Fortune by Jen Turano
jenturano.com

◈ BETHANYHOUSE

Stay up-to-date on your favorite books and authors with our *free* e-newsletters. Sign up today at bethanyhouse.com.

Find us on Facebook. facebook.com/bethanyhousepublishers

Free exclusive resources for your book group! bethanyhouse.com/anopenbook